By the Feet
of Men

49

By the Feet of Men

Grant Price

COSMIC
EGG
BOOKS

Winchester, UK
Washington, USA

JOHN HUNT PUBLISHING

First published by Cosmic Egg Books, 2019
Cosmic Egg Books is an imprint of John Hunt Publishing Ltd., 3 East St., Alresford,
Hampshire SO24 9EE, UK
office@jhpbooks.com
www.johnhuntpublishing.com

For distributor details and how to order please visit the 'Ordering' section on our website.

Text copyright: Grant Price 2018

ISBN: 978 1 78904 145 3
978 1 78904 146 0 (ebook)
Library of Congress Control Number: 2018943945

A CIP catalogue record for this book is available from the British Library.

Design: Stuart Davies

UK: Printed and bound by CPI Group (UK) Ltd, Croydon, CR0 4YY
US: Printed and bound by Thomson-Shore, 7300 West Joy Road, Dexter, MI 48130

We operate a distinctive and ethical publishing philosophy in
all areas of our business, from our global network of authors to
production and worldwide distribution.

For Christopher and Amanda.

Acknowledgements

My thanks to Liam Price, Fraser Patterson, Emma Hall, Ciarán Fleck, Ania Wachnik, Ashley Godfrey, Elsa Monsch, Hamed Karimi, Jennifer Hackney, Toby Russell and, above all, Chiara Tormen.

"Only those who still have hope can benefit from tears."
Nathanael West, The Day of the Locust

Part I – On the Edge

1

It was the perfect time and place for an ambush.

A pitted gravel track unravelled amid sickly trees and undergrowth that devoured anything not strong enough to withstand it. The ghost of tyre treads in mud suggested the route had not been abandoned altogether, though the imprints had long since dried and hardened. The remains of a plastic bag clung to a branch that bent towards the road. Other than the cicadas that buzzed softly, all wildlife was either dead or elsewhere. Clouds obscured the stars overhead and the air was thick and warm and wet.

A mechanical whine interrupted the stillness and a vehicle rounded a bend in the track. Large enough to scrape the bark from the boughs, its six oversized wheels ate the gravel at a steady rate, kicking up dust that clung to the windows of a boxlike cab. Behind the cab sat a cargo bed with a ribbed metal frame over which a dull tarpaulin skin had been stretched and sutured to the tailgate to shield the cargo from view. Every surface of the vehicle was scratched and chipped and dented. Daubed in crooked white brush strokes on the driver side door was a name: Warspite.

Two male faces hung like orbs inside the cab. The driver gripped the steering wheel and scanned the few metres lit by the headlights as the vehicle bit forward. In the passenger's seat, his companion studied a map spread out on the dashboard, a sinewy arm resting lightly against the window frame.

The driver's lean fingers pressed against foam pads taped to the wheel. The darkness had been slow to arrive, but now it was suffocating him. He switched off the barely functioning A/C unit, rolled down his window and listened hard. Hot air buffeted his cheeks. Cicadas sang to one another in the brushwood. There was nothing else out there. His cap, faded by a lifetime's exposure to sunlight and sweat, made his temples itch, but he kept it on out of superstition. He took a sip of water from the bota bag above his head before breaking the silence.

'Ghazi?'

'A marker should be coming up on your right soon.' The voice of his co-driver was muted, unhurried. Liquid eyes followed the lines on the map. 'After that it's just another three kilometres to Verne.'

'We should've made it before sundown.'

'We'll be fine.'

'Not if they cause trouble.'

'It's a new settlement. They'll want to keep things above board.'

The man at the wheel grunted. 'Two things people are good at: selling themselves a lie and making stupid decisions for quick gain.'

His point made, the driver wiped the sweat from his palms and settled back in his seat. Some Runners thrived on driving at night, but he wasn't one of them. The risk of attack wasn't much greater, but now he had to keep the rig in low gear. The track was too pocked with holes to be able to put his foot down and trust his instincts like he would if it was daylight. And moving at a crawl was an invitation for slingers to throw their hooks onto the cargo bed and board them from the rear. All they had to do after that was lean out and slash the back tyres and the pantech would be a sitting duck. The crew was always expendable.

The hood trembled as the potholes tested the suspension springs. The heat from outside was rapidly replacing the recycled air in the cab, but the driver made no move to roll the window up. He wanted to hear the demons if they cried out in the night.

'Where's the marker?'

'Just relax. There's nothing to worry about.'

'Sure. Jinx us, too.'

'You're winding yourself up.' Ghazi rubbed at the white strip of hair running from his brow to the nape of his neck. Then he pointed. 'It's there.'

The carcass of what was once a two-seater car lay in rigor mortis by the tree line. Every part worth salvaging had been stripped long ago. Warspite edged by without stopping. Shortly afterward the gravel ended and the truck turned onto a rock-hard path that sent shockwaves through the driver's arms. No rain in the area for months. It was clear why Verne needed water rations. He put his foot down and the whine under the hood increased. He wanted to cover the last stretch and be done with it. The optimism he'd felt when they'd set out had died at some point in the afternoon, along with one of their precious batteries. Two hot, dull days kicking their heels in a filthy nowhere town before taking the first contract that came their way, and then the old rig had lost power just a few hours down the road. The battery, an old lithium-ion roadster model, had drained its charge, so they'd had to switch it out for the reserve. Now he checked the meter. Down to thirty percent. They wouldn't get far if the delivery in Verne fell apart.

'Still set on the cargo?' he asked, one eye on the road, another on the sullen trees.

'Yes. That water's ours. The hemp we can trade.'

'Good.' He hesitated. 'What about the battery?'

'I'll take a look at it first thing tomorrow. Today was warm. It may just've overheated.'

'Verne's too small to have a repairs and spares yard.'

'We'll be okay.'

The driver's eyes itched. His arms were cramped and his neck was stiff. As much as he loved the Old Lady, he couldn't wait to get out. Up in the cab he could feel every bump in the road, and a full day of it was more than enough. He tried to ignore his reflection in the windscreen. Heavy brow, dirty tanned skin, cobweb veins creeping in at the corners of eyes with mismatched pupils. Above all, he was gaunt. Neither he nor Ghazi had been eating well of late. But they were holding on. He pushed his cap back and rubbed at the stubble underneath. Sweat dripped from his temples. The eternal heat was its own brand of torture, but there were ways to mitigate it. Keeping his head shaved was one. In the long summer months, they regularly came across pantechs and other vehicles that had gone end over end, the driver in pieces against the windshield or thrown out face-first onto the road. People like that always had hair tickling their ears.

Warspite swatted more branches aside. Keeping a hand on the wheel, he fished around inside a pouch on his belt until his fingers closed around a small piece of root. As he chewed it, a stream of ice water trickled through the centre of his skull and his nerves died, replaced by an artificial calm that would see him through the next few minutes. He offered a piece to Ghazi.

'Not now.'

'Suit yourself.'

'Lights beyond those trees. Electric.'

He eased off on the accelerator and the whine lessened. Ahead, two lamps hung from wooden stakes on either side of the trail and a sign announced their arrival in Verne. They squeezed through and pulled up inside the perimeter. The driver removed the key that activated the pantech's system and looped it around his neck, then reached under the seat for the pedal lock and secured it before flicking the kill switches for the battery. He jumped out of the cab as a tallish man wearing a handlebar moustache and a bush hat strolled towards them. The barrel of an ancient rifle peeked over his shoulder. Lurking in the gloom behind him was a cluster of lean-tos, tents and shacks.

'You Cassady?'

'That's right.' He took off his cap and stared the man down.

'How-do. Name's Quentin. Welcome to Verne. We was beginning to think you was lost, or worse. But our spotter tagged you out on the track and morsed it in. We got him sitting up in a tree a couple hundred metres down the road.' The man stood with the confidence of a ruler in his kingdom. A thickness around his waist indicated that he ate well.

'Lonely job.'

'We all gotta do it from time to time. How about that cargo? Got everything we asked for?'

'It's all there.'

'Great. Cost us enough. Two boys. Just for a little rope and water.'

Cassady's eyes lit up at the hint of a contract. 'Water's scarce. You want us to take your boys to Souk?'

'Naw. We ain't got nothing to give you in return. We'll take 'em on a quad. It'll be hell for 'em, but that ain't my problem. Things are ugly enough around here as it is.'

'How bad is it?'

'We ain't having any luck. River bed's drier than the gap between a crone's legs. Hasn't rained since we last sent for a Runner, and we been rationing like you wouldn't know how. We dug a well and got it going, but it's an ornery son of a bitch. Ain't bringing up anything but black. Wouldn't even be fit to grease your axles with. Plus the stills are only capturing enough to wet our lips. But we'll turn it around soon enough.' Laughter leaked from the back of his throat and he eyed the truck that sat dormant on the track. 'Say, what're you driving there anyway?'

'A 939. Six by six, five tons,' said Ghazi, coming around from the passenger's side and shaking hands with Quentin. As a mechanic, he never shied away from reeling off the Old Lady's measurements. 'Just over seven metres in length. Around three high if you don't count the top lights. Armoured cab. Beam axle on leaf springs. EV conversion with manual gearbox. Brushless DC motor.'

'She ain't pure electric?'

'No. She's at least twice as old as any of us. We had to mod her after the gas ran out.'

'Ever think about trading her? We could use a machine like

that. Our quads don't carry nearly a thing.'

'Not a chance.'

'How fast can you get her?'

'She can edge a hundred on tarmac.'

Cassady offered a thin smile. 'Unlike whatever it was we just drove in on.'

'That was my doing,' said Quentin. 'I had some of the young-uns tear up the track with pickaxes. We was getting too many unwanted visitors in the night. Red carpet all laid out for them. And we ain't exactly got the hardware to drive off more than a few at a time.' He dipped his shoulder to show the rifle.

'Makes it harder for us, too, you know.' The beginning of a breeze touched the back of Cassady's neck. This was the good time, the few hours before the world woke once more and fire rained down from above. The cicadas continued to make their music.

'Sure, but you can handle it. A few holes ain't gonna stop you.'

'True.'

'You boys decided what you want to do with your percentage?' The settler eyed them with an eagerness that betrayed his hand.

'We're keeping the water. What will you give us for the hemp?'

'How much is there?'

'Our cut works out at a box.'

Quentin made just enough of a show of calculating a fair trade in his head. 'I can't offer you any food. We're all of us going to bed on empty stomachs at the moment.' His gaze flickered to Warspite. One of the plates along the side of the cargo bed was black and buckled. 'Looks like you boys've been playing in the wrong neighbourhood. What'd you say to a couple of sheets of metal? Nice and strong. I was gonna use them on my own foxhole, but it can wait.'

Cassady listened to his partner drag his foot across the dirt, which meant he was on board with the offer. 'Deal.'

'Sure you don't wanna hand over your water? Give you boys a good return for it. Couple of new tyres, for example?'

'Ours have some life in them yet,' said Ghazi.

'Plus any items of clothing you want. You name it. We got ourselves a good guy in camp. Makes some durable stuff.'

Cassady spat out the root pulp. 'No.'

'Well. You can't blame a man for trying. You boys make yourselves welcome in the camp. Verne ain't exactly Prestige, but it's got diversions enough. Either of you want a boy? A girl?'

'Not today.'

'Let me know if you do. Got a few decent ones with us. And tell me if you have any trouble.'

Cassady narrowed his eyes. 'Why would there be trouble?'

Quentin grinned. 'Runners find trouble. How long you gonna stay?'

'Until tomorrow morning. Soon as we're recharged and ready to go.'

'You need us to hook you up?'

He was quick to shake his head. 'We'll use our turbine.' He didn't want to be in the man's pocket for anything.

'Well, we're pleased to have you, long as you want. Without the water we'd be in trouble. I'll get a few of my boys to unload it now.' He turned and whistled. Malnourished faces appeared in the dark. They were young, no older than sixteen, and their eyes were blank. They waited for orders.

'Do as these men say. Take everything to the store. If even one cask goes missing, I'll lay a beating on you so hard, the noise you make'll scare the maneaters away. You hear me?'

Quentin pinched the brim of his hat and wandered back down the main thoroughfare of the camp. After the boys had finished unloading the cargo, Ghazi climbed into the back and gave the faulty battery the once-over. Cassady ran his hands over the tyre treads. They weren't bald yet.

Ghazi poked his head out. 'It looks fried. I'll try to charge it, but don't hold out much hope.'

Cassady closed his eyes for a moment and quelled the spark of anger that wanted to take hold. 'How?'

'Can't tell. Pushed her too hard in the heat, maybe. Or it might just have been its time. Old model. Anyway, looks like we're running on a single until we find a proper town.'

'Wind's picking up, so at least we can charge the other one. We may need to leave at short notice.'

'You don't trust him.'

'That man is too accustomed to giving orders and being obeyed for his hospitality to benefit us.'

While Cassady worked a splinter from between his teeth, Ghazi took the wind turbine from its storage tube and set it up on the roof. He pulled the blades into position and fed the lead through an opening at the top of the hood into the cab and then into the battery. The vanes began to chase one another and the yellow LED winked on.

'When it's charged I'll try the other,' Ghazi said, closing the cab door and locking it. 'I'm going to see if I can find a book.'

Cassady smiled. When he wasn't behind the wheel or repairing the rig, his co-driver spent his time reading anything he could get his hands on. He was one of the few who still bothered. Books couldn't be eaten or traded or used as weapons. They were only good for burning. In the early years of the Change, the survivors had thrown them onto fires to make it through the still cold winters. As a younger man, Ghazi had gone into the dead cities in search of untouched libraries and bookstores. Cassady had put a stop to it when they'd joined forces. It wasn't worth the risk.

'Not hungry?' he asked.

'I'll eat when I'm done. I guess it won't take long.'

'Then I'll take a look around the camp, too.'

Ghazi nodded at the rig. 'Okay leaving her on her own?'

'She's all locked up. Meet back in ten.'

Ghazi ghosted between the shacks and disappeared. Cassady sighed and stretched his arms. He was beat, but the thought of the faulty battery wouldn't allow him to relax. He couldn't remember when they'd come by it. His memory was getting worse with each summer that passed. There had been a time when he'd only needed to hear a name once for it to stay lodged in his head. Now he was already struggling to recall the name of the head honcho of this pitiful camp.

A cough that started deep in his chest had him doubled over with his arms wrapped around his stomach. His lungs were on fire. After a minute of agony it stopped. He took a drink of water from his canteen and leaned against the hood of the rig. The road was getting to him. A few days in a larger settlement would be no bad thing. All he wanted was a river to wash away the lice, a warm meal that tasted of something other than grease and Cosinex, and a night of uninterrupted sleep.

He struck out along the main path that cut through Verne. The camp was quiet. Places like this always were once night fell. Only a fool advertised their position when they could no longer see well enough to protect themselves. Dwellings fanned out on either side: corrugated iron shacks, wooden huts, vehicle bodies, canvas bivouacs designed to be taken down in a hurry. Squat solar stills that were little more than a black tray with a plastic cone and a spout at the top had been set up wherever there was a free space to distil the water they had managed to collect. The air was heavy with sweat and incinerated plastic and illness. Few lights burned inside the shelters. As he walked past the doorways, he caught snatches of conversation. The water shortage was on their minds. Verne was vulnerable. He didn't hold out much hope for it. Setting up a new camp always came with a cargo full of risk. A lack of food and water, disease, infighting, flash floods, dust storms, the baking sun. They were a prime target for nomadics too. Virtually no defences to deal with, and Quentin hadn't even put sentries on the gate. One guard watching the road from a tree house didn't cut it. A few men with rifles and bows could take this place. The settlers would be cut down where they stood and the dwellings would be razed. Cassady shivered. As soon as morning broke, they were getting out.

At the end of the trail was an old windowless substation that had been turned into a bunker. Behind it, pylon legs jutted out of the ground, rising to a height overlooking the station's flat roof. A lamp hung from one of the legs and a limp flag from the other. Two generators thrummed next to the squat building and thick cables disappeared through a small hole in its side. Loopholes had been hacked into the brick and a sandbag fortification, vacant now, had been set up on the roof. Next to the entrance was a crude metal barricade that could be dragged in front of the opening in the event of an attack. One of the boys who had helped to take the cargo from Warspite stood by the door, leaning against a crude pike with a look of boredom on his face. When he spotted Cassady approaching he straightened up and stared at him with cold interest. The Runner stopped and plugged a new stick of root in his mouth. The stench of Verne's latrine pits drifted over from their location in the forest. He spat a long stream of saliva into the dust. It wouldn't take a minute to walk over and take a look inside the bunker, but that would mean dealing with Quentin again. The man might not be so easy to shake a second time. The boy's hands wrung the body of the pike like it was a wet rag. Cassady winked at him, turned away and started back to his rig.

As he neared the end of the thoroughfare once more, he spotted movement near Warspite. It was too furtive and unsure to be Ghazi. Keeping low and on the balls of his feet, Cassady left the track and squeezed between a tent and a lean-to. The trees whispered with the wind, damping the sound of his boots hitting the ground. He peered into the shadows and recognised the rig's bulky form and the blades spinning on the roof. And there, by the hood, the silhouette of a man. He ducked back behind the tent, blood pounding in his temples. Either the man was friendly or he was not, but he would have to find out either way. Another peek. Some kind of tool glinted in the man's hand. As Cassady watched, the man bent over, wedged it into one of Warspite's headlight sockets and yanked the cover off. A cold fury made rational thought impossible. Cassady fished the wad of root out his mouth and dropped it on the floor. From his belt he took a switchblade knife and snapped it open. If the thief damaged or stole the light, it could be weeks before they found a replacement. But if he made too much noise trying to take the bastard out, the whole settlement could come down on them, which meant they probably wouldn't make it out alive. He focused on the back of the man's neck, knife held in a tight grip, and covered the dead ground at a jog.

The thief spun around, eyes dilated with surprise. He had a scavenger's face, thin and hollow and lacking a conscience. He swung at Cassady with the sharp-edged tool and bared an incomplete set of brown teeth. Cassady stepped back, keeping his body loose and his eyes on the tool. The thief darted forward and swung once more, slicing the air as Cassady rocked on his heels. Before the thief could bring his arm around again and regain his balance, Cassady stepped forward and led with his elbow. The thief's head snapped upward. He grabbed the wrist holding the tool, plunged the knife into a bloated stomach and pulled hard. The blood ran hot and slick over the hands of both men. Cassady yanked the blade out, held the thief by the hair and plunged the knife several times into his neck.

It was over. The scavenger dropped to the floor, bubbles forming at the corners of his mouth, dust puffing against his cheeks. Cassady picked up the tool and cracked it across the back of the man's skull to make sure. He turned the body over, wiped the blade clean on his tunic and then rifled through the pockets, which were empty except for a fire steel. Light footsteps sounded behind him and he spun around, the handle of the knife feeling inadequate in his bloodied palm.

Ghazi glanced at the body and holstered his pistol. 'Dead?'

He nodded. 'Where were you?'

'Watching from over there. You were too quick. You spooked him.'

'I didn't ask for a review.'

'Let's get rid of the body before anybody else decides to visit.'

They lifted it by the arms and legs and carried it into the forest. It didn't weigh much more than a child.

'Do we cover him?' asked Ghazi.

'No. We're out of here once the battery's charged.'

'First light, then. I'll check the maps.'

'Good. I'll give the Old Lady a once-over.'

Cassady rubbed his eyes and cursed the thief. As soon as dawn diluted the sky, they would be bouncing over the excuse for a road once more. There would be no sheets of metal to patch up the rig and no sleep for either of them. He climbed into the cab and took a blitz pill from the bottle under the seat. The miserable camp crowded the windshield. A few metres away, a body lay in the trees. He suppressed the urge to retch. Then he got to work.

2

The road played hell with the suspension and the tree branches flogged the Old Lady like she was a sinner. Behind the wheel, Ghazi did his best to keep the truck on an even keel, but it was tough work. They had to put as much distance between them and Verne as possible. Just in case. There had been a couple of shouts when they'd rolled out of the camp, but none of Quentin's men had taken a shot and they'd made it through the gate and back along the gravel trail without being pursued. Then, as soon as the chance arose, Ghazi had guided Warspite onto a track that bent north. There were more settlements up that way.

Cassady hunkered down in the passenger seat, hands gripping one of the maps as he searched for a likely destination. Ghazi kept his eyes on the trees. He had a few suggestions on where to go, but for the moment he stayed quiet. The ration boxes rattled in the back. The run to Verne had left them with enough water to last a week, but beyond that they were struggling. Breakfast had been hardtack biscuits and dried rabbit meat. The pangs in their stomach kept them alert, but they weren't much good for anything else.

The map fluttered and fell onto the Runner's lap. 'That thieving parasite,' he said. 'I can barely keep my eyes open.'

'After we're off this track, you can sleep.'

'We need a plan first.'

'You want to go to Souk?'

'There's nothing there.'

'Okay. On a day's juice, we can get to the Eisernstadt, Catun or Brunna. In two, we could make it as far as the Complex.'

'And do what there? Watch the machines tear up the earth? Schlep rubble for a meal a day? Forget it. We're not that desperate.'

'So tell me your idea.'

'I was thinking about what that settler said last night. He mentioned Prestige. Why don't we head there?'

Ghazi wrestled down a gear and considered the proposal. Prestige was as pre-Change as they came: a stable economy, supplies, jobs, a freshwater source and a swollen population of refugees. It was well-defended and a good place to land a contract to run supplies to the north, south, east or west. Or at least it had been until a recent coup had stained the dusty streets and favela hovels with blood.

'What about the uprising?'

'It's over now. They've had the executions. All back to normal.'

'That's what Faustine and the others would like us to think.'

'It's less than 90 kilometres due north from here and we can take the Watched Road for most of it.' It was obvious Cassady had already made up his mind.

'I'm not exactly keen on driving into a warzone, Cass.'

'We won't be. Look, we need food. You want to go someplace else, I'm open to it.'

They fell silent. The whine of the transmission raced in front of the truck, encouraging them to follow. With the sky now grey enough to see the road, Ghazi switched the headlights off.

'Okay,' he said against his better judgement. 'But I want to hear a report first.'

'You'll place your faith in that?'

'Please don't start.'

'I'm not starting anything.' Cassady checked the map. 'Track should finish soon. Mud for a K or two. Then we're back on asphalt. We'll stop there and catch your report.'

Ghazi patted the steering wheel, his apprehension appeased. Despite the danger, it was likely no worse than any other plan. And driving on a paved surface was something to savour. Pre-Change blacktops were becoming rarer all the time. They usually had to make do with broken, weathered roads, old farm tracks and post-Change routes that had sprung up out of necessity. Much of the infrastructure built before the temperatures and oceans rose had been reclaimed by nature or torn up for use by gangs and settlements. He and Cassady sometimes encountered highways that had toppled over, legs broken and cracked and useless. Other routes had been buried by rocks or mudslides, never to be used again. Of the passable roads that still existed, many were regularly blocked by desperate individuals waiting to liberate a vehicle of its occupants and gun it north to where the water supplies were more plentiful.

Despite the early hour, the day's heat pressed against the windows, but the A/C sat quiet. They couldn't afford the juice to switch it on, not with only one battery working. It would be hell to drive come the afternoon. While he guided Warspite over the mud, Cassady opened the armoured box under the dash, took out a ledger and skimmed through the pages. Scrawled on the pages in jagged handwriting were the broadcast frequencies of the listening stations.

As promised, the mud gave way to a tarmac road that whip-cracked between the trees. Warspite's tyres dug in and the vibrations receded. Ghazi sipped lukewarm water from the bota bag hanging above his head and kept an eye on the surroundings as the world beyond the windshield heated up. Plastic debris in the road was chewed up under the treads.

Cassady snapped the ledger shut. 'Closest station will report in fifty-seven minutes. Call sign Poor Yorick.'

'When was it last verified?'

'As if it matters. Around three months ago.'

'Better get some sleep in the meantime. I'll wake you in forty.'

Cassady pulled his cap over his eyes and within a couple of minutes his chin was resting against his chest. Ghazi stretched his neck muscles. An hour was a long time to wait. If it was bad news or Poor Yorick had switched frequencies in the past three months, the distance they'd travelled in the meantime would be for nothing. But that was the gamble. The stations had their schedules and the Runners had to obey them. Other than sharing information at the settlements, it was the only way they could find out about road conditions. Cassady didn't trust them one bit, but Ghazi had gleaned enough useful intelligence from the reports to be convinced of their worth.

The early morning sun poured death onto the asphalt. Ghazi frowned. Few of the trees on either side showed any green. If there was a spark, the forest would burn until there was nothing left. He'd driven through a forest fire once. No other choice. Flames had set the tarp alight and the smoke had come close to taking him. Almost unconsciously, he pushed the pedal down and Warspite leapt to the challenge. The rumble of the tyres against the ground undercut the whirring engine. He wiped the sweat from his eyes and reached for the sun goggles. The strap bit hard into the back of his head, but they were all he had.

There was a flash of movement as something crossed the road in front and disappeared into the brush. Ghazi tensed, but kept Warspite steady. He was about to rouse Cassady when a dog jumped out from the trees and nearly fell under the wheels. It raced after the truck. Ghazi watched it through the side mirror. A bloodhound, eyes red, foam dripping from the corners of its mouth, fur caked in dust. He was acutely aware of the wheel in his hands. A jog to the left was all it would take to put it out of its misery. He studied the reflection in the mirror. Then he dipped the pedal again. The dog stopped running and stood in the road, watching the vehicle as it picked up speed and disappeared.

He woke Cassady just before the report was due and pulled over. The drowsy Runner unlocked the storage box above their heads and took out the telescopic antenna. Outside, he uncovered the jack mounted near the hood and screwed the antenna home, then climbed back into the cab and yanked the door shut. He wiped his brow.

'The days aren't getting any cooler.'

He checked the ledger once more and read out the code. Ghazi dialled it in and turned up the volume. A sound like rain hammering against iron sheeting filled the cab. 'Here we go,' he murmured.

A low whistle cut through the rain and a few bars of a tune rang out, cold electronic splinters that got under Ghazi's skin and pulled his muscles taut. As a synthesised voice reeled off a series of letters in blocks of four, Cassady dotted boxes in the ledger. The voice repeated the message three times and was followed by the tune and the interval signal. White noise flooded the cab again.

'Got it?'

'Yes.'

Ghazi switched off the radio and waited for his partner to decipher the message. Without the solution in the ledger, the letter blocks were meaningless. Each station used a substitution cipher, and each one had its own ciphertext alphabet. Runners received the solutions from the merchants, who traded them with the stations for whatever the stations needed. Nobody knew who ran them or if they were even part of the same network. But it gave the operators a purpose, and that was all anybody wanted in the world.

Once the antenna was back in its box, Ghazi manoeuvred Warspite back onto the road and eased through the gears until they were cruising.

Cassady grunted. 'It says there's no flooding in the area.'

'With this drought I'm not surprised.'

'Route 25 is out of action. Rock fall.'

'I heard the same news back at that last town we were in. Anything about the Watched Road?'

'No. But there's a group causing trouble. Hang on.' Cassady unfolded the map and laid it against the dash. 'Near Prestige. Remnants of the uprising, I guess.'

Ghazi's jaw tightened involuntarily. Cassady caught it.

'Near, I said. Not in the actual camp. If we go in via the Watched Road, we won't have to deal with them.'

'Anything else?'

'That was it. Glad you pulled over?'

He ignored the jibe. 'Let's make it to Prestige before sundown.'

'You want me to take over?'

'Get some more rest. You're the negotiator.'

Cassady settled back in his seat. For the first time in days, the creases on his forehead disappeared.

'Follow this route until you reach the marker,' he said softly. 'Old power plant with a chimney stack. Take a left and then a right at the next crossroad. Keep going until you hit the Watched Road. Wake me then.'

'Understood.'

Cassady covered his face with his cap again. Ghazi took another sip of soupy water and rolled his neck from side to side until something clicked. An ancient urge for a cigarette stirred within him, but he quashed it. No chance of that. Nobody bothered to grow tobacco plants anymore.

3

Cassady knew the hand was reaching out for him before he opened his eyes. He grabbed it.

'I'm awake.'

He pushed his cap off his face. A paved road twisted through the washed-out brush. His throat was tighter than an engine nut. A mouthful of chlorinated water loosened it a little.

'Any trouble?'

'Overturned four-wheeler half an hour back. Already stripped. No bodies, but signs of a struggle. At least a couple of occupants, I would reckon.'

'Enough meat for a week or more, then.'

As usual, Ghazi said a prayer in Farsi under his breath. Cassady yawned. For a long time the mechanic's need to say a few words had annoyed him, but the man's respect for the dead had succeeded in making him a little less desensitised as well.

'The toll is coming up.' Ghazi swept the steering wheel left to avoid a hole. 'What do we give the Agis?'

'One of the water carboys should be enough.'

'I heard they're starting to ask for more. And not just in the north.'

'We'll see soon enough.'

Cassady poked his head into the back and counted the precious water vessels. Asking for more. They'd be lucky. In a previous lifetime, he'd wanted to join the Agis, a loose association of men and women who controlled the Watched Road. The road itself was an old highway that started at the lagoons in the north, just beyond the ruins of Hanover, and twisted south for four hundred kilometres. The only way to get on or off was through the gates guarded by the Agis. Ramshackle watch posts sat at remote intervals, each manned by a few devotees who kept the highway safe to drive on. From time to time a band of nomadics would become desperate or brash enough to block the road, and the Agis would have to take it back. He'd changed his mind about joining them after he found out the devotees almost never left their posts. They were married to the highway and the system they'd created and so they simply waited, contending with the heat and the flies and the monotony and the sudden violence, until death came for them.

Warspite sang as it took the contours. The asphalt shimmered. A film of sweat covered the scalps of the Runners.

'Pull up here. Let me drive a while, would you?'

'You sure? I've got it.'

'I've slept all I can.'

The truck rolled to a halt and Cassady slid into the driver's seat. He felt rested, though his stomach was growling. As they bore down on the Watched Road, his movements were mechanical, yet fluid, as though the wheel, the stick and the pedals were extensions of his own body. He'd been driving since he was a child, and the Old Lady was his life. Now, before the monotony kicked in, he was able to relish the vibrations passing through his arms and the fact that he was in complete control of five tons of metal and rubber. Sometimes at night, after surviving another day, he would sit in the cab listening to the rig cool down and slow his breathing until his body and the machine became one.

The gate blocking the way to the Watched Road consisted of stacked metal containers and a portcullis strung between them. On either side, foliage and hills of rubble prevented any vehicles from simply driving around the gate. A couple of rusting motorcycles sat nearby. The Agis standing in front of the gate wore a black keffiyeh and a pair of goggles and hugged a riot shotgun against her chest. Another, hair braided in tight rows, trained a rifle on them from a sandbag fortification on top of the gate. Her eyes didn't leave the two men behind the windscreen.

Cassady switched off the engine and opened the door, keeping his movements as relaxed as possible. The air was thick and unmoving and the music of the mosquitoes faded in and out. He held out his hands, palms forward, in greeting.

'Trade?' asked the Agis. Her voice was muffled.

'Water. Five litres.'

Barely a pause followed. 'Unload. Leave it there.' She pointed at a barred metal door in one of the containers.

Once they had the water, two more figures appeared on the container roof and heaved on hemp ropes wrapped around a winch. The portcullis rose. The Agis with the shotgun stood to one side and waved the vehicle through. Cassady stabbed the horn as they cleared the gate and rolled onto the asphalt. Compared to the previous night, it was more like floating than driving.

Ghazi loosened the laces on his boots and leaned back against the headrest. 'Rather taciturn today.'

'Better than the ones who keep you standing there for twenty minutes while they talk at you. Lonely bastards.'

'How's the juice?'

'Halfway gone. We should make it fine.'

Ghazi took out a knife and a piece of basswood he'd half-carved into an elephant, an animal he'd once seen a picture of in a book. Cassady didn't understand why he'd been so enraptured by it. It was just another reminder that they lived in a deader world. The creatures were gone, and the last few humans clinging onto existence would join them soon enough.

Warspite devoured the highway, and he raised a hand in greeting each time they passed one of the watchtowers. A fly landed on his cheek and he waved it away, but it kept coming back for more until finally he swatted it. The things feasted on human sweat and mucous and were more than capable of turning the days into a living nightmare. He wished he could gas them all.

Before the turnoff to Prestige, they bore down on an orange muscle car hugging the shoulder of the road. Supplies in jerry cans were lashed to the roof and a small motorbike, its wheels barely clearing the floor, was mounted to the rear fender. The car's battery poked through a hole cut in the hood. Music drifted from an open window.

'I don't believe it,' shouted Cassady. 'What's that crazy bastard doing this far north?' he shouted, and stabbed the horn three times.

'Trouble at the plantation, maybe,' muttered Ghazi.

Cassady wound the window down and shouted over the music and the keening engines. 'What's the story, Wyler?'

A massive bearded man, mostly naked except for a pair of tiger shorts and red sunglasses, leaned out of the window. He lifted the glasses and screwed up his eyes.

'Cassady, the high priest of the wheel! And Ghazi, my man from Afghanistan. What's happening?'

The two vehicles pulled over. Wyler couldn't stop laughing as he embraced them. His teeth, all present and intact, were as white as bleached bones.

'Ain't that something, meeting you two out here? Tell a brother the news.'

'Not much to tell,' said Cassady. 'We were run out of a two-bit camp last night and now we're hustling to Prestige for some chow.'

'What happened to the farm, Wyler?' asked Ghazi. The huge man's smile became a grimace. He tugged at his beard.

'Bad luck, man. Some evil sons of bitches paid us a visit one night. Nothing left for me there now. Figured I'd head north, see if there's any action.'

'I'm sorry,' said Ghazi.

'I ain't dwelling on it now.'

Cassady let it drop. 'How about coming with us to Prestige? Food and a place to sleep. It's the next exit.'

'Sure, brother. Sure. Be good to spend a night among friends. I'll follow you, okay? Don't leave me in the dust. The old heap ain't cut out for speed.'

'Yeah, right. I'll take it steady.'

Warspite rejoined the road. The muscle car, all sleek lines and raw power, followed close behind.

The exit from the Watched Road was marked by two rusting containers and a sedan sitting lengthways in the road. After a brief exchange with the guard and another few litres of precious water, the Agis shifted their car. The asphalt ended a couple hundred metres from the gate, and Warspite shuddered as it moved across the beaten earth. Cassady's gaze kept flitting to the mirror and the muscle car close behind them. He tried to recall the last time they'd taken the rig as far south as Wyler's plantation. The wild man's farm had been self-sustainable with enough food all year round, even in the burning months when the land offered little more than dust and misery, and he'd always made Cassady and Ghazi welcome. Now he was on the road just like them, driving naked through the dirt and the heat and the emptiness to find a reason to keep going and survive another day.

Prestige appeared without warning. One moment the ground was hard and barren; the next they were hemmed in by a favela. Plastic turned the road a greyish-white. On either side were single-storey shelters thrown together with tarpaulin, timber, plastic, netting, corrugated iron, nylon and anything else people could lay their hands on. Although it looked like chaos, Cassady's practised eyes identified the markers and signposts hammered into the ground and the narrow channels running between the structures. These homes belonged to the latecomers and refugees who had fled something, somewhere, and who now clung to the city as though it was a lifeboat in a boiling sea. The stench of faeces, sweat and fat clogged the air. Skinny children picked through mountains of refuse, hoping to find a scrap of food or something useful to trade. Haunted

24

and hungry faces appeared in dark openings as the two-vehicle convoy drove by. A few had the look of a survivor. Their skin was leather, their eyes stone, and they were driven solely by a desire to outlast the others around them. Ghazi unbuttoned the flap of his holster and rested his hand on the butt of his pistol. Both men kept an eye out for slingers and climbers. Most of the people in the favela were sick. Some lay outside on the ground, too weak to search for food anymore.

'Worse than death,' said Ghazi. Cassady didn't reply. It was true. The ones on the ground would be set upon and cut up for meat once they became too weak to fend off attackers. There was a rule against cannibalism in Prestige, but it didn't apply in the slums. He looked on with detachment. He'd been lucky not to end up in a place like this. Ghazi had grown up in one with the rest of his family, and he didn't speak about it.

The favela gradually gave way to pre-Change concrete and brick buildings that had been built to last for two hundred years. Some bore the marks of the recent failed uprising. Colossal water cones sat on the roofs, condensate dripping from the plastic inner walls. Banners hung from some of the buildings, each bearing a name, drawing or dictum. Cassady's gaze lingered on one displaying a vivisected man. Two guards armed with axes stood outside the structure. The fighting was over, but Prestige was still on edge.

People moved with purpose. These were the scavengers, mechanics, doctors, drivers, explorers, soldiers, farmers, opportunists, murderers and the lucky ones who were never short of something to trade. Cassady spotted a few pantechs clustered outside the only bar in the settlement. His stomach throbbed. He wanted a drink, but they had to sort out business first. He guided Warspite to a spot by a four-storey building, its heavy doors drawn shut and windows mostly covered with sheets of metal. This one had no banner hanging from its walls. More pantechs were lined up here, along with a few quads and buggies and even an exo-suit. The two Runners hopped out and locked the truck. The muscle car idled in the road, music still blaring from inside. When Wyler leaned out of the window, his twisted grey beard fell almost to the floor.

'Any place to get a drink or some herb?'

'Over there,' said Ghazi, pointing at the bar.

Wyler lifted his sunglasses and looked at the low, dark structure. 'Family place, is it?'

'Just be careful,' said Cassady. 'Don't go talking yourself into trouble.'

'Don't worry about me, babe. I didn't drive all the way up here to start fighting. Not unless somebody picks one.' He laughed.

'That's exactly what I mean.'

'See you over there.' The muscle car wheezed as it pulled away.

The Runners turned to face the sealed building. It had a few more holes in it than they remembered.

'We'd better hope she's still in business,' said Ghazi in a low voice. 'Or we could be here for a while.'

'If she's half as smart as I think she is, she would've seen the trouble coming before anyone else. In fact, she probably twisted it to her advantage.'

'Let's see.'

Cassady rapped on one of the rusted doors and a slot at eye height opened a few moments later. He passed a card through the gap and it closed again.

'Must've been bad for Wyler to leave his farm,' Ghazi said, pinching the flesh near his shoulder.

'I don't know what he thinks he'll find up here.'

'Same as what all refugees hope for.'

Metal ground against metal and they stepped away from the door. A concrete pillar of a man appeared in the gap. Livid tattoos scarred his skin and an eye patch dug into the meat below the socket.

'Cassady.'

'What happened to the eye, Sergei?'

'Carelessness. Faustine will see you both.' He handed the card back. They followed the giant inside, and a guard yanked the door closed behind them. Sergei led them up flights of rusting stairs to a drab third level where flies dive-bombed every surface. Two more guards flanked an opening into a harshly lit room. The Runners paused before the door.

'Waiting for an invitation?' called a voice from within. 'Mon dieu. Come through.'

'Go on,' said Sergei. He limped back down the stairs.

A woman dressed in a grey hemp smock and khakis waited by a window frame fitted with wooden planks instead of glass. Pencil stubs protruded from a tight black bun at the back of her head. She was thin, but wiry, and moved with the cold grace of a killer.

'Hello, Faustine,' said Cassady.

She gripped the pair of them in a strong forearm handshake. 'As always, it is good to see you both.' The way Faustine spoke made it sound as though she'd filed down the words until no ugly corners remained. They curled around peoples' ears and held on tight. Most of the time, all she had to do was talk until she got what she wanted. Runners called her the Siren.

'How's business?' asked Cassady.

'Good. Where have you been hiding the past few months? Tell me this. You missed some inviting jobs.' She flashed a set of pointed teeth. 'But no matter.'

Cassady appraised her without staring. She looked more drained than ever. Deep lines were etched into her forehead and around the mouth. Nevertheless, she radiated control. She strode over to a table covered with ledgers and beckoned for them to follow.

'Looks like you rode out the storm well enough,' said Ghazi.

'Oui. But it was a close run thing for a while. Sergei suffered worst. You saw his eye? Of course you did. He saved my life. I owe him. I told him I would give him anything he desired, but he simply said he wants to keep doing what he is doing. That is loyalty.'

'Or he knows a good thing when he's got it,' replied Ghazi mildly. Faustine shot him a glance.

'Perhaps. Still. All quiet now. The leaders have been executed. We're back to normal.'

'That's why we're here,' said Cassady.

'Busy day for good Runners. Brandt was here earlier.'

Ghazi smiled. 'How's he doing?'

'Working hard like an ox. People left their bunkers just to look at his pantech. Très formidable.'

'Where did you send him?'

'North. Where are you arriving from?'

'Verne,' said Cassady.

'With Quentin? That abruti is something short of a full tank. Did he try anything on with you?'

'We didn't exactly hang around. What's the deal?'

'Twenty wives, too many children to name. He believes he can scratch out a city in the middle of a basin and become its emperor. He can get quite violent if he doesn't have his way. We've had some trouble with him in the past.'

'The man who would be king,' said Ghazi.

'Pardon?'

'Just something I read.'

'Never a good idea. What are you looking for now? Long haul or short trip?'

'Either,' said Cassady before Ghazi could speak.

'Let me see what I have.'

The Siren took a grimy notepad from her pocket and leafed through it. 'That has been resolved,' she muttered. 'This one was cancelled today. Ah, here. I have a red run. Four deuces northeast to Syntovia. They're desperate for Gro-crop, food supplies are almost gone. Heavy flooding around the camp. Could get a touch difficult.'

'We don't need that right now,' Ghazi interjected. 'One of our batteries blew on the way to Verne.'

Cassady narrowed his eyes, but said nothing. Ghazi was right. It was too far to go without a backup.

'Dommage. I will have to find another couple of lunatics. Okay, how about this: green run, religious camp, half a deuce from here.' She unfolded a map and showed them the location. 'They call themselves the Gaeans. They need explosives to make a cave so they can pray in it.'

Cassady raised his eyebrow and Faustine smirked. 'I just send the supplies. It is not my concern what people do with them.'

'So what are you giving them?'

'Some sacks of ANFO and a handful of cast boosters.'

He whistled. 'What are they paying you for that?'

'Nearly everything they had. They brought it all in on the back of an ancient pantech and then sold it, too. Had to return to their camp on bicycles.'

'What shape are the explosives in?' asked Ghazi, waving away a fly that was determined to land on his eyelid.

'Safe. Old, but in good condition. You would not be able to detonate them if you dropped your Warspite off a mountain.'

'Cut?' asked Cassady.

'All the rations you need. No cargo.'

'Deal.'

'When's the go-date?'

'Tomorrow. I've had it on the books for a few days. Perhaps they are praying for a sandstorm to come and give me a new complexion.'

'I thought they only dealt in forgiveness.'

'Not in this world.'

Cassady offered a tight-lipped grin. 'By the way, you know anybody in Prestige with a spare battery?'

Faustine laughed and revealed her needle-like teeth. 'It is as simple as that? You must find a mechanic and hope she has the parts to fix it. Perhaps you can pick it up on your way back.'

'Who says we're coming back?'

'There is nowhere else like Prestige. You know this.' She gave a dry chuckle. 'And before you go,' she said, opening a small wooden box, 'have some root.' Cassady added a few sticks to his pouch.

'Not for me,' said Ghazi.

'Then take a water ration on your way out. Pick up the cargo tomorrow morning at daybreak. Sergei will be waiting. Do you have a place to sleep?'

'We'll park the Old Lady nearby.'

'Cą marche.' They shook hands again before parting. On the ground floor, Sergei loomed next to the open door. The sun had dipped below the horizon. It would still be hot for a couple of hours.

'Stay outta trouble,' said Sergei as the door slammed shut.

Cassady kicked up a plume of dust. 'The battery,' he said simply.

'Ease up.' Ghazi scraped a sliver of black out from underneath a nail, studied it, and wiped it on a trouser leg. 'The Old Lady's in good shape. We know the terrain. We aren't going to run into trouble.'

He pursed his lips. There was little point discussing it further. 'Let's go to the bar.'

'Not a good idea. You should rest.'

'I want to catch up with Wyler. One drink.'

Ghazi frowned. 'It's your health. I'll meet you there after I see a couple of the junkers. Maybe I can scrounge a piece of metal to patch the truck.'

'You want me to come with you?'

'I've got it. Find some food if you can.' He set off across the dusty square in the direction of a building with piles of rusting and broken parts stacked outside.

Cassady bent over until his fingers brushed the top of his boots. Something cracked in his back. It felt good. He headed for the bar. He wasn't worried about leaving the Old Lady unattended. Invisible eyes kept watch from Faustine's bunker and Sergei would step in if anybody was stupid enough to try to harvest the parts.

People walked by in ones and twos, silent for the most part. Nobody paid Cassady a second glance. He pressed his abdomen to stop the hunger pangs. He hadn't eaten since the hardtacks at daybreak. Still, they would have new rations tomorrow. The deal they'd made with Faustine was a good one. No danger, no pressure. The hands that had been twisting his insides since Verne relaxed their grip.

The air in the bar was thick with body odour, dust and unrefined alcohol. Runners, traders and drunks who could pay their way collected around empty metal drums turned on their heads. One of the Runners recognised Cassady and called him over to trade news. There wasn't much to be had: a group of fanatics was causing trouble in the south, a battle had been fought with the Agis somewhere on the Watched Road, a useful highway had been swallowed by the great lagoons in the north, and there were food shortages everywhere.

'Same as always,' said Cassady.

'Not exactly. Joe's got a story for ya.'

'Oh yeah?'

A tall man with a face caked in grime leaned over the barrel. 'Took the Bull Bitch to the Russian Wall.'

'Why?'

'Call it curiosity. We was well stocked an' close enough.' Joe jerked a thumb at his co-driver. 'I said to Ryman tha' we should take the Bull Bitch an' go for it. Dig around, maybe find summat to salvage. Wasn't worth it though. Closed up tighter than the Alps an' barren as the Bowl.'

'What did it look like?'

'Felt it 'fore I saw it.' Joe's eyes shone. 'Blocks out the sky. Swear. Metal an' concrete, mostly. Far as I could see in both directions. Barbed wire an' all kinds of traps along the top. Some kinda sandbag bunker for a cannon or suchlike. Gun was gone though. Give you summat to think about if you went an' decided you wanted to climb up there. A few signs tha' people had tried to get in. Wrecks all along the black, too. Pantechs, four-wheelers, heavy military rigs bigger 'un the Bitch. All blown outta existence. Years ago, like as not.'

'See anybody around?'

'Naw,' said Joe. 'None. I even worked up the courage to shout an' pump the horn. Got me wonderin' if there's anybody left inside. Eerie, it was. When we got there, it was jus' gettin' on for dusk, but we didn't wanna make camp. Death was hidin' behind every rock. Won't be goin' back, that's for sure.'

'Somebody told me the border's open if you follow the Wall south.'

'Sure. If you wanna try your luck pokin' around down there, go ahead. There's a reason scavengers an' Runners an' the rest never come back. Radiation hits hard.'

Cassady withdrew and made his way to the bar. Wyler's hulking form filled the far corner of the room, hands wrapped around a tin of pulque. He stared straight ahead. Nobody came close to him. Cassady swept his sweat-stained cap from his head and rapped his knuckles on the bar top. The owner, Teju, was hovering beside his tubs of pulque and fiddling with the casing of an old lamp.

'Business so good you don't need to serve your customers anymore?'

Teju looked up, lips set in a grimace. When he saw the mismatched eyes flashing in the dim light, he clicked his tongue against his teeth and laughed.

'What are you doing here? You look like hell.'

Cassady smiled. 'Thanks.'

'Where's Ghazi?'

'Taking care of something. He'll be along.'

'What's the story?'

'We were in the area and we needed a contract. Faustine had something for us.'

'The Siren has something for everyone.'

'True. And you? You look like you're still in one piece.'

'Many aren't. It was a bad business, Cassady. Cleansing in the favela. People being chopped up left and right. Those damn fanatics decided we'd raped the Earth and had to answer for our sins.'

'Sounds like they knew what they were talking about.'

'We hoped they'd move on once they'd finished their business in the slums, but they raided the town. That's when Faustine raised a militia with a few of the other entrepreneurs and put them down. We had three days of hell and then it was over.'

'And now?'

'Things have been quiet. Traffic passing through has dropped off. Fewer Runners and refugees. Faustine and the others have been spreading the word, but it's taking time.'

'We're here.'

'You are.' Teju grinned again. 'What can I get you?'

'A meal if you've got it.'

'All I have is Gro-crop and a few strips of meat. Tough as hell, but it's edible.'

'Where's the meat from?'

'You don't want to know.'

'As long as it's not human, I'll eat it. Will you do some for Ghazi too?'

'Sure.'

Cassady reached into a pocket on his utility belt and took out the fire steel he'd liberated from the thief in Verne and a few other trinkets. 'Will these cover it?'

'Works for me.' Teju took the fire steel and the other items and poured Cassady a tin of pulque from the tub. Then he disappeared to prepare the food. Cassady grabbed the tin and walked over to Wyler's corner. The wild man continued to stare straight ahead, seeing nothing.

'Your beard's in your drink.'

Wyler looked up. He blinked several times and the muscles around his jaw loosened.

'Cassady,' he said, as though remembering a name he hadn't heard for years.

Cassady took a seat across from him. 'Tell me what happened at the farm.' He swallowed a mouthful of milky pulque and blanched.

'You want to know?'

'I'm asking.'

'Fine, but you ain't going to like it.' Wyler took a deep breath. 'I took the car out to collect supplies and while I was gone, some bikers came to the farm. They'd been watching the place. They murdered my poor sweet girls, Cassady. Raped them, beat the hell out of them, cut them up and hung them from the walls while they were still alive. I've seen some things, but that was a new kind of evil, brother. Afterwards, they burned all my crops.'

Cassady stared into his drink, sickness rising in his chest. He'd known the girls. Not well, but enough for it to hurt. 'Did you know the bikers?'

'No. They were young guys, feral almost. Didn't speak any language I'd ever heard. More like grunts. I went after them, found their camp in an abandoned town.'

'And?'

'I took care of them. All of them. Some were young. Children. When I got back to the farm, I cut down my girls and buried them. I couldn't stay there any longer. I burned what was still standing, packed up the heap and hit the blacktop.'

Cassady waited a few moments before he spoke again. 'I'm

sorry. The girls were good people. They didn't deserve that.'

'It's the hand they were dealt.'

'And now?'

'It was a long journey. Not just the distance, if you dig me. I don't know if I made the right decision. You know what's naïve? I always believed in, like, a core of goodness in every human being. We're all creatures of the same family, I thought. But after seeing what those bastards did, it ain't true. Some people are born evil and die evil. Some learn how to become evil. Others react in evil ways as a response to evil. This is how we murdered the only world that was given to us. A pure, beautiful gift and we tore it apart. If there were two people left on the planet, they'd end up fighting just to take what the other has. It's in our nature, man.'

Cassady sipped his pulque. 'Maybe you're right. But I have to believe in more than that. Not every human is good, I get it. But some are. Ghazi has helped me to understand that. The good ones are those who turn life into something greater than scrabbling around in the dirt, knifing each other in the back for half a canteen of water.'

Wyler looked at him. 'And what about you, babe? Are you hacking at the branches or striking at the root?'

'I don't know. Both. Neither. I took a man's life just last night. Maybe I didn't need to, maybe I did. All I have is what I do now. Running. It gives me purpose. Somebody needs water, I bring them water. Somebody else needs grain, I bring them grain. And I get enough in return to survive and keep going. That's the cycle.'

'And you ain't looking for more than that?'

'If I am, I haven't found it yet.'

'Amen to that.'

Their tins rang against one another and they drank until the pulque was gone.

'This stuff is something,' said Wyler.

'Helps you see in the dark, too.'

'Good job. Ain't much more than shadows out there. How long are you hanging around here for?'

'We're leaving tomorrow morning. Back in a couple of days, I think.'

Wyler's face became serious again. 'Then good luck, brother. And don't look the devil in the eyes if you see him.'

4

Warspite rolled out of Prestige just after daybreak, her cargo hold laden with explosives, water and 24-hour ration packs. Ghazi was tense. He hadn't managed to find a piece of metal in good enough shape to patch up the gash in the side of the truck. As Faustine had suggested, he'd left the broken battery with one of the more reliable mechanics and asked her to do what she could. The plan was to deliver the explosives to the Gaean camp, recharge overnight, and return to Prestige to check back in with the mechanic. Then they would take a break for a couple of days. He'd insisted on it. A single evening spent drinking pulque wasn't enough time for either of them to get their heads screwed back on properly. If anything, it had made things worse.

Now they forced their way along a track being slowly consumed by a near-black mess of roots and branches. It was a typical post-Change situation. Areas that hadn't been scoured by drought, desertification or flooding now thrived in subtropical conditions. Entire towns had been swallowed by the natural sprawl, and roads and tracks sometimes abruptly ended in a wall of brambles and undergrowth, never to be used again.

Ghazi raised his voice over the grumbling tyres. 'Do you see how the forest looks?'

Cassady, one hand on the wheel, stared through the windscreen with listless eyes. 'So what?'

'Sometimes it gives me the feeling we don't exist. Do you know what I mean? Or that we're echoes of lives already lived.'

'So maybe we don't exist,' replied the other Runner wearily. 'Maybe this is all part of a dream in somebody else's head. The road, the forest, Warspite, us. No way to prove any of it's real. In which case there isn't much of a reason to keep going on like this, is there?'

'I'm being serious. Anyway, what about doubting your

existence being proof you exist? The thought itself has to come from somewhere. That somewhere is you. A being that thinks and feels.'

'That's nothing new. One of your philosophers in the container out back said that.'

Ghazi glanced across at Cassady, who wiped his mouth with his hand. The hint of a smile remained on his lips. 'I never remember the names when I read your books. But I do read them. What do you mean by us being echoes?'

'Well, let me take the Old Lady as an example. She's tied up with the road. The way we understand her, how we see her, what she does, depends on how we see everything else around her.' Ghazi paused, struggling to order his thoughts. 'It works the same with us. For so long our understanding of the world was tied up with our position compared to everything else. We were the rulers. Humanity's a grand word, isn't it? We were the subject at the heart of the universe and everything else was just an object or a resource to be used. Take nature in general. It was a store where we could buy anything we needed. We needed shelter; we chopped down trees. We needed fuel; we dug holes in the ground. We needed food; we dipped a net in the ocean or grew it in factories. Like the Old Lady driving from A to B, our identity was based on these things. But what about now? Nature is turning its back on us and we've fallen. That means we aren't the subject anymore. We're an object. So what does 'human' mean now? Do we need to redefine what we are?' He pointed to his left and right, colour rising in his cheeks, his voice louder. 'Look at this forest. It doesn't need us and we don't fit into any ecosystem. We're surplus to requirements. Perhaps we're no longer human.'

Cassady sighed. 'Yeah, and maybe a hundred years from now, there'll be nobody to ask these questions. Are you trying to make me depressed?'

Ghazi shook his head and caught his breath. He did his best

not to sound irritated. 'If you don't want to talk, just say so.'

'I don't want to talk.'

They fell into a silence that held for the next couple of hours. Leaving the larger issues to one side, Ghazi focused instead on making an inventory of Warspite. Aside from the gouge in her side and the broken battery, they were in fairly good shape. The engine was sound. They'd been lucky enough to find a pantech on the road a few months back and cannibalised it for parts. The suspension needed an overhaul, but it would keep until they had enough time and supplies to work on it. They also had plenty of sub-oil, water and grease to keep her ticking over.

And he had ammunition for his pistol again. He didn't like the vulgar lump of metal hanging by his side, but it had saved him more than once. Five cartridges sat in its single-stack magazine, his reward for poking through a deserted, disintegrating camp whose stench had saturated the surrounding area. He'd also found a pile of yellowing bones in a pit inside one of the buildings and a vicious dog he'd had to put down. They'd left before any nearby scavengers or gangs had arrived to investigate the sound of the pistol shot. It never paid to hang around in one place for too long.

In mid-afternoon, they emerged from the forest. Grasslands stretched out into the distance on either side of the cracked, faded road. The Runners switched places. Ghazi coaxed Warspite along, his gaze sweeping the tarmac for potholes, rocks and other obstacles that might damage the vehicle. Once in a while he had to swing the steering wheel around, jolting both men from the hypnotic state they fell into most days. At one point, a motorcyclist approached from the opposite direction and sped past Warspite without trying to make contact.

A station broadcast was due at three o'clock, and Ghazi insisted on listening in. They stopped at the side of the road, and the sun scoured the top of the mechanic's head as he attached the antenna. Back inside the cab, he waited with his hand on the dial as Cassady pulled the ledger out. Reams of code had been jotted down, scratched out and rewritten so many times there was almost no space left on the pages.

'Laika-3,' he said. 'Frequency 15.867.'

Ghazi tuned the radio in. The familiar unsettling soup of white, thermal and electronic noise filled the cab. Cassady glanced at the timepiece above the juice meter. 'She'll be on in five minutes. Enjoy the music.'

They waited, listening to the howl that heralded the slow death of the universe. Ghazi kept his eyes on the road and the mirrors. The timepiece ticked off five minutes and then five more. Cassady drummed his fingers against the ledger and checked the list again.

'Maybe the frequency's changed,' he said.

'Unlikely. Faustine would have mentioned it.'

'Somebody could have retired it, then.'

Ghazi frowned. Once in a while a station was discovered and the operators were murdered. But finding one was more luck than design. And the sites were well defended against that kind of threat.

Something whispered to them between the static. It was almost inaudible. Cassady pressed his ear against the transmitter and then reached over and dialled up the volume until they could both hear it. It was a human voice, male, accented and nothing like the synthesised messages sent by the stations. The words were clear.

'...must find the intruder. All agents have been activated. They understand the importance of the task. This technology could restore nature's balance and repair the damage wrought on a global scale. It is imperative for us to seize it. The threat is—'

The broadcast went dead. Cassady's hand leapt to the dial, but Ghazi grabbed his wrist.

'Leave it on for a minute.'

White noise ricocheted off the cab walls. Outside, heat waves made the air shimmer and the road became a shifting, drifting river of bitumen. Finally, Cassady switched off the radio.

'That wasn't Laika-3,' murmured Ghazi.

'No.'

'So what was it?'

'I don't know.'

'Sure it's the right frequency?'

'I'm sure.'

Cassady turned to the back of the ledger and wrote down the message.

'So what happened to the station?'

'I don't know. Pick a reason. Maybe it was a rogue signal from a settlement that interfered with the broadcast. Or tropospheric ducting bent the signal hundreds or thousands of kilometres from wherever it was sent. Happens once in a while. Or a geomagnetic storm ate up Laika's message. Or the fool in the operator's chair flicked the wrong switch.'

Ghazi sat back, staring at nothing. 'Did you get it all down?'

'I think so. "This technology could restore nature's balance and repair the damage wrought on a global scale."'

'What do they mean? What kind of technology can do that?'

Cassady's voice was strained. 'How should I know? We don't even know who 'they' are. Maybe somebody's making a bad joke.'

Despite the heat, Ghazi's skin was cold. 'If it's a joke, why are you writing it down?'

'Just in case.'

'What do you want to do?'

'What do you mean? We're going to the Gaean camp. And we keep quiet about whatever this was until we find out if anybody else heard it. No use drawing attention to ourselves.'

'Fine.'

Cassady shifted in his seat to face him. 'What's gotten into you?'

'That wasn't a normal broadcast. You know that.'

The sinewy Runner lifted the peak of his cap to reveal his eyes. 'It hasn't got anything to do with us. Let's just get to the camp. I don't want this dynamite in the rig for any longer than it needs to be. And we haven't got much of the afternoon left.' He checked the map. 'A marker will be coming up in 30 to 40 minutes. Some kind of military bus. Then it should be another twenty Ks to the drop-off point.'

Ghazi pushed the button next to the wheel and the low whine returned. They rejoined the road. He threw the truck into the next curve, replaying the message in his head. He couldn't share Cassady's pragmatism. Technology to reverse the Change. A snatched message broadcast on a frequency reserved for a listening station. He didn't believe in coincidences. Either the universe meant for them to hear it or it was a poor omen. Whichever it was, it left him restless.

The grass gave way to scrubland, with plants that looked like mould growing on a brick of orache bread. Deep in the hills, the road finally fell apart and became a barely visible dirt track. Both men became more alert. The shadow of the truck stretched further outward. Ghazi had to shake his arms to relieve the cramps in his elbows. The pain was something he and Cassady had to live with, like the heat and the constant throb of hunger. He sipped thick water from the bota bag and ran his tongue over his teeth. He detested the chlorine tang. Cassady insisted on treating all water they collected with a puritab, but he didn't think the chemical made it much safer. Every water supply was probably contaminated by radiation anyway.

A band of cloud obscured the sun. The A/C rattled on a low setting. Flies buzzed inside the cab, but neither man attempted to brush them away. Then Cassady sat up straighter.

'There.'

The back end of the marker, the military bus, was visible ahead. Like a sinking ship, the front was submerged in a sea of dust and earth. The paint had flaked away, leaving only a brown husk. Devoid of wheels, axles and windows, the ragged holes in its sides had been blocked with planks of wood, rusted chicken wire and other flotsam. Ghazi eased off on the pedal. Cassady pressed his forehead against the glass.

'Ground's disturbed by the back doors. We'd better take a look.'

They stopped. 'Let me go first,' said Ghazi. He looped the ignition key around his neck and flipped the kill switches. Then he threw open the heavy door and jumped out, his hand on his pistol. He scanned the scrub. Nothing moved except the flies and the lizards. He moved around the hood of the truck. Cassady was right. The ground near the rear doors of the bus was scuffed. An incomplete boot print stood out like an accusation in the dust. He motioned for his partner to join him.

Cassady pulled out an old, scarred machete from underneath the passenger seat, left the truck and approached the back doors while Ghazi covered him. He yanked the door open and the sound of screeching metal disturbed the silence. With his machete raised, he peered inside. Then he turned away and suppressed a retch.

'Wasted. You can put your gun away.' He returned to Warspite for a couple of respirators and threw one to Ghazi. The plastic cup was uncomfortable and barely worked anymore, but it was better than nothing. Cassady climbed into the remains of the bus first. The shell creaked under his weight. Ghazi took another look up and down the road, wary of a trap, and followed him inside.

The air was ripe enough to burst. A sweet, putrid stench clung to their throat and nostrils. The bus was a grave. The drone of a thousand flies disturbed from a banquet filled their ears. There were no seats or frames bolted to the floor of the bus, only dead scrub, a layer of earth and handfuls of rags. Lying in the middle of the space were two decomposing bodies.

'How long?' asked Ghazi, his voice muffled. Cassady crouched beside one of them.

'Three or four days. Starvation, probably.' He scratched the back of his glistening head.

'We should leave.'

'We will. Go back to the rig. I'll check them.'

Ghazi's eyes lingered on the bodies and he whispered a quick prayer. At least they hadn't been mutilated or the bones picked clean. But it was a miserable way to go. Middle of nowhere, nobody to hear their cries as they died. He didn't want to know how they'd become stranded in the bus like that. He climbed out and stripped off the respirator, then wiped his lips and forehead and blew hard through each nostril. The rotting stench would stay with him now for the rest of the day.

Warspite was idling by the time Cassady climbed back into the cab. He slid the machete back under the seat and dropped a couple of razor blades into one of the holders next to the dash.

'Found them under the rags.'

'Anything else?'

'That was it.'

Ghazi's boot touched the pedal and Warspite leapt away from the forsaken bus.

'Still another two hours before we hit the settlement,' said Cassady. 'Hungry?'

Ghazi's fingers tightened against the wheel. 'You're joking.'

'We haven't eaten since daybreak. Don't tell me a bit of carrion can put you off your food.'

The lean Runner reached behind him and grabbed a metal container that was sealed tight. He popped the lid and took out a small red cake of pemmican. The meat had been dried out in the midday sun, crumbled up into pieces, formed into a rough ball

44

and bound with melted animal fat. He held out a piece to Ghazi, who shook his head and winced.

'Sometimes I don't understand you.'

'Human fertiliser. That's all they were. Don't think about it.'

Cassady tore into the flesh-coloured cake. Ghazi moved Warspite up through the gears, wound down the window and drove with his head leaning out of the cab. It was the only way to blast the stench of death from his body.

5

The Gaean camp was on a plateau, with good views of the land in every direction. The few trees and bushes that had been growing near the top had been cut down to give a clear line of sight, and the settlement was protected on all sides by a palisade fence, the top of which had been cut and honed into a row of serrated teeth. The fence hid everything inside from view, making it difficult to guess the camp's strength. The only way to reach it was to follow a narrow track that wound its way around the hill to a crude metal gate. Once inside, it would be impossible to leave in one piece unless the Gaeans allowed it.

Warspite halted in front of the gate. Rifle barrels and arrowheads protruded from loopholes, but nobody appeared on the track.

Cassady eyed the hardware and ignored the sweat that rolled down his back. 'Be ready to cut out.'

'They're just flexing their muscles.' Ghazi's hands massaged the wheel. 'I hope.'

'I know that.'

'So why do you look so tense?'

Cassady grunted. It was the rifles that were making him sweat. All it would take to set them all off was a single nervous kid fondling the curve of a trigger too much. He and Ghazi would be dead before they could throw the Old Lady into reverse.

A hatch in the bulwark opened and a woman wearing a pale robe emerged. She stood with her arms out and her palms facing the truck to show the Runners she was unarmed.

Cassady kicked open the door. 'Wait here.' He jumped out of the cab and mimicked the woman's stance. The air on the plateau was cooler than he'd been used to for the past few weeks. It was almost bearable.

'Identify,' she rasped. Dark blue tattoos formed geometric

worlds on her forehead, chin and neck. Somebody had cut open her cheeks and sewn them back together to leave behind vivid tribal welts. Long grey hair collected at her shoulders.

'Cassady, Warspite. ANFO delivery from Prestige.'

The woman walked up to him, so close that he could smell the sourness of her. She reached out and they gripped forearms.

'Follow the path to the end of the stockade. A disciple will be waiting. Remain here for the night. Your safety is guaranteed. Does your vehicle require recharging?'

'Yes.'

'We will make our energy available.'

'Thank you.'

'We are indebted to you. We can now continue our journey.'

'What journey?'

'To meet the Mother. We shall dwell within Her and we shall hear Her voice. She will tell us how to repent our sins. We shall be born again.'

The woman held his gaze for a moment before turning away. The conversation was over. Cassady returned to the cab.

'So?' asked Ghazi.

'All clear. She guaranteed our safety.'

'I think we can believe her.'

Any further conversation was cut short by the sound of the bulwark being dragged out of the way. Warspite entered the camp. Beyond the palisade wall, large and small tents were laid out in clusters across the plateau. Each cluster had a tangle of Gro-crop and a solar still next to it. Men, women and children eyed the truck with simple curiosity and then returned to their tasks. Cassady relaxed. A glance in the mirror showed the metal shield being pushed back into place.

They continued straight ahead, passing turnoffs to the left and right until they reached a large round tent in the centre of the camp. A bald man in a tunic hobbled out of it and signalled for them to stop. Cassady stuck his head out of the window.

'Follow,' said the man, jerking his thumb over his shoulder. He led them along the track and then down a side path that terminated in a bay shielded by a canvas screen. The palisade wall and a squat black solar still lay just beyond it. After Cassady had dropped the hatch at the back of the truck, the man called out a command in an unfamiliar language. The flap of a nearby tent was thrown open and eight women filed out. Without paying any attention to the Runners, they carefully unloaded the sacks of explosive and the boosters and set off along the track.

'Charge battery there,' said the man, pointing to an old energy storage unit. He sounded as though he was chewing gravel. 'Remain at all times this area. No communication with persons. Understand?' He stared at the two sun-burnished men, evidently not trusting them, and shuffled back in the direction of the main track.

'No friends here,' said Ghazi. He stretched his back and tensed his right arm until his elbow crunched. 'How large do you think the camp is?

'Four hundred. Five, maybe.'

He ran his nails along the canvas screen hiding the ancient truck from view. 'Wonder why they felt the need for this.'

'To keep us away from the true believers.'

'Are you hungry?'

'Always.'

While Ghazi busied himself with the rations, Cassady retrieved their entrenching tool and dug a shallow latrine near the palisade wall. When he was done, he took the storage unit provided by the Gaeans over to Warspite and hooked it up to the depleted battery. It would take most of the night before they were back to full power. A tiny display indicated the cells were charging. He wished they had a backup.

Next he checked the solar still. He lifted the cone and ran his finger along the trough at its base. It was dusty. He was thankful they had enough water in reserve.

'Chow,' called Ghazi softly.

Cassady took a seat on one of their collapsible stools and watched the mechanic tear open one of the 24-hour boxes Faustine had given them as payment for the run. He reached over and picked up a piece of cardboard. The expiry date was seven years ago. According to the label, the contents had been treated with Cosinex, which meant they would still be edible. Or at least he hoped.

Ghazi checked off the items. 'Biscuits, meat spread, jam, peanut butter, tea, coffee, sugar, salt, chocolate, creamer, beef tea, soup, gum, dextrose tablets and powdered lemon. Take your pick.'

'Toss the jam, the chocolate and the creamer. Divide the rest. I'll heat some water.'

They ate in silence. The tang of the Cosinex overpowered everything, but neither man complained. Their stomachs were full for the first time in weeks.

Afterwards, Ghazi lay on the floor and joined the stars with an invisible thread. Cassady rummaged around in a kit locker until he found a half-full canteen. He poured a mouthful of the liquid into a cup and sniffed. It didn't need chemicals to stay good.

Ghazi broke the silence. 'I was thinking about the transmission we heard earlier.'

Cassady hesitated. The clear, urgent voice echoed inside his skull. He couldn't say exactly why it had made him feel so uneasy, and he had little desire to discuss it now. 'What about it?'

'I think it was real. Something to take seriously.'

'How can you know?'

'I can't. But the voice was human. You heard it. The words it used were precise. It knew what it wanted to say. We weren't the only ones listening in. It had an audience. And it has support behind it.'

'You're guessing.'

'It said 'we', not 'I'. It spoke of agents. And the matter was urgent. Only a group with enough resources would be able to take a technology by force and hunt down an intruder before a deadline.'

The food congealed into a cold, hard brick in Cassady's stomach. 'Pointless to waste energy like this,' he said quickly. 'You're reaching for conclusions.'

'Don't you want to know what it meant?'

When no response came, Ghazi lapsed into silence. Cassady closed his eyes and listened to the world. The palisade wall creaked in the breeze. Footsteps carried over the tops of the tents. An engine whined for a moment and then died. He was surprised there were any other vehicles in the camp.

When he came to, his chin was resting on his chest and it was dark. Ghazi leant with his back against one of the tyres and ran his precious whittling blade over a piece of wood. Cassady lifted his head and struggled to work some moisture around his mouth. 'Turning in time,' he said hoarsely.

Without using a light, they strung tripwires and laid mantraps around the truck. Then they laid their sleeping mats on the cargo bed and strung up a mosquito net from the central rib. Cassady looped the strap on the handle of his machete around his wrist. He listened to Ghazi's breathing become deep and slow, and waited for sleep to come to him.

6

Dawn was on its way, but the camp remained dormant except for one man. Ghazi jogged along the track, kicking up plumes of dust that coated the toecaps of his boots. His hand gripped the handle of the bayonet hanging from his belt. His shifting, liquid eyes were little more than slits. He didn't know what to make of what he'd just seen, but he wasn't about to jump to any conclusions. He had to speak to Cassady.

When he neared the end of the trail, he slowed and shifted his weight onto the balls of his feet. Sitting in the porch of the tent closest to Warspite was the bald man who had directed them to the berth the night before. A rifle, old and discoloured but well maintained, lay across his thighs. His head rested on his shoulder and his eyes were closed, just as they had been twenty minutes earlier. Ghazi walked by without making a sound, climbed into the back of the truck, and dragged the mosquito net aside. Cassady's eyes flicked open.

'What is it?'

'There are other Runners here. Three rigs.' His voice was scratchy.

Cassady sat up, skin taut against his jaw. 'Together?'

'No. Hidden behind screens, same as us. North, south, east and west. Guards watching each one.'

Cassady wiped the sleep from his eyes and reached for his vest.

'Recognise any of them?'

'Two. Brandt is here with Renfield.'

'Faustine said she'd sent them north.'

'I remember. Why would she lie?'

'I don't know. Who else is here?'

Ghazi hesitated. 'Orion.'

'They're here? You're sure?' Despite the situation, the news made Cassady smile.

'Difficult to mistake that beast.'

'What about the third one?'

'I don't know. Looks like a bunker on wheels. Newer model, probably post-Change. Automatic transmission for sure. Painted black. I didn't see the drivers. Know anyone who would drive something like that?'

'I don't think so. Any of the guards spot you?'

'No.'

Cassady rubbed his chin, stood and launched himself over the tailgate. Within a minute he was back. 'The battery's charged. If we need to make a break for it, the Old Lady's ready to go.'

'What are you thinking?'

'That we're being set up.'

'Me, too.'

It couldn't be a coincidence. The camp was too small and the drivers were too good to be sent to the same place simply to deliver supplies.

'Do you think Faustine wants the pantechs?' continued Ghazi. 'Maybe the fighting hit her harder than she showed and she needs to restock her fleet.'

Cassady shook his head. 'If she started killing off Runners whenever she was short, she wouldn't be in business for long.'

'The Gaeans, then. They've orchestrated it. You heard what Faustine said. They sold everything just to get those explosives.'

'So why didn't they cut our throats last night already?'

'I don't know. In any case, we should speak to Brandt and Renfield. Four heads are better than two.'

Cassady weighed up the decision and reached for his machete. 'Then let's go.'

The bald man was still dead to the world. They retraced the boot prints that were visible in the dust, following the camp trail until it forked off to the left. Ghazi winced as Cassady's boots thudded against the ground. The noise was loud enough for him to squeeze his partner's wiry arm and raise a finger to his lips. He earned a scowl in response.

As they approached the eastern edge of the camp, they dropped to a crouch. Flies settled on the backs of their necks and hands. They left the path before they could be observed by the guard and ducked between cramped tents and patches of Gro-crop. Keeping low, Ghazi led Cassady in an arc until they reached the palisade wall. The smell of the cut wood cooled his thoughts. They could see Brandt's vehicle, Telamonian, looming over the tents, an eight-wheeled tank that was too large to be fully concealed by the screen. Hollow bars had been welded to the cowl to give the monster a set of tusks. It looked as though it could knock Warspite aside without moving into second gear.

The camp was beginning to stir. The sky was grey now. They didn't have much time. They skipped over guy-ropes that seemed to have been thrown in their way on purpose, but froze when one of the tent flaps opened. Ghazi's hand snaked to the bayonet on his belt. A hooded disciple strode out without noticing their presence and joined the path. They continued on until they reached the edge of the clearing, where they spotted Renfield. A tall man with long, spider-like limbs and not a hair left on his head, the Runner's attention was on a can bubbling over a small, wood fire. Ghazi's features softened at the sight of him.

'The old buzzard looks calm,' muttered Cassady.

'He always is.' Ghazi made a quick assessment. 'If we stay low, we should be able to make it behind the screen without the guard noticing. He's looking at the trail, not the tents behind him.'

'Lead the way.'

He dropped to the floor and pulled himself forward over brittle ground that rubbed the skin from his elbows. He kept his eyes on Renfield, who stirred the contents of the can. He was much older than him or Cassady, with wrinkled skin that collected in sacks around his neck and arms. The sun's touch through the driver's window had left one half of his face more mottled than the other. A couple of years ago he'd lost his pantech in a rockslide and been lucky to escape, and a short while later he'd joined up with Brandt. The two veterans worked well together.

As Ghazi reached the screen, Renfield finally raised his head. A slight twitch of the lips was the only indication that he'd seen the two men crawling towards him. He stopped stirring the food and, with some difficulty, heaved himself into the back of the monster rig. Ghazi dragged himself behind the screen and scrambled to his feet. Cassady was right behind him. No shouts came from the track.

Renfield emerged once more, dropping to the ground with a quiet groan and straightening up until his knees clicked. Behind him was an even taller man, shirtless, with a muscular chest and arms showing early signs of disrepair. They walked over, both limping slightly.

'How's the old boys' club?' asked Cassady.

'Been expecting you,' muttered Brandt, and stuck out a hand for the pair of them to shake. A thick German accent twisted the words into unfamiliar shapes. Ghazi hadn't seen the grizzled old Runner for a while, but his appearance had changed little in the meantime: flat grey eyes, a halo of grey hair, sharp-angled face, broad shoulders. A real block of granite.

'We clocked you coming in last night,' said Renfield. He smiled. 'Jürgen called it. Said by the sound of the engine that the rig was yours.'

'Impressive,' said Ghazi.

'Every engine has its own heartbeat,' said Brandt. 'Yours beats faster than most.'

'Scares away rabid dogs,' said Cassady. 'How long have you been here?'

'We turned up a couple of hours before you did.' He spat out a wad of root pulp. 'Directed to this spot, told not to leave the area. I went anyway. A few of those fanatics showed up. They weren't so threatening, but I got the idea they wanted us to stay put and wait.'

'You want to try for the gate?'

Brandt folded his arms. 'I'm not in any hurry.'

'Why?'

'I'd say we're here for a reason.'

'Is that what the Siren told you?' asked Ghazi.

'She told us this was a milk run. That was all,' said Renfield. 'We simply have to be patient, boys.' He walked over to the fire again and poked around in the tin with a knife. Ghazi's stomach twitched at the smell of Gro-crop heads caramelising. He hadn't eaten yet. Around them, more flies were waking up.

'You know there are two other crews here besides us?' said Cassady.

Renfield glanced over his shoulder. 'No. We didn't hear them. They must have arrived before us. Did you get the chance to identify the pantechs?'

'One is Orion.'

Brandt's features softened for a moment. 'Die liebe Katarina. I wonder how Hearst is taking her captivity.'

'Not well, I would guess.'

'And the other?'

'Unknown,' said Ghazi. 'I didn't get a good look at it. But it's a tank. Newer than our pantechs.'

Brandt scratched at the white fuzz on his chin. 'Strong group. Do you have an idea what for?'

Ghazi glanced at Cassady, who chewed his lip and said nothing. He always did that when he was mulling something over. He drifted over to the palisade wall and rested a hand against one of the wooden stakes. 'We could climb out,' he said quietly. 'Circle the camp, link up with Hearst and Katarina. They might know something we don't.'

Then a rough voice rang out. 'Runners.'

The four men turned around to find the bald man standing by the canvas screen. Flanking him were four robed Gaeans, all with rifles pointing towards the ground. The early sun cast long shadows behind them.

'Remove weapons. Place on floor. No harm.' The bald man spoke without intonation.

Ghazi immediately looked to Cassady. One hand was wrapped around the handle of his machete and the veins jumped on his forearm.

'Don't do anything,' he said. 'You heard what Brandt said. We're here for a reason.'

'Mr Ghazi is both correct and sensible,' said Renfield. 'There's no need for bloodshed this early in the morning, either.' He held out his hands towards the bald man. 'I'm not carrying anything.'

Brandt reached behind his back and pulled out two gimlet knives that he tossed on the floor. The bald man pointed at a holster on Brandt's belt. 'Pistol.'

'It isn't loaded. I don't have any bullets.'

'Pistol,' said the man again. The German threw the firearm next to the knives.

Taking care not to make any quick movements, Ghazi drew his firearm from the holster, released the magazine and placed the pistol next to Brandt's. There was no round in the chamber. He stuffed the magazine into a pocket.

Only Cassady remained. His body vibrated with energy and beads of sweat dripped from his head. He didn't want to give up so easily, but he unbuckled the machete holder from his leg anyway. The metal rang out as it hit the floor. The four guards moved in and stuffed the weapons into a bag, which they then threw into the back of Telamonian. The bald man jerked a thumb over his shoulder.

'Follow.'

Renfield kicked dust over the flames of the fire, scooped one of the crop heads out of the pan, and juggled it from hand to hand until it was cool enough to eat. Then, sandwiched between two guards at the front and two at the rear, the Runners walked in single file along a dusty path that wound its way towards the centre of the camp.

7

Two men and two women waited outside the stockade's main tent, and a handful of robed Gaeans with blank expressions watched over them. The men were strangers, but Cassady recognised the women as Hearst and Katarina. He tried to crush his fear into a ball, but it was proving difficult. He shouldn't have given up the machete. Now he was at the mercy of the fanatics with rifles and the limping bald man who kept turning around to check they were following.

Brandt fell into step with Cassady, who dug his hands into his pockets. He hoped the old man hadn't seen them shaking. Brandt spoke quietly. 'Bleib ruhig, friend. Whoever brought us here needs us more than we need them.'

'I know that.' He didn't try to disguise the irritation in his voice. Brandt raised his eyebrows, but said nothing.

The bald man turned around again and pointed at the tent. 'Stay there. Return soon.' He hobbled away along another path. The four Runners joined the group. For a moment there was silence as the men and women eyed each other up, and then Brandt grinned and stepped forward to embrace Katarina. Older than any of them, her hair was as white as a salt pan and wrapped in tight braids that fell down her back. He kissed her on the cheek.

'Hello, Kaja,' he murmured. They broke apart and he studied her face. 'So lange. You are in good health. Better than me, that's for sure.'

'We've been lucky. Food and rest go a long way.' She smiled and took Renfield's arm. 'Länge sedan sist. It is good to see you both. Truly.'

'Isn't it time for us to retire yet?' said Renfield with a laugh.

'Speak for yourself.'

Cassady turned his attention to Hearst, who had taken a step back from the others.

'Keeping up okay?' She inclined her head slightly and looked away. The long scar running from her temple to her jaw gleamed in the morning sun. It had been stitched together badly, and it made her face appear crumpled. Like Ghazi, a short strip of hair ran across the top of her otherwise shaven head, while brutal geometric tattoos covered the back of her scalp. Hearst was probably the best driver Cassady had ever run with. Orion was her rig, and it was a toxic insect in mechanical form. Hearst never seemed to tire, had the reflexes of a viper, and rarely said more than a few words at a time. Only Katarina was able to get her to open up even a little.

He was aware the two strangers were staring at him. They were young. One had a shock of blonde hair, quick eyes and a dangerous smirk. The other, tall and gaunt and dressed all in black, with his hands out of sight behind his back, hadn't moved a muscle while the others talked. Neither man looked as though he had eaten much in the past few weeks. But before Cassady could ask them their business, Katarina gripped his arm and drew him close, and he allowed himself to enjoy the old woman's embrace. She whispered into his ear. 'You look tired, Edward.'

Cassady grimaced. He felt the blood rise to his cheeks and he pulled away.

'Busy schedule. You know how it is.'

'Not every day has to be a battle.' She turned to Ghazi. 'Salam, my friend. Is he getting enough rest?'

'He would if he ever let go of the wheel.'

The braids swayed as a laugh escaped her body. 'Ah, yes. He still believes himself to be an island.'

Cassady bit off his retort. He didn't appreciate being spoken about as though he wasn't there, but it wasn't worth picking a fight over already. Instead, he fixed his mismatched eyes on the unknown crew.

'What's the story with you?'

The boy with the blonde hair stepped forward and held out his hand. 'My name's Victor,' he drawled. 'I know who you are. No need to waste words.'

Cassady frowned, unsure whether the kid was testing him or if he was just arrogant. He nodded at the other newcomer. 'What about you?'

The other man offered the shortest of bows, but his hands remained clasped behind his back. 'Hideki Tagawa.' He paused for a beat. 'Pleasure.'

'How long have you been running?' He hadn't meant it to sound like a challenge, but there was an unmistakable edge to his voice.

The skin creased around Victor's eyes. 'A little over two years, all told. Drop in the ocean compared to you, Cassady. But we all gotta start somewhere.' He became mock-serious. 'Wanted to meet you for a while, by the way.'

'Why?'

'Pick a reason. Driving into the ruins of Berlin and making it out alive. Breaking the blockade at Souk. Those ain't things you can shrug off like they're nothing.'

'Drivers like to stretch stories further than the Watched Road. Free advice: don't trust what you hear in the watering holes.'

'Even so, there's no smoke without fire,' said Tagawa.

Victor cuffed the hair away from his forehead. 'So are we done with the introductions now? Don't you wanna find out why we're all standing here? We ain't got any weapons and we ain't getting near our rides unless these wackadoos want us to.' He folded his arms. 'You wanna tell us what you know?'

Cassady bit the inside of his cheek. The boy was too sure of himself.

'No more than you do, I should think,' said Renfield. A grin played across his lined face. Unlike the others, he was clearly enjoying Victor's performance. 'Jürgen and I came in from Prestige with a cargo from Faustine yesterday evening. Simple run, no problems. Same for Warspite.'

'Us, too,' said Katarina. 'But we arrived yesterday morning. Our hosts told us they were waiting on three more rigs and that we were invited to stay. Nothing more. And here you all are.'

'Did you get the feeling we're in danger?' asked Cassady.

'No. In fact, I believe they know about as much as we do.'

'You're saying they don't have anything to do with it.'

'Not beyond keeping watch on us. Somebody else is pulling the strings.'

Brandt cleared his throat and jerked his head towards the path. 'I believe we may be about to find out who.'

The head of a giant bobbed above the tents. There was a patch over the hole where his left eye should have been. Cassady exchanged a glance with Ghazi, whose features remained neutral. He dug his sweating hands further into his pockets and tried to ignore the feeling that the situation was spiralling beyond his control.

From somewhere down the hill came the sound of a bag of ANFO being detonated. None of the Runners flinched. Sergei broke between the tents and stalked towards them, a metal case clamped in one of his scarred hands. Behind him stumped the bald disciple, supporting a gaunt, pallid man with a head wrapped in bandages. From inside the tent, two robed figures appeared bearing a table. Sergei slammed the metal case down onto it.

'Let's get to it,' he growled as an introduction.

'What the hell is going on?' snarled Victor.

Sergei gave him a look that suggested he change his tone. Cassady took a step forward, wishing he had his machete. The dread was solidifying into a hard ball of anger.

'Answer him,' he said.

Sergei drew himself up to his full height. He was easily a head taller than Brandt. 'All of you watch it. You ain't the only ones feeling tender. I want two minutes now to tell you what's what. So be quiet.' He stared at Victor. 'Hear me?'

The boy gave a short nod.

'You all know each other by now. What I gotta tell you might be difficult to understand, but these are the facts. I ain't gonna water it down, because there ain't time. A little while ago, we found out about a settlement deep in the Italian desert. Seems it's some kind of geo-engineering research facility, set up while the Change was shaking us back to the Dark Ages, and the people there have been working their asses off on all kinds of different technologies ever since. Clean energy, sustenance, terraforming, that kinda thing. For the past few years they've been developing some kind of machine that could, if it works, clean up the mess we've made of the planet. Turn back the clock, I mean. Sea levels, rainfall, jungles, animal life, the deserts, all reversed. But now the settlement has hit a big damn snag and they need help from outside to get them back on track. We're that help.'

Sergei paused to draw breath. It was the chance Victor needed to jump in.

'Where's the joke?'

'No joke, boy. You're on this hill for a reason.'

'How can you prove what you're saying?' asked Katarina.

Ghazi spoke up. 'I can.'

Cassady's eyes bore into him. He was going to tell them about the broadcast. Throwing away their bargaining chip before they even had a chance to work out what they could get from it. Sometimes the man was too quick to do the honest thing.

'We heard a transmission on the road. Yesterday afternoon.'

'What did you hear?' asked Sergei.

'We were keyed into a station frequency, but there was no report. A message was broadcast instead. A man's voice, not encrypted.' He dug a small notebook out of a pocket.

Cassady shook his head. He must have copied it down sometime during the night.

Ghazi read aloud from the page. 'This is how it started "...

must find the intruder. All agents have been activated. They understand the importance of the task. This technology could restore nature's balance and repair the damage wrought on a global scale. It is imperative for us to seize it. The threat is—" That was all it said before it cut out.'

A new voice spoke. 'When did you hear that message?'

The gaunt stranger who had been following Sergei stood leaning on a cane, his gaze firmly on Ghazi. Deep lines were cut into either side of his mouth, as though he'd spent most of his life laughing or in pain. A wave of brittle hair sat atop his head, while an iron-grey moustache fanned out to the middle of his cheeks.

'Yesterday afternoon,' said Ghazi.

The man winced. Cassady wasn't sure if it was due to the words or the discomfort he had to be in. A dark patch showed on the bandage wrapped around his temples. 'The machine is real,' he whispered, the words thinner than paper curling in a fire. 'And the intruder was me.'

Nobody in the group spoke. The pregnant silence stretched until they could feel it scratching at the hairs on their skin. The man swayed on his feet. Cassady prepared to dart forward and catch him before he hit the ground, but he steadied himself and used the cane to limp over to the table.

'I will take it from here,' he said to Sergei. The giant clasped his hands together and stepped back. 'My name,' he said, shifting his gaze to each Runner as he spoke, 'is Lupo. I am a scientist, and I am here with a plea for help. I come from a settlement, a research facility, in the deserts of Italy. We call it La Talpa. It is my home. Two weeks ago I set off on my journey, along with three others. I faced death several times, but I survived. My comrades were not as fortunate.

'Just under three months ago, the first of us at La Talpa fell ill with the disease that has brought so much misery to our community. The symptoms are mild at first. Localised bruising coupled with insomnia. Later on, the bruising spreads. The body is in a state of constant pain and is unable to heal itself, and the patient is exhausted from the lack of sleep. At the end, the body bleeds internally. It cannot be stopped. Before I left, we had lost nearly sixty people. Among these were twelve engineers who had been working on the machine.

'Our efforts to combat the disease were initially unsuccessful. We could slow the spread of the bruising, but the internal bleeding was something else.' Lupo paused. 'My daughter, too, fell ill. She was part of the first group.' He sighed and shook his head. 'But this isn't relevant. Three weeks ago we made a breakthrough. We created a serum, a coagulant that stimulates platelet activation, combined with a sedative that places the patient into an induced coma. We tested it. The serum reversed the effects after two days. After coming out of the coma, the patient made a complete recovery.'

Lupo rested his hands against the table and squeezed his eyes shut. Cassady watched him. The man was a step away from diving off the deep end. Italy to Prestige in six days, all while injured. He wasn't sure he could believe it.

'I apologise,' he said in the same thin voice. 'I am still somewhat short of energy. After we concluded the tests, we found we had enough supplies for only two more patients. We used them immediately. For days afterwards we travelled far and wide looking for supplies, but we failed. Eventually we realised we would have to go further north. I and three others volunteered to go. While we prepared, our head researcher reported to sick bay with a bruise on her arm. We left that afternoon. When we made it to the walled zone around the Alps, we split up. We were supposed to rendezvous on the other side, but I was the only one waiting.

'I continued alone. At a settlement in your south, I spoke to a Runner who directed me to Prestige. This is where I found

Faustine. She believed my story and agreed to help. The medication is now ready to be delivered. It must be brought to La Talpa while there is still time. If we lose more people, it might take years for the machine to be completed. Many of us have dedicated our lives to it. When it is finished it will work, I promise you. It is the best chance we have of removing the burden our ancestors gave us to carry.'

The sound of more ANFO being detonated drifted over the plateau. Mosquitoes staked their claim in mahogany flesh. None of the Runners moved or looked at one another. It was as though asking a question would turn fiction into reality. Cassady waited a few beats longer and then took the plunge.

'You made it through the Alps?'

'Yes.'

'How? It's impregnable.'

'No longer. I passed through almost without detection. The route I took was difficult, but passable. There was much snow, but few soldiers.'

Cassady narrowed his eyes. 'The temperature is too high for snow.'

'Outside the zone, yes. Not inside. For years the corporations that set up shop there had the best geo-engineers in the world working to find ways to sidestep the Change. Until they tried to enslave us, we too had an agreement with them to help develop their technologies. They deploy drones to draw a sulphur dioxide blanket above the mountains. It reflects enough sunlight to keep the snowpack in place. They have wind barriers, artificial trees, clouds that block out the sun, fan walls, protected biotopes. A huge number of different technologies that allow them to maintain a steady pre-Change climate, more or less.'

'My mother worked on some of these projects,' murmured Katarina. A lock of hair fell across her eyes and she swept it back. 'You say 'They.' Are the corporations still around?'

'No. They merged a long time ago. They're called the

Koalition now,' said Lupo. 'And the Koalition controls the zone and everything in it.'

A snort came from Victor. Here, at least, was something he could dismiss. 'The Koalition is a myth.'

'Somebody is running things behind that wall,' said Ghazi.

'The Koalition is a name people throw around because they ain't got a clue what's actually going on down there.'

Lupo wheezed. 'I assure you it is not.'

'Yeah, and maybe that knock on the head screwed you up a little.'

Brandt straightened up and squared his shoulders. 'Show some respect.'

Victor's smile vanished. 'You ain't running things here, old man.'

Brandt's lip twitched. 'Do you wish to test me?' Cassady watched them size each other up. The kid didn't seem unsettled by Brandt's size. The quieter one, Tagawa, kept his attention on Renfield, who looked on with amusement as though the whole scene was being staged just for him.

'It wouldn't be a test,' said Victor.

Brandt took a step forward. The younger man barely reached the top of his chest.

'Not many young men on the road. Too arrogant and too foolish to survive for long.'

'Pretty words. Make a move.'

Before Brandt could react, Lupo rapped his cane on the table. The group's attention returned to him.

'I did not drive nearly two thousand kilometres to watch you beat your chests at one another. This matter is urgent. Please.' He pointed at Brandt. 'Now is not the time for this.'

'He is right, Jürgen,' said Katarina, placing a hand on his arm.

Brandt's features softened. 'Klar. It isn't a problem.' He backed away from Victor and didn't look at the boy again.

Renfield chuckled, shaking his head. Then he became serious.

'Let us assume, for argument's sake, that the Koalition does exist. What does it want with the machine?'

'They either want to destroy it or take it for themselves. The Koalition state exists because our world – the world beyond the walls it has constructed to keep out – is an unforgiving one. As long as they have water, food, structures and the rest, the Koalition's rule is preferable for the people who live within its borders. But if we activate the machine, the land beyond the walls would become bountiful again. The Koalition's alternate reality would become obsolete. And they would lose their grip on the people.'

'How strong are the Koalition's forces?'

'I do not know.'

'I have seen the wall,' said Brandt. 'And I saw no breaks. Only scorched earth and barbed wire and death.'

'The walls in the south are unguarded. There is nothing left to watch over. My land is barren. There are few people still alive. Most, like us, live underground to escape the sand and the heat, and we leave only to scavenge and barter. We are not concerned with the Plato's cave the Koalition has created.'

'But what about the defences in the north?' asked Katarina. 'Anybody who drifts too close is dealt with.'

Sergei crossed his massive arms across his chest and spoke up. 'Some time ago, maybe. But it ain't like that anymore. Most of the towers have been abandoned. They rely on old minefields, blockades, bunkers and other traps. The guards they have are for show, mostly.'

'How do you know that?' asked Ghazi.

'Faustine has eyes everywhere. She's been watching the wall for years. Just in case. People have made it in and out from time to time. Lupo here ain't the only one.'

'I ain't buying that,' said Victor.

'I don't give a damn what you're buying,' he growled.

'Well,' said Brandt, turning back to Lupo. 'How many soldiers did you see?'

'Except for one time, I saw their soldiers only from a distance. A few troop transports, some smaller four-wheeled vehicles. They mostly use drones to defend their lands and quell unrest.'

'When did you see them up close?'

'I ran a blockade at the northern border. I managed to break their line. This is where I was wounded. They followed me, but I escaped.'

Cassady had to stop himself from reaching into his pouch for a stick of root. It was obvious what the man wanted from them. A movement from Hearst drew his attention. Her lips formed silent words as she looked at the floor. She did it when she wanted to be sure a sentence was correct. After a few moments she raised her head. 'Whole state could be on alert.'

'Probably,' said Lupo.

'You want a pantech to take supplies to your base.'

'Not just one. I want all of you to go.'

She made a clicking sound with her tongue and her face wrinkled in disgust. Lupo continued, undaunted.

'If a single machine leaves this camp and fails, my people will die. If four go, the chance is greater that one will be able to slip through.'

Katarina folded her arms. 'While the rest perish.'

'The risk is high, certainly. The roads are dangerous. You will have to contend with extreme heat, extreme cold, unwanted attention, poor roads and people who want you dead. If the Koalition seizes the medicine, I believe they will attempt to hold us hostage. The machine in exchange for the lives that are left.'

The heat was already advancing up the hill to the plateau, but Cassady's brow was cold. Clammy palms left faint imprints on his khakis.

'Is your base safe?' asked Ghazi.

'Yes. La Talpa is deep underground. It has never been discovered. The Koalition tried its best in the past, but did not succeed. Let me show you.'

Sergei cracked the case and took out a large piece of paper, which he unfolded. It was a detailed map of the continent. Lupo placed a crude cotton map over the Alps area. The Runners crowded around the table on which their world was laid. Cassady followed the lines on the paper.

'We are here,' said Lupo, pointing at a spot in northern Germany. His finger drifted south until it hovered over the square of cotton. 'I was able to cross the wall somewhere here. I am not sure where exactly. This line is the approximate route I took through the mountains. I was only able to make a rough sketch. The road is wide enough for your vehicles, though I presume there are others if you wish to find an alternative route. I also passed three abandoned settlements. These I have marked here, here and here.'

He paused and gritted his teeth. He had to force the next words out. 'Once you exit the zone, keep going. There is a single track bearing south. You should not encounter any difficulties. La Talpa is here. You will be intercepted on approach. They are expecting you. All you need is my name and the name of the settlement.'

'Wanna take a break?' asked Sergei. Lupo waved him away.

Each Runner took their time consulting the map. Cassady's eyes traced the crudely drawn lines. The intel was weak, the conditions beyond dangerous. Hearst grunted a couple of words that confirmed it.

'Suicide mission.'

Lupo's response was immediate. 'I still live.'

'You were on a bike,' said Katarina.

'True. But this is why you are here. I asked Faustine to find me the best drivers around. If I did not believe this to be a matter of life and death, I would not ask you to risk your lives. I am not an egotist. But we are desperate. My people need you. If we do not act now, the machine may never be completed.'

Katarina waved a fly away from her cheek. 'How does it work?'

'It serves no purpose for me to tell you.'

Victor stepped forward. He did not look to the others. The disdain was gone.

'You guarantee the machine'll work?'

'Yes.'

He waited until the sound of a detonation had passed. 'The Silkworm will get your supplies to La Talpa. We're ready to go.'

Leaning on the cane with one hand, Lupo held the other out. Victor grasped it.

'I cannot thank you enough.'

'We ain't there yet.'

'Forgetting something?' asked Renfield, his bare head reflecting the light of the sun. 'What's the payment?'

Lupo reached into a knapsack that hung by his hip. He withdrew a handful of yellow capsules.

'For now, this is all I can give you.'

'Blitz pills? We have quite enough of those, my friend.'

'Not quite.' He handed one to Renfield. 'Swallow it.'

'I didn't reach this age by acting on the suggestions of strangers.'

'If my intention was to harm you, this is not the way I would do it. These pills are a form of sustenance. We produce them at La Talpa.'

Renfield reached out and took one of the pills. He placed it on his tongue and held it there.

'Now swallow it,' said Lupo.

He did as he was asked. A smile cut across his weathered face. 'Astonishing.'

'What?' asked Brandt.

'I can feel it in my stomach.'

'You only need four for a complete meal,' said Lupo.

With the exception of Hearst, each Runner plucked the yellow pills from the scientist's hand. Cassady forced the pill down and waited for the effects. Slowly, the hunger that had been gnawing at him since he awoke receded.

'Nice trick,' he said.

'It is not a trick. We engineered it to cover everything the body needs,' said Lupo. 'Now you see what we can do. Once you reach La Talpa, we will repair and upgrade your pantechs. We can increase the capacity of your batteries and their charging speed. We have also designed a lightweight para-aramid synthetic fibre weave. Impregnable to blunt force. This we can apply to the body of your vehicles.'

Brandt and Renfield retreated from the group and spoke in low voices. Cassady could see from their expressions that they would go for it. He glanced at the map once more and balled his fists. It just didn't look possible. The old Runners returned to the table.

'You use your words well,' said Brandt, 'and we're prepared to believe you. We'll be the convoy's shield.'

'It'll make a change from running hemp to nowhere,' added Renfield with a smile.

As with Victor, Lupo gripped Brandt and Renfield by the hand and thanked them both several times. The hairs of his moustache quivered and a tear fell from the corner of his eye.

Brandt disengaged from the gaunt scientist and stared at Victor. 'I'll be seeing you, boy.'

The younger man smirked. 'You got it.'

'We'll have the cargo over to you this afternoon,' said Sergei. 'Prepare your rig and get some rest. Briefing at dusk.'

Brandt and Renfield shuffled away. Cassady wanted to ask them to look after his machete until he came to retrieve it, but he didn't trust his voice not to waver.

Victor shook his arms out by his sides before swiping the shock of blonde hair from his forehead. 'Well, we gotta fine-tune the Silkworm. We gonna leave at daybreak, I guess?'

71

'Yeah,' said Sergei.

'Good.' He winked at Cassady and left with Tagawa, who didn't give the others a second glance.

Lupo rested his hand on the cane and waited. A fly buzzed near the dark patch on his bandage. Without warning, Hearst spat in the dust at Sergei's feet and stalked away. Katarina looked at them all, the creases on her forehead deepening. 'I'm sorry.' She walked quickly to catch up with her partner.

'Pity,' whispered Lupo.

Cassady exchanged glances with Ghazi, who closed one eye slowly. They had to talk to Sergei. 'We need time to discuss this,' he said to the gaunt scientist.

Lupo looked into his mismatched eyes. 'Of course. And I must rest. I will wait for your answer in my tent.' Then he said something odd. 'You could be our saviour.' Leaning on the cane for support, he followed one of the paths leading between the tents.

Only when the man was safely out of earshot did Cassady offer a response. 'Not likely,' he muttered.

8

Ghazi traced the lines on the map with his finger, mind already turning as it sought the best route south. If Warspite volunteered to go with the others, they would have to avoid all major camps and settlements. Three trucks travelling together would be too much of a target to pass up. The Watched Road was out, too. The Agis weren't the only ones with their eyes on the asphalt. So they would have to stick to the back roads and trails half-digested by nature.

'What if we say no?' he murmured, almost to himself. 'Will you make us disappear?'

Sergei's remaining eye showed surprise. 'What do you think this is? You don't wanna take on the contract, you can go. You ain't hostages.'

'Then why did you keep a guard on us?'

'Precautions. Just precautions. Didn't wanna spook you.'

'Why didn't you tell us about this in Prestige?'

'Spies. Prestige ain't safe. Information is worth more than water, you know that. We wanted to keep a lid on things.' Sergei caught the sceptical look on Cassady's face. 'I'm telling the truth, damn you. It's part of the show. People are always gonna sell others out if they can get something outta it.'

Cassady bit back. 'And you think this stockade is safe?'

'Ain't a place in the world we can call safe anymore. We do the best with what we have.'

'And what's Faustine's end in this?' said Ghazi, cutting in again. An argument would get them nowhere. 'Does she know Lupo?'

Sergei sighed. 'No. Look. Lupo shows up and tells us about the machine and the drugs he needs for his serum. We don't know what to believe. But we've got a couple of guys listening to the traffic on the shortwave, right? Always do. We know which frequency they broadcast on down there, and we got transmitters and receivers that can overcome all the collisional damping.'

'You mean to say you knew about the Koalition already?' asked Cassady.

'Yeah.'

'Christ.'

'So our guys pick up a few references,' continued Sergei. 'The Koalition is using code, but we work out they're talking about the machine. And then their comms guys get excited. They start scrambling search teams and breaking radio-silence rules they've kept up for years. You wanna know why? They're looking for Lupo.'

'So that's why you believe him,' said Ghazi. He tried to keep his mind from racing in ten different directions.

'You said you heard a broadcast yourself somehow. That thing didn't appear out of nowhere, did it? What you gotta understand is that Faustine's an intelligent woman. She listens to the broadcasts. She understands the trouble this guy's causing. And Lupo's descriptions of what it's like inside the state check out with ones we've heard before. So she figures this guy is telling the truth. Yeah, it's a gamble. We don't know him and we can't pin his story to the wall, not with any certainty. But we're gonna take the chance.'

'Because it isn't your life on the line,' said Cassady.

'What else do you want me to say? Lemme give you both a piece of advice. If you join Brandt and that kid – and I hope to hell you do – be on your guard 24 hours a day. Watch out for each other. Help each other. And forget what you think you know about the south. It's the Wild West down there.'

'No different to up here, then,' spat Cassady.

'How long have you been driving that rig?'

'Twenty years. More.'

'Then you know what to expect. If you grew up in the Wild West, it ain't wild. It's home. You understand what I'm saying?

Different game. Now listen: there's some kind of civil war going on down in that place. Their comms guys are trying to keep it quiet, but it's got everybody damn excited.'

Cassady laughed without humour. 'This just keeps getting better.'

Ghazi ran his hand over the strip of hair on his head. The pessimism that came naturally to his partner wasn't anywhere close to his thoughts. A civil war might just provide enough of a distraction to let them slip through without being detected. If the Koalition's eyes were directed inward, it might not see them coming. It was a big if, but it was something.

Cassady wasn't done yet. 'You say you hope to hell we go with them. Why do you want us on this convoy? Do you gain something from seeing us dead?'

Sergei slammed his hands down on the table.

Cassady stopped short.

'I'll tell you why, damn it. Before you turned up, Faustine was desperate. We had the other crews, but we needed a leader. Somebody's gotta take that convoy into hell and they need to not flinch when they do it. The Silkworm boys are too inexperienced. You saw them. They got a lot to prove to themselves and they'll gamble everything and they'll end up dead.'

'So what about Brandt? He's been doing this twice as long as we have.'

The giant pointed to the patch over his empty socket. 'The old man's got an eye on getting off the road for good. He and Renfield are burning fumes. You gotta be able to see that. They're too cautious, too slow. Comes with age, and I ain't got anything against that, except when it interferes with the work I gotta get done.'

Ghazi shook his head. 'I don't agree with your assessment.'

Sergei flashed him a look. 'I wasn't asking for your opinion.'

'And Hearst?' asked Cassady. 'She's tougher than any of us.'

'She ain't going, or didn't you hear? Besides, she doesn't look out for anybody except herself. No, we need the pair of you. You two can lead. You've done enough jobs for us and guided enough caravans in your time. The Strasbourg run, that manoeuvre outside Warsaw, it all counts. You got a reputation, you got a vehicle that can cut it, and you've been working together longer than any of the others. If you set the example, they're gonna follow you. With you two at the helm, the rest of them might make it through the mountains. If you cut out now and go back to running parts and rations, I know they ain't gonna get to La Talpa. They'll try, but they'll fail.'

Ghazi said nothing. He understood what Sergei was saying. Delivering crates of expired food to a settlement clinging to life in the Bowl was one thing. This was something totally different, which is why somebody needed to take charge. Somebody good. He glanced at Warspite's owner, who looked beyond Sergei with unfocused eyes. Which Cassady would be chewing the issue over now? Would it be the reliable man he'd driven with for years, the one who would bare his teeth and dig in and fight? Or would it be the Cassady of late, the one he didn't want to admit he shared a cab with, the barely recognisable spectre who was all paranoia and quick temper?

'One more thing,' said Sergei. 'We'll give you a new battery for your rig. A third generation Milutin. It's already here. Just need to hook it up.'

Ghazi blinked in surprise. Faustine really was banking on Warspite leading the group. A battery – a good one at that – didn't come cheap, not even for her. 'And what about Lupo?'

'What about him?'

'Is he going too?'

'No. We had to pump him full of stims just to keep him on his feet. He's in a bad way. Spilled the red stuff all the way to Prestige. He's gonna stay here until he's recovered. Can't say how long that's gonna be.'

Cassady cleared his throat. His gaze was hard and focused

again. The other two fell silent. 'Me and Ghazi are going back to the Old Lady to talk. I'll give you our answer in an hour.'

With the deception no longer necessary, the Gaeans had taken the canvas screen down. Hunkered against the palisade wall and with the sunlight pooling on its metal surfaces, Warspite was a glistening beast, cornered but more dangerous than ever. Every scratch and every dent in the metal was a badge of honour. Ghazi was itching to get back out on the road. That was where things made sense. He opened the cab door on the passenger side and took out the half-carved wooden elephant, then sat with his back against one of the thick tyres. The scent of rubber and dry mud took some of the sting out of his uneasiness. He shaved the basswood with long, clean strokes. The carving was the closest he could come to bringing the animal back, for all that was worth. Neither he nor Cassady had been around to help destroy everything, but he'd inherited the guilt. And now, as the planet tried to rid itself of the poison, it was forcing them to the edge of the abyss, too. Sooner or later they would have to jump or fall in.

At least, those had been the only two choices before this morning.

Now a third option dangled before them on a string as delicate as gossamer. If they reached the scientists before the disease decimated them, they might be able to pull the world back from the brink with their machine. And then he could put the whittling knife away.

Cassady took a long draught from one of the bota bags and leaned against the hood, his eyes on the palisade wall. Ghazi worked the blade into the hunk of wood and brushed shavings from his lap. Lice, the eternal companion of the Runners, ran over the back of his neck, and he caught one between his finger and thumb and squeezed. They hadn't smoked their clothes for a month. The seams were packed with eggs.

Cassady cleared his throat. 'So.' The declaration was dead on arrival.

Ghazi blew dust out of a groove. 'So what?'

'You're just going to sit there in silence until I say something?'

He chose his words carefully. 'It's your truck. You tell me what you think.'

Cassady wore an expression that was part resignation, part determination. 'We have to do it.'

'Have to?'

'"I must create a system or be enslaved by another man's". Remember those words?'

'Blake.'

'Previous generations enslaved us. They made us like this, gave us a life where we kill each other for headlights and hubcaps. Maybe this is our chance to change that.'

Ghazi ran a palm over his scalp. 'Why not the other crews instead?'

'They need us. We make the difference.'

'Those are Sergei's words.'

'But he's right.'

'You think the machine exists?'

Cassady sighed. 'Do you?'

'I want it to.'

'Exactly.' He paused for a moment. 'But it's not even about that. Not really. If I turn my back now, this thing will stay with me for the rest of my life. These past months have been hard.' He spoke with hesitation, as though he wasn't sure how much to reveal. 'I haven't been the same. I know you've noticed it even though I've tried to hide it. I'm slipping. It's getting away from me. This, now, is the real test. Even if I fail, it's better than not trying at all.' He blew out his cheeks. 'But we can make it. I know it.'

He slapped at a mosquito on his neck. The detonations that had punctuated their thoughts all morning stopped suddenly, and snatches of conversation and commands carried over the tents.

Ghazi turned the block of basswood over in his hand, his mind made up. 'Do you really believe we can make it?' His voice was no louder than the breeze.

'Yes.'

'This is going to be rough. If we're in, then we're in all the way.'

'I understand.'

'Do you? We'd be risking everything.'

'I know.' Cassady pushed himself away from the hood. His wiry frame tensed up and his voice became harder. 'If you don't trust me, you don't have to go. I'll arrange it with Sergei to get you to Prestige. No hard feelings. If I make it, I'll come and find you on the way back.'

Ghazi stood and brushed the dust from his trousers. The man liked his ultimatums. He held out a hand. 'No need for any of that. I am with you. Same as always.'

Cassady returned the grip. 'I was hoping you'd say that.' A faint smile showed on each man's face.

'We'd better start looking at that map. And Sergei needs to know.'

'Not yet. First we tell the crews.'

A few Gaeans stopped in their work to watch them as they walked with purpose between the tents. The hammer blows of the ANFO resumed. Ghazi winced. The noise would be heard for kilometres around. He hoped any groups in the area would be dissuaded by the stockade's strong position on the plateau. Beside him, Cassady wiped the sweat from his lips and angled the peak of his cap lower over his eyes. He'd been unusually upfront about his fears, and Ghazi respected that. He wouldn't leave the man to face his demons alone, not even if it meant his own death in the process. Perhaps that was the point anyway: to be prepared to sacrifice oneself in service of something greater. The higher understanding was on the horizon of his existence, and he had to close that distance. His connection with Cassady would help him do it.

There was another reason, too. He was curious to see what lay beyond the mountains. There were three ways to get to the south, but threading the eye of the needle through the Alps was the only viable one for them. Cassady would never guide Warspite into the wastelands that had once been called France. Nobody knew how bad the radiation levels there were. Some towns managed to hang on, which proved it wasn't all death and desolation, but it wasn't worth the risk. Some of the younger or more foolish Runners didn't care. They took the cargoes and laughed at the drivers who refused. But their smiling faces vanished from the watering holes much quicker than those who stuck to the safe areas. The third option was to use the network of trails that criss-crossed the centre of the continent like hardened veins, but it would take more time than Lupo's people had before they bled out.

Brandt was perched on the hood of Telamonian, watching a couple of boys trying to strike each other across the cheek without moving from the same spot. They crouched and twisted their bodies to avoid the blows from their opponent. The smaller of the two leaned back so far Ghazi was sure he'd lost his balance, but he sprang forward again and his hand crashed against the other boy's face. The taller boy spun around and fell to his knees. The victor remained where he was, not celebrating. The loser dragged himself to his feet, his right cheek glowing red.

'Taking a time out?' asked Cassady.

'Gladiatorial combat,' grunted Brandt. 'Free of charge.'

'We're coming with you.'

Brandt jumped off the hood. Even he was dwarfed by the mammoth machine. He folded his arms across his chest.

'You're sure?'

'Yes.'

'Hearst?'

'I'll speak to her.'

'What about the new boys?'

'I'll deal with them. I'm leading the convoy. Out on the road, I make the decisions. That's the way it is. If they don't like it, they're out.'

Brandt hocked a wad of phlegm into the dust. The chest hair poking out of the top of his vest glimmered with sweat.

'What if you make a decision I don't like?'

Cassady's voice was level. 'You've got the experience, Brandt. I need your help. I'm not going to make any rash calls. You don't like the way something sounds, you tell me and we'll work it out. This is a team thing all the way. Otherwise we'll get strung out and picked off one by one. You understand?'

Brandt's heavy eyebrows shifted. He smacked his lips and then chuckled. 'Okay, Cassady. Good speech. You have a deal.'

'Where's Renfield?'

'He's gone to scrounge what he can from the crazies. We'll be there for the briefing.'

'Brandt?' said Ghazi. He had to say something. 'Is there going to be a problem between you and Victor?'

'Not unless he makes one.' Ghazi's expression elicited another laugh from the old man. 'Schlechter Witz. I've got no quarrel with him. But listen, those boys look hungry. They're desperate. They signed up to this run before Lupo said anything about payment. You'd better watch out for that.'

Ghazi accepted a stick of root from Cassady as the boxy truck came into sight. He usually abstained, but special circumstances called for special measures. He chewed the stick a few times to ease out the flesh and then pushed the wad under his top lip. A cool wind whistled through his skull.

Victor's head was in the engine when they reached the other

side of the camp, but he straightened up to receive them. Tagawa crawled out from underneath the truck. Bones danced under their skin. Brandt had a point. Neither spoke as Cassady and Ghazi surveyed the pantech, a fully enclosed black metal shell sitting on four wheels.

'You're right about it being a bunker,' muttered Cassady. Aside from the scratches and dents, the shell was smooth on all sides with no hand grips or footholds. The weapon loopholes along the sides and at the back were closed up tight. At the front, a set of spikes had been welded to the bumper, and a winch with a spool of high-tensile wire sat just above them. A silver symbol in Japanese script gleamed on the hood.

'What does it say?' asked Ghazi, nodding at the symbol.

'Kaiko,' replied Tagawa. 'It means silkworm. The name spoke to me. Victor says I should cut my links to my forebears, but I believe it important to remember where one came from. Keeps one grounded.'

Victor offered a short laugh. 'Sure, stability. Just what a guy needs when he's living out of a box on wheels.'

'It's an impressive one at least. Auto?'

The boy nodded.

'We're here about the convoy,' said Cassady.

'Gonna come along for the ride?' Victor flashed two rows of crooked grey teeth. Without meaning to, Ghazi recalled a starving man he'd once stumbled across in a yard belonging to an old farmhouse. He'd been stripping the flesh from the bodies of two men and singing to himself when Ghazi had fired an arrow into his chest to bring an end to the ugly scene. The man had been wearing a discoloured dental prosthesis. While Ghazi had stood over him, his mouth had been twisted open in death, silent laughter pouring out, mocking Ghazi for setting him free while he stayed behind to struggle on. The man still came to him in his dreams from time to time.

'No,' said Cassady. 'I'm leading it.'

Victor swiped at the hair plastered against his brow and scowled. 'Who says?'

'I do.'

'What if we don't wanna follow you?'

'Then you pack up your things and return to whatever backwater it is you came from,' said Cassady. 'I haven't got time to play games. If you can't get a handle on your ego, that's fine. You won't be joining us. Ask Sergei for some supplies before you leave. He'll give them to you. You boys look hungry.'

'We have endured leaner times than this,' said Tagawa. The hollow cheeks made it look as though his face was cast in shadow.

Cassady scratched at his chest, drawing attention to the knotted scars sewn into his skin. 'Sure.'

'This contract is nothing to us,' said Victor slowly. 'We can find plenty more in Prestige.'

Cassady continued to scratch. He yawned, putting on the full show. 'Right you are. Good luck, boys. See you out on the road some time.'

They left the berth. The stunned silence was quickly followed by a flurry of words in a foreign tongue between the two young Runners. Ghazi smiled. They had them. Sure enough, Victor's drawl rang out in the heavy air. 'Wait.' They turned. 'I know what you're doing, Cassady. A damn fool kid could see it. You need us and I know you know it. But either way we accept your terms.'

'Until the end of the line.'

'Yeah, till then.'

'Briefing's at 1900. We leave at dawn. Be ready.'

Victor threw Cassady a lazy salute. 'Sure thing, boss.'

Tagawa watched them until they were out of sight.

'Two down,' said Ghazi. He spat the root pulp onto the path and waved away the offer of another piece. He was already sweating with energy.

'That kid's going to be trouble,' muttered Cassady.

'We'll keep him in check.'

'I hate these dances.'

'Only the ballet to go.'

'I haven't got a clue what I'll say to her.'

'Just make it quick. And make it convincing.'

'Thanks. You're a real help.'

When they arrived at the berth, Hearst was throwing supplies into the back of her pantech. The red paint job burned in the sun. Katarina, standing beside her, clicked her fingers as she saw them approach. Hearst stopped what she was doing and turned her crumpled face towards the Runners.

Katarina's features were set. 'Will you be leaving with us?' Her hemp robe, which fell to just above her ankles, trembled in the breeze.

'No,' replied Ghazi.

'So you're joining the others.'

'I'm leading them,' said Cassady.

Hearst snorted.

'Why don't you stick around for a while?'

She leaned against the truck and spat on the floor.

'And you, Katarina?' asked Cassady, keeping his eyes on the younger woman.

'Orion is not my vehicle. I do not make the decisions.'

'But what do you think?'

'Does it matter?'

'Humour me,' he said, and sat next to the remains of a fire that had been built the previous night.

Katarina dropped to her haunches. 'As you wish. A long time ago, something happened to me that left me hovering between life and death. The two paths were open to me. I could have chosen the latter. It would have been simple. But something brought me back, and since then I've had the idea it was for a reason, that I'm here to make a difference. By this I do not mean transporting a few barrels of water to murderers or rapists or fanatics. That is a question of compromise for the sake of one's own survival. A man whom we have never met is asking us to risk our lives to save a community of unknowns. He appears with a fantastic story about a machine that could reverse the Change and he hopes we'll make a leap of faith. I'm not willing to jump for him – men with promises are not to be trusted – but I would do it for myself.'

Hearst made another dismissive noise that Katarina ignored. 'But, as I said, I am not the owner of this pantech,' she continued. 'And so it is not me you have to convince.'

Cassady nodded. He allowed the silence to linger before addressing Hearst. His voice grew harsh. 'We're going to the Alps and we need you with us.'

'Why?'

'Because you're the best driver in the group.'

'Words.'

'It's the truth. Nobody drives a rig like you. And nobody is more pragmatic. If you don't join the convoy, we won't make it.'

'Not my problem.'

'Maybe not. But I know you don't want to see us dead.'

She tapped the tattooed skin near her ear. 'You do not know. You cannot see.'

'Then I hope.'

'Too much unknown. Too dangerous.'

'We never know what's on the road until we're out there.'

'Only suffering for you all.'

Cassady took his hat off and rubbed his forehead. He looked to Ghazi. All he could do was shrug his shoulders. There was nothing he could add. They had never won an argument with Hearst before, and it was no different now.

'Fine,' said Cassady, standing up and walking over to Orion. Up close, the abuse stood out against the red paint. He brushed the outline of a long scratch with his finger. 'Before you pack up the rest of your stuff and ball it back to Prestige, just do me one favour. Think about how it'll feel knowing you turned your back on the greatest challenge anybody ever asked of you. You had the chance to compete with six other drivers and you said no. Really think about it. Because when you're back out there, especially on those long stretches when you've got no distractions to stop you from confronting your fears, you're going to end up asking yourself anyway. Trust me.'

Without another word, Hearst climbed into the back of the truck and slammed the door. Cassady shook his head and chuckled despite himself. Ghazi rested his hand on Katarina's shoulder. 'Take care, mamani.'

'I will. Look after yourself. Both of you.'

He waited until they were out of earshot of the truck before he addressed Cassady.

'You did what you could.'

The other man scowled. 'She's more stubborn than tyre tracks on tarmac.'

'Maybe she'll still change her mind.'

'No point wondering.'

When Warspite's tarpaulin cover came into sight, Ghazi asked the only question that mattered. 'Are we still on?'

Cassady didn't hesitate. 'Get her ready. Once we hit that road, we're not stopping. Not even if Death tries to get in the way.'

Part II – On the Trail

1

Hearst came to Warspite's campsite, alone, before dawn. When he spotted her, Cassady dropped the torque wrench he was holding and wiped his hands on his already filthy trousers. His pupils were the size of buttons and an electric current scratched under the surface of his skin. After the briefing, he'd spent an hour interrogating Lupo for every scrap of information the scientist had about the Koalition and its Alpine state. Then the bald man had turned up at their berth with the medical supplies bound for La Talpa, and he and Ghazi had placed them in crates and secured them in the cargo hold. They had taken it in turns studying the maps while the other slept for a couple of hours, before both dropping a blitz pill so they could work through the night. The Old Lady was in sparring shape now. There was little more they could do except get out on the road.

In the dawn light, Orion's owner was a spectre from a nightmare, all dirt and ink and scars undercut with anger at the world and everything in it. She waited for Cassady on the path. With the blood audible in his ears, he approached and stared her down.

'You're still here.'

Hearst glanced beyond him to Ghazi, who was running a cloth over a set of immaculate plugs and humming softly to himself. Then her eyes were on his once more. 'My decision. Ours.'

'Yes?'

'We go with you.'

His breath boiled in his throat. With some effort, he kept his voice steady.

'Then get ready,' he said simply. 'We leave in an hour.'

She held his gaze for a moment longer and left. The blood continued to throb in his head and a muscle in his cheek trembled. His relief at her decision was so strong that it soured and turned to shame. He told himself to get a grip. He walked back to the berth and, retrieving the wrench, bent down to tighten the lug nuts that held the Old Lady's wheels in place. Out of the corner of his eye, he could see a smile on Ghazi's face and he did his best to relax. Hearst and Katarina were coming with them.

By the time the trucks lined up in formation by the gate, the sky had been slashed open and the darkest blue poured from its wounds. The temperature was already on the wrong side of comfortable. The ancient, indomitable Warspite sat at the head of the convoy, her new battery safely stowed between the seats in the cab. Orion tucked in just behind her, a fat red beetle ready to bite anything that stood in its way. A few metres further back was the battering-ram outline of the Silkworm, while at the rear, the massive Telamonian attempted to block out the dawn. The crews waited in silence outside their cabs. Each Runner ran through their pre-road ritual, hoping it would be enough to keep them alive for another day.

Cassady stood next to Sergei, taking in the sight of the rigs. Lined up like that, with the crews ready to go, it looked as though nothing could stop them. And he would be leading them out.

'Faustine's paid a tribute to the stations,' said Sergei. 'It didn't come cheap. But you can count on reports until you hit the Alps.'

'Vultures preying on people's superstitions,' said Cassady. He always had to laugh whenever another Runner trotted out the old line about the stations being their guardian angels. If a station didn't receive enough donations, it stopped broadcasting until the drop points filled up with supplies. It was as simple as that.

'If it keeps your drivers satisfied, you oughta listen in to those broadcasts. Don't underestimate the strength of belief.' Sergei handed Cassady a piece of fabric containing the frequencies.

'Anything else?'

The giant looked down at him through his remaining eye.

'You ain't gonna be able to use those medical supplies you're schlepping if you run into trouble. They ain't exactly bandages and painkillers. If you don't know how to mix them right, they're useless to you.'

'Right.'

'Well. Good luck. Work as a team. Keep your head. And don't think that anyone's gonna help you down there. We're counting on you.'

He nodded. It was time to go. 'Okay,' he shouted. 'Let's mount up.' The crews jumped into their vehicles. As he went to join Ghazi, Cassady's attention was drawn to a solitary figure leaning on a cane near the gate. Lupo wore a fresh bandage around his head.

'In bocca al lupo,' he shouted. 'Good luck. May God be with you.' The scientist coughed and his battered body heaved with the effort.

'Which God is that?' Cassady muttered. He swung himself into the cab, adjusted his cap and exchanged glances with Ghazi.

'Show us the way,' said his co-driver.

The sterile whine of the electric engines drew some of the disciples from their tents. They watched as the Runners, faces lined with concentration, ran through their final checks. Four sets of headlights turned the earth the colour of dried blood. Metal bodies shuddered. Then Cassady coaxed the gearstick into first and applied pressure to the pedal. Warspite crunched over the plateau. One by one, the heavy trucks slipped through the gate and left the stockade behind.

The sun was about to reach its high-water mark. Warspite rumbled along at a steady speed on a track heading south. The landscape was a sea of scrubland. Jagged metal pylons that predated the Change marched off towards the horizon. Cassady's gaze flickered to his mirrors every few minutes. Hearst was keeping pace. The Silkworm and Telamonian were somewhere further back. Excessive ionisation in the atmosphere put a stop to radio transmissions. Once they were out of sight, the trucks had no means of contacting one another.

The Old Lady obeyed his every command like she'd been put together yesterday, not over a century ago. It gave him some comfort, but the uncertainties continued to twist his thoughts in different directions. He was already worried about Telamonian. The beast was too much of a heavyweight to match the speed of the others. There wasn't much he could do about it other than set a rendezvous point every evening and hope each rig made it before dark. At the briefing Victor had protested about the plan, arguing they should continue through the night, but the other Runners had dismissed the idea. They would need all the rest they could get before they hit the mountains. Of that Cassady was sure.

Ghazi shifted in the co-seat.

'What?'

'Something that's been playing on my mind,' he said slowly. 'I think those boys in their black box would rather break before they bend to us.'

'What do you mean?'

'They're hungry, like Brandt said, but there's more to them than that. Somebody has lit a fire inside them, and that means we should watch ourselves – how we speak to them. You, me, Brandt and the rest. A mind with something to prove is rarely the most rational one.'

'Is that a warning?'

'No. I just want us to be facing in the same direction. Even so, they aren't your enemy. Remember that. We'll need them out here.'

'I know.' Cassady pressed down on the accelerator, signalling an end to the conversation. He jammed a piece of root into the space between his gum and his cheek and felt his mind become clear.

They passed the occasional vehicle heading in the other direction but didn't slow down or stop to make small talk. When they hit a two-lane tarmac road that hadn't yet disintegrated, Orion drew level with Warspite. Hearst was a statue in the driver's seat. Ghazi wound down his window and Cassady flicked the A/C off. Katarina grinned at them, her white hair sitting atop her scalp in thick, oily braids. Both drivers slowed their pace so the co-drivers could hear each other over the biting tyres.

'Chetori?' shouted Katarina by way of greeting.

Ghazi chuckled. 'Khoobam.'

'Silkworm fell back to run with Tela.'

'I hope they behave themselves.'

'Did you listen to the station report?'

Ghazi read from the sheet. 'Activity quiet up and down the map. No inclement weather. No other issues.'

Katarina nodded. 'Right. That puts us clear while we go around Motze.'

Cassady had made sure they wouldn't be driving into that bleak town. Too many people knew their faces there.

'Anything else?'

'A request from my partner here. Okay if we take the lead?'

Cassady raised his thumb. He'd led them out of the camp, but there was nothing to gain from holding Hearst back.

'Go ahead,' shouted Ghazi.

'See you at the rendezvous.'

'Good luck.'

The squat eight-wheeler streaked ahead and grit rapped against the Old Lady's bumper. Cassady kept his eyes on Orion as the gap between them gradually widened. Hearst had grudgingly given him the details on her pantech once. Parabolic tapered leaf springs and telescopic shock absorbers made it a smoother drive than Warspite, and Hearst could rely on a seven-speed transmission to get her out of trouble. The cargo bed was closed on all sides with plates of heat-treated carbon manganese steel, and she'd stripped the chassis and cab as much as possible to make the truck more manoeuvrable.

Orion danced around a couple of burnt-out wrecks without slowing down. Cassady's mouth bent into a tight smile. He was good at what he did, but she turned driving into an art form. Having her with them was good, no doubt about it, but it added pressure, too. If he made a mistake, she would be gone before he had time to switch off his engine. And she wasn't alone. Victor and Tagawa were waiting to pounce on the slightest weakness. But he had to stop dwelling on the negatives. He pushed the worries into a dark corner of his mind and put his foot down.

When his hands started shaking so badly that the Old Lady weaved to the left and right, he switched with Ghazi. His body was running on root and blitz pills and his head was stuffed with what-ifs and maybes. In the co-seat, he checked the report from the station again, idly noting how poor the intelligence was, before staring at a map of the surrounding area until the lines fused together. Then he put his cap over his eyes and waited for sleep to come.

Warspite passed the next marker an hour later. It was an old gas station, no more than a shell, with a towering billboard nearby that had been claimed by climbing vines. Cassady stared at the building with lamplight eyes, mechanically chewing on another piece of root. Then his breath caught in his throat and he recoiled. Ghazi was jerked from his hypnotic state.

'What is it?'

'Nothing.' Cassady slumped in his seat. 'Nothing. I thought I saw a face in the window of that building.'

'Maybe there was one.'

'No. There were flames. It was burning.'

He kept his attention on the dashboard to avoid Ghazi's probing gaze.

'Are you okay?'

'Yes,' he muttered. 'Just keep going. We only have three hours of daylight left.'

'Maybe you ought to take it easy with that stuff. Try to get some rest.'

Cassady glowered at his reflection in the long, rectangular side mirror. He wanted to slap himself around the face. Ghazi was right. He had to lay off the root. The chemicals in the genetically modified plant were messing with his mind. He wound down the window and spat out the pulp before retrieving the maps that had fallen to the cab floor. He glanced at the pages. They could only go as fast as the slowest rig, which was Telamonian. La Talpa was right in the middle of the Italian desert, approximately 1,500 kilometres away by the route he'd sketched out, though that didn't account for detours. Over the next couple of days they would follow a narrow route through a minor mountain chain and then switch to a highway Brandt had told him was still in drivable condition. Although it would take them to within spitting distance of one of the dead cities, the route cut straight through the Bowl, which meant they should avoid contact with the tribes that somehow scratched out a living from the dead ground. If everything went to plan, they would hit the Alps four days from now. After that it would have to be guesswork. They couldn't plan for what they would find down there, where the mountains rose like so many shadowy wraiths. They didn't even know if there was a way in. Lupo had marked his supply road through the mountains and assured Cassady it was unguarded and passable, but he needed more proof than the word of the scientist. Besides, a motorcycle wasn't a pantech. He folded the maps and stowed them in the locker beneath his seat. Automatically, his hand reached for the pouch on his belt. He stopped himself. Forget the root. Get some rest. He drank a few mouthfuls of water to appease his throat and then leaned against the window. Orion was long gone. Telamonian and the

Silkworm chased Warspite's tail. He imagined a silver thread linking them all together over kilometres of road. And he held the spool in his hand.

The odour of death tainted the air. Flames framed the face in the window, a woman's face, her skin melting and dribbling off the bone. She was not in pain. A pair of red eyes, full of hate, bore into him. He wanted to scream, but he didn't have a tongue.

'Cassady, wake up.' Ghazi's voice was tense.

'What is it?'

'Exos to our left. Possible hunters.'

The light was beginning to fail. They had left the paved road and were now churning up a trail of mud. The rendezvous was close. Cassady could see the fresh welts that had been left by Orion's eight wheels sometime earlier. The trail was hemmed in on both sides by ranks of hardwood trees with leaves injured by acid rain. From the sound of the engine, Warspite was thrumming along at a steady rate of 40 km/h. A flash of movement between the trunks drew his gaze. Something out there was keeping pace with the truck.

'I see them. How long have they been on us?'

'A couple of minutes, I think.'

He concentrated. 'I make four of them.'

'Yes.'

'Single crews.'

'Right.'

Cassady unclipped a pair of binoculars from above his head and held them up. Bipedal metal forms darted between the trees. They were close enough for him to see the pistons moving up and down in the legs and the barrels of rifles strapped to armour-plated backs. Each oversized robotic suit cradled an operator made of flesh and blood. Helmets obscured their faces, and chest guards, greaves and other metal plates protected their bodies. From the mismatched outlines, it looked as though the exoskeletons had been cannibalised many times over. Cassady had never learned how to operate one. Too cumbersome, too dangerous. He encountered them out on the road from time to time, blocky humanoid shapes lurching from one settlement to another, carrying warnings, summons, pleas and threats. It was difficult to tell if these ones were hunters or farmers. Farmers used them as lifting equipment and for defence. Hunters tracked vehicles in packs before swarming to take them out.

'What do you think?' he asked Ghazi.

'Unsure. Could belong to a camp watching its territory.'

'Let's wait. If they keep following, we'll send them a warning.'

'You think they tracked Orion, too?'

'Probably.'

Cassady wound up the timepiece next to the juice meter and watched the seconds tick over. His eyes had stopped burning and his skin no longer itched. The A/C had dried out his throat again, so he took a sip of water. Judging from the sky and the thickness in the back of his head, he couldn't have been out for more than a couple of hours. He tracked the exoskeletons through the binoculars. For some reason, he was sure they weren't hunters. Four was too few for an attack, especially for a truck the size of Warspite. Ghazi was probably right about the camp.

The clock wound down and the hand stopped moving. The exos were still visible in the trees.

'Hit the lights,' said Cassady.

Ghazi twisted a dial next to the steering wheel and flicked a switch. Outside, the world around them glowed red. Halogen lights positioned on top of the cab, under the chassis and on the drop hatch burned with an intensity that couldn't be ignored. Now the exos would know for sure the pantech had seen them. And they would know the crew was ready to fight if they tried to attack.

Almost immediately, three of the exoskeletons peeled away and headed back in the direction they had come. The fourth continued until the trail made a sharp left turn and then stopped in its tracks. Warspite lumbered on. Cassady pressed the binoculars to his eyes and, craning his neck, managed to catch a view of the crude suit slipping away between the trees.

'They're gone.'

Ghazi's hand snaked out to flick the switch. The surroundings became a murky yellow-grey soup again.

'Not hunters, then.'

'Guards, I would say. Wonder what they'll make of four rigs passing through their turf on the same afternoon.'

'That's valuable information.'

'Nothing we can do about it. How much further?'

'End of this trail. I estimate 40 minutes.'

'Markers?'

'Dead town fifteen minutes back. Some kind of industrial job.'

It took a few moments for him to find it on the map. 'Forty is right. Thirty if you stop letting the road whip you.' He glanced at Ghazi. The mechanic's lips twitched.

'Glad you found your wit while you were sleeping.'

The Old Lady jogged from side to side. The track was disintegrating into a mess of ruts, holes, plastic and dead wood. The trees soaked up the light, and branches lashed the edges of the windshield and scraped against the tarpaulin cover. Ghazi switched on the headlamps. Cassady watched the speedometer. The needle remained steady. He might have chanced fifth gear, but Ghazi wouldn't. There wasn't a reckless bone in the man. His thoughts drifted to the rendezvous point, a handful of buildings Sergei had marked as probably safe. The stimulants had released their grip on his stomach and he was growing hungry. Neither of them had eaten since throwing back a few of Lupo's pills at midday.

Without warning, Ghazi grunted and slammed on the brakes. Their harnesses bit into their shoulders. Cassady had just enough time to spot a huge pothole before they slid over it. Warspite's wheels struck the lip and the vehicle lurched like a dying man. As quickly as he could, Ghazi hit the accelerator. The tyres bit and spun and the engine droned. Warspite dragged herself forward until her front half was back on the road. Cassady pounded the dash.

'Go, go,' he shouted. The rear wheels attacked the hole and she juddered as though she was trying to tear herself apart. He held his breath, fearing the worst. But Ghazi's brow was clear. He waited a split second and hit it. The back end bounced free of the hole. Warspite stumbled along the track. Cassady breathed again.

'Stop the rig,' he said. He jumped out and crawled underneath the cab, hands reaching to open a small storage box as the evening's heat wrapped itself around him. He unclasped the rusting lock and rummaged around inside before rolling back out from under the creaking pantech. The trees leered at him as he jumped up and hurried along the trail, sweat running in unbroken lines down his back. Visibility was low without Warspite's headlights to paint the surroundings. His sticky hand gripped a chemical snaplight. At the edge of the hole, he wiped his top lip against the collar of his tunic and paused to listen. The Old Lady breathed behind him. Cicadas called out from all around. The trees shushed one another. He snapped the cylinder and threw it over the hole, and it landed on the trail on the other side. Fluorescent light spilled out into the dirt. That would have to do. Brandt and Victor wouldn't be able to miss it, as long as they turned up before the stick died. As he headed towards the Old Lady, the darkness flooded in. He froze at the sound of something moving in the forest and whipped his head around. Panic bloomed in his chest. Go, said a voice. Now. His boots tramped against the dirt and he ran for the red globes suspended below the cargo bed. He pulled on the door that always required so much force to yank open and dived in. He stuffed his trembling hands under his thighs and stared straight ahead. Ghazi threw him a quizzical look, but said nothing. The dark-eyed Runner slipped Warspite into gear and guided them further into the forest.

The rendezvous was a medley of half-collapsed concrete structures a few hundred metres downhill from the edge of the forest. It wasn't ideal. Sergei had said it was safe, but his information was a few weeks old already and life moved fast on the edge of the Bowl. Ghazi cycled down into first and guided them in. Cassady kept his eyes open for danger.

But there was no need. 'There,' he said to Ghazi, pointing. A blood-red piece of fabric hung from one of the dilapidated structures. Hearst and Katarina were waiting. They nosed through the structures until they reached a quadrangle. A female form cradling a crossbow stood in the doorway of a building that was mostly intact. White hair, released from its braids, fell down around Katarina's shoulders. She pointed to her left and Ghazi guided Warspite into a concrete building which still had a roof. Orion hugged one of the walls. They set to work removing the battery from its crib and hooking it up to the wind turbine. Cassady strapped the black tube to his back, attached a set of cleats to his boots and scaled the outside of the building. Orion's turbine had already been set up on the flat roof. He unscrewed the end cap from the tube and extracted a smaller cylinder that split into four hinged legs at one end and curved blades at the other. The spiked feet dug into the rooftop. Finally, he took the cable that was hooked onto his belt and plugged it into the base of the turbine. The cable snaked over the lip of the building and down to where the battery waited.

'Yellow?' he shouted from the roof.

'Yellow,' came the muffled response. He picked up the turbine case and climbed back down in time to find Ghazi setting up the pedal lock and flipping the kill switches. He threw the case into the back of the rig.

'Think we need to mantrap her?' Ghazi asked.

'Wire the tailgate. Hearst probably has a bunch of traps around the perimeter already.'

'Better check anyway.'

After setting the tripwire, they crossed the quadrangle. In the doorway where Katarina had stood, Cassady paused and listened for the sound of incoming vehicles, but there was nothing but silence. He scratched at his neck and pinched a louse between his thumb and forefinger. He hoped the others weren't far behind.

Hearst and Katarina were sat on the floor near a dying fire, over which a cooking pot hung from a tripod. Something bubbled inside. Wisps of smoke escaped through a hole in the roof. The fire had made the room sweltering and it smelled of burning air and unwashed bodies.

A maternal smile crossed Katarina's face. 'Hello boys. Food in the dixie.'

The new arrivals loaded their mess tins and shovelled the contents into their bitter stomachs.

'Nothing like home cooking,' said Ghazi.

Cassady paused in his mechanical digging to hold a spoonful up to the light. 'What's in it?'

'Roots, acorns, herbs, boletus, water. A stone for flavour and minerals. All you need to be fighting fit in the morning.'

'Started using Lupo's pills yet?'

'No. Not when there's food all around us.'

'It's good,' Ghazi said. 'Thank you. Have you wired the perimeter?'

'Of course. Any news on the others?'

'Haven't seen them.'

Ghazi set his tin down. 'Were you out of the forest in time to hear the second station update?'

'No news,' muttered Hearst, her gaze trained on the powdery

white ash in the fire pit. 'Quiet.'

Cassady nodded, satisfied. Their luck had held so far. He ate without worry. The stew tasted better than anything they usually relied on. When he was finished, his stomach was full and he permitted himself to enjoy the luxury of it. He stretched out on the cool floor with his palms laid flat on the stone. The tension of the day was like a suit of armour he had to take off piece by piece. He closed his eyes, hearing only the spitting fire, lost in thought about the future. One day he would climb out of Warspite for the last time and live out his remaining days on a farm. He couldn't keep running forever, not like Brandt or Renfield or Kaja. His body wouldn't have the strength to take it. It was like the grip on a set of tyres. Once it was gone, it was gone.

For a moment he saw the burning, hateful face in the window again. Cold hands wrapped themselves around his throat and forced him to sit up. He thumped his chest and the image dissolved. He'd startled the other three and now they watched him. He frowned. To hell with their judgement.

Ghazi broke the awkward silence. 'Which one of you is taking first shift tomorrow?'

'Me. Hearst had the wheel today,' said Katarina. 'Guided us all the way. Danced around those potholes back there like they didn't exist.' Hearst nodded at the compliment.

'No break?' asked Cassady. The tattooed head shook from side to side. He grunted to show he didn't care one way or another, but he couldn't fool himself. If she could last the day, so could he. Next time he sat in the driver's seat, he wouldn't give it up so easily.

'Did you see the exos?' asked Ghazi.

'Yes,' said Katarina. 'They kept their distance. And they dropped us when they saw we weren't looking for a fight.'

'Must've been watchdogs.'

Hearst tensed, angling her head towards the open doorway.

'Quiet.' Then she relaxed. A second later, Ghazi smiled. Cassady waited, wishing his hearing was as sharp as theirs. A faint noise carried through the door: the whine of two powerful engines in conversation with one another. He sprang to his feet and headed outside.

On top of the building, the turbines cut circles in the darkness, recharging the depleted batteries that would serve as a backup the next day. With rapid strides he crossed the quadrangle and followed the road until he reached a building at the base of the hill. He peered through a windowless opening. The mobile pillbox was in front, the monster just behind, both vehicles creeping down the hill like they were trying to sneak clean through. Victor's mess of blonde hair was luminous behind the wheel. Cassady stepped into the road to wave them in. The Silkworm's headlights flashed as they lit up his body. He jumped back out of the way, and the rigs trundled past. Neither vehicle showed any signs of damage. Renfield gave him a quick salute from Telamonian's cab. Cassady grabbed a rail on the back of the massive truck and planted his feet against the bumper. As they bounced towards the quadrangle, he idly lifted the tarpaulin flap and looked at the cargo bed. Bungee cords secured the crates of medicine. Everything was as it should be.

Renfield guided Telamonian into one of the empty buildings. The Silkworm kept going, eager to find a spot away from the others. As Cassady jumped down from the bumper, the doors were flung open and the two old Runners emerged. Brandt held a wind-up flashlight in front of him, and its light danced across Cassady's face.

'Cut it out.'

Brandt laughed. 'You look just as good as I feel. Verdammt warm today.'

Renfield placed his palms flat against the side of the truck and pushed until his back clicked. His spindly frame didn't have a gram of fat on it. 'Twelve hours in the boneshaker.' He sighed.

'Tell me again why I agreed to this.'

'Any problems?'

'Aside from being too old and too slow? No. Thanks for the warning about the hole back there.'

'What about your new friends?'

'Didn't hear a peep from them, but they kept us in view the whole time. Even stopped when we had to switch one of the batteries, but they didn't say anything. Jürgen has no problem with them keeping their distance.'

'I bet.'

Renfield yawned. 'Those boys have much to prove to themselves. I've seen it all before many times. One day they'll realise that.' He took a battered flask from a trouser pocket, unscrewed the cap and took a long drink. Brandt grabbed the flask, had a swig and held it out to Cassady.

'What is it?'

'The finest malt.'

'Not today.'

Renfield laughed. 'One of the only things left in this world to enjoy and you turn it down.'

'If I start now, I won't want to stop. You'd better sort out your rig.'

'Later,' said Brandt. 'Is there food?'

'Yes. Kaja took care of it.'

'Meine Heldin.'

Brandt handed the flask back to Renfield, and the three of them made their way across the quadrangle. Their attention was drawn to the businesslike movements of Victor and Tagawa as they set up their turbine on the roof of the building they'd chosen to house their vehicle. Victor crawled over the structure like an insect, all jerking, nervous energy. Tagawa moved at his own pace, languid and confident, as though his way was the only one worth knowing.

Brandt and Renfield spoke a few words to Katarina and

served themselves a bowl of stew. Renfield sat with his back against the wall and took out a decaying paperback. He found his page, perched a pair of glasses on his nose and read while he ate.

'What have you got?' asked Ghazi.

The old man grinned. 'You'd like it. The Shape of Things to Come, H. G. Wells. The destruction of Europe, a plague that decimates the population, and the birth of a utopia.'

'When can we expect the utopia to find its feet?'

'Look around you, Ghazi.' Renfield waved his hand at the room. 'Food, warmth, no fighting, security, friendly faces. This is as close as we'll ever get. Enjoy it.'

Cassady closed his eyes once more and let the calm settle on his skin. They had all survived the first day. He repeated it to himself several times as though it was a mantra.

A pair of boots slapped against the earth, and Victor entered the room with a theatrical yawn. 'It's hotter than the Bowl in here.' Tagawa followed, his gaze eluding them all.

Cassady forced himself to sound friendly. 'How was it?'

'Why? Were you worried?' A mean grin cast a shadow over Victor's boyish features. He spied the food and Katarina told him to help himself. He dived in, his spoon a blur as it dipped in and out of the pot. Tagawa sat near the fire in silence. Cassady felt the lines of electricity running under his arms and breathed hot air through his nostrils. He told himself to keep cool.

'You want to take point tomorrow?'

'Oh sure,' said Victor. He threw back a spoonful of the stew and wiped his chin. 'But who's gonna keep watch over the buzzards?'

Brandt stopped mid-chew and set his plate on the floor. 'Boy, you'd better start watching what you say. I have a few sticks of dynamite in my supplies that I've been saving for something special. If you want to be that something, keep talking.' He pressed his knuckles against his palms until they popped.

Victor carried on eating as though he hadn't heard him. After a few moments, Brandt picked up his plate again. Renfield glanced at Victor over the top of his reading glasses, once more not bothering to disguise his amusement.

Katarina tied her flowing hair behind her head. 'There's a long way to go yet, gentlemen. You would all do well to keep your heads.' Her tranquil eyes found Victor. 'Can you manage that for us?'

He stepped away from the pot and wiped his mouth. 'I ain't promising anything, lady. But tonight you can have your wish. Seeing as you cooked and all.'

He made his way to the doorway. Before he disappeared, Cassady called out. 'Telamonian will take the lead tomorrow.'

Victor hesitated, hands gripping the door frame, and then ducked into the night. Tagawa remained where he was, his eyes searching the embers. He leaned over and reached into the pot. After a few spoonfuls, he stood and walked to the door.

'Thank you for the food.' He turned to Brandt. 'Don't dismiss him. He doesn't make idle threats and he's gunning for you.'

'What do you care?' growled Brandt.

'I watch his back and he watches mine.'

'Are you threatening me now, too?'

'No. I'm simply making things clear between us. Oyasuminasai.' Tagawa slipped out.

When he was sure neither of them was coming back, Renfield placed the book down and peered over his glasses at Cassady. 'That wasn't necessary.'

'What?'

'You know what, Edward.'

Cassady kept his voice low. 'They aren't leading us out if they can't show you respect.'

'We can fight our own battles, boy. We don't need you drawing lines in the sand. And this isn't a procession. 'Leading us out'. Forget about that kind of ceremony. We're in the Bowl now.'

The old man groaned as he hauled himself upright. He beat the dust from his patched clothes. 'Anyway, I've said my piece. Time to turn in.' He shuffled over to Brandt. 'Long day tomorrow. And we still need to charge the batteries, which means one of us has to get up on that roof. I believe it's your turn, my friend.'

Brandt frowned, but accepted the veined hand held out towards him. 'You know where I am, Katarina,' he said. She waved him away.

For a while the four remaining drivers sat in silence. Then, one by one, they slipped out of the room until Cassady was the only one who remained. Except for the occasional tremor of fatigue that passed through his body, he was still. He watched the entrails of the fire until the embers stopped glowing and the sky outside paled from black to dirty grey.

2

The cry rattled the foundations of the buildings. A bird shot into the air and flew towards the safety of the trees. Inside the belly of Warspite, Ghazi threw off his sleeping sack and shook Cassady.

'Wake up. Trouble.' Even as the scarred Runner's mismatched eyes fluttered open, Ghazi was reaching over to unclip the tripwire and jumping out of the truck, his foot barely clearing the drop hatch. He raced across the quadrangle in the direction of the noise, a distinctly human articulation of pain, despair and defiance. It was coming from somewhere out on the road they'd taken to reach the abandoned settlement. Magenta lines lanced the sky and the warm morning air filled Ghazi's mouth and nostrils. As he ran, he struggled to release the clasp that would free the pistol clattering against his rib cage. Before he reached the road, he risked a glimpse over his shoulder. Cassady emerged from the building with Hearst by his side, the crossbow slung over her shoulder. Then he skittered around the last building and hit the bottom of the hill.

A moment was all Ghazi needed to assess the situation. Halfway up the hill, Brandt stood over a long, thin, spider-like body crumpled on the ground, his pistol gripped in two hands as he pointed it at three strangers. They looked like what they were: ravenous animals hunting their prey, with faces hollow and bodies brittle from a lack of food. One, a tall, grey-haired man with a distended stomach, hefted a rusty pipe between thick hands. Another, a woman, wielded a pickaxe and hissed. The third, evidently the leader, was a younger man whose head was a mess of scars. A machete in his hand dripped with fresh blood. Brandt aimed the pistol at each attacker in turn, and they ducked and weaved. The leader swung at him and the towering Runner jumped back just in time.

The gun was empty. That was why Brandt hadn't fired. It

would only be a matter of seconds before his attackers realised it too and overwhelmed him. In a single motion, Ghazi drew his own firearm and aimed it at their backs. He hadn't fired on another human for over a year, but he wouldn't hesitate now. He could hear Cassady and Hearst pounding the asphalt behind him.

'Put the weapons down,' he shouted.

Three startled heads turned in his direction. In that split second, Brandt made his decision. He thundered towards the grey-haired man and barrelled into him, but as he drew back his fist to follow up his attack, the woman swung her pickaxe in a wild arc. The flat side caught Brandt full in the shoulder and he crumpled. The grey-haired man staggered to his feet, lifted the pipe over Brandt's head, yanked it back across his neck with both hands and forced the Runner up onto his knees. The German's desperate fingers scrabbled at the bar and his flat grey eyes moistened in preparation for death. Ghazi gritted his teeth. The trigger was cool against his finger.

The group's leader pointed his machete at Ghazi.

'Gun down.'

Ghazi kept the pistol trained on the grey-haired man as Cassady and Hearst appeared by his side. The scarred man was incensed. 'No further or he die. Drop weapons.' He pointed again with the machete.

'Do as he says,' muttered Cassady.

'No,' said Hearst. 'Best chance. Fire.'

Cassady ignored her. 'Wait for my signal, Ghazi. We'll take them together.'

Ghazi allowed the pistol to fall to his side. The scarred man grinned in triumph.

Cassady pointed at Brandt, whose eyes were rolling into the back of his head. 'Tell your man to release him.'

'We take with. You stay.'

'Hand him over right now and we let you go.'

The tattoos became an ugly blur as the man shook his head. 'He come.'

'Last chance.' Then he muttered out the side of his mouth. 'The one on Brandt.'

'Right.'

Cassady indicated behind him with his hand. The sound of Hearst loading the crossbow was brutal in Ghazi's ear.

The scarred man was about to scream at Hearst to stop when a heavy thud cut him short. The woman with the pickaxe moaned and gobs of blood fell down her chin. She dropped her weapon and toppled over. A wooden stake quivered between her shoulder blades. The scarred man spun around and watched in horror as an immense form, head wrapped in a keffiyeh and body sporting a suit of leaves and moss, burst from the undergrowth and ran at them. Brandt's captor released him and brought the pipe up to meet the new threat. The old Runner rolled onto his back and sucked in air.

Cassady's voice was calm. 'Ghazi. Take the leader.'

Time slowed. Ghazi's heartbeat was a metronome. The pistol's ugly barrel wavered. He saw only the scarred man's back. Don't miss. Se, do, yek. He squeezed the trigger.

The explosion was loud enough to flatten the trees. The bullet plucked at a spot under the scarred man's shoulder and he dropped. Even as Cassady broke away and ran up the hill, Ghazi switched his aim to the grey-haired man. But there was no need. The camouflaged form was already on him, rocking on its heels to avoid a wild swing of the pipe and then darting forward and yanking a blade upwards through the grey-haired man's pelvis and stomach until it became lodged in his ribcage. The subdued attacker doubled over, trembling fingers finding the handle of the blade and recoiling as though burnt.

Cassady stood over the leader, who was trying to crawl away as blood drained from the hole under his shoulder. The wiry Runner gripped the back of his knotted head and brought it down against the track again and again until a sound like glass being ground under a boot was the signal to stop.

The grey-haired man lay where he'd fallen, his gaze fixed on the sky. His sobs carried down to Ghazi, whose stomach roiled. He wanted it to be over now. He shouted up the hill to the camouflaged form.

'Finish it.'

The blade came free from the grey-haired man's chest with a grinding sound and the sobbing became a gurgle as the metal sliced through his mottled neck. Then there was silence.

Reluctantly, Ghazi trained his pistol on the camouflaged form. It dropped the blade again and stood with its hands up, palms facing the group. Cassady went over to Brandt, who was on the ground massaging his neck.

'You okay?'

'Renfield's dead.' The two words were heavy and ugly. Brandt dragged himself over to the long-limbed form that lay face down in the road and turned it over. Ghazi edged forward with caution, his gun still trained firmly on the newcomer.

Renfield's cheek flapped obscenely. One of his eyes had been hammered shut and heavy liquid dripped from his temple. Ghazi muttered a prayer and tried to dam the emptiness flooding his chest. It wasn't the time or place to mourn the old man. They had to sort the mess out and get out of there before more unwelcome faces appeared at the top of the hill.

Brandt waved away the hand Cassady offered him and struggled to his feet. His face was white, but the bruises on his neck glowed red and purple. Purposefully, he walked over to the woman with the stake between her shoulder blades.

'You'd better still be breathing.' He kicked at the stake.

'She's dead,' said Cassady.

Brandt growled. He raised a well-worn boot and brought it down on the woman's skull. Then he took out his gimlet knives and slashed at the body until blood pooled under his feet.

'Enough,' said Cassady, marching over. He dodged the knives and shoved Brandt away from the corpse. 'I said enough. Get control.' He stared the larger man down.

'Don't do anything stupid, Jürgen,' said Ghazi.

Brandt's eyes bore into Cassady's. He raised his head to the sky and screamed until his voice failed. Then he wiped his mouth with the back of his hand.

'Okay.'

Cassady was still tense. 'Are you calm?'

'Don't ask again.'

'Tell us what happened.'

Brandt flicked the blood from the blades. 'We were looking for food. That was all. We don't sleep as much as we used to. These Schwein were waiting for us.' He nodded at Renfield's body. 'Went on ahead, never saw it coming.'

Ghazi's eyes flickered over the bodies lying in the road. The blood from the scarred man was already drying in the morning sun. There was nothing worth salvaging except the machete. Desperate people. Hungry, cold, hopeless. And now dead. Maybe they had once lived in a commune or been farmers whose crops had crumbled before their eyes. Maybe they'd been a family who had lived through better times. There was no way of knowing, and it didn't matter. Renfield was gone. A man with an understanding of the world like he'd had deserved to go out without aggression or fear. But deserve didn't factor into it.

A new voice, young and jumpy, joined the conversation. 'Just who in the hell are you?'

Ghazi glanced over his shoulder to see Victor, Katarina and Tagawa approaching. The latter held an old bolt-action rifle. The shout had come from Victor, who was pointing at the stranger.

Before the newcomer had a chance to answer, Cassady bellowed at the boy. 'What the hell do you think you're doing? Go and guard the rigs. There could be more of them.'

Victor stopped in the dirt. 'You don't get to talk to me like that.'

Cassady bore down on him like a truck with no brake. 'While you're shooting your mouth off, they could be raiding our supplies.' He spat the next words out. 'Go back. Now.'

The boy wavered and then did as he was told.

'You need the rifle?' asked Tagawa, holding it out in a lazy grip.

Cassady shook his head. 'Take it with you.'

Katarina went to Brandt, who crouched in the road with his head in his hands. She put her arms around his shoulders and spoke softly in his ear.

'Put the gun away, Ghazi,' said Cassady. He turned to the camouflaged figure. 'You can lower your hands. We have no fight with you.'

A deep baritone voice emerged from the depths of the keffiyeh. 'I know, man. I know.'

Ghazi's mind cooled to sub-zero. He recognised the voice. Cassady did too.

With massive hands, the figure drew back the folds of the keffiyeh and pulled out a twisted grey beard that had been hidden inside the camouflage suit. Droplets of blood left trails on dark skin. Cloudy eyes flickered from Ghazi to Cassady and a set of straight white teeth flashed at them.

'What's the news, brothers?' asked Wyler.

3

Cassady stared at the man they'd last seen drowning his demons in Prestige. Ghazi fidgeted beside him, the pistol pointed at the floor, but ready to be raised in an instant. Brandt sat in the road with Katarina and looked at Renfield's spindly body as though he expected him to sit up and laugh and tell him it was just a joke. The death of the old man had Cassady sick with fear. Day two and he'd lost someone. He didn't have a grip on anything. And now there was Wyler. The situation didn't sit right. He had a hundred questions to ask, and he had to start with the right one.

'How did you find us, Wyler?'

He laughed. 'You'd have to ask the Almighty. I didn't mean to. I've been tracking these jackals since last night.' He nodded at the bodies.

'Why?'

'Tried to get the jump on my camp while I was sleeping. I scared them off easy enough, but they took some of my things. Doesn't look like I'll be getting them back now.'

'Where's your car?'

He winced. 'Wrecked. Made an enemy in the big city just as soon as you left. Didn't like the way I gambled so they lit her up. By the time I got to her, I only had time to pop the trunk and drag out what I could before the fire burned her black. A real shame, man. All I have left is my bike. Back up the hill about a hundred metres.'

Cassady listened to the words without hearing them. 'Who sent you?' His voice shook.

The grin on Wyler's face dried up. 'What do you mean?'

'Who sent you to find us?'

'Sent me? Nobody sent me. I'm looking for a new place to settle, babe. You know that.'

'So what was wrong with Prestige?'

'That place is a nest of rattlesnakes and I don't have your connections. Remember what I said about the different kinds of evil? Well, I saw them all there, clear as day. I made a mistake. It wasn't the place for me. I thought about going further north, finding something by the lagoons, maybe catching a ship to one of the islands, but the boys in the bar said things are tougher up there than they are down here right now. So I started south again. It's what I know best, anyway. Past two days I've been cutting along the roads. I'm heading for the Complex. Might be able to get something going. Now I got a question: what's with the interrogation? Why are you looking at me like I'm one of the jackals? And who are these people? Lay it out for me.'

Cassady wished to hell he had a stick of root to help him think more clearly. But the pouch was in the rig. 'Are you being straight with me?'

The wild man took a step forward. Ghazi snapped to attention, bringing the pistol up until it was pointing at Wyler's chest. He stopped. 'What is this? What's happened? Are you in trouble?'

'I've always liked you, Wyler,' said Ghazi. 'And neither of us have anything against you. But right now you've got about thirty seconds to tell us what you know.'

'About what?'

Hearst appeared next to him. She held the crossbow in front of her. A quarrel lay on the stock.

Wyler faltered. 'I don't know what you want. I'm on the road. You're on the road. Here we are.' His eyelid twitched.

'Of all the roads and trails leading south,' said Ghazi, 'why would you take this one?'

'I could ask you the same thing. It's quiet. I can keep a low profile. I thought it would keep me away from punks like that.' He indicated at the bodies on the floor. 'The bike doesn't provide much protection.'

Cassady squared his shoulders. He had to get control. 'Back

off,' he said to Ghazi and Hearst. Then he turned to Wyler. 'I'll ask you once more. Are you being straight with me?' He paused. 'Brother.'

Wyler looked at him. His eyelid stopped twitching. The tension left his body. When he spoke, his voice was calm. 'I've told you the truth. If you can't be persuaded by it then I'm ready to die. I've lived deep and sucked out the marrow of life. I never thought you'd be the one to send me into the darkness, but that's how it is. So do what you have to do.'

Wyler lowered himself to his knees and waited, seemingly content in the face of death. The tip of his beard dragged in the dust. A battle raged within Cassady. This wasn't how it was supposed to be. These weren't the kind of decisions he had any right to make. But perhaps this was exactly the kind of test he'd wanted, and now he was about to lose his nerve.

A hoarse shout came from behind them. 'What are you doing?'

Cassady didn't bother to look. 'Stay back, Brandt.'

'That man just saved my life.'

'I said stay back.' He motioned to Ghazi to give him the pistol. It was cold, dead, unfamiliar. Nothing like the machete hanging from his belt, an intimate weapon whose handle was for his hand alone. He aimed at Wyler's chest and stopped breathing.

'Do it,' whispered the giant.

The barrel dipped and wobbled. Cassady waited five long beats. Then he lowered the gun. He breathed again. He held out his free hand to Wyler, who looked at it as though it was an arrow dipped in poison.

'Get up.'

Wyler remained on his knees. Cassady handed the pistol back to Ghazi, who holstered it. With reluctance, Hearst made the crossbow safe.

'I'm serious. You can get up.'

Wyler rose slowly. His body shook. 'Man, I don't know what game you're playing, but it ain't funny. Not a damn bit.'

'It's not a game,' said Ghazi. 'You'd have done the same.'

'Are you going to explain what's going on?'

Hearst scowled and stepped in front of Ghazi and Cassady. 'No. Back to your bike. Long drive to Complex. Better start now.' She pulled out a small, button-sized compass and rested it on her palm. 'That way.'

He tugged at the strands of his beard. 'Just like that?'

'Yes.'

'As you wish.'

Cassady rubbed the top of his head and felt the sweat against his palm. They should have left the area by now. It was dangerous to hang around after a shot had been fired. 'Wait. Wyler, stay a moment. I want to talk to my partners.' He gestured for Ghazi and Hearst to follow him away from the stinking bodies. They halted at the bottom of the hill.

'Need to go now,' said Hearst. The ugly lesion on her face was black with dirt. The sourness of her body caught in the back of Cassady's throat.

'I know. What about Wyler?'

'What about him?'

'He just saved Brandt's life. The least we can do is give him some supplies to help him on his way.'

She didn't respond. He turned to Ghazi. 'What do you think?'

'I think he's in the wrong place at the wrong time. He's showed us hospitality when we needed it. Brandt's still here because of him. He's lost everything. Your proposal is fair.'

Hearst clicked her tongue and glared.

Cassady spoke firmly. 'That's how it's going to be.'

She bared her teeth and stalked off in the direction of the buildings. He hoped she wasn't about to reconsider their deal. He and Ghazi retraced their steps to where Wyler waited with a wary look on his face.

'Get your bike. We'll give you some supplies.'

'Great. But are you going to tell me what's going on or not?

Starting with why you nearly dropped me a minute ago.'

'I had to be sure.'

'Of what?'

'That you weren't sent by someone to follow us.' Shame bloomed in his chest. How quick he'd been to give in to mistrust, to steel himself to pull the trigger and end the life of a man who had shown them only hospitality in the past. He wouldn't make the same mistake again. He couldn't afford to.

'Who? I don't understand.'

'Let's go to our camp and I'll explain everything.'

Footsteps scraped against gravel. Brandt pushed his way past Cassady and held out his hand to Wyler, who took it without hesitation. The old Runner was in pain and looked as though he had aged another fifty years in the past hour. But at least he was still alive.

'Danke. I owe you a debt. What is your name?'

'Make it Wyler.'

'If there's anything I can do for you, tell me.'

'Come on,' said Cassady.

'What about Renfield?' asked Ghazi. 'We can't leave him here like this.'

'He's mine,' said Brandt. 'I'll take him.'

Four bodies lay pale in the morning sunlight. Bloody footprints disturbed the dirt around them. And already the flies were gathering at the wounds.

4

'You can't be serious.'

'That's how it is.'

'And you actually think you have a chance of making it.'

'We'll do what we can.'

The day's heat hadn't yet found the inside of the building. All of the Runners were present except for Brandt, who was outside digging a grave.

Wyler's muscles shifted under the fabric of his camouflage suit. 'Babe, I've got to tell you: it ain't going to happen. You think you get by riding your luck up here? Wait until you're in the south. I've seen the wall. The ground is choked with skeletons and wrecks. Trucks like yours, Cassady, lined up like they're waiting for a green light. Except they ain't going anywhere. Not now, not ever. Whoever owns that land controls its borders like a king.'

'The king's losing his grip.'

'Right. According to a man you don't know from a hole in the ground. Ghazi, aren't you questioning any of this?'

'I believe the man was telling the truth. I trust him enough.'

'Trust. Belief. Difficult words in this world, brother.'

'We are committed now.'

Hearst worked up a wad of phlegm and spat into the ash of the previous night's fire. 'Need to leave.'

The Runners fidgeted. She was right. They had some decisions to make, and they needed to make them now.

'So what about Brandt?' asked Tagawa.

Katarina stirred. 'You would talk about him when he isn't here?'

'We don't have time for niceties.'

'It's over,' said Victor. 'He ain't gonna make it alone. The rig's too damn slow, even with two drivers. He's gotta turn back.'

'That's exactly what you've been hoping for,' said Cassady.

'You know I'm right, boss,' he sneered. 'The old man ain't got a hope in hell of keeping up with us on his own. This is why we've got four crews. If something goes wrong, we drop them. We ain't got time for soul searching. He's lucky he's still breathing. You only get a certain number of lives out on the road, and he's just used up another one.'

Silence followed the speech. Ghazi grimaced, wishing the boy wouldn't speak so harshly. But he was right all the same. Brandt wouldn't make it. He'd try, but he'd slow them down and he'd do more harm than good.

Cassady had reached the same conclusion. He kept his voice low. 'Will you tell him, Kaja?'

'Yes. But I don't agree with this.'

'We'll give him all the supplies he needs,' said Victor.

Katarina headed for the block of light that was the doorway.

'Wait a second.' All eyes turned to Ghazi. A half-formed idea fell out of his mouth before he could think about what he was saying. 'Wyler could take Renfield's place. He wants to go south again. That's where we're going.'

Leaning against a wall, the plantation man shook his head and pulled at his beard until his dark skin became taut. 'No chance. I'm a lover, not a fighter. This mess you've driven into, you can reverse out of it without me. I already lost nearly everything once this moon. I don't need to make it a full house with my life.'

'I see,' said Ghazi, pressing on with the thought. 'So what do you intend to do?'

'I told you. I'll try the Complex. I reckon those boys working the machines could use an extra hand.'

'Only the desperate go there. What if you don't cut it? Will you go from camp to camp until you run out of things to trade? Or until you starve?'

Wyler offered a wry chuckle. 'I'm already at that point, brother. Everything I had went up in flames.'

Cassady looked up at the roof of the building as he spoke. 'So you'll steal and kill like all the rest.'

'I never said that.'

'There are four trucks,' said Ghazi. 'If we send one away, we slash the odds of us making it to La Talpa.'

'What you're talking about is suicide, and you all know it. I can see it in your faces.' He looked at Hearst. 'Even you. I see the fear. None of you think you'll make it. That's the truth, isn't it?' He focused on each of them in turn. 'Well? I thought so.'

Ghazi spoke quietly. 'Remember what we talked about in Prestige after I joined you and Cassady at the bar that night?'

Wyler wrinkled his nose.

'You were talking about the idea of the soul. About good and evil and how people succumb to the shadows. You've been through hell. I know that. But now you have the chance to redress the balance. You can score a victory for the good people left in the world. Yes, we're scared. Of course we are. The abyss is looming and we're heading straight for it. But you heard what's at stake. You know why we're doing this. Don't be one of the ones who succumb.' He held his breath.

Wyler crossed his arms over his vast chest and studied the ground. The sound of a shovel tearing into the Earth's flesh carried through the doorway. A mosquito buzzed from Runner to Runner as it tried to find a landing site without being killed. Time they couldn't afford to waste continued to evaporate. Somewhere, thousands of kilometres away, people were dying of an illness in an underground base and hoping their cries for an antidote would be answered before it was too late.

Wyler shifted his stance. 'Right.'

'What?'

'You got yourselves another fool. But that's the last time any of you holds a gun on me if you want to live.'

Ghazi squeezed the man's shoulder. 'You're doing the right thing.'

'We'll see.'

'Can you drive a pantech?' asked Katarina.

'I can learn.'

'Then it's settled,' said Cassady.

Victor broke in. 'Wait a minute. You ain't the only ones here.'

'Until the end of the line, remember? Those were my terms. I'm in charge.'

'This is different. This ain't about choosing a route or picking somebody to take point. This is gonna change things completely. You ain't a dictator, Cassady. So we're gonna take a vote.' Victor looked around at the others, becoming emboldened when none of them dismissed the proposal. 'Yeah, we'll take a vote. Then we'll see if he comes with us. Right?'

'Okay,' said Cassady evenly. 'That sounds fair. Raise your hand if you agree to Wyler joining the team.'

Ghazi's hand was the first in the air. For a moment he thought he might be the only one in favour. Hearst stared pointedly at Wyler without moving, as did Victor. Katarina's outstretched hand blocked out the light streaming through the door. A moment later, Tagawa indicated his consent. Victor stared at him, but Tagawa held his ground. Finally, everybody looked to Cassady.

'Three against two. So if Brandt agrees, Wyler comes along with us.'

'What about you?' said Victor. The mop of platinum hair crackled with energy. 'You didn't vote.'

Cassady's gaze became hard. The boy had burned through all of his patience. Victor shifted his weight onto his other foot and swept the hair out of his eyes. 'Fine. Forget I said anything.'

'Mount up. We're getting out of here. Rendezvous is Werner Creek. You have the coordinates. Orion is the lead rig.' Cassady turned to Hearst. 'Go hard.'

The grave was an abscess expanding under the crust of the

earth. Stripped to the waist, sweat streaming off his body, Brandt shovelled great chunks of dirt with each swipe of his fold-away spade. As Ghazi, Cassady and Wyler approached, he paused in his work to swig from a bota bag and squirt a jet of water against his neck. Renfield's corpse lay at an unnatural angle near the grave. Brandt had covered his face with a piece of cloth. His pockets had been turned out.

'Decided on my future?' he grunted.

Ghazi smiled. The man was sharp.

'Something like that,' said Cassady. 'How would you feel about Wyler joining you in Telamonian?'

Brandt looked the plantation man in the eye. 'That what you want?'

'Prospects ain't leaving us much of a choice, it seems.'

Brandt nodded. 'Alles klar. I said I owed you a favour. You want to come along, it's okay with me.' The strength the man usually radiated was missing. 'You want to bring your bike along?'

'No. I'll leave it. It's more trouble than it's worth.'

'Then grab your things. I'm almost done here. Then I'll show you Tela.'

Brandt returned to his digging. Wyler and Cassady dispersed. Ghazi crouched by the lip of the grave.

'Jürgen.' The shovel continued to gouge at the dark soil. 'Are you okay?'

'I will be.'

'He was a good man.'

Brandt nodded once. The bruises on his neck looked like rotting fruit. Ghazi stood, wiped his brow and went to prepare Warspite for departure. He flinched when he heard Renfield's body thud against the bottom of the grave.

The low-pitched moan of Telamonian's engine rolled through the opening in the hanger and snapped at Ghazi's ankles. He wiped his hands on his trousers. The batteries were fully charged and everything was ready. He wandered outside to where the others stood by their vehicles, waiting for Wyler to try his hand behind the wheel. Renfield's grave had been filled in. Brandt hadn't turned the burial into a ceremony. Now he stood behind Telamonian and waved into the huge ear-like mirrors hanging from either side of the cab. Wyler edged out of the building and reversed over the quadrangle to where the hill began. He threw the pantech into gear. Telamonian bit hard and crossed the quadrangle again at speed as it heading for a concrete wall at the other end of the abandoned settlement. The sunlight turned the warthog spikes to liquid mercury. Ghazi looked on, a futile shout already dying in his throat because Wyler had lost control and was about to die. But just before he smashed the pantech into the wall, the wild man engaged the handbrake and threw the shuddering monster to the left. One half of its body left the ground and for a moment it balanced on four wheels. Then it came crashing back to earth. Dust and gravel flew into the air. The vehicle stopped with a whisper. Wyler jumped out of the cab and casually walked over to the others.

'What the hell was that?' shouted Cassady.

Ghazi couldn't tell if he was furious or amazed.

'I had to test her out.' He handed the keys back to Brandt. 'She's good.'

'The best. Never moved like that before though.'

'You just have to teach her the rhythm.' Creases appeared around the cloudy eyes. Brandt clapped him on the back.

'Just keep the stunt-driving to a minimum from now on,' said Cassady.

'You got it, babe.'

Victor leaned against the Silkworm and laughed quietly. Hearst stared at Wyler like she wanted to tear his throat out.

'Mount up,' shouted Cassady. He turned to Brandt. 'You need anything, let us know.'

'I can take care of myself.' He marched away towards the eight-wheeler. Wyler flashed his pure white teeth and followed.

Cassady sighed and closed his eyes. 'Christ.'

'Forget it,' said Ghazi. 'Time to go. I'll take the first shift.'

As the convoy sped away from the crumbling buildings, Ghazi spotted two buzzards above them. They would eat well today. He hoped the grave was deep enough for Renfield's body to remain undisturbed. Hacked down by a few desperate people on a gravel track. A bleak way to go. He shifted gears and the Old Lady picked up speed. The trees flanking the trail became dusty smudges on the windows. They continued south.

5

Warspite slid along the dirt road, tyres looking for purchase where there was none. The shriek of the wind fused with the keening engine and made it sound as though the world was screaming in unimaginable pain. Fat raindrops smashed into the windshield like a fist, and the wipers raced back and forth to try to create an opening wide enough for Cassady to peer through. His knuckles were white against the steering wheel. The storm had been hammering at them for hours now. He was trying to keep it together, but the effort was wearing him out. To his left was a dense line of trees that swayed drunkenly. To his right, the road quickly gave way to a sheer drop. Deep grooves in the mud indicated Orion and the Silkworm had passed the same spot some time previously. He checked the clock. It was after midday.

'Wake up, Ghazi.'

The mechanic's voice was thick with sleep. 'What is it?'

'Station report. I'll attach the antenna. You get the ledger out.'

'You sure?'

'Let's just get it done.'

Cassady stopped the vehicle and cut the power to the wipers mid-stroke. He wouldn't have admitted it out loud, but he was glad of the broadcast. It meant he could wake Ghazi. After removing his cap and tugging a balaclava over his head, he rooted around in the space behind the driver's seat for a plastic sheet to wrap around himself. Then he opened the door and stepped out into the storm. The wind tried to rip the sheet from his body and push him to his knees. With water streaming from every surface, he screwed the antenna into place and dived back into the cab. Ghazi pored over the figures in the ledger.

'Keyed it in?' Cassady asked as he removed the soaking balaclava. He shivered. At least the murderous heat of the past few weeks had finally broken.

'Double-checking. Yes, we're good to go. Call sign is Helios. Five minutes.' Ghazi was understandably groggy. He'd driven most of the previous day and tinkered with the rig late into the night after the brakes had started to feel gluey.

They switched on the short wave and waited for the report. Cassady checked the mirrors again. No sign of Telamonian. The beast would be scraping its wide flanks against the trees all the way, but Brandt knew how to tease his rig along a track this narrow. He had Wyler's quick reflexes to rely on, too. The wild man was filling the vacancy well so far, it seemed. Brandt hadn't raised any complaints when they'd rendezvoused the previous evening. For the hundredth time, he tried to blank out the ugly scene that had played out on the hill. He'd come close. Much too close.

'Tell me something,' said Ghazi.

'Go on.'

'Why didn't you vote on Wyler?'

Cassady coughed. Sometimes he was sure the man was a mind reader. 'You wait two days to ask me that?'

'I wanted to see if you would bring it up. And you haven't.'

'If I came down on one side or another, somebody would be left feeling pretty sore about it. That's not something this circus needs. I'm not under any illusions. We're just about keeping it together, but a wrong word or decision will spell the end of it. I'm not giving Victor or Hearst any more fuel for their fires.'

'Nothing you can do about Hearst one way or the other. The boy's young, that's all. He needs time to work things out.'

'It's time we don't have. I need to rely on him now and I can't.'

They fell silent as the opening bars of an unknown tune emerged from the speaker. The tune repeated itself twice more, and then a synthesised human voice reeled off a sequence of vowels and consonants. After the second run-through, Helios signed off. By the time Cassady had cursed the rain and retrieved the antenna from the hood, Ghazi had decoded the message.

'Bad news.'

'So are you going to tell me or do I have to ask?' Cassady threw the plastic sheet in the back and wiped the slimy water from his eyes.

'Flooding and landslides all around this area.'

'That's news? Anything else?'

'There's a group making waves further south of here, and they seem to be heading north.'

Cassady frowned. 'Could be the Zuisudra. One of the flies mentioned it back in Prestige. Remember the stray we picked up last year?'

'Of course.'

'Let's worry about that later. We have to make it off this mountain first.'

Cassady peered into the side mirror. The surroundings were barely visible beyond the driving rain. The real question was whether the road ahead would still be in one piece or underwater. He tried to guess how the other crews would respond to the report, and concluded none of them would want to retrace the same ground, not while there was still a chance of making it through.

He pushed the starter button and strained his chest until something in the centre clicked.

'You want me to drive for a while?' asked Ghazi.

'No. I've got it. Get some more rest'

'Take it slow.'

'Thanks for the advice.'

Cassady's shirt was still drying when he spotted a flash of vivid red in the murk. Orion sat in the middle of the road. The tail lights were dead. He eased off on the accelerator and stopped twenty metres short of the devil truck. He sensed Ghazi's hand straying to his holster.

'We'll go together.'

'Okay.'

After locking up, Cassady went to the lip of the road and peered into the abyss, but the rain and the swaying tips of more trees made it impossible to see the bottom. No lights burned below.

They set off for Orion. Their boots sank into the mud and the rain clung to their eyelashes and wet their mouths. Whip-thin branches slapped together in wet applause. At the rear doors, Ghazi pointed at a cluster of boot prints and the barely visible flicker of a tripwire. Cassady indicated for him to go around to the left. Under the plastic cape, he held his machete tight against his body. The wind screamed at him. He patted the blood-red body and swallowed hard. Keep calm, he told himself. It didn't make sense to lose it. It never did. At the front of the vehicle, he crouched down to check the steps leading up to the cab doors. Another tripwire had been strung across them. He turned at the sound of a low whistle. Ghazi stood a few paces further along the road.

'Look,' he said, pointing. 'Over there.'

Something was visible behind the curtain of rain. They pushed on until the apparition became a boxy pantech with a silver symbol painted on its side. Cassady unsheathed his machete and rapped the hilt against the Silkworm's rear hatch. It swung open with a rasping sound, and the business end of Hearst's crossbow greeted him. A tangle of blonde hair and Victor's grinning face followed.

'You look like your engine's flooded, boss.'

Cassady growled and climbed into the vehicle. Ghazi pulled the hatch shut behind them. Even with the crates of medicine laid out in the centre of the bed and six people inside, the pillbox felt spacious. Hearst sat closest to the rear hatch, the crossbow across her chest. Leaning against one of the crates was Katarina, a smile on her lips and a tin mug of something clutched between calm hands. Tagawa perched on a small fold-down seat next to a periscope that could be raised through the roof to check the surroundings. Victor ducked his head and retreated to the far end of the bed, where he rested against the back of the driver's seat. He took a sip from a canteen before throwing it across the length of the box to Cassady. He caught it before it hit the floor.

'The road is blocked,' said Tagawa without emotion. He crossed one leg over the other and studied the new arrivals. 'By a tree. One of the GM strains. Slid down the slope and hit the road. We thought it wise to wait for you. See if you had an idea on how to proceed.'

'You need kindling, in other words,' said Ghazi.

The Japanese chuckled. 'Right.'

Before speaking, Cassady tried the liquid in the canteen. Pulque. The back of his throat burned. Not wise, but welcome. He took another mouthful and hurled the canteen back to Victor.

'How does it look?' he asked the boy.

'It ain't good, that's for sure. There's gotta be enough timber out on that road to build a house. The end with the roots is still sitting pretty on the slope, but the gap ain't high enough to squeeze through. If we use explosives, I guarantee we're gonna trigger a landslide. So it's your call, chief.' He grinned, clearly enjoying himself.

'The tree which moves some to tears of joy is, in the eyes of others, only a green thing that stands in the way,' said Ghazi.

Victor's brow wrinkled. 'What are you gabbing about?'

'Something I read. It's a useful one for making sense of things.' He glanced at the others, but nobody spoke. 'In a way, it's saying we sacrifice the old for the new. Always chasing after the future, always convinced we can push on and think our way out of a jam. When we butt our heads against the trunk of the tree to knock it down, we blunt our ability to understand what the tree actually means.'

Tagawa rested a hand on the periscope. 'Enlightening indeed.'

'Sounds like a load of bull,' said Victor.

Katarina cleared her throat. 'Couldn't you say we're doing the same in service of the machine?'

'I don't think so,' replied Ghazi. 'We took on this run – or at least I did – because we want something more to hold on to. Not because of the material rewards.'

'That's where you got me wrong,' interjected the boy. 'When we get there, they're gonna fix us up with all kinds of pretty gizmos for the Silkworm. You heard what that old fella with the cane promised.'

'We shall see.'

Cassady listened to the drumming on the roof and felt the overwhelming urge to close his eyes, lie down on the cargo bed and sleep the sleep of the dead. His limbs were heavy from the pulque. He wanted another mouthful. He shook his head and forced himself to think.

'We can't go back,' he said.

'Could,' countered Hearst.

'Even if you managed to reverse the rig all the way back down the mountain without killing yourself, you wouldn't avoid Telamonian. Try convincing Brandt to turn around. And if you do somehow manage that, we'll still lose a day or two.'

Katarina stirred. 'We could wait for the rain to stop.'

He shook his head. 'This storm might not blow itself out for hours yet.' He nodded at Ghazi and Victor. 'We can't sit around here until then listening to the two of them talk philosophy.'

The boy scowled. 'You actually got a plan in mind or are you just happy to knock other people down?'

He didn't have one. But he thought fast. 'The tree's on an incline, right? Warspite has a winch. So does the Silkworm. We could tie the cables around some of the branches at the end closest to the drop and drag the trunk towards us. Then we just roll it off the edge and we're free to go.'

Victor exchanged glances with Tagawa, who nodded once. 'I guess it could work. If the engines can take it. That's a big son of a bitch out there.'

'We'll soon find out.'

'How are we gonna tell if we're both yanking the chain at the right time?'

'Ghazi will stand next to your rig and direct us with hand movements. Kaja, I want you to climb one of the trees close to ground zero. Take a piece of fabric with you. White. Wave it if the root end of the trunk starts to slip down onto the road. Ghazi will see it, I think.'

'What if the engines overheat before we shift the thing?' asked Victor.

Cassady raised an eyebrow. 'Then we're out of luck. Or do you have another suggestion?'

The boy shook his head.

'Then let's do it.'

'Now?'

'Want me to write you an invitation?'

'Fine.' Victor stood and pushed through the gap between the front seats into the Silkworm's cab.

Cassady turned to Hearst. 'I need you to move your rig as far over to the tree line as you can so I can get by in Warspite. After that, stay clear.'

Katarina touched his arm. 'Be careful, Edward.'

'And all of you stay out of the way of the cables,' he warned. 'I don't want anybody getting decapitated if they fail.'

While Ghazi ran back to Warspite to unwind the cable from the spool, Cassady went to take a look at the tree. It was unnaturally large, with purple and white roots as thick as his arm exploding from its base. The ridged bark was a suit of armour. Trees like that populated quick-grow GM forests, the product of a desperate idea clutched at by governments willing to try anything to save the planet. Katarina had once told him about the measures her mother had worked on with other scientists to try to slow the Change. Controlled volcanic eruptions, reflective crops, cirrus cloud dilution. And these forests. The problem was the formula hadn't been perfected before it had been rushed into production. Within months of being planted, the GM trees had multiplied out of control and destroyed even more of the continent's already-fragile ecosystems. The napalm fires that were supposed to check their advance simply cleared the way for them to eat up more land. Other measures were taken with negligible results. Finally, after all the resource wars had fizzled out and the population had shrunk beyond even the most extreme estimates, the trees had been left in peace to thrive as the forerunners of the new world.

Footsteps sounded behind him. Ghazi struggled through the puddles and potholes with Warspite's steel cable, which was looped at the end and tied off with a metal binder. As the rain streamed off them, they passed the cable around several branches near the lip of the road, lowered the looped end over the bough and tightened the binder until it cut deep into the flesh of the tree. Tagawa appeared noiselessly.

'Taking your time, I see.' He deftly tied off the Silkworm's cable further down the trunk. When they had made certain both cables were secure, they retreated. Cassady climbed up to the Silkworm's cab and rapped on the glass. Victor rolled down the window.

'Take it slow and steady, okay?' he called over the wind. 'Don't gun it unless you see Ghazi raise his fist. We need to be in sync if we're going to get her to move.'

'No problem.'

'If you feel her sliding away from you, detach the cable immediately.'

'I can't just cut it, Cassady. I ain't got anything fancy down there.'

That was a problem. He suppressed the urge to shout at the boy for not telling him earlier. 'Then get ready to jump clear.'

'Yeah, right. Hideki will take care of it.'

He jumped down and ran over to Warspite, cursing the rain as he slipped and nearly fell on his face. Hearst had moved her pantech as far over to the left as she could and Ghazi had brought the Old Lady up until she was sitting just behind the Silkworm. In the driver's seat, he knocked his sodden cap to the floor and wiped his eyes. He pumped the starter button and dragged the stick into reverse. Ghazi, pelted by the rain, stood to one side of the Silkworm with his arms above his head. With a sweeping motion, he signalled for them to start pulling. The cable lying in the puddles lifted off the ground and became taut. The transmission whined and Warspite juddered as it engaged with the tree. Both vehicles inched backwards. Cassady pressed his foot down, feeling the weight of the trunk in the pedal and the steering wheel. Ghazi held out a hand and he eased off. His partner disappeared behind the curtain of rain and then appeared again, a hand making a scooping motion above his head. He dipped the pedal once more. The tyres spluttered as they tried to find some purchase in the slick mud, and he prayed he wouldn't become stuck. The Silkworm's taillights burned. Warspite trembled, the chassis groaning with the effort of dragging the great load, and the dials behind the wheel tick-tocked. Cassady muttered an apology. He wanted to stop torturing her, but he couldn't. Ghazi raised his hand above his head and made a circling motion. He pressed the pedal to the floor and the engine whirred in double time. Warspite rolled back and the cable remained rigid. Thin-lipped determination played across his face. It was working. They were moving the tree.

A jolt shook the cab and the rig slithered forwards. Through the windshield, he could see the cable swaying up and down, but Ghazi had disappeared again. Something was pulling Warspite forward through the muck. He pumped the brakes, but the locked wheels were dragged along anyway. His dread mounted. He held the accelerator to the floor and the hood dipped with the effort. Ghazi came into view once more, now racing towards him with his hands cupped around his mouth. He kept a hand on the wheel and frantically wound down the window. But the wind snatched the words away and he heard nothing until Ghazi had reached the hood.

'Cut the line!' he shouted before diving to the ground.

Without hesitation, Cassady yanked the lever below the wheel to his right. At the front of the rig, a pair of powerful cutters swung together to slice into the cable. Butchered metal strands fanned out in front of the grille, but the cable held. He lifted the lever again and pulled it down. On the third try, there was a whipping sound as the cable flew free. Warspite stopped dead. Before Ghazi had even picked himself off the floor, Cassady had dived out of the cab and was running in the direction of the Silkworm, which was being dragged towards the chasm at speed.

'Get out!' he screamed, skidding to a halt near the bulky rear of the vehicle. The edge of the cliff had crumbled, and the tree slid slowly over the edge. Its roots were a mass of intestines that glistened in the rain. The passenger door flew open and Tagawa dived out and hacked at the cable with a machete, but it held firm. Victor's door remained shut. The pillbox squealed and bucked as it tried vainly to stay on the road. Tagawa brought the machete down on the cable over and over again. Time became warped and the seconds slowed until it was possible to see individual drops of rain strike the ground.

He had to get Victor out of there. He took two steps towards the cab of the black truck when a force yanked him back. He spun around and found himself looking into a pair of dull black eyes that showed no emotion. A long scar trickled from temple to jaw.

'What the hell are you doing?' he shouted, trying to shake his wrist free from Hearst's pincer grip. 'We've got to help them.'

'You'll die too.'

His hand clenched into a fist. He was about to swing for her when a metallic death rattle made his mind go blank. He turned in time to see the winch being ripped free from the front of the Silkworm. With inhuman reflexes, Tagawa dropped flat on the ground. The winch cleared his head by millimetres and disappeared into the abyss. The Silkworm leapt backwards across the road and came to a halt just before it ploughed into the slope of the mountain. The engine murmured for a few seconds and then died. Behind the glass, Victor slumped in his seat, head on the wheel, body shaking with adrenaline. Tagawa lay in the mud with his eyes open to the twisted sky and breathed.

Hearst let go of Cassady's wrist. He raced over to the Silkworm. The vehicle was hurt. The grille, bumper and winch were gone. Part of the engine compartment was visible. He climbed the steps and yanked the driver's door open. Victor was still hunched over the wheel, his skin as pale as his hair.

'You okay?'

'Yeah,' Victor muttered. Then he sat bolt upright as though emerging from a trance. 'Where's Hideki?'

'He's okay. Never seen anybody move as fast as that before.' He looked at the boy and struggled to find the right words. 'You're a brave man.'

The muscles in his face remained slack. 'Sure.'

'She's a little banged up, but it's nothing that can't be repaired.'

The younger man leaned against the headrest. 'I thought we were all done.'

'I know.'

'Guess I'd better take a look at her.'

'Easy. Rest first.'

Without thinking about it, Cassady placed a hand on his

135

shoulder. Now Victor broke into a weak grin. 'Feeling paternal?'

He withdrew it immediately. 'I'm going to check the road.'

'Should be clear now,' Victor managed to say, before dissolving into laughter. Cassady stared at him for a moment and then jumped to the ground. Ghazi was helping Tagawa to his feet.

'Is he okay?' he called. Ghazi gave a short salute. Tagawa set about brushing the worst of the mud from his dark uniform as though nothing had happened.

Cassady's hands trembled. Too close again. He tried to calm his breathing, but it was no good. He slipped a stick of root into his mouth. The rainclouds continued to slug it out overhead, battered and bruised but still burly enough to keep going. As he made his way over to where the great tree had lain in the road, his foot connected with the side of a submerged hole and he clattered to the ground. The root fell out of his mouth. Water and mud splashed his face.

'Goddamn it,' he shouted, pushing himself out of the muck. He wanted to hit somebody. He wiped his eyes and picked his way through the gloom.

Hearst and Katarina were standing where the tree had been. The path was clear.

'Are they okay?' asked Katarina. Her clothes were smeared with moss and bits of bark from where she'd climbed the tree. The rain had plastered a lock of white hair to her scalp.

'They'll live,' said Cassady. 'The pantech's taken a bit of a beating.'

'That was too close.'

He grunted.

'Are you okay, Edward?'

'I'm fine.'

'Do you want to wait for Jürgen? Or should we go on?'

'It doesn't make sense to wait. Push on to the rendezvous. You lead. We'll check the damage on the Silkworm and then follow.'

'Give them the time they need. They'll be more shaken than they make out.'

'I know that,' he snapped. Hearst growled at him in warning. He held out his hands. 'I'm sorry, Kaja. Adrenaline's still calling the shots. I was sure they were going over the edge.'

Her eyes roved over the lines on his face. 'Maybe you should let Ghazi handle Warspite for a while, Edward. You look like you could use a rest, too.'

'It's this damn rain, that's all.' He plucked at the plastic sheet that covered his body. 'I'll be okay.'

'Don't overdo it. There's a long way to go yet.'

'I know.' Her expression didn't change. 'I do.'

She touched his arm before heading back along the waterlogged road. He stood alone with Hearst. Raindrops cut through the geometric patterns on her head. 'Hearst.' She looked at him out of the corner of her eye. 'If you grab me like that again, it'll be the last thing you do.' He paused. 'But thanks for stopping me.'

The trace of a smirk was unmistakable as she walked away.

Once they had finished helping Victor and Tagawa patch up the Silkworm, Cassady and Ghazi returned, thoroughly wet, to the comparative comfort of Warspite. Ghazi pumped the starter and guided the Old Lady onto the road. He flashed the headlights as they slid past the pillbox. Cassady sank into the co-seat and rubbed his palms together. His boots were heavy and his skin was ashen and ugly. He checked the clock. Mid-afternoon. Still no sign of Telamonian.

Towards evening, the half-submerged road sloped downwards. Warspite's headlights struggled to pick out the route as the grey sky became deader. A serrated band of lightning lit up the world. Beyond the valley, to the east, a clutch of cinderblock towers without roofs cowered in the crevice of another mountain, unreadable banners and humanoid forms hanging limply from the exteriors. A small fire burned inside one of the towers, turning the window frame orange. When the road curved away from the valley, the buildings were swallowed up. Little by little, they left the drowned mountainside behind.

6

The trees cowered and groaned under the weight of the water falling from the sky. Ghazi sat cross-legged on the ground, using his whittling knife to chip shavings from a bundle of wet wood. When he was done, he took the shavings, placed them inside a modest stone pit and scraped the spine of the knife along his fire steel to generate sparks and ignite the tinder. He added kindling until a compact fire burned in front of him. He held his palms out and appreciated the warmth of the fizzing flames so close to his skin. All they needed now was some wild meat to roast on sticks.

The storm had slowed their progress to a crawl. The rendezvous had been under water and the trail had become near impassable, so they had struck camp in a clearing at the side of the road. Now they waited for Brandt and Wyler to appear. A shortage of power in the batteries played on their minds. The conditions were too hazardous to break out either the turbines or their few precious PV panels. The enforced inertia affected Cassady most of all. He paced underneath the sloping, lightweight plastic sheet that he and Katarina had slung between Warspite and Orion when they'd stopped. A few metres away under another canopy, Tagawa and Victor made repairs to the front of their truck and talked to each other in low voices. Victor had brushed Ghazi off when the mechanic had offered to take a look at the Silkworm.

'Maybe you should sit down, dostem.' Ghazi kept his voice quiet.

Cassady made no indication that he'd heard him.

'The rain will stop when it stops.' He pulled his hands away from the fire and stretched. 'You know that. We have no control over it. So why wear out your boots?'

'Can't I walk around a little without you making a comment?'

139

'Something is pulling at your thoughts. You've barely slept in two days and I haven't seen you eat since morning.'

'That isn't your concern.'

'It is if you close your eyes behind the wheel.'

'When was the last time that happened?'

He swept his hand over the flames. 'Sit by the fire. Switch it off for a while.'

'I don't need your spiritual crap right now.'

Despite his vitriol, Cassady dropped down next to a pile of unused firewood and swept his cap from his head. He reached over to a leather pouch by Ghazi's foot, took out a few of Lupo's pellets and gulped them down with a swig of pulque. His mismatched eyes focused on the leaf-shaped flames that writhed on top of the wood.

'You want to know what's on my mind?' he asked in a monotone. 'Why do we do this? That's what I'm thinking about. Why do we keep going?'

'It's like you said before – what else can we do?'

'So I could kill myself now and be done with it.'

'You could, and your search for whatever it is you're looking for would end right there. Or you could simply accept that you're not going to find a meaning to any of it, and then you'll be free to do what you want. No burden.'

'And that's it?'

Ghazi frowned. 'That's everything there is and ever was. Think of it this way: this, now, is a clean slate. We're freer than previous generations because we aren't petty conquerors any longer and we don't have the luxury of distraction. We can confront ourselves.'

'Sure. Until we drop dead from heatstroke. Or take a knife to the chest. Or swan dive off a mountain.'

'Maybe. But we don't sit and wait to find out, not if we want to get the most out of our time here. Each day when I wake up, I seek to improve my connection with everything around me.

Humans, animals, trees, rocks, the stars. Yes, my material needs sometimes take precedence. I won't stand idly by and let myself or others be slaughtered, for example. And I won't starve if I can help it. But beyond this, my mission is to understand what I call the soul.'

'What if we don't have one?'

'We do,' Ghazi said simply. 'There can be nothing without it.'

Cassady took a branch from the pile and threw it into the fire. 'Well, I don't see a greater goal in the distance. We're racing towards our end, that's all. Willingly, knowingly, without pause. All of us have a death wish. Victor and Tagawa were ready to go over the edge just a few hours ago. We both know Brandt is desperate for an honourable death. When Renfield was killed, he was full of rage, but I also saw jealousy. Even Hearst is only here out of curiosity, to find out whether she'll survive or not. Doesn't that seem wrong to you?'

Ghazi looked at him across the fire. 'And what about you?'

'The idea is to keep running until the day I'm slower than the next person and she takes me out, right? That's how it works. But I don't want to wait. I don't want to spend the rest of my life looking over my shoulder. I want to face it sooner rather than later, and I want to know if I'll flinch when it happens.'

A steady metallic thud resonated behind them. Ghazi looked over his shoulder. Tagawa wielded a hammer, its head wrapped in cloth, and brought it down onto a warped piece of metal. Victor, eyes shielded behind an oversized pair of goggles, connected an arc welder to one of the Silkworm's batteries. He dragged on a pair of filthy gloves and switched on the device. Tagawa moved out of the way, and fireworks exploded as the welder came into contact with the metal.

Cassady sat up and drank from the canteen of pulque. 'The day I watched my father and mother die, I didn't feel fear or remorse or despair.' He shook his head. 'It's strange how the mind works. I forget many of the runs we've made. I bury them

141

under a stone in the desert of my mind and walk away, never to come back. But this memory is as clear as spring water.'

Ghazi watched him, not moving for fear Cassady might close up.

'I barely remember being a kid, but I know I was one that day. My father had fried a big piece of game on the stove, back when we still had propane. He had canisters of it hidden away in caches all over the north. Near the great lagoons, mostly. Fuel, tinned food, winter clothes, spares for the rig. After he died, I only managed to find a couple. Anyway, he was dishing up the meat. My mother was taking apart a radio set. The sun was strong and the way it hit the Old Lady made her look new, proud, invincible. I sat in the trees, keeping a lookout, listening to my stomach. I had no reason to be fearful. My senses had been blunted by weeks of isolation in the wilderness. I couldn't wait to eat that game.

'The arrow that hit my mother in the back knocked her to the floor. My father didn't notice until she called to him. He kicked the stove over as he ran to her, and barely registered it when a second arrow tore a chunk out of his arm. When he reached her, he took her by the hand and tried to drag her under the rig. He was so calm about it, like it was happening to somebody else. She looked up at him and said something I couldn't hear. The next arrow went through his shoulder. That stopped him. I watched him try to pull it out with hands that were slick and red. My mother watched him too, her face white. And I could see the acceptance in her eyes. She'd already let go.

'They finished them off with knives. Two men, small, skinny, no different to any of the spectres lurking in the shadows by the side of the road. Just before they cut my father's throat, he lifted his head and smiled, because he knew I was watching, because he wanted to show me everything was okay. Neither my mother nor my father showed any fear. They saw death and they didn't flinch. They embraced it. And they went out knowing they'd passed the test.'

Ghazi added a couple of sticks to the fire. Cassady had alluded to what had happened a few times before, but never like that.

'Do not wish for it to come to you,' he said after a pause. 'Death will find you soon enough.'

'I need to know.'

'If you follow that path, you may lead others down it as well.'

A furrow appeared on Cassady's brow. 'That's how it is on this bitch of an earth.'

Ghazi nodded. 'But you are not the blind man. Now is not the time to put your doubts ahead of everything and everyone. You are connected to us all, Cass. This is what you should remember.' He stood. 'I'm going to sleep for a while. Wake me if you need anything, dostem.'

At the back of the truck, he heaved himself over the tailgate. Before he pulled the tarp down over the opening he regarded his friend once more, frame outlined by the flames that wrapped around charred entrails. The surface of the canteen winked as Cassady drank deep.

Telamonian arrived at the makeshift camp as night fell. In silence, the Runners watched the monster tuck itself in beside Warspite. A long gash had puckered the metal in the driver's side door. Brandt and Wyler exited the cab, the older man arching his back as he walked over to the congregation sitting under the plastic sheet.

Katarina's alert eyes searched Brandt's body for signs of injury. 'What happened?'

'Nothing to worry about, meine Liebe. The price of ambition.' Brandt accepted a stick of root from Cassady and chewed it while he told his story. 'The rain was bad up there, so we had to stop. I didn't set any traps. Just didn't think it was necessary. Resting in the hold when four of them tried to ambush us. I think they wanted parts. One went at my door with an axe. I dropped him and Wyler took out another. The two still standing disappeared in the rain.'

Wyler peeled off a wet flak jacket. 'These are the badlands, alright.' He jammed a branch into the ground near the fire and hung the jacket from it. 'Desperate men on the road to hell.'

'Will you be ready to go in the morning?' asked Cassady.

'Cosmetic damage only,' said Brandt. Wyler took out a pipe, packed the bowl with herbs and bark shavings and used a twig to light it. A bitter, fresh scent settled on the camp. He passed the pipe to Katarina.

A slurred voice rang out. 'Sounds like you're using up your lives pretty quick.' Over by the Silkworm, Victor raised a canteen and drank.

'If he keeps pushing me, he'll have one less to count on,' said Brandt quietly. 'I guarantee that.'

Ghazi gestured to the fire. 'Forget it. Make yourself comfortable instead.'

Victor jumped up. Before he could take another swig, Tagawa leaned over and plucked the canteen from his grasp. He held out his hand, but Tagawa shook his head and placed the canteen by his feet. Victor mumbled something in Japanese and staggered out from under the Silkworm's canopy. Rain plastered his unruly hair to his forehead. Brandt stood with his legs apart, head brushing the plastic sheet, the fire forgotten. Knotty hands hung loose and ready by his sides.

Victor ducked under the canopy slung between Warspite and Orion. His thin-lipped mouth twisted into a sneer. His eyes had lost some of their sharpness. 'If you set off now, you're only gonna be an hour late getting to the camp tomorrow. It's that way.' He pointed at the trail that disappeared into the gloom. 'But maybe taking the lead ain't for you. I'll tell you what. We'll clear the way and you can drive as slow as you want. Because we're just gonna wait for you anyway. Right, boss?'

Cassady eyed the boy. Lines cut into the pale skin between

his eyebrows. 'Now is not the time.'

'When is the time? When another one of us is dead? When we're all dead and he's the only one left and there ain't anybody else to point out how stupid this whole damn setup is?'

'He hasn't done anything to you. You can't blame him for what happened today.'

'I don't. I blame you, Cassady.' Victor spat out the words. 'You cut the line and you cut us loose.'

'That tree would have dragged us both over.'

'So you saved yourself as soon as you could.'

Hearst, silent since they'd stopped and made camp, chose the moment to let out a dry laugh. The shadows from the fire merged with her tattoos. 'Way of things.'

On unsteady legs, Victor spun around, glowering at each Runner in turn. He was ready to explode. 'This ain't a team. All you care about is not biting it before the day is through. Yeah, we're heading in the same direction. But that's it. If we'd gone over the edge, would any of you have climbed down to check if we were still breathing?'

Hearst answered a split second before Cassady. 'No.'

'Yes.' Cassady threw her an ugly glance. 'It isn't like that, Victor. I wanted to help. I did. But I had to cut the line.'

'We ain't anything other than pawns to you.' He turned his attention back to Brandt, making sure to hold his gaze as he made a fresh attack. 'What I don't get is why he has special privileges. Why does he get to take his time at the back, slowing us down, turning up after the work is over?'

'You see the size of that rig compared to the others,' said Cassady. 'It can't go as fast as us. Anyway, look at the door. They were attacked.'

'Another reason to drop him. He's attracting all the wrong attention.'

Ghazi slowly got to his feet, making sure to be ready for whatever came next. The boy was spoiling for it. Long, monotonous hours of driving were perfect for scratching away at the surface of a thought until it became a festering wound. Sometimes the bad blood simply had to be let, and afterwards they could all move on. He wouldn't step in unless either Brandt or Victor threatened to go too far. He admired the younger man's courage. He hadn't been eating properly for months and Brandt was close to twice his size. He could only see one outcome.

Brandt hadn't moved while Victor spoke his mind. Now he waited for his opponent to come to him and concede the psychological advantage. Whether due to indifference or ignorance, Victor obliged. Before either man could make the next move, Katarina placed herself between the two. Weathered hands pressed against their swelled chests. 'Violence is not the path we need to walk here. Jürgen, think about what you're doing. We live in a world saturated with pain already. Do you want to contribute to that? And Victor, look at yourself. You're drunk. Bed down and sleep it off. Don't take the easy route.'

Victor pushed her hand away. 'I ain't got a quarrel with you, old woman. Stay out of this.'

Brandt jerked his head and clicked his tongue. Katarina looked to Cassady to intervene, but he remained seated by the fire.

'I will not be part of this.' She turned away, climbed into the back of Orion and closed the door.

Brandt stared Victor down. 'I'm here. What do you have to say to me?'

'I'm done talking.'

Cassady beat his palm against his chest and frowned. He tried a final time. 'This isn't going to solve anything.'

'Give me your best,' said Brandt. As he brought his guard up and shifted his weight onto his back foot, Victor sprang forward in a blur and threw a solid left that landed on Brandt's cheek. He staggered back, surprise still registering as a right connected with his skull and sent him reeling. He fell against Warspite with a thump, and his head was yanked from side to side with an invisible string as he tried to recover from the blows. Victor backed off into the middle of the makeshift fighting space, cracked his knuckles and swept back his shock of hair. He'd shaken off his inebriation quickly and was focused on taking the big German down. Brandt pushed himself back upright. Warspite creaked on her suspension.

'Those were your free ones.' He probed his teeth with his tongue and brought his fists back up. The pair circled the space, each waiting for the other to show a chink in their armour.

Ghazi casually edged around the space until he was closer to Tagawa. The other Silkworm driver hadn't moved yet, but he would be ready if the Japanese tried to step in. On the other side of the space, Hearst bared her teeth in a grim rictus, a lion watching two hyenas snap at one another. Wyler worked his pipe from one side of his mouth to the other. Cassady kept his features blank. That meant he was irritated.

Brandt threw a punch with his right that Victor blocked with a strong forearm. The response was a low jab that hit the old Runner in the kidney and forced him back again. A confident smile was evident on the younger man's lips. As long as Brandt kept underestimating him, he would continue to pick out the spots where it hurt the most.

But the old German wasn't a fool. With a cry, he charged shoulder-first into Victor and sent them both sprawling to the sodden ground. Brandt was quick to rally, rolling the boy onto his back as he gasped for air and then trapping his arms under his knees. A heavy punch to the jaw knocked the fight out of Victor. A second hammered his left eye shut. Brandt's jabs were spiteful and designed to humiliate his opponent. The third punch split Victor's lip, and the blood ran slick against his knuckles. The last sent the boy under the waves.

Now Tagawa stood, rolled up the sleeves of his black tunic and left the cover of the Silkworm's canopy. Ghazi ghosted in front of him to block the way. Cassady sprang to his feet.

'Enough, Brandt. You win. Get off him.' He turned and pointed at Tagawa. 'You. Back off. Now.'

Calmly, Tagawa looked at his stricken partner on the floor. 'I warned you all this would happen,' he said.

'It was a fair fight,' replied Cassady. 'He knew what he was getting into. So don't do anything foolish.' He signalled to Wyler. 'Help him up.'

'You could've prevented it,' said the Japanese quietly. 'Let me take him to our rig.'

The wild man tapped his pipe against his boot and slipped it into a pocket. Then he gripped Victor by the wrist and hauled him to his feet. The boy's hair was caked with mud. Blood ran down his chin and the skin under his eye was already puffed up. Wyler slapped him across the cheek. He groaned and lifted his head, unsure of what had happened.

Ghazi stepped aside to let Tagawa pass. 'Let me know if you need anything.'

'I won't.'

Wyler helped Tagawa drag the boy over to the Silkworm. Brandt watched them go. He wiped his bloody knuckles against his trousers and muttered under his breath.

Cassady glanced at him. 'Proud of yourself?'

The old man's mouth opened and closed, but no sound emerged. He stumbled away into the rain.

For a minute, only the fire spoke. Then Hearst stirred.

'Better man won.'

The evening station report crushed any hope they had of making up for lost time. Heavy flooding had washed away roads and destroyed settlements, swelling the ranks of the transients on the hunt for food, water and transport. Any vehicles capable of moving would now be prime targets. The report had signed off with the news, again, that an unknown group was pushing up from the south.

Ghazi sat close to the fire with Cassady, Hearst and Wyler. The report had left them restless. Katarina had taken the first watch, sat in a hidden spot close to the trucks with Tagawa's bolt-action rifle, which he'd given her before returning to the Silkworm to tend to Victor.

'If it is the Zuisudra,' said Ghazi, 'we need to avoid them.'

Wyler lit a stick of bud, took a long drag and passed it. 'Before I left the south, all talk in the town was about those fanatics. They talk about cleansing the Earth of 'the disease'. They renounce all forms of technology and trust only in whichever God it is they've hijacked to support their cause.'

'What disease?' asked Ghazi.

'Us, brother. We're the plague. We destroyed the Garden. You know what they do to the ones who don't repent and join their group? Castration. They slice them up and leave them to bleed out. It'll be a graveyard down there right now.'

'They think what they're doing is right,' said Ghazi. 'In a way, I understand them. We went as far as we could with technology, and now they want to head in the opposite direction. Man-made systems and automation corrupted us, enslaved us and destroyed the world.'

'We picked up one of theirs a while back,' said Cassady.

Wyler raised his eyebrows. 'And?'

'We were running a cargo of generators to a settlement somewhere in the Bowl,' said Ghazi. 'It was the middle of the day in the middle of nowhere, and we rounded a corner to find a man hobbling down the road on foot. So we gave him a ride.'

Cassady cut in. 'You insisted on it.'

'He was desperate and exhausted. It wouldn't have been right to leave him. When he'd recovered enough to speak, he told us he'd been with the Zuisudra, but had managed to get away while on watch and had been walking for three days straight. Fear gave him the strength to keep going. He said the group is controlled by a caste of priests who keep everyone in line through a combination of amputations, cannibalism, rape, torture and executions.'

'Usual tricks,' grunted Hearst.

'Before they attack a settlement, the men mate with the ground and the women with plants and trees to absorb nature's vitality. They have shamans who speak to their God to find out what steps to take next. Our man was terrified the God would help the Zuisudra find him.'

Cassady leaned in to take the stick of bud from Hearst's outstretched hand. 'We messed up though. When we made it to the settlement we were headed for, we told the council who he was. They executed him before we could intervene. Too superstitious.'

'Put to death for escaping hell,' muttered Ghazi. He leaned back and eyed the sagging canopy. As much as he wanted to believe otherwise, maybe the killing and the misery would never end. He only had to look to the convoy to know it was true. If the eight of them couldn't work together without spilling blood, what chance did the rest of the world have?

'We should stay closer together from now on,' said Cassady. 'I don't want us getting picked off one by one. I've taken a look at the map, and I estimate the highway to be around half a day's drive from here.'

Hearst growled in response.

Cassady sighed. 'We have to take the highway. We're losing too much time on these roads. It won't be affected by the floods and it'll get us to the other side of the Bowl. Plus we'll be less likely to run into any transients.'

'No promise,' said Hearst.

'I want you to take the lead tomorrow. Tela will be behind you. Then the Silkworm. Ghazi and I will be rearguard.'

'If they stay,' said Hearst.

Wyler chuckled, revealing his straight white teeth. 'I don't think you need to lose sleep over it. That boy ain't got any more negativity stored up. Humility and peace is what'll repair his wounds, not a disappearing act in the middle of the night.'

Hearst squinted at his mouth and pointed without shame at his teeth. 'How do you have these?'

'Call it luck. Had a granddad who was a dentist before the Change. Taught my father about proper hygiene, and my father passed the facts on to me.'

'None missing.'

'Not yet.'

Hearst edged forward until she was millimetres from his mouth. Ghazi winced, but Wyler's face showed no discomfort. Finally, she sat back again, her eyes still on the ex-farmer. Wyler frowned for a moment before turning to Cassady.

'I'll let Brandt know the plan.' The old Runner had returned to the camp a half-hour after he'd left it, but had shut himself away in Telamonian.

'The two of you seem to be getting on well enough.'

'We've talked. You know how it is, sitting in a pantech. You spill anything and everything. He's been through a hell of a lot in his life, most of it bad. But he keeps going anyway.'

'We all do.'

Ghazi stretched out a hand beyond the canopy. The rain was in its death throes. It would stop before morning. He stood and arched his back. Katarina was probably freezing out there.

'I'll go and relieve Kaja,' he said.

He was gathering what he needed when the cab door to the Silkworm creaked open. A mass of luminescent hair appeared and a thin form dropped gingerly to the ground. Victor walked with stiff strides over to the group. By the fire, he crouched down and warmed his hands. His cheek had ballooned and his bottom lip was a wedge of spoiled flesh.

'You okay?' asked Cassady. Victor nodded. He rose, ducked under the canopy and disappeared into the darkness. Katarina

appeared a few minutes later. She stretched out by the fire and
closed her eyes.

'Did he say anything?' asked Cassady.

'Only that he was there to relieve me and there would be no
trouble. I checked his injuries. They'll heal quickly enough.'

'You think it's a good idea to let him sit out there with a rifle?'

'It belongs to him.'

'Maybe I should go and speak to him.'

'Leave him, Edward. He'll be okay. The watch will do him
good. Give him time to think.'

'Exactly right,' said Wyler. 'I'll relieve him in a couple of
hours.'

'And Brandt?' asked Cassady.

'Jürgen knows what he did wasn't okay,' said Katarina. 'I'm
sure he'll apologise to the boy in the morning. I think this will
be the end of it.'

Hearst shrugged off her blanket and draped it over Katarina.
She retrieved a few utensils from her truck and brewed a pan of
acorn coffee, which she shared out between the Runners. The
heavy aroma of burnt sugar settled on the camp.

When the wind picked up they turned in. As he bedded down
next to the crates of medication, Ghazi's ears remained pricked
for the sound of a crew preparing for departure. He hoped
they wouldn't wake to find a flattened patch of grass where the
Silkworm had been.

7

The four-lane highway was a grey brushstroke against the plastic-infected scrubland. The storm had blown further north, taking the last of the rain with it and leaving puddles that stretched like mirrors across the ground. Husks of ancient vehicles sat with their shoulders against the side barriers. Remains of former barricades and road blocks pointed to a time when the road had been a rat run for fugitives, exiles and survivors heading north or south. Now the cracked and crumbling surface was devoid of life save for the four trucks that raced along in the weak afternoon sunlight.

The Silkworm was the size of a matchbox in Warspite's windshield, dipping in and out of view as the two vehicles dodged various obstacles. Cassady guided the Old Lady around a laceration without jabbing the brake before bringing her back onto the centre line. For the first time in days, the needle on the speedometer quivered a few points below red. He sucked on the tube snaking out from the bota bag to rinse the dust from his mouth. Although they'd lost half the morning waiting for the batteries to charge, they were finally making good time.

Victor hadn't spoken to any of the Runners in the morning, instead waiting inside the Silkworm until it was time to depart. As Katarina had predicted, Brandt had been keen to make peace, but Tagawa had advised against it and told him to wait until Victor was ready. Despite his dislike for the boy, Cassady hoped he was okay. His pride had been stung more than anything else, and that was the kind of wound which could take an eternity to heal.

But something else was bothering him more than Victor. Before the convoy had headed out, he'd gone to Katarina for advice on how to deal with the tense situation. She kept her thoughts clearer than most others, uncoloured as they were by anger or superstition or petty rivalry.

'You may not like what I'm about to say.' She'd been braiding her long hair and coiling it on top of her head in readiness for the day's run.

'I'm asking you.'

'Then you must let me speak and not interrupt. You have changed, Edward, and not for the better. I noticed it at the stockade, I have seen it on the road, and I observed it last night when you sat and did nothing while two men under your charge fought between themselves. The boy was looking for someone to blame. He was nearly dragged over a cliff and he was shaken by it. When a man comes to you with desperation in his eyes, you don't blink or look away, no matter how much you may want to. Brandt should know better, but he's dealing with Renfield's death. He's hurting too. You don't have the luxury of that excuse. Everybody is looking at you to lead us. If you can't keep somebody like Victor in check without things spiralling into violence, how do you expect to make it through the Alps? We don't know what's there. You have to be ready for it, Edward. You have to be ready for everything this run throws at you. Now I'm going to ask you: what is wrong? What's happening inside there?' She'd pressed her cool fingertips to his forehead.

'There's nothing wrong.' The words had been insubstantial, meaningless, and had been snatched away on the breeze.

'You can tell me.'

He'd stared with lips pressed together and sweat dribbling from his temples as he debated whether to tell her. Finally he'd blurted it out.

'I've lost my nerve.'

The confession had triggered a wave of nausea. The only thing that had stopped him from turning away and retreating to Warspite was the way she'd regarded him. There was no pity, no disgust, no resignation. Every line, every pore on her face had radiated understanding. And she'd wrapped her arms around him and held him tight against her. Her comforting scent had filled his nostrils and he'd breathed deep to chase away the shadows. Afterwards, she'd taken his hand and asked him the difficult questions.

'How long have you felt this way?'

'Weeks. Months, maybe.'

'How bad is it?'

'I question everything I do and I don't know why I'm here. Back at the stockade I thought it made sense. Now I see we haven't got a hope in hell. I want to run and not look back.'

'Have you spoken to Ghazi about this?'

'A little. But he's the only one.'

'I won't say anything to the others. Can you continue?'

'I don't know. I keep jumping at shadows.'

'Listen to me now. I don't have any magic words that can shake you out of this, but I saw how Hearst had to hold you back yesterday when those boys were being dragged over the edge. Those are not the actions of a man who has lost his nerve. When the time comes, you'll know how to act. I believe it.'

'Easy to say. You're not the one living inside my head.'

'The mind is a repository of convictions and fears and you are the sole gatekeeper. Remember that, Edward.'

Replaying the conversation in his head now made him grip the wheel until his skin protested. He thought ahead to what the borderlands, and the Alps beyond that, might hold. Fear chewed at his stomach, his neck, the hairs on his arms. He ran his palms over his head to dry them.

'What's bothering you?' asked Ghazi

'Nothing.'

'Come on.'

'Just forget it.'

'Do you think Victor will settle down now?'

'If he's smart.'

'Intelligence is in short supply in this world.'

'You have everybody worked out.'

'Something has you wound up and it's not me. If you want to tell me anything, I'm right here. You aren't alone.'

'That's where you're wrong. All of us are.'

His hand slipped from the wheel to his belt and caressed the top of the pouch where he kept his root. No. Not yet. It was too early. He had to maintain control.

The whir of the engine kept time for the orchestra of vibrations and rattles that played from one end of the pantech to the other. They were deep in the Bowl now, and the land was dead. Forest fires, plastic saturation, topsoil erosion and the effects of photochemical smog had left only parched and poisoned ground. No animals ran or flew or slithered across the open landscape. They'd migrated to the green belts further north long ago. Despite the desolation, there were still some signs of human life beyond the highway. They passed a compact hub of brick buildings and corrugated iron lean-tos that lay just a couple hundred metres from the road. A flag on a roof bore an image of a star. Standing in one of the entrances, watching the convoy speed by, was a dark-skinned man with a rifle cradled against his chest. Two children burst from behind a giant clump of ditch weed, raced over to the building and hid behind the man's legs. Cassady kept his eye on them as Warspite rumbled by. Alone and surviving. That was all.

In late afternoon the remains of Frankfurt, one of the great cities, appeared on the horizon, a mouthful of broken teeth that smacked its lips in anticipation as the convoy dangled closer. Cassady's mind became cold, his grip on the wheel a little tighter. Revolts, war and fatal efforts to control overpopulation had turned the cities into bone houses; flooding, fires, radiation and erosion had turned them into graveyards. Most Runners made sure to go around places like Frankfurt, even if it added an extra day or two onto their run. Anything was better than contending with streets so clogged with vegetation, rubble, wreckage, rusting carcasses and surface water that it took hours to find a way through. Only the bravest and most foolish drivers went in. When he'd been younger and more reckless, he'd been no different. He'd raided garages and supply depots and department stores. He'd seen buildings collapse without notice, sturdy one minute and a mushroom cloud of dust the next. And he'd laid eyes on the kind of people that now called the decaying metropolises home.

Buildings spilled out to the left and right, devouring the landscape and scratching the streaky blue sky. Ghazi pulled the maps out from the box under his seat.

'We're not going through it,' said Cassady. 'I don't know why you're checking.'

'I just want to make sure. Some of these maps tell more lies than truth.'

'It's a highway. The route's fixed.'

Ghazi traced the sinewy line with his finger. 'We rub shoulders with the western edge.'

'No other choice. We've lost too much time as it is. Put the map away, would you? I need you to spot.'

He kept his foot down on the pedal and swallowed to clear the tightness in his throat. Ghazi's concern was a valid one. Once the road curved closer to the city, anyone with a high-powered rifle could take pot shots at the rigs. They would be in range for at least a few minutes. It was part of the gamble.

When they came close enough to make out the details, their mouths fell open. It was a mortuary. Every building had faded to the colour of dried blood, as though smeared when fresh and never rubbed off. The thick outer skin of the dead giants had sloughed away to expose the metal bones and gristle underneath. Rain and wind and sandstorms had tenderised their faces until they were unrecognisable, and in some places their skulls had caved in altogether. Other buildings had been disembowelled, their guts spilling into the surrounding streets. This was the extinction they were always running from. An ancient flying machine sat on the roof of one of the taller structures, its beak protruding from the concrete lip. Closer to street level, oleaginous growth covered the walls and gummed entrances shut, and creeping vines hung from glassless windows. The heat haze threw everything in and out of focus. A city this size would take centuries to be reclaimed by nature. But the process had started.

The number of stripped and destroyed vehicles on the highway increased, some fresher than the rest. Cassady spotted a pantech whose crew he'd once run a convoy with. They'd gone missing a while ago. He eased off on the accelerator and swerved left and right around pools of water, wary of any holes they might be concealing. Even as he willed the convoy to push on until they were well clear of the sinister necropolis, the Silkworm's brake light flickered on and the pillbox slowed and stopped.

'What the hell are they playing at?' he growled through clenched teeth. He judged the distance between the trucks and the forest of high rises ahead. They were still out of range, but only just. Victor emerged from the cab and crouched down, his eyes scanning the asphalt.

'He's found a note,' muttered Ghazi.

The boy jogged the hundred metres to where Warspite sat idling. Cassady wound down the window as he climbed the steps.

'What is it?'

'Message from Hearst on the blacktop. Road is booby-trapped. Starts a few hundred metres further up.' He pointed behind him with his thumb. 'Explosive tripwires, apparently. The kind meant to cut our legs off and bring the natives running.' Victor swiped at his hair. The swelling under his eye had receded a little, but the casual arrogance hadn't yet returned.

'Anything else?'

'Yeah. Kaja's guiding us through. I guess she's gonna disable them and we follow.'

Ghazi unclipped his harness. 'She doesn't have to. I can do it.'

'They'll be way out ahead by now.'

'We can catch up.'

Victor shook his head. 'No,' he said, his voice level. 'One of us out there alone ain't gonna draw much attention. Two or three will. We've gotta stay with the rigs and be ready to move. That's how it is. You don't get to choose who lives and who dies.'

Before he could jump down again, Cassady's hand shot out and grabbed Victor around the throat.

'What the hell are you doing?' gasped the boy.

Dirty nails dug into his skin.

'Let him go, Cass,' shouted Ghazi.

White noise in Cassady's ears drowned out the words. He clenched his teeth and tightened his grip. Orbs of energy exploded at the edges of his vision and the boy melted away into rivers of colour. The world no longer existed.

A hand crashed into the side of his face. He let go. Everything swung back into focus: the city, the wrecks, the hot dead road surrounding the vehicle. Victor dropped down from the cab and doubled over.

Ghazi drew his hand back. 'Get control,' he said. 'Right now.'

Cassady tried to slow his breathing. He leaned his head out the window and looked for the boy. 'I'm sorry.'

Victor raised his middle finger, confusion and disgust naked on his face, and stalked back to the pillbox.

'What are you doing?' demanded Ghazi.

'I don't know. I saw red.'

'Listen to me.'

He looked into Ghazi's liquid eyes.

'Victor's right. You can't save them. Any of them. They're not yours to save. Your job is to get the cargo to the destination. Nothing more. Get a grip of yourself now or we aren't going to make it.'

Cassady stared straight ahead, struggling to find a way back to reality.

'You hear me?'

'Yeah. I'm sorry.'

'Forget it. Start her up.'

Out ahead, the Silkworm pulled away, and he put Warspite into gear and followed. His skin burned. He half-expected to see the pillbox make a U-turn and blaze past them, and it would be his fault if it did. Some leader he was proving to be, lashing out because he couldn't keep his emotions in check, afraid of his shadow and terrified the others would find out. Kaja and Ghazi were both right. He needed to get his head straight, fast, or it would be over.

To calm himself, he checked and rechecked the meters and dials quivering behind the steering wheel. The battery bar was still green. Providing they made it through the tripwires in one piece, they would have more than enough juice to gun it away from the area. Not much of a silver lining, but it was all they had. When next he swallowed, he almost gagged on the taste of copper. Evidently, there were high levels of chemical residue around the city. He took a sip of water from the bota bag above him, swilled it around his gums and spat out of the window. Ghazi did the same. They wound up the glass and tried not to think of Katarina breathing in the tainted air.

Their view of the highway was limited to the back end of the Silkworm. The rusted vehicle bodies made it impossible to pull out and look further down the road. Cassady stopped the truck when Victor stopped and kicked her into gear again when the pillbox jerked forward. His eyes darted to the clock every few minutes. They were burning through time like it was gasoline. He gauged the distance to the buildings.

'We're in range.'

'I know.'

Ghazi unclipped the binoculars from above his head and

scanned the facades as Warspite crawled along at walking pace. Most of the buildings were too damaged to be inhabitable, but some were still intact. Cassady muttered curses as Victor stopped yet again. Maybe taking the highway had been a bad idea after all. Almost on cue, Ghazi's voice rang out and he went numb behind the wheel.

'Turret, 11 o'clock. Building with the jury-rigged balcony and the hole in the centre. Approximately four floors down from the top. You see it?'

Cassady ducked over the wheel, pushed back the peak of his cap and searched for the threat. His gaze rested on an outcrop of wooden boards that didn't belong to the concrete exterior. The snout of a heavy-calibre gun, large enough to put all four vehicles in the convoy out of commission, protruded from the balcony.

'I see it.'

He shifted his attention back to the road and counted the seconds while Ghazi surveyed the building.

'Looks like it's rusted to the spot. No movement behind the windows or in the doorway.'

Cassady unclenched his jaw. 'Keep an eye on it.'

They rolled over a section of road spider-webbed with cracks. A glint of metal drew Cassady's eye. An ammunition box sat on the hood of a car, its lid propped open and a slack length of wire emerging from its guts. Katarina's work. The box was probably filled with stubs of scrap metal and other shrapnel that would shred tyres and tear a few holes in the driver.

'Reminds me of the Berlin run,' he muttered.

'At least we're only dealing with tripwires.'

'I hope so.'

It had been the worst run he'd ever been part of. A settlement on the outskirts of the old capital had been under siege and in need of supplies. Cassady and Ghazi had volunteered to join the convoy of eleven rigs on its way there because they knew the leader, a good woman who had helped them out in the past. They'd driven night and day to reach the settlement, but by the time they'd reached Berlin the inhabitants had already been massacred. In their place were tripwires, pressure mats, spring-loaded bombs and landmines designed to turn vehicles into scrap. The first explosions had destroyed three trucks outright. An attack had come soon after. Only two out of the eleven trucks had managed to escape, and both had been severely wounded. Warspite had limped to safety on two flat tyres and the windshield, along with Cassady's nerves, had been smashed to bits.

Somewhere ahead, Katarina crept forward through the debris field, scouring the area for gossamer tripwires and booby traps. And all the while, the pantechs growled and snorted and pawed at the ground as the sun turned the world to liquid.

Stop. Start. The clock hands gradually toppled over. Ten minutes. Twenty. Half an hour. The trucks dipped in and out of ruts and crushed rocks and flora under their tyres. The shadows on the asphalt became grotesque as the sun drifted towards the horizon, and the drivers reached for tinted goggles whose suction caps bit into their skin and filled their noses with the scent of rubber. The metallic tang entered the cabs even with the windows rolled up, and so the occupants swilled out their mouths and spat water onto the floor. The heat sat heavy on their skin.

Life in the city had been extinguished. Warspite passed building after building that showed no movement. The debris field thinned out, the mountains of rubble that blocked the lanes became hills, and the distance from one charred wreck to the next increased. The space on the road gradually became wide enough for two vehicles to drive side by side. Frankfurt fell away. A final copse of creaking high rises was all that remained, and then the convoy would be safe.

Ghazi twisted in the co-seat. 'Movement.'

'Where?' said Cassady, his chest suddenly tight.

'Fourth building. Blue paint near the top, hole on the right-hand side by the corner. There's a person standing in the middle of it.'

He followed Ghazi's instructions, running his eyes over the high-rises.

'Are you sure? They look too unstable.'

'Fourth building,' he insisted. 'Near the roof. It's a man.' A pause. 'At least it was once.'

Cassady kept the rig on an even course, his gaze occasionally flicking to the building with the blue paint. The goggles made it more difficult for him to see. Ghazi rarely made mistakes, but he hoped he was wrong all the same. He increased their speed.

'Now two. Both males. Maybe others inside.'

Ahead, the Silkworm rumbled on at the same pace. Cassady held his breath, sensitive to everything.

'They've seen us.' He paused. 'They're tracking us with a telescope.'

Without waiting for more information, Cassady guided the rig out into the lane beside them and jumped on the accelerator. They drew up alongside the Silkworm. In the cab, Tagawa had a pair of binoculars trained on the structures. Victor and Ghazi wound down their windows.

'Blue building,' shouted Ghazi.

'We see it.'

Tagawa barked a warning. 'They're armed'.

Ghazi brought the binoculars up again. 'It's a rifle. Scoped.'

Cassady clenched his teeth and Warspite pulled away. They had to get to Kaja. They would target her first. The needle ate through the numbers on the meter, but it felt as though they were churning through a waist-high river.

'Come on,' he barked, throwing the rig from one side of the road to the other to avoid the rubble and metal. 'Faster.'

The huge back end of Telamonian slid into view.

'They're judging the distance.'

Cassady's hand hovered over the horn. If he used it, it would warn Kaja, but it would also draw the attention of anybody else in the vicinity. He hesitated. It went against every instinct.

'Where are they aiming?' He wanted it to be at them.

Ghazi tried to steady the binoculars while the vehicle bounced up and down. 'Hard to tell.' They drew closer to the monster, which leaned to the left as Brandt finally noticed them in the side mirror. 'But not us.'

Warspite streaked past Telamonian. There was no time for an explanation. Now Cassady could see the blood-red beetle scuttling along asphalt. Beyond it, a human silhouette stood out against the dying sun.

'Go, go, go,' yelled Ghazi. The pedal was on the floor. Cassady fought with the wheel. Turn around, he thought. Get back to the rig. Find cover. Anything. He willed Hearst to notice the shooter in the building. But her attention would be on the road and the woman who meant so much to her.

'They're sighting.'

He punched the horn with the flat of his hand. The sound travelled up through the belly of the Old Lady. He hit it again. It was an ugly noise, a last resort only, and now it was drawing attention to them all. The rig scudded along the road and ticked and blared and groaned. Orion picked up speed. The silhouetted form turned its head in the direction of the noise.

The first shot was almost swallowed up by the wind shrieking through the windows. But they both heard it. Cassady's only reaction was to grip the steering wheel tighter. Ice water dripped through his ribcage into his stomach. The second shot came as they flew past Orion. He swung in front of Hearst. Katarina was on her knees, hair unbound and spilling out around her. As Warspite strained to reach the spot, she managed to roll herself over until she lay protected by a chunk of highway barrier. Confused hands sought a hole in her shoulder that pumped out a thick hot stream of red.

The Old Lady screeched and the tyres left a scar on the road. Cassady ripped off his goggles and his cap, threw open the door and rode the shockwave as his feet connected with the brittle floor. The rifle sang again, and a bullet chimed against Warspite's hood. Katarina reached out with a bloody hand and he grabbed at it and dragged her towards the rig. Ghazi appeared beside him and shouted at him to keep his head down. Together they lifted her and carried her around the back. Orion pulled in, shielding the tailgate from view. A fourth bullet tore into Warspite's tarpaulin roof and exited out the side. Cassady's breath emerged in ragged gasps. His hands were warm and wet and he looked down at Katarina. Her eyes, so clear and focused, drilled into him. She said something he couldn't hear. Ghazi released the tailgate, threw himself onto the cargo bed and reached out for her. Cassady lifted until she was taken from his arms.

He raced back to the cab where the door still hung open, doing his best to ignore the blood soaking into the road and the metallic taste that caught in the back of his throat. Telamonian drew close and he raised his hand to wave them on, on, away from the danger. Somewhere at the back of his mind he registered there had been no further shots, which meant the figures in the tower had either run out of bullets or were saving their ammunition. Other hostiles could be on the way. The Silkworm with its patched-up front swept past like a rabid dog, the threat of the tripwires forgotten.

Cassady hauled himself into the driver's seat. In the back, Ghazi tore up pieces of cloth to press against Katarina's wound. Orion sat in the road, waiting for him to get going. He slowed his breathing, checked he was in gear and pulled away. If the bullet had hit anything important underneath the hood, the trip would be a short one.

'How are we doing?' he called behind him. No answer. Ghazi's movements were those of a caged animal as he moved back and forth over the bed. Katarina moaned. He glanced at his hand resting on the wheel. The creases had been poisoned brown. A long strand of white hair was caught under the leather strap around his wrist and he clawed at it until it fell to the floor. His whole body itched. He retrieved his cap from the passenger seat and jammed it onto his head. Despite his efforts to keep the Old Lady steady, she shook on her chassis. Other than Orion, no vehicles were yet visible in the mirrors. He could only guess how Hearst was feeling.

The copse of buildings melted away, replaced by an open expanse of brown and yellow land on which nothing grew. The road was open and clear. They hadn't triggered any explosions. The Runners fled into the approaching dusk while one of them slowly bled out on a cold, uncomfortable cargo bed.

8

It was Tagawa, alert to everything around him, who spotted the entrance to the train tunnel. Disappearing into the side of a mountain, the narrow mouth was obstructed by a lattice of branches and vines. He, Cassady and Brandt attacked the undergrowth with machetes while Victor stood guard. Moonlight gilded the surface of the blades as they rose and fell.

Katarina lay on Warspite's cargo bed, skin pallid, head propped up on a duffel bag, eyes following the movement of a snaplight hanging from the roof. Hearst watched without expression as Ghazi and Wyler tried to stop the blood trickling out of the hole in the top of her partner's chest. A hill of soaking rags lay next to the crates of medication bound for La Talpa. Wyler pressed three fingers against Katarina's arm, searching for an artery, and took her in a firm grip. Ghazi ignored the fear in his chest and continued to murmur in Katarina's ear to keep her alert and calm as he held her left arm high by the wrist and pushed down on the wound.

The flow of blood slowed. Wyler told Ghazi to switch places with him, then unclipped a nylon strap hanging from one of the roof ribs and fastened it around the top of Katarina's left arm. He turned her head from one side to the other, searching for signs that one of her lungs had collapsed, but her breathing was normal and the veins on her neck were barely visible. He took a piece of foam, placed it on the wound and secured it with a bandage. Finally, he sat back and wiped his hands on his trousers, his eyes on the old woman lying before him. Ghazi pretended not to see the resignation there.

'What about removing the bullet?' he murmured.

Wyler shook his head. 'We won't find it. And it might be plugging a vessel for all we know.'

'What do we do?'

'Can we use any of the medical supplies in the crates?'

'They're useless to us. They're for preparing a serum, not for patching up wounds.'

The snaplight swung back and forth, spilling crimson everywhere. Katarina whimpered. Wyler placed a palm on her forehead.

'Quiet now, sister.' He turned to Ghazi. 'Then I'd say we make her comfortable.'

'Isn't there anything else?' asked Ghazi, knowing the answer already.

'No. I ain't a doctor. None of you are either. And we won't make it to a settlement in time.'

Hearst sprang to her feet and squeezed between the seats into the cab. She quickly reappeared with a threadbare map and held it up to the light. When she found what she was looking for, she headed to the rear of the truck. As her heavy black boot hit the tailgate, Ghazi called out.

'It's too far.'

She paused, raw hands gripping the top of the gate. The twilight dipped her outline in silver. She looked across to the blood-red truck that might just have enough juice to take her and Katarina to a miserable camp somewhere out in the desolation. Ghazi wouldn't have blamed her if she'd gone for it. He would have done the same for Cassady.

'It's too far,' he said again. 'And too dangerous.'

Hearst made to jump.

'Where are you running off to?' Katarina's voice was paper-thin.

Slowly, Hearst lowered her foot to the bed, crept over to the makeshift cot and dropped to her knees. Her fingers brushed the other woman's cheek.

'Don't leave, min dotter.'

'Town hundred kilometres from here. We can make it.'

'No.'

'Not done yet.'

'Yes we are. I am ready.'

'I can save you.' Hearst pressed her forehead to Katarina's and held a white hand between hers.

Ghazi's eyes sought the tarpaulin. His chest burned. He was an intruder. Outside, one of the trucks was still switched on, its engine sighing over and over.

'I am saved.' The words were barely audible. 'Now you need to finish what you've started here.' The tips of her hair were clotted with blood.

Hearst didn't move. Her forehead remained glued to Katarina's, as though in an attempt to transfer her vitality to the fading body.

Boots thudded on mud and Brandt's glistening face appeared by the tailgate. He glanced at the two women. 'Entrance is clear. Tunnel's empty. We should get inside. We'll cover the entrance again once we're out of sight.'

'I hear you,' said Wyler. He placed a hand on Hearst's shoulder. 'I'll drive your ride into the tunnel. You stay here with her.' Ghazi expected her to shake him off, but she nodded. The wild man lifted himself out the truck with a grace that belied his bulk. In the night air he stretched, huge arms reaching to the sky, before heading for Orion.

Ghazi squeezed Katarina's hand once before pushing his way between the seats into the cab. Beyond the windshield, Cassady used his machete to direct the Silkworm into the tunnel. Warspite was last in line. Ghazi concentrated on the sound of his own breathing until he could hear nothing else. But he couldn't stop his mind from replaying the horror of the afternoon on a loop. He saw the well-maintained rifle resting on the sandbag and the blunt scope keeping the target in sight. He saw the long clumps of hair, the pitted yellow skin, the tattered clothing, the feverish, ravenous gestures of the hunter and the spotter. He saw the frustration when the first round fell short. The elation as the second bullet thumped clear of the barrel and whistled home. The fragments of tooth visible through a hole in the hunter's face and the ecstatic screams of the spotter. Their cold composure before the third shot. And then all he could see was the woman lying on the ground with her arms outstretched.

'Ghazi? What are you waiting for?'

Cassady stood by the window, an impatient look on his face.

'Sorry. I was miles away.'

The Runner's voice softened. 'Get inside, partner. Come on. It isn't safe to be out here.'

With mechanical gestures, Ghazi warmed up the truck and drove towards the charcoal entrance. Cassady hopped onto the running board. The train tracks and sleepers in front of the tunnel were still in place. Inside, the headlights of the other pantechs lit up the walls. Victor and Tagawa were already working to get a fire started. Ghazi pulled in alongside them. No sound came from the cargo hold. He left the cab and followed Cassady back to the tunnel mouth, where they piled branches and plastic debris to create a makeshift wall. His bones ground against one another. Perversely, he was desperate to eat something.

'How does she look?' asked Cassady in a dull tone. He threw an armful of thick vines onto the pile.

'She's lost a lot of blood. Wyler says there's nothing we can do.'

'And what do you think?'

He hesitated, feeling it start at the edges of his eyes. 'It's true.' Pain pulled the muscles in his throat tight and he swallowed hard. Somewhere out on the arid plain, creatures shrieked as they found or became food.

Cassady hefted a large branch onto the blockade. 'That'll do it,' he said. 'Let's get over there.'

'You okay?'

'We'll talk later.'

Shadows battled on the walls behind the fire. Brandt and

Hearst carried Katarina out of Warspite and laid her by it. Her eyes opened when she felt the heat of the flames, and her skin became taut and her cries echoed through the tunnel. Hearst gripped her hand.

'Look at me,' she commanded. When Katarina turned away from the fire, she relaxed.

'I thought I was in hell.'

'No. Not for you.'

'I have done terrible things.'

'Yes. To survive.'

Ghazi stood nearby with Cassady. He didn't want to listen, but the conversation was the only one that mattered in their world. Victor and Tagawa sat on the hood of the Silkworm with their hands entwined. Brandt had backed away and was now perched on the hood of Telamonian with his shoulders slumped. Wyler used his curved blade to dig out blood and dirt compacted under his fingernails. Ghazi squinted at his own hands, but the tunnel was dark and only their outline was visible.

'I did not want to leave you, min dotter.' The words were weightless. 'I am sorry.'

'Don't.'

'I thought death would hurt. But there is no pain.'

On Katarina's cheek, a bloody fingerprint stood out like an accusation. Hearst rubbed at it until it was gone.

'Where is Jürgen?'

'Near.'

'I want to speak to him.'

Hearst lifted her head and scanned the faces of the Runners who stood or sat in the shadows. Brandt jumped down off the hood and approached the fire.

'Katarina.' With a grunt, he dropped to her side. His vision blurred when he saw the colour of her skin.

'You'll have to find somebody else to retire with you, farbror.' She managed a faint smile.

'Don't say that.'

'Next time.'

The German's shoulders heaved and tears fell onto Katarina's arm. He squeezed her hand.

'Jürgen.'

He tried to speak, but his throat was clogged.

'Don't fight with the boy anymore. Keep a calm head.'

He cuffed at his eyes until the backs of his hands glimmered.

'Jürgen.' She sighed and her lids drooped. Brandt pressed his lips to her hand and stumbled away towards the mouth of the tunnel.

Ghazi looked around, noticing that Victor and Tagawa had slipped away to their truck in the meantime. Wyler twirled his knife in his hand and slotted it home on his belt. He nodded at Ghazi and disappeared inside Telamonian.

'Let's wait in the cab,' he muttered to Cassady, whose entire body trembled with terrible energy as he tried to hold something back. The Runner said nothing. Ghazi hesitated, then went to the cab and took out a couple of blankets. After the stench of blood, the stale scent of the fabric was a comfort. He draped one over Cassady's shoulders and wrapped the other around himself.

They sat in silence, heads leaning against one of Warspite's great tyres, and watched the fire.

Katarina's eyes closed for the last time at dawn. As the branches at the tunnel entrance scrambled the light, Hearst pressed her lips to Katarina's head and held her in her arms. Ghazi and Cassady lifted their tired bodies off the floor and crossed the rusted tracks. Hearst rose to her feet.

'With her family now,' she murmured.

'I'm sorry,' said Cassady. The words were too loud, too quick, too bloated with selfish remorse. The apology was not for Hearst.

'Not about you.'

Ghazi grimaced. They had to be careful.

'I didn't say it was.'

'Would prefer it to be.'

Cassady's mouth fell open. 'How can you say that? I know you're upset—'

'You do not know how I feel.'

Ghazi placed a hand on his shoulder before he could make the situation worse. 'Stop,' he whispered. He turned to Hearst. 'We should bury her.'

She hissed and moved closer to him, crushing her fingers into ugly fists. She was as tall as he was and for a moment she became a wraith, wild, unreasonable and unkillable. His hand automatically snaked to his holster. When she spoke, her fetid breath was a veil that covered his face.

'I decide.'

With some effort, Ghazi allowed his hand to drop to his side. His temples throbbed and his stomach growled. Lupo's pills weren't working like they had before. They were all strung out. He had to keep things under control.

'I know you're hurting right now, and you want to destroy something. Maybe that something is us. And after you're done you'll jump in your truck and smash through that pile of branches and we'll never see you again. But this wouldn't help anyone. We still have a run to finish, and if you lose it now then we're done. And her death will have been for nothing.'

Beyond the rage and the hostility and the survival instinct, Ghazi saw his words connect. Her heaving chest fell still. Her fists unclenched and she took a step back.

'Help me bury her,' she said.

None of them wanted her final resting place to be in the tunnel, so they took her outside. Cassady, Wyler and Tagawa manoeuvred the pantechs into the light, set up the turbine chargers and took stock of the supplies. For the second time in a week, Brandt attacked the earth with his entrenching tool, this time helped by the man he had knocked to the ground two nights before. Now the quarrel meant nothing at all.

Ghazi and Hearst wrapped the body in a piece of tarp donated from Telamonian's supplies. When the grave was ready, they lowered it in and Brandt and Victor shovelled the earth on top. The Runners stood around the fresh scar, shifting their weight from one foot to the other as Ghazi said a brief, ancient prayer in Farsi. Somewhere on the mountain, a bird called without receiving a response. Hearst bowed her head, took out a knife and cut her palm. She squeezed a few drops of blood onto the earth. Then she bound her hand.

'Speak now or do not,' she grunted. Her obsidian eyes skewered each man in turn.

'Can you keep going?' asked Tagawa.

She squared her shoulders. 'Yes.'

'It's a long drive.'

'No further than before.'

Brandt spoke up. 'She'll make it.'

Tagawa nodded. 'I believe it.'

Cassady took the chance to outline the plan. 'We're running low on water. Food is down to half.'

'Lupo's pills ain't working,' said Victor slowly. 'An hour after I eat a handful, I'm hungry again.'

'That's true,' said Ghazi.

'Then we'll keep them in reserve,' said Cassady. 'The batteries aren't fully charged, but we don't have time to sit around and wait until they hit green. We're still too close to that city and we need to keep moving.' He drew out a map and they crowded around it.

'We aren't getting back on that highway.' There were murmurs of agreement. 'There's a road here we can take. Looks to be single lane, probably pre-Change. This is some hairy country we're running. There are bottlenecks here and here.'

Tagawa drew a thin finger across the map. 'If the Zuisudra

are still moving north, we may encounter them.'

'I'm willing to take that chance. We use this route and we'll be at the Alps two days from now. What do you say?'

'We follow you,' said Tagawa immediately. Victor nodded. Cassady glanced at Hearst, who said nothing. He didn't press it.

'No rendezvous today. We've lost too much time.' He stabbed at a point on the map that was a thumb's breadth away from the Alps. 'Here's where we'll regroup. Try to keep each other in sight as much as possible. Rest up at dusk and don't advertise your position. If you find water, leave a marker for the others and fill up as much as you can for the stills. Use your dew-catchers and transpiration bags. And stay on your guard.'

The Runners dispersed to their trucks. Ghazi ran around to the hood and propped it open. He'd forgotten the Old Lady had taken a bullet as well. The slug had gone clean through the metal and made a dent in the top plate protecting the engine cylinder. He rubbed it with his thumb. Lucky. Any closer and she would have been disembowelled.

Pebbles spilled down the mountainside. He jerked around, his hand already sliding the pistol out of the tough holster, and dropped into a kneeling position. His eyes darted from one outcrop to the next. His finger rested on the trigger. He waited. One second. Two seconds. Three. A bird gave a forlorn cry. Then nothing. He was jumping at shadows. He holstered the weapon, slammed the hood shut and dragged himself into the co-seat. Fatigue nipped at his muscles. He snapped open the blitz bottle, fished out a pill and threw it back just as Cassady appeared by the door.

'Chetori?'

Ghazi blinked, surprised by the word. Cassady only knew a few phrases in Farsi and he rarely used them. 'I've been better.'

'I know. I've spoken with Hearst.'

'Go on.'

'I'll drive with her today and tomorrow.'

'Are you sure that's a good idea?'

'Why not?' the other man snapped. 'I don't want her doing anything stupid.'

Ghazi took a deep breath. 'Do what you think is best.'

'Christ. I'm sorry.'

'It was a long night for all of us. I can't believe she's gone, just like that.'

Cassady reached in through the window and placed a hand on his shoulder. 'I know. Keep it together for a little longer. We're getting closer. Here, pass me the pills.' He rattled a few into his palm. 'Don't think about Kaja. Not now. Stay focused. We'll rest before we hit the mountains. I promise.' He jumped down from the cab and was gone.

The pill kicked in as Ghazi slid across to the driver's seat and the lethargy melted away, replaced by a chemical high that aligned his thoughts and numbed his back teeth. He sucked on the tube snaking out of the bota bag. Only a few mouthfuls left. They needed to find a water source soon. He pumped the starter button and put Warspite into first. It would be a long two days.

9

'Want to talk?'

The question slipped, unanswered, through the crack in the side window. The bug-eyed cab was too cramped for Cassady to be comfortable. The sun hammered against the glass and he fidgeted in his seat for the tenth time that hour, trying to find a position which didn't make his thigh muscles or tailbone ache like hell. The heat wasn't helping either, a dense block that pushed his entire body down. Each time they took a corner, he had to grab the window frame to stop himself from sliding onto Hearst's lap. The chair's cracked leather cover was torture. His shirt was soaked through with sweat and his tongue was fat and heavy. They needed water soon. They hadn't found any pools or streams in the past 24 hours and the dew-catcher and transpiration bags had only managed to collect a mouthful of water each. That's how it was in the Bowl.

Hearst hunched over the steering wheel. She threw the truck left and right, Orion's tyres hurling chunks of mud into the tangled shrubs as they followed a ribbon road that wound through the forest-spattered hills. Cassady watched her out the corner of his eye. She'd said only a few words since leaving the tunnel the morning before. When they'd reached the road and found it to be in good condition, he'd been so relieved that he'd shouted aloud. Hearst's blank expression hadn't changed. He'd hoped she would take it steady and stick close to Telamonian, but she'd overtaken the larger vehicle in the afternoon and they'd been out of sight since. At dusk they'd stopped to recharge the batteries, eat a few old rations tainted with Cosinex, and grab some sleep. When they'd rejoined the road in the morning, a layer of mist had tied the trunks of the trees together. He'd offered to drive, but Hearst kept the reins in her hands, almost as though she had something to prove to herself.

His mind drifted to Ghazi guiding the Old Lady through the forest alone and wished he could check how his friend was holding up. It hadn't been fair to leave him like that, but he needed to watch Hearst.

'Tell me what's on your mind.'

He snapped open his belt pouch and pinched one of the few sticks of root he had left. The lack of saliva in his mouth made it difficult to get it started, but the sweet numbness came soon enough.

'If you don't want to talk then I will.'

She stretched her arms until her elbows clicked, but remained silent.

'Fine. How about this: I saw a helicopter once. I was alone, in the south, not too far from here and I remember hearing the hacking sound of a fuel engine working overtime. At first, I looked in front of and behind me and prepared for an attack. But it didn't take long to realise the noise was coming from above, so I stopped the Old Lady and got out. The helicopter hovered just behind me, close enough to hit that swollen bug on the nose with a rock. It was old. The body was dented, twisted and covered in rust. I couldn't see who was inside because the windows were dark.'

The road declined. He held a hand out against the window frame to stop himself from sliding forward on the leather. 'I didn't know what to do. It just hovered there. Not friendly, not hostile. I remember thinking that if whoever was in there had a gun on me, I was finished. I wouldn't have made it back to safety. So I waved. I held my arms above my head and I waved to the machine.'

He paused. A muscle in Hearst's scarred cheek quivered. He took it as a sign to continue.

'Then I saw a hand pressed against the glass. Just for a second or two. After that it left. Headed towards the horizon and disappeared. I thought it might have come from the Alps, but I couldn't work out why it would have crossed the border. I don't know. Maybe it was looking for something out here.'

Hearst said nothing. He arched his back, massaged his thighs and grunted. He had one more angle to try, and it would cost him a lot to reveal it.

'The last time I spoke to her, the morning before we joined the highway, she gave me some good advice. She told me I was the master of my fears. She said I'd been holding back since we left the stockade. I didn't thank her, but she was right. Telling her made the fear real. It somehow became something I could face. And do you know what I did about it?' He paused. 'I strangled Victor on the highway.'

A bark of laughter escaped from her lips. The noise startled her, and she choked it off. He smiled inwardly. It wasn't much, but it would do. He gazed through the unfamiliar windshield. The trees were unbroken streaks of green against the glass. The bleak road dipped and kinked and turned, and the engine hummed. They could have been the only people left on Earth. With a dirt-darkened finger, he eased a sliver of pulp from between two of his teeth. A headache gnawed at the back in his skull. He was about to reach for the map and check once more for water sources when she spoke.

'Only person I ever picked up.'

He stopped chewing.

'Many people need help. Families, children, ghosts. I don't stop.' She spoke roughly, as though she wanted the words to be gone from her as quickly as possible. 'She was different. Head down, hood over face, walking in a place where body and mind are apart. Drove next to her. Didn't look up. Rain started. Pulled her hood down, shook out her hair. Pure white, long, beautiful. Stopped in middle of road, eyes to sky, arms held out. No fear. I wanted that. She saw me. I opened the door. Climbed into that seat and stayed. Taught me enough for decision to be a good one.'

Cassady didn't know how to respond. He'd never heard her speak more than a few words before. He rubbed the stubble on his skull, coating his palm with a gluey film. His mind was muddled and bitter. His attention was drawn to her reflection in the windshield, and he focused on the scar that pulled her features tighter on one side.

'So what do you do now?'

She narrowed her eyes. 'Keep going.'

'Why?'

'What?'

'Why do you keep going? What stops you from driving this rig off a cliff?'

She prepared the words in her head before she spoke. 'To have five more minutes to breathe the air.'

'Is that enough?'

'Better to exist here, now, than to not.'

'Consciousness is its own reward?'

'Yes. This,' she said, waving a hand at the cab, 'whole world. Better than nothing. She helped me understand that.'

Cassady thought for a moment. 'My whole life I've felt like I'm on the run. From hunger, drought, violence, other people. From myself. And ever since I could remember, I've wanted to escape that feeling. I always hoped there was something more. But I'm starting to think maybe there isn't.'

He rubbed his eyes and struggled to work some saliva around his mouth. She reached underneath her seat and threw a canteen onto his lap.

'Drink.'

'What is it?'

'Water.'

'It's yours.'

'Drink.'

He tossed the dead piece of root out the window, unscrewed the cap and took a sip. The liquid was warm and foul, but it wet his mouth and opened his throat. He held it out to her.

'Keep it. You need strength, Cassady.'

10

'I had a family once, Ghazi.'

'I didn't know.'

'A husband and a baby boy. They were taken from me long ago, when I was little more than a child myself.'

'What happened?'

'When the refugees first crossed the northern waters into Scandinavia, we welcomed them. We tried to help them and accommodate them, but it did not last long. The hotter it became, the more bombs were dropped, the more communities collapsed, the more refugees we found on our shores all wanting to head further north. There were just too many. We didn't have the resources. The bloc's infrastructure was pushed beyond breaking point. That's when the government set up the other camps, in secret. For the executions. Did you read about them? It was the only way to control the influx. At least, that's what they hoped. They ran liquidation shifts day and night and the skies turned black with incinerated flesh. But the boats kept crossing the waters and the people kept choking the roads, destroying the landscape, filing into the cities like a conquering army because it was all they could do. Petty battles flickered like fires between the population of the bloc, the army and the refugee groups. Even far in the north I saw the snow painted blood. It didn't take long for the collapse to happen: the government, law, order, society itself. Chaos became normal.'

'Didn't you try to get out?'

'Only when I could see there was no hope of staying. You have to realise that the days and nights in Sweden were still cool. We had ample freshwater supplies, too. To give that up and move south wasn't an easy decision to make. But at least in the south the dead outweighed the living. We thought we might find a place where we'd be left alone.

'The same boats that had been used to take refugees from the south to the north were now being commandeered to ferry people in the other direction. There were many bodies on the shore. The smell was like the flesh of the Earth itself had turned gangrenous. My husband didn't like it, but I made a deal for a skiff to take us across. For the sake of my child.'

'What was the deal, Kaja?'

'I will not say. But after I paid what I agreed, we were betrayed. There, on the shore. They used axes to chop my husband down where he stood. He didn't see it coming. They pierced my stomach and left me for dead. And they took my son. I do not know what for. But I am sure he did not live long.

'I hovered between worlds for a week before I chose to remain in this one. I sterilised the wound, bound myself, and returned to the place where everything had been taken from me. I buried what was left of my husband. I looked for my son, but I did not find him. What I did find was a small motor boat hidden in a hut. It didn't have much fuel and I nearly capsized it more than once, but I managed to cross the sea and one of the great lagoons and landed on a spit of land thick with possessions, bodies and waste. That was how my new life started.

'I walked for a long time in search of purpose. The external material world faded. It held little importance to me. I ate and I drank and I rested, but other than that I lived inside my head. I don't think I talked to more than three or four people during these two years, but I had conversations with myself – with my soul – which helped me to understand the meaning of existence. One day I knew I was ready to return to this reality. A week later, Hearst picked me up on the road and I've been running with her ever since.'

'Do you still think about your husband and son?'

'Every day. I see them at night when I close my eyes.'

'If you had lost everything, why didn't you let go? You were hovering between life and death. It would have been easy.'

'Because it was not my time, Ghazi. As I walked the lands, I gradually understood that I hadn't lost my family at all. My husband and my son are waiting for me. When my time to leave here comes, I will see them again.'

'You believe that?'

'I know it.'

11

It was time to knock on the door to the closed land. The moisture on Cassady's hands made the map wilt. Sketched on it in pencil was Lupo's trail, a single-lane tightrope between the peaks. The old scientist had said the road was safe, unwatched and in good enough condition for the rigs to use, but they would only know for sure once they found a way in and began their climb. He could send one of the pantechs ahead to make sure the road was clear, but if it wasn't, it would be the same as singling out one of the crews to die. It wasn't an option.

That was if they even found a way in. He ran his finger along the northern edge of the mountain range. He'd been this far south just twice before, and Brandt was the only one in the group who ever had laid eyes on the wall. He'd said it was easily twice as high as Telamonian and bristling with razor wire. The ground in front had been ripped up and was studded with barriers, obstacles and destroyed vehicles. They'd all listened to the stories of how, in the first years of the Change, desperate armies and militias had tried to force their way into the zone, but had been decimated by IEDs, camouflaged bunkers and the soldiers of the corporations. Cassady hated the uncertainty. The deaths of Renfield and Kaja couldn't be for nothing. He wished somebody would tell him what to do next, how to keep the rest of them safe.

He glanced in the side mirror. Still no sign of the others. Hearst wasn't letting up. Their rendezvous point was an old refinery marked on the map just a few kilometres further on from where they were now. Soon they would have to navigate the second of two bottlenecks. The first had been clear. The area was dead.

'You want me to take over?'

She shook her head.

'You need a pill?'

Her reply was drowned out by the sound of something bouncing off the side of the truck.

'What was that?' he shouted. Hearst wrenched the wheel to the left to take a tight bend. Cassady checked the mirror and caught a glimpse of a spear lying in the road and three figures emerging from the undergrowth. The rig screeched around the corner.

'We've got trouble,' he said, ducking back into the cab. But Hearst wasn't listening. Her body was rigid. He peered through the windscreen and understood why.

The second bottleneck closed around them. Vehicle hulks dotted the road, dragged into place to form a rough gauntlet. Behind them, armed men and women in loincloths waited behind a barricade flanked on either side by a pair of crude towers.

Hearst stamped on the accelerator. Cassady buckled his harness and held on to the door frame. They smashed into one of the vehicle bodies, sending it spinning. Orion lurched to her right, but a flick of the steering wheel put her back on course. Hearst swerved around the remains of a pre-Change tank, but clipped a car beyond it. Cassady clenched his teeth and tightened his grip. In the towers, human forms aimed longbows at the rig, holding off until they could do maximum damage. The barricade filled the windshield. A man in a green robe stood on top of it. He whirled a staff, pointed at the truck and shouted to the defenders.

The engine click-clacked and the wheels kicked up plastic and stones. The needle on the speedometer twitched into the red. A vein quivered on Hearst's temple. They braced themselves for impact. The robed man leapt from the barricade and moved off the road, and the others followed his example. An arrow thudded into the hood. Orion barrelled into the bulwark made of wood and plastic and metal and Cassady and Hearst were thrown forward in their seats, belts biting far enough into their collarbones to draw blood. Hearst wrestled to keep control of the truck as it bucked. Debris spilled over the hood and bounced off the windshield. The engine hummed once more and switched off, but the momentum continued to carry them along the road. Then the shouts of the people outside were replaced by a metallic screeching noise. Tremors shook the vehicle's occupants to the bone.

'The tyre,' shouted Cassady.

Hearst hit the brake. The screech became a wail. Orion wheezed once more and stopped dead some distance from the barricade.

'Secure it,' said Hearst. 'Quick.'

They locked the cab doors and attached metal plates to the windows and windshield. They wouldn't hold forever, but they offered more protection than the glass. Hearst squeezed between the seats into the cargo hold, reached up to the ceiling and pulled the crossbow free. She hooked a piece of tubing to the bow and dragged it around to the notch above the grip. After pulling the tubing back until the bow locked into place, she flicked on the safety, slid a bolt into the channel and secured it. She handed it to Cassady as he joined her, and lifted the lid off a storage hole next to a crate of medical supplies. Cassady moved to the back door and placed his ear to it. They had seconds left to prepare. Hearst appeared beside him with a cudgel wrapped in barbed wire and an ad hoc metal shield large enough to cover his chest.

'Swap.'

Cassady gave her the bow and slipped the nylon straps of the shield over his forearm, then picked up the cudgel. His machete lay on the floor beside him.

'Don't you have a pistol? Or a rifle?' His mouth was dry enough to hurt.

'No.' She stripped down to her vest. Cassady unbuckled his utility belt and tried to slow his breathing.

Rocks and other projectiles rained down on Orion. Somebody

screamed commands. The tramping of boots against the road sounded like a rockslide.

'It's the Zuisudra.'

'Yes.'

'See the crank in the green robe?'

She grunted.

'I'd say he's one of their priests. Go for him if you can.'

'If I'm hit, close door. She tapped the bed with the bow. 'Hollow under here. Space for one.'

He nodded. 'You ready?'

The voices screamed murder.

'Open left door.' She hefted the crossbow. 'Keep me covered. No sudden movements.'

He grabbed the door handle. Despite the fear, his hand didn't shake. Hearst's determination helped. He crouched, covered his body with the shield as best he could and pushed the handle.

Even before the door had fully opened, the first bolt whistled past his shoulder and buried itself in the forehead of an onrushing figure in rags. He gasped. A group of twenty bore down on the pantech, faces ulcerated and dirty and distorted with bloodlust. The priest in the green robe stood near the destroyed barricade, surrounded by a cluster of armed children and adults, and shouted commands.

An arrow slammed into the door, but failed to pierce the plate metal. Cassady looked past the attackers on the ground to the towers, where a pair of archers aimed at Orion's back doors. They were a problem. Another arrow thumped into the ground in front of them. The sound of Hearst clicking the second bolt into place rang in his skull and he tensed and leaned to his left. She fired. Another attacker dropped. Terror wrapped itself around him.

The horde halted their advance, a few paces out of range of Cassady's cudgel. The attackers hissed at the bald, scarred man standing in the doorway and waited for somebody else to be the first to take him on. A toothless woman screamed and she and three others dived forwards. Cassady's mind became blank. He no longer saw people, only targets. He lowered the shield and whirled the cudgel. It crunched into the head of a tall man and he fell. An arrow intended for him hurtled into the back of the toothless woman and she collapsed. Blows from a bat rained down on the shield and his arm shuddered with the impact. He bellowed in pain and swung again, hitting nothing. To his right, a blunt dagger lacerated the air, on course for his arm, but he managed to bring the shield around in time to stop it. His chest heaved. Sweat burned his eyes. More blows pummelled the metal. His shield arm felt as though it was broken. The blunt dagger found his trouser leg and tore a deep gash in his thigh and he fell back and screamed because he was about to die.

Hearst's crossbow sang again. The bolt took a chunk out of the man wielding the dagger, and the weapon fell onto the cargo bed. Desperately, Cassady dropped the cudgel and grasped the blade, then lifted the shield just enough to glimpse a sight of hard flesh. He lunged with all his strength and dragged and twisted the dagger until the body fell away. Nobody else tried to attack. He clambered back to his feet and tested his shield-bearing arm. It wasn't broken. An arrow hit the shield and the force of it pushed him to his knees. He threw himself forward and hid by the back door that was still closed.

Now four more attackers peeled away from the main group and closed in. Hearst fired. 'Three bolts left.'

A woman swinging a chain raced to Orion's rear doors. Cassady leaned out and slammed the shield into her head. As she fell, he narrowed his eyes and looked beyond the dwindling group. The bowmen in the towers prepared to fire.

'Get down,' he shouted, ducking back behind the door. Hearst rolled to the side. An arrow flew through the opening and buried itself in the medicine crate. The second glanced off the top of the truck. The attackers seized their chance and climbed onto the cargo bed. With movements born of defiance and desperation, Cassady jumped up, dodged a wild swipe of a sword and butted a man under the chin. His hand found his machete and he roared, ducking, pushing and slashing. Hot metal bit into his arm, but he ignored the pain and kept punching and cutting until only one attacker remained. Blood stuck to his eyelashes and ran down his neck and he didn't know whether it was theirs or his, but the thought of dying now gave him strength and he seized the final man by the throat, bludgeoned his head against the side of the rig and hurled him at another fanatic who was trying to climb inside. Panting and shaking, he beat his chest with the hilt of his machete and shouted for them to keep coming. His thigh burned. He looked down. His trouser leg was dark and soaked through. He tested his weight. He would manage.

'Raise the shield,' shouted Hearst. She appeared beside him and pulled back the tubing until the bow locked. He lifted the shield in time for another arrow to thump into the edge of it, bending the metal inward. The noise of the mob had died down. The attackers hung back, unwilling to grapple with the demons in the red truck. The priest continued to twirl his staff and scream commands. He pushed the throng of children towards the poisonous vehicle, urging them to join the attack. They stumbled forwards, dragging weapons that were too large for them.

'Him,' said Hearst, looking down the body of the bow at the priest.

'Do it.'

She waited, the meat around the crooked scar twitching. An eternity passed as the attackers searched for their misplaced courage and edged closer to the vehicle that dripped with the blood of their fellow zealots. The children came closer. Cassady suppressed the urge to tell Hearst to fire. Dull pain rolled over him in waves. The straps on the shield cut into his skin, and the tape wrapped around the machete handle was wet and sticky.

A body hanging out of the door gurgled, but didn't move. He peered out. In one of the watchtowers, a white-haired man frantically tried to restring his broken bow. In the other, the bowman called for somebody to bring him more arrows.

Hearst held her breath and squeezed the trigger. The bolt jumped away from the block and flew. For a moment it looked as though it would hit the target. But one of the children moved at the wrong moment and the bolt sheared through her cheek. Her scream roused the attackers into action again. They raised their weapons and charged.

A horn boomed and the priest whirled around. Hurtling towards the bottleneck was 12 tons of armour-plated tactical vehicle. It batted the blackened wrecks aside like they weren't even there and trampled over the remains of the blockade. The brakes squealed and Brandt dived out while Telamonian was still moving. The old Runner rolled on his shoulder, sprang to his feet and ran at the robed man. Gimlet knives flashed between his knuckles. The few men and women still near the smashed barricade brought their weapons up, but Brandt didn't stop. He slashed the knives across a man's eyes, and a one-two combination to the midriff knocked another to the floor. The priest gnashed his teeth and raced towards him, whirling the staff above his head. Brandt checked his run and dropped to his knee, and the man's staff sailed overhead. A powerful fist to the stomach bent the priest in two. The staff fell from his hands. The vicious gimlet blades opened his throat. The Zuisudra followers backed off, staring in terror at the golem who had just murdered their leader without breaking a sweat. And now another one emerged from the rig, a curved blade in hand and a grin on his bearded face. Wyler and Brandt stood side by side and begged for the mob to attack.

Cassady peered out from behind the door, transfixed by the brute strength on show. Hearst nudged him.

'Cover me.'

She aimed the crossbow at one of the watchtowers and followed the movements of the white-haired bowman, who had repaired his weapon and was now turning his sights onto Brandt and Wyler. She fired. The bolt hit the man in the side. He reeled, staring at the wound with disbelief, and fell over the side of the tower. She reloaded quickly and loosed her final quarrel into the mass of bodies. Then she leapt out without another word, not once breaking stride as she scooped up a club and slammed it into the skull of the nearest threat.

The children lifted their weapons. Cassady hesitated, still standing on the cargo bed. Their eyes rolled around at the bottom of scooped-out sockets and their bones were visible under their skin. But they hacked at Hearst with quick movements and so Cassady lifted the machete high and ran at them. Pitiful yells stained the air as the blade connected with flesh and bone. He wanted to gag. The attacks of the youngest were easy to avoid. Hearst engaged them one at a time until none were left standing. The last adults in the group closed around Cassady, and as he lifted the shield to meet a blow from an axe the blade punched a hole in the metal above his forearm. He wriggled free and the shield fell to the floor. He jumped back out of the way. Cries of desperation mixed with the sobs of the wounded. Hearst scratched and bit and whirled her club, and the bodies piled up in the road.

A high-pitched whine floated over the screams. Warspite rounded the corner and followed the path cut by Orion and Telamonian. Cassady wanted to shout with joy. Then a balled fist hit him square in the jaw and he fell. White fireflies buzzed at the edges of his vision. He struggled to focus on the face of a snarling woman raising a jagged rock, but he was too shaken to truly feel any fear, so he closed his eyes and missed the blur of motion that was Hearst barrelling into the woman. Once the threat was dealt with, she dragged Cassady to his feet and ran to find another opponent.

A gunshot made a dent in the sky. Brandt fell back and landed heavily on his side. Still dazed, Cassady jerked his head around in search of the threat until he found it. A bald woman leaned against the bucket of an ancient excavation vehicle with a rifle clasped between wiry hands and the stock lodged against her shoulder. She aimed at Wyler, who stood over Brandt, and pulled the trigger again, but the hammer clicked and nothing happened. Cassady sprinted across the tarmac and careened into her. Her body smacked into the metal. Even as she shrieked, he grabbed her wrist and snapped the arm. The woman retched and fell unconscious. He scooped up the rifle and ran his eyes over the body. An old carbine with a deformed stock. The misfired bullet was probably lodged in the bore. Keeping an eye out for incoming threats, he closed the stock, slammed the butt against the ground and stamped on the operating rod. The chambered round flew out of the carbine. He brought it up again and aimed. Hearst wrestled with a tall, raw-boned man over the long wooden handle of an axe. The man kicked at her legs and knocked her to the floor. Cassady hoped to hell the rifle wasn't jammed any longer and squeezed the trigger. The carbine bucked against his body and the bullet impacted between the man's shoulder blades. The axe landed on the ground, centimetres from Hearst's head. She rolled over and snatched up the weapon.

Another gun fired, and Cassady held the rifle tighter. But this time it was Ghazi. A boy staggered away from the battle holding his stomach. Ghazi gave Cassady a short salute and ran across open ground to join Hearst. Cassady adjusted the sliding sight and dropped the remaining archer and his loader in the watchtower before they could scramble clear. He sighted again, but the pin clicked on an empty chamber, so he threw it to the floor. A weak hand grabbed his ankle. The woman had recovered consciousness and now tried to sink her teeth into his flesh. A swift kick to the temple dealt with her. Ghazi's pistol cracked and another body went down. Panic rippled through the last of the Zuisudra. Their ranks had been decimated. As though a signal had been given, they turned as one to run for the tree line. Hearst launched the axe at their backs, but it missed and clattered on the road. They flitted between mutant tree trunks and disappeared. Hearst retrieved a machete from one of the fallen bodies and headed after them.

'No,' shouted Cassady. 'Let them go.'

She took another few steps, but stopped and dropped the weapon. She held up a hand to shield her eyes from the glare. 'You're bleeding. Are you okay?'

His mouth opened and closed in surprise. He wiped at his forehead. 'I'm alright.'

She waited, saying nothing more.

'We need to be ready to go as soon as possible. Do you have a spare tyre?'

'Yes.'

'Good. Change it. Ghazi can help if you need it. We'll search the bodies afterwards. And thanks for saving me. Again.'

Then he remembered Brandt. He ran, vaulting bodies that twitched and moaned in the dying sun. Mounting despair turned his vision hot and filmy. Wyler was on his knees, stained fingers pressed against the old man's neck, and an image of Katarina lying on the highway flashed through Cassady's head.

'Is he gone?'

Wyler moved his fingers away. Muscles rippled under his shirt. 'Relax, babe. He's alive. The bullet only creased him. Take more than that to finish off this beast. He'll wake up with some headache though. I can handle the rig until he comes to.'

Relief filled Cassady's lungs and he exhaled slowly. He surveyed the scene. Bodies lay like islands on a frozen river. The stench of fresh blood and long-unwashed skin clogged his nostrils. 'Can you get him back to Tela alone?'

'Yes.'

'Good. Mount up.' He held out his hand to the other man.

'We owe you one.'

Wyler clasped it. 'Just glad to be part of the team, brother.'

He crossed the road to where Ghazi stood by the children. The mechanic's eyes were ringed and bloodshot and his dark skin was as dull as ash. The bodies scattered everywhere caused him untold pain. The two men embraced.

'Some fight you started here.'

'Yeah. I thought we were all done. Are you hurt?'

'No. You? You look terrible.'

Shaking fingers prodded the flesh around his jaw and he winced. 'One of them clocked me pretty good when Brandt showed up. Got a few cuts, too. Have you seen Victor and Tagawa?'

'They were a few minutes behind me. They should be here soon.'

Cassady reached to his belt for a stick of root, but he'd left it in the back of Hearst's rig. It was a charnel house in there now. He'd have to help her clear out the bodies after she'd finished changing the tyre. She was busy levering the shredded tyre free of the rim with two lengths of metal. An axe protruded from one of the rear doors, and a severed hand clung to the handle.

'Cass.' Ghazi checked the magazine in his pistol as he spoke.

'What?'

'We need to finish off the wounded. It isn't right to leave them like this.'

His stomach heaved as he assessed the bodies. Any meat-eaters in the area would have a field day when they found the blockade. Three of the Zuisudra were still moving, including the woman with the rifle whose arm he'd broken. He grimaced. It was a bad business, but Ghazi spoke the truth. He picked up a shovel which had been honed until the three sides of the blade were sharper than his machete and trudged over to the woman while Ghazi took care of the other two. She lay in the shadow of the excavator, broken arm trembling. He stood over her. Her eyes pleaded and her mouth opened and closed, but no words emerged. She held out her hand. He closed his eyes and lifted the shovel. Don't think about it. There was a crunching noise and a soft plop. He bent over and vomited.

On creaking legs, he threaded his way through the bodies to the robed priest, who lay on his back with pupils frozen in horror. The wound in his throat was already congealing in the heat. Cassady checked the pockets of the robe and found a water filter, a piece of paper with a few markings on it and an expired pack of painkillers, which he deposited in his shirt pocket.

He took a seat on a rusting drum and taped up the gash on his calf with a rag that looked clean enough. Hearst's air compressor emitted a loud crack as she pressurised the new tyre. Her movements were a blur. He didn't know how she had the energy. It took all of his strength just to help Ghazi make a search of the camp for supplies. He dug through crates while the other man checked the vehicles scattered along the road. There were no more bullets for the carbine anywhere. All he managed to turn up were a few meagre food rations. He gagged again as he ran his hands over the foul bodies that carried nothing of use. His temples throbbed and the fibres of his body screamed for sleep. But there was no time for rest. They had to get away.

As he finished his search, Ghazi called out a single word. 'Water.'

'How much?'

'Two barrels.'

'Fill up the bags and the bottles. Quick as you can.'

The minutes fell away. Orion reversed over the bloodied ground until it lined up in front of Telamonian. Hearst leaned out of the window and flashed three fingers at Cassady as he loaded the water into the back of Warspite. The battery had thirty minutes of power remaining. It would be enough. Behind her, Telamonian ticked into life. One of the headlamps sputtered and died.

Another mechanical whine signalled the arrival of the Silkworm, which rounded the hairpin and halted next to Warspite. Victor climbed out.

'What the hell happened here?' he said, inspecting the devastation. 'Looks like we missed Judgement Day.'

Cassady threw the last bota bag onto the cargo bed and turned to face the boy. Somewhere along the way, he'd hacked off his hair, and now only blonde stubble remained.

'Zuisudra, we think. We're okay. Brandt was hit.' Victor's face became tense. 'Don't worry. The bullet barely creased him. He's sleeping it off. Where were you?'

'Tyre blowout. Bad luck. Took us a while to change it.'

'Should've asked Hearst. She just did one in ten minutes after taking out half their soldiers.'

Victor grinned. 'You sure you're okay?'

'Why?'

'You've got a hot look in your eye.'

'Running on empty right now. Don't worry about it.' His gaze flickered to the top of Victor's head. 'Why the cut?'

'I dunno. Call it a change of mindset.'

'It suits you.'

Victor nodded. 'We can take the lead. Ain't a problem.'

'Good. We drive for thirty minutes. That's all the juice we've got. The road should end somewhere beyond the next corner. Follow the track that breaks left. Keep your eye open for any strays. A few made it to the trees, but I think they'll be too busy licking their wounds to bother us again. Once you hit thirty minutes, stop and set up camp.'

'I hear you.'

Victor clapped him on the arm and returned to the Silkworm. Cassady took a last look at the blockade. One of the children's bodies quivered and became still. He ignored the voice that told him to check. Instead, he hobbled over to Warspite and dragged himself painfully into the co-seat. When he heaved the door closed, the ringing in his head stopped. He was home. Ghazi punched the ignition and followed Orion. The convoy slipped through the debris and left the battlefield behind.

12

The vehicles sat nose-to-end in a laager formation. The air smelled burnt. Wind turbines spun on the roofs and solar kits sat splayed on the hoods. In the centre of the laager, the Runners patched up holes, checked the crates of medicine, wiped engines down, added coolant to thermal management systems and replenished brake fluid. They swilled out their dusty mouths with the water taken from the Zuisudra. Wyler treated Brandt's head wound while he lay unconscious on Telamonian's cargo bed.

When they were done, they dropped to the ground and stretched and massaged their muscles. They were battered and bruised, but there was a new sense of determination within the group. They had been lucky to escape the blockade with their lives and trucks intact and they knew it. Tagawa unravelled a bundle of cloth to reveal an extremely old pot of raw honey, and they took turns dipping sticks into it.

'Put it on your wounds,' he said to Cassady. 'It'll take care of bacteria. Something my mother taught me.'

The Runner did as he was told, dabbing the honey on his arm and thigh before heading over to Warspite and disappearing inside.

Ghazi took out his whittling knife, but couldn't bring himself to start working on the elephant. The rolling rattle of the cicadas mixed with his steady breathing. His thoughts were blurry and his soaked shirt clung to his back. He needed to let go, if only for a few moments. Forget the road, forget the mission. But he couldn't. Beyond the laager, on the other side of the gravel track, was the fuselage of an airplane, long and tubular with creased metal skin and twenty blank eyeholes. Vegetation grew around, inside and on top of it. He stared at it, captivated by the notion that it had once flown high above the earth, able to cross seas and mountain chains and deserts. In another reality he might have been a pilot. Here, the Old Lady was the closest he would ever get.

Warspite's cab door creaked open and Ghazi regarded the thin, worn-out form that emerged with maps in hand. The peaked cap was back on his head. It made him look more like Cassady. He sat with his back to one of Warspite's tyres. He'd kept it together well, drawing on the old fire to emerge from the battlefield alive. Perhaps it would prove to be the turning point.

Ghazi walked over and sat down next to him. 'Are we using Lupo's road to get in?'

Cassady set the map down on his lap. 'I don't know. I don't trust it.'

'The Koalition probably has eyes on it.'

He nodded. 'And they could have mined the road all to hell by now.'

'So what do you want to do?'

'Listen to the station report first, I suppose. Unless you've given up on them, too?'

'It's the last one we'll get. Let's hear what it has to say.'

When it was time, they set up the antenna and sat together in the cab. Cassady spun the dial for the shortwave and opened the ledger.

'Algernon. Never heard of it.'

The storm of static beat against the walls. Ghazi consulted the timepiece. They had an hour or so of daylight left. Cassady would want to try to cross the border while it was dark, and he would want to do it tonight.

'Algernon, Algernon.' A metallic voice rasped the call sign, and several beeps followed. Then came the sequence of numbers and letters. The voice repeated it twice more and signed off. Cassady killed the radio and pored over the code, making notes in the corner of the page with a dirty pencil stub.

'Same news they've been peddling all the way,' he said, puffing out his cheeks. 'Zuisudra pushing up from the south.'

'Anything else?'

'Runners are advised to stay away from main roads near the Alps due to hostile activity.'

'That's it?'

'Yes.'

Ghazi shook his head. 'Some report.'

'I told you.' Cassady closed the ledger and pushed it into the dashboard. He leaned back and rested his chin on his knuckles. 'Now we have to decide. Let's take it to the others and see what they have to say.'

The Runners convened in the back of Telamonian so Wyler could keep an eye on Brandt. Hearst glowered at nobody. Victor ran his hand through hair that was no longer there. Tagawa leaned against one of the walls and hummed a tune under his breath, apparently unconcerned about what was to come. Cassady spread Lupo's cotton map on a crate and pressed his finger against it.

'You all know that according to Lupo, this is our best chance of getting in. It's not much to go on, but I don't have any other ideas. So I want to hear what you have to say.'

Ghazi struggled to recall the features of the scientist, his accent, the words he'd used. But he couldn't, not properly. He and the others had lived an eternity since leaving the Gaean camp.

'What about hitting one of their main entrances?' asked Victor. 'This monster can take down the gates, no doubting that. Then we'll go straight on through and stop for nothing. Or we blast them outta the way. The old man's got some explosives around here somewhere, remember? Dynamite.' He licked his lips and grinned and for a moment the hubris was back. 'Said he wanted to use them on me.'

Cassady eyed the boy. 'No chance. We don't know their numbers. Count on them having a ton of hardware with them. They'll shoot out the tyres before we make it a hundred metres.

Even if we did punch a hole in one of the gates, they'll block the road further on and trap us. But if we take Lupo's road and we go when it's dark, we might be able to slip by unnoticed.'

Tagawa spoke up. 'There's a Japanese saying that applies here, Cassady. Day may have its eyes, but night has its ears. Even if we use the road when it's dark, they may hear us. I would prefer to face my enemy in the light. Then I'll know whether to attack or to run.'

'Hideki's right,' said Victor. 'If the road's under surveillance, we're only putting ourselves at a disadvantage by running blind.'

'Agreed,' added Hearst.

Cassady rubbed his jaw and turned to Ghazi. 'And you?'

He didn't answer immediately. They would be driving through unknown mountainous terrain. Maybe the Koalition would hear the convoy at night and maybe it wouldn't, but the risk of one of the trucks taking a wrong turn off the side of a cliff was too great. 'It makes sense.'

Cassady turned to Wyler, who rested on his haunches and stared at the unconscious form of Brandt. 'You haven't weighed in.'

His response was soft. 'No. I haven't.'

'So?'

He placed a wide, flat hand on Brandt's forehead before making his way to the crate and bending over the map. The twisted grey beard brushed against his stomach. A wormy vein stood out on his neck. His heavy eyelids fell closed.

A shadow passed over Ghazi. Something was off. 'What is it, Wyler?'

The cloudy eyes remained shut. 'I know another way in.'

'What do you mean?'

He lifted his head and looked at the assembled faces. 'There's another road. The entrance is hidden well enough, but it's there. I can take you to it.'

Ghazi's hand ghosted to the pistol. Wyler caught the

movement.

'Please, brother. You ain't in any danger from me.' Ghazi kept his hand where it was.

A heavy silence stretched and nobody moved until Hearst slapped her thigh. The other Runners jumped. 'You're an agent. You work for them.'

Wyler nodded. Cassady let out a moan of disbelief which was quickly drowned out by a bark of laughter from Hearst. 'Knew it. Never seen teeth like yours.'

The wild man's eyes found hers. 'Why didn't you say anything?'

'Figured it didn't matter either way.'

Ghazi's hand fell to his side. He felt no rage, no confusion, no aggression, only a jagged blackness that threatened to cut his faith to ribbons. 'So we had you pegged right from the start?'

'I'm sorry, brother.'

'But we talked ourselves out of it.'

'Not me,' said Hearst. Somehow she was pleased with the situation.

Cassady recovered enough to sputter a question. 'You work for the Koalition?'

'I did. Now I don't.'

'Do they know we're here?'

'No.'

'How can you be sure?'

Wyler smoothed his beard against his chest and rested his palms against the crate. 'It'll take a while to explain. If you'll give me the chance. But I mean what I say. There ain't any danger to any of you right now.'

After the attack by the Zuisudra, none of the Runners had any stomach for further violence. Instead, a great emptiness filled the space. Ghazi walked to the back of the cargo bed, sat on the floor and stared hard at a twisting scratch along the metal frame. The others leaned against walls and stuffed their hands into their pockets, unsure of how to act.

'Okay. Let's hear it,' said Victor finally.

'They call me a sleeper. The Koalition has a network of spies outside the state that it uses to collect information and keep eyes on threats. They've got them all the way up to the lagoons in the north, and I know they've got a few agents still working in the deserts to the south. They plant us in settlements or set us up to be self-sufficient, like me and my farm, and they leave us to live our lives. You don't hear from them from one year to the next. You got something to report, you record it and you take it to a drop-off point. That's it.

'A few weeks ago everything changed. A couple of the Koalition's top intelligence guys paid me a personal visit. They'd never done that before. They told me they'd picked up a couple of intruders in Novus who had spilled their guts about a machine.'

Tagawa raised his head. 'Novus is the name of the state?'

'Right. They made me go to Prestige and listen out for news about medical supplies being taken south. If I got lucky, I was supposed to follow the carriers. Those boys were agitated. I could tell the news of the machine had shaken them. But it wasn't my concern. Not anymore. And I told them so. I hadn't been back to Novus in ten years and I was happy where I was. I had my girls to look after. I couldn't just uproot and go north because some uniform in a room told me to.

'The Koalition didn't accept my – what do you call it – my resignation. When I was out finding supplies, the bikers came.' A heavy gaze found Cassady. 'I wasn't totally honest with you, brother. They only murdered two of the girls. They took the other three. After that those bastards from intelligence returned and told me if I didn't do my job, they would carve up the girls and do the same to me. I don't know if they're still alive. I reckon they ain't. It doesn't matter anymore. I'm through.'

Another silence filled the space as the Runners processed the information.

'Tell us about the Koalition,' said Tagawa. He was less rattled than the others.

'I ain't got all the details. There's a lot of secrecy. Chain of command is long enough to tie you up in knots. What I know is the corporations ran Novus during the Change, and after a time they merged to form the Koalition. It has absolute power, keeps life going in the state, minimises the effects of the Change. They ain't got to deal with starvation or nomadics or the heat like out here. There are five cities and everybody lives in them except the synth-farmers, a few geo-engineers and the military. The rest of the land is deserted. Makes it easier to control, you know. The cities have electricity, sanitation, medicine, education, hospitals, food and water rations. Even art, after a fashion. And on all sides the state is protected by walls. Physical and not so physical. Much of the population works in factories. They build and fix the turbines, the machines, the pipelines and the other connective tissue that keep Novus ticking over, and in return they get just enough food and water to make it through another week. All the Koalition cares about is climate engineering, the military and total control.'

'How did their men know to send you to Prestige?'

'They didn't. It was a guess. Lupo had to get to a supplier who had the reach to secure the medicine, right? The Koalition knows about all the big-time dealers. Faustine, too. They've done business with her a few times.'

At that, Ghazi looked up. The others were as surprised as he was.

'Son of a bitch,' spat Victor.

Cassady rubbed his temples. 'Christ. So she's in on this as well?'

'I don't reckon so. They were worried about her. Knew she would probably try to help Lupo if he got in contact with her. That night in the bar in Prestige, one of her guards came in. It was late, after you and Ghazi had left. It only took a couple of drinks to loosen his tongue. He told me about you being sent to the camp to join a convoy. After that it was easy. I waited on a road I knew you'd have to take and I tailed you.'

Ghazi couldn't remain silent any longer. 'You said Novus has food, water, medicine, education, things like that.'

Wyler shifted his weight until he was facing him. 'Yeah.'

'So why leave in the first place?'

'Brother, you've got to understand that life in the state ain't exactly sunshine. Your world might be hard and full of misery, but at least you control your fate. The Koalition uses anything and everything to make sure Novus stays under its control. Executions, labour camps, propaganda, you name it. Sometimes they infect the food supply and withhold medicine just to cut down the population if the numbers are getting out of control. Anybody who speaks out is murdered. A long time ago, before I left, I was one of the clean-up guys who made people disappear. I didn't want to do it, but I had no choice. If you don't do exactly as they say, you disappear, too.

'But their grip is slipping. I hear things from time to time. Rebellions, protests, rumblings about a resistance. All the people want is to live free. At some point those bastards just ain't gonna have enough brainwashed devotees anymore to keep their system alive. And it wasn't until Kaja died that I truly realised it. I didn't have to stand with them any longer. I could stand with you instead.'

Wyler struggled with further words that refused to emerge. Questions and snapshots and information drifted through Ghazi's head and he fought to understand it. He'd made the wrong call. He'd trusted the man when the others had wanted him to leave, and this was the result. But Wyler wasn't evil. He could see that. Every one of them could. The wild man had made the wrong call, too. The world was brutish and solitary and poor, and they were all casualties of it.

A blunt voice rang out in the confined space.

'Why Renfield?'

Ghazi jerked his head around. Brandt had regained consciousness. He raised himself to a sitting position. The German looked older than ever, colourless and bandaged, leaning to one side as though half of his body was made of lead.

Wyler turned to face him.

Brandt's tone was measured. 'Answer me.'

The agent's cloudy eyes became clear. 'I was desperate. I didn't know the man, and I thought only of my girls. It was easier to join the convoy than follow it. He was my way in. I'm sorry. I wish I had a better explanation, but I don't.'

With a grunt, Brandt struggled to his feet. His bulk filled the space and he swayed on his feet. A gnarled hand found something to grab hold of and he steadied himself.

Cassady stepped forward, placing his body between Brandt and Wyler.

'Don't do it.'

Brandt looked down at him. 'Don't do what?'

'Don't kill him.'

Brandt's jaw went slack. He gazed beyond him to Wyler. 'Do you remember what Katarina said? There is too much violence in this life already. I won't add to it. But I don't want to be in here right now. So stand aside.'

Cassady waited a few beats, but did as he was asked. Brandt shuffled along the length of the cargo bed, using the wall to support him. He brushed past Wyler without another word.

'Help me,' he said to Ghazi, who opened the door and held Brandt's arm steady as he climbed out. The door clanged shut behind him.

Resignation hung thickly inside the truck. Ghazi surveyed the others. Even Hearst showed no desire to be rid of the man standing in the middle of the bed. And Wyler could sense it.

Victor rubbed his scalp. 'So what do we do now, boss?'

Cassady's fingers flipped open the pouch on his utility belt, but closed it again. He moved to the crate where the map lay. 'Are you with us?' he asked Wyler.

'Yes. I am. We get these supplies through and it might make up for some of the stuff I've done.'

'Then show us where to go.'

He spent a minute staring at the map before pointing at one of the crude markings. 'Here. This is where we need to go. There's part of the wall that isn't the same as the rest. Looks like the real deal, but it's a gate. The trail behind it will take us into the mountains.'

'Is it guarded?' asked Cassady.

'The gate? No. Like I said, they ain't got enough bodies to watch everything anymore. Besides, it's supposed to look low key. Guards would draw attention.'

'Is the road mined?'

'No. At least I don't think so.'

'That's reassuring,' murmured Tagawa.

Ghazi approached the crate. 'What about the trail? Are we likely to encounter trouble once we get inside?'

'It depends on troop movements. And if you're spotted. They rely on a whole lot of drones to keep the state under its paranoid control.'

How far will the trail take us?'

'If we link up with the scientist's supply road, it'll take us all the way, more or less.'

'And at the southern border?'

'That's something we'll have to find out together. I've never seen it.'

Cassady took it all in, reading the lines on the map while he chewed at his bottom lip. He lifted his head until he was eye to eye with Wyler. 'How can we trust anything you say?' he said quietly.

'Look. I'm being straight with you. Here are the facts: I saved

Brandt's life back there. I came to your aid. I did what I could for Kaja.' His shoulders slumped, as though the effort of recalling the image of Katarina was too much for him.

Hearst made to speak, but hesitated.

'If you can't trust me now,' continued Wyler, 'then you'd better end it. Because I ain't got anything else to keep me going anymore.'

His cloudy grey eyes were serene, his beard matted with dust and sweat. The great chest muscles relaxed under his shirt. His sense of calm affected them all, and in that moment Ghazi forgave him. The darkness lifted.

Hearst clicked her tongue and the Runners turned to her.

'Right about Katarina. Made her comfortable, did what he could. Made a mistake. Now has to live with it.'

Victor's mouth fell open. Ghazi did his best to hide a smile.

'Thank you, sister,' said Wyler.

Cassady looked around the truck bed. 'Okay. This is what's going to happen. Wyler, you ride with Victor for now. Tagawa, you're with Brandt. Does that work for you two?'

'If he stays with us,' said Tagawa. 'He's been through hell already.'

'He will. Everybody get some rest. I'll take the first watch. We leave at dawn. Once we start the climb, we're not stopping until we see the desert. Understand?'

The meeting was over. Cassady folded up the map and slipped it into a pocket. Ghazi opened Telamonian's rear door.

'I'm going after Brandt,' he called. 'I'll be back.'

He jumped out before Cassady or any of the others could respond. He stepped over the warm earth and slipped between Orion and the Silkworm onto the gravel track that coiled upward through the rocky landscape. A gust of wind rattled the tree branches and froze the sweat on the back of his neck. The first drops of night were beginning to dilute the sky.

Brandt wasn't far away. He sat on a flat rock further up the track, at the point where it disappeared around a tight bend. Ghazi approached with caution, not wishing to interrupt the man's thoughts. His ears pricked at a faint boom from somewhere in the distance. Trouble on the road, maybe. The air became still. Brandt glanced over his shoulder at the sound of footsteps. Ghazi took his lack of response as a sign to join him.

'I keep going over it,' Brandt murmured. The bandage was bright in the dusk. 'He saved my life, but Renfield died because of him.'

'There's no easy answer.'

'Out here, our wits are all we have. Mine are blunt and rusted. I let my guard down too easily. Wouldn't have happened in the past.'

'You saw somebody you thought you could rely on. We all did.'

'You can't rely on anyone. Not in this world. Everybody is too concerned with looking out for themselves. The whole thing stinks. Victor had it right.'

'About what?'

'Using up my lives on the road. I can't count the number of times I've cheated death. Like this,' he said, pointing to the side of his head. 'I owe a debt for each one.'

'What are you saying?'

'Nothing. I don't know. Maybe it's better to go out on my own terms.'

'Don't talk like that. Wyler made a terrible mistake and he'll pay for it. Of that I'm certain. But it doesn't mean you should beat yourself up about it, too.'

'I should be in the ground. Katarina, Renfield, all the other shadows I've buried. When will it finally be my turn?'

'You don't have to keep running. Quit if that's what you have to do. Quit and find peace while you still can.'

Brandt shook his head. 'There's no such thing.'

Ghazi felt the blood beginning to burn in his veins. 'You need to get your head together.' Brandt looked up. 'You allowed a man to deceive you. Yes. But he deceived all of us. That's no reason to fall off the edge. And you have no right to talk about death in this way. There is no 'should'; there are no debts. Death is something we'll never understand. This,' he said, spreading his arm out, 'is all we have. Every single day. It's something to work with, not against. You'll die one day, but as for right now you're among friends. And we need you.'

He looked back down the trail. Nobody else had followed them.

'I don't know if you can forgive Wyler, not yet, but he's trying to do what he can to make things a little better. Like all of us.' He laid a hand on the old man's forearm. 'Now come back to the camp. Rest for a few hours more.'

Brandt remained motionless, looking past Ghazi at a mass of dark foliage. Then he rose. Ghazi offered his arm, and he leaned on him for support. The old German spoke only once more as they trudged back to the laager.

'Into the brood of vipers, then. The sentence of hell is upon us.'

13

The wall was three times as high as Telamonian and at least as wide. Humans and the elements had both launched waves of attacks against it, but it was still taut and dangerous as it followed the contours of the hills and mountains, jutting out from slopes that were already difficult to scale. Razor wire swirled over the wall's battlements, and rusting spikes pointed towards the earth and the sky. Pillboxes, perched like growths, offered sweeping views of the surroundings. In the no-man's land in front of the wall, old mines and other explosive devices waited patiently under the soil or else had risen to the top and protruded through the crust. The heat haze blurred the land.

The convoy sat a few hundred metres away, hidden from view by an outcrop of rock. Stone embankments hemmed them in on both sides. Following Wyler's instructions, the Runners had taken the paved road before turning onto a gravel trail and then a barely visible mud track. They had climbed higher into the mountainous landscape, remaining alert all the way. Then it was there, in the distance: the wall that hid a pre-Change world from their post-Change reality.

A dark, colossal form stepped out of the Silkworm and headed over to Warspite. Wyler grabbed the handrail and hauled himself onto the top step of the cab.

'This is it, brother. Let's go.'

'Yeah,' said Cassady.

Ghazi leaned over and pinned the wild man with his gaze. 'Don't come back without him.'

'I won't.' He dropped to the ground again.

Cassady removed his hat and uncoupled his harness. Blood pumped in his chest and head.

Ghazi slid his pistol out of its holster and handed it to him. 'Success, dostem.' There were deep lines around his mouth.

Cassady stuffed the squat lump of metal into his waistband. 'If I'm not back in ten minutes, turn her around and don't stop until the batteries are dead.'

'You know I won't.'

'Please.'

His boots hit the mud. He and Wyler marched shoulder to shoulder, passed the Silkworm and rounded the outcrop of rock. The wall loomed at the end of the near-invisible mud track. The larger man tucked his chest-length beard into his shirt. He did not sweat.

The wall inched ever higher as they approached. The concrete was pitted and pale and the coping stones were crumbling. There was no movement anywhere along the battlements. The pillboxes on top of the wall watched them through notched eyes.

'You're sure there's nobody in those boxes.'

'Can't be sure about anything in life. But they look dead to me.'

Cassady tried to swallow, but his throat was pinched tight. Neither the pistol nor the machete hanging from his side gave him any confidence. He expected to be plugged by a bullet at any moment. A voice inside his head urged him to run. Clear out, forget the whole business. But he continued to put one foot in front of the other, stepping on ground strewn with plastic, metal, stones and branches. They sped up, covering the last few metres at a run, and stopped only when they reached the wall's shadow. Cassady rested his hands on his hips and peered at the structure that towered over him. Something was off. He raised his hand and placed his palm flat against the wall.

It was made of wood.

The facade had been expertly painted to resemble the concrete blocks stretching away to his left and right, but it was definitely wood. Without getting up close, it was impossible to tell the difference.

Wyler looked on with a faint smile on his lips. 'Smoke and

mirrors. It's what they're good at.'

'How do we open it?'

'We climb. There's a ladder over that way. Stick close to the wall, babe. Everywhere else is mined.'

They left the track and scrambled up the embankment. Wood gave way to concrete again. Cassady kept his eyes on Wyler's broad back. His legs shook, his shoulder brushed the wall and his clumsy boots knocked loose stones back down the incline. He cursed. He couldn't see a ladder anywhere. His mind raced and now he couldn't remember why he had decided, once again, to place his trust in the man in front of him. If Wyler still wasn't playing it straight, they were finished. Or he was at least.

'Here.'

Wyler stopped by a tangle of foliage clinging to the wall and pushed aside a few of the branches. 'Take a look.'

Bricks no larger than the heel of a boot extended from the concrete in two rows to the top of the wall. It was a crude way to break into an isolated state, but it would do. The wild man took the lead. Cassady observed Wyler's deft climbing technique, steeled himself and started his ascent. The bricks were spotted with moss and mould. Despite his size, Wyler managed to swing himself onto the battlements with ease. Razor wire plucked at his clothing. Cassady followed at a slower pace. His face and hands were wet. Grit landed in his eye. The wall's mouldy scent filled his nostrils. Near the top, a few handholds had been worn away and he found himself struggling to hang on. Desperate fingers dug into the masonry. He grunted, trying to find the reserves of strength that would propel him to the top.

A massive hand stretched out towards him.

'No,' he said through clenched teeth. His grip was slipping.

'You don't need to fear me.'

He reached out. Wyler grabbed his wrist and hoisted him onto the top of the wall. Together, they slid between the rolls of razor wire and dropped from the battlements onto a lower level.

Cassady shivered as he took his first proper look at Novus. He was inside. From where they stood, he could see the mud track unfurl between folds of rock and turn a corner. The pillboxes, open on this side, were vacant. There were no signs of human activity anywhere. They found a ladder and descended to ground level, then followed the wall back to the hidden entrance. The gate hadn't been camouflaged on this side, and the wood stood out in sharp contrast to the concrete. A heavy metal bar sat in two brackets, and a chain had been strung across the gate and the wall and locked with a padlock for good measure. When the gate was open, the space would be just high enough for Telamonian to pass through without scraping the roof of its cab against the concrete. Next to the gate was a windowless cabin with its door closed. Cassady moved past Wyler and unsheathed his machete. If anybody was inside, he had to deal with them now. His hand found the door handle.

'Don't!'

He spun around, the blade jumping in his hand until it was centimetres from Wyler's neck. The larger man stopped where he was.

'Easy, babe. Easy. Odds are the door's rigged. The gate, too. Your world ain't the only one with scavengers. You can see they don't have any eyes down here right now. So they wire the place instead.'

'Is there anyone in there?'

'It looks like a supply hut to me.'

He lowered the machete. 'Do you know where the system is to disable the wire?'

'No. But we need to find it if we want to get the gate open without bringing the whole of the Koalition's army down on our heads.'

They didn't have to search for long. Wyler's practised gaze zeroed in on a clump of undergrowth growing near the gate and he pushed it aside to reveal a small black box. He unclipped a tool from his belt, removed the cover and yanked a pair of red and black wires out. Cassady held his breath. The tool snipped the red wire in half.

'She's dead.'

'That's it?'

'Ain't a reason to make it more difficult. Come on. They're waiting, brother.'

At the gate, Cassady used a pick to make quick work of the padlock before unthreading the chain. Each man gripped one side of the metal bar shackling the wood to the concrete, lifted it with some effort, and dumped it at the side of the trail. They heaved on the liberated brackets. The wooden gate scratched against the ground and edged back. Cassady gritted his teeth and dug in and pulled until his feet hit grass. Sweat streamed down both their faces. They doubled over, sucking in cool air. The gateway to Novus was open.

'Let's check the hut,' said Cassady, panting.

There wasn't much to look at: three crates containing paint and tools, a couple of storage racks, a few bales of razor wire and some wooden beams. Cassady, aware their ten minutes was up, was ready to leave empty-handed when Wyler emerged from the back of the hut holding a small radio.

'Can you get it working?'

'I reckon so.' The former agent extended the antenna, checked the battery, flicked a switch and adjusted the dials.

'Shortwave?'

'VHF. They've got batteries ten times as powerful as yours. The one in here,' he said, pointing at the radio, 'could power Telamonian for 48 hours if you worked out how to link it up.'

The radio crackled. A voice that sounded as though it was being forced through a narrow tunnel disturbed the quiet. It spoke in a tongue Cassady didn't recognise.

'What language is that?'

'Sursilvan.' Wyler cocked his head and listened. 'And mine is rusty. But they're searching for us. All along the wall, sounds like. They found the Zuisudra camp. They know we blazed through.' He paused. 'They're still looking further north. They think you'll try one of the gates up there. That buys us some time. But we ain't got long before they start searching down here, too.'

'Keep listening. I'll bring the rigs up. You and Tagawa take the lead. Do we close the gate after we're inside?'

'No point. They'll see the tracks anyway. Don't waste time.'

'Okay.' He hesitated, wanting to thank the man but still not trusting him. Wyler didn't miss it.

'I understand, Cassady. I'd feel the same in your position. Before this is over, I'll convince you I'm on your side. Count on it. Now go and get them. One more thing – when we start to climb, it's gonna get cold. Real cold. They use a screen of clouds to stop the heat from getting through. You'll notice it soon enough.'

Cassady turned on his heel and ran through the gate. Seeing the convoy disappearing down the mountain would break him. He sprinted to the bend in the road, ignoring the dizziness that tried to take his feet from under him.

The rigs were still there. He called to Tagawa in the Silkworm. 'Pick Wyler up at the gate. Stay close. I'll flash twice if I want you to stop. If you get tired, switch. Or hit the blitz pills. We can't stop for anything now.'

'Are you okay?'

'Everything's under control.'

Tagawa woke the Silkworm. A smile flickered. 'Try to keep up.'

Ghazi's gaunt face leaned out of the driver's window and broke into a grin when he spotted Cassady. He ducked back inside and opened the passenger door. The engine sighed and the lights flashed twice. Further down the trail, Orion and Telamonian stirred.

'This is it,' said Cassady as he jumped into the co-seat and slammed the door. The Old Lady groaned as she rounded the bend and rolled towards the wall. The Silkworm had already passed through the gate. Wyler leapt onto the pillbox's running board, radio tucked under an arm, and threw open the cab door. Orion and Telamonian chased Warspite's shadow.

Cassady wound down the window. He could already notice a slight difference in the temperature. He reached behind the seat for his flight jacket and beat the dust off it. His hands shook with adrenaline. The remnants of a world they'd never experienced were hunting them. The real battle started now.

The mountain trail promised death at every turn, folding around on itself like a tangled length of rope as it climbed higher into the peaks. As promised, thick clouds whose edges were tinged with green filled the sky and blocked out the sun. Warspite laboured up the narrow incline. In the co-seat Cassady stared straight ahead, eyes wide open, as though to look away would send them to their deaths. If they did go over, there wouldn't be enough time to jump clear. He couldn't even open his door without slamming it into the rocks. He'd stopped counting the hairpin turns that had Ghazi pulling the wheel all the way over just to keep them on an even keel. The mechanic hadn't said a word for more than an hour. His gaze strayed to the side mirror every few seconds. The tyres were on the verge of slipping off into nothingness. Ahead, the Silkworm's brake lights flickered like dying stars.

They hit a plateau and the black pillbox shivered and stopped. Ghazi switched off the engine, let go of the wheel and looked at his hands as though they belonged to a stranger. Tagawa slipped out of the cab and buttoned up his tunic against the cold. He crept to the edge of the track, lay on his stomach and poked his head into the void.

'What's he doing?' asked Ghazi.

'Maybe he's spotted a drone.'

They were almost on top of the Japanese when he sprang to

his feet.

'Look,' he said, throwing a ball of something towards them.

Cassady caught it. It was cold and wet. He held it up to the fading light. Sunlight exploded in every shard. 'Snow,' he whispered. He pressed it to his lips and ice-cold heaven trickled down his throat. 'Take ten. Fill the canteens.'

While Ghazi went to pass the command back to the other pantechs, Cassady joined Wyler in the Silkworm. The headset was clamped to the huge man's ear.

'Any news?'

'Not much. They're drifting south, trying to scare us out from wherever we're hiding. Sounds as though half the military's on the hunt. Once they discover we're inside, they'll have the drones up and sweeping. Then we'll be riding our luck.'

'It's held so far.'

He'd never seen a drone, but he didn't want to ask Wyler for a description. There were none further north, not that he was aware of. Even Faustine didn't have one in her arsenal. He supposed he would find out what they looked like soon enough. More importantly, aside from Tagawa's rifle they had no way to shoot them down. They would have to run.

Messages continued to buzz in the receiver. He leaned over and listened in.

'What did you say it was called?'

'Sursilvan.'

'Is it a code? Like what the stations use?'

'No. It's a dialect of an old language. Mountain people spoke it. They translate some of the words literally and for the rest they choose terms that mirror their essence. Kind of beautiful in a way.'

'Can you teach me it?'

'Not unless you've got a few years to spare.'

Cassady knocked his head against the back of the seat and sighed. 'Strange world you live in.'

'Ain't been my world for a long time.'

Before he could respond, Wyler sat up straighter and held up a hand for quiet. He pressed the radio against his ear, lips twitching as he made sure of the message.

'They've found the gate. They're coming. Advance party.'

'How long do we have?'

'With their vehicles? One hour, ninety minutes at the most.'

'Get ready to move.'

Cassady ran to where the others were pushing snow into canteens and passing around barely edible rations, and relayed the news. Brandt threw a look at the Silkworm's cab, but said nothing. They mounted up.

Getting back on the trail, Cassady thought, was like closing his eyes again after waking from a nightmare and being thrust right back into the middle of it. He would have taken over the driving, but Ghazi was in sync with the rig. It had become an extension of his body, every tick and vibration flowing through his veins. He had become the mass of metal distributed across six wheels. Warspite slid and spun on mud and then sleet as they climbed higher. More than once, Tagawa had to slam on the brakes, and Ghazi had to be just as quick. Cassady stretched his jaw to prevent it from locking up tight. He was desperate to chew on one of his last pieces of root. He wanted the numbness, the shards that were colder than the snow coating the slopes around them. But he had to hold on to all of his senses. The enemy was coming.

The next time the Silkworm stopped on the trail, Tagawa and Wyler both emerged from the cab and stalked to the edge of the cliff.

Cassady zipped up his jacket. 'Switch her off. You stay here, take a break.'

Ghazi simply nodded and closed his eyes.

He trudged up the slope. The wind cut into his skin. Isolated trees bent towards him. Green was losing ground against white up here. Back in their world it didn't become this cold until deep winter, which meant the technology keeping Novus shielded from the effects of the Change had to be more powerful than anything he'd ever dreamed of.

He joined the two Runners and looked out over a sea of rock. 'What is it?'

'Bridge,' said Wyler, pointing down.

Thrown across a gorge at a lower altitude were two concrete bars. Without binoculars, he couldn't tell how wide each bar was or how far apart they were from each other. There were no other man-made structures around.

'I wouldn't call it a bridge,' he muttered. 'More like the start of one.'

'It's how we get across, in any case.'

'You're sure?'

'I don't see any other option. This trail is going to take us down there.'

Something glittered in the sky and the three men instinctively threw themselves flat on the floor. A tubular black machine with vast wings glided above the tree tops. It banked left and made a lazy circle before passing over the concrete bars and disappearing behind the serrated outline of a mountain.

Footsteps slapping against the trail brought them to their feet again. Victor ran up the slope, arms pumping at his sides.

'Engines,' he shouted. 'Petrol-fired.'

'How many?' asked Wyler.

'I ain't sure. Hearst reckons a dozen.' His face was white. He stopped and bent over to catch his breath. 'Thought they were right behind us, but it was the cliffs. They're making a hell of a racket.'

Wyler turned to Cassady. 'Count on them using quads. Maybe exos following up behind. They're way more agile than us. We've got to get across that bridge before they catch up, or we ain't going any further.'

Cassady stared at nothing. His rig sat in the middle of the track, trapped between an army and an abyss. His legs threatened to buckle with the realisation.

'Brother?' A dark hand closed around his forearm and shook him. 'You in there?'

'Get back to the rigs,' he said in a monotone. Victor retraced his steps at speed. Cassady forced himself into a jog and didn't stop until his hands found the cold chassis. He hauled himself into the cab just as Warspite rolled forward.

'Ready to drive through the valley of the shadow of death?' called Ghazi over the keening engine.

Cassady didn't answer.

14

The concrete girders were two stitches tying together a jagged wound. It was the start of a bridge, nothing more, perhaps once intended to serve as the foundation for something much greater, but now left to rot under the snow. The Runners stood by the precipice, a chill wind slapping at their skin, and sized it up. A hundred calculations ran through their heads, but the only one that mattered was the odds of their survival. Hearst spat into the chasm and offered a curse that echoed off the cliff walls. Brandt and Wyler stood together a few paces away from the group. Neither man had spoken to the other, but their body language indicated a renewed understanding between the two as they assessed the obstacle before them.

'I reckon we can make it,' said Victor slowly. 'Width is okay and the bars are far enough apart.'

'Not possible,' said Hearst.

'Only one way to find out.' The boy grinned. 'Besides, I thought you were supposed to be the best. I guess maybe that ain't true after all.'

She scowled. 'You go first. Then we'll see.'

Ghazi sat on his own a few paces away, not listening to the conversation. He pressed his hands to his temples, then swallowed another blitz pill and chased it with the freezing mountain air. His entire body was shaking. Before the long incline that had taken them down to the half-bridge, he'd come to within a hair of dragging Warspite off the edge. Cassady had had to reach out with a wild hand to keep them on the mountain. He couldn't get the truck across to the other side. Not in this state. Cassady would have to do it.

The other man stood leaning against the trunk of a tree, binoculars angled up at the mountain they'd left behind. He'd barely glanced at the girders since they pulled up in front of them. Ghazi forced his aching limbs into motion and limped over.

'Cass?'

'I see movement,' he muttered. 'Back where we stopped before.'

Ghazi held up a hand to shield his eyes. Vague outlines flitted at the limit of his vision.

'Quads and exos. Wyler called it right.'

Ghazi waited for him to bark out commands to the others. An eternity passed in the meantime. 'We need to get moving, Cass,' he prompted. 'Either we try for it now or we prepare for a fight.'

That broke the spell. Cassady lowered the binoculars and shouted across to the group. 'Who's going first?'

Tagawa stretched out his limbs and buttoned his tunic. A streak of grease ran from his chin to his hairline. His eyes were glazed with fatigue, but the confidence was still there.

'Better show you all how to do it, I guess.'

'We're going together,' Victor added. 'Or we ain't going.'

'Then get ready. And good luck the pair of you.'

While they warmed up the Silkworm, Brandt trudged to his cab and retrieved a flask that sat inside the door. He unscrewed it, pressed it to his lips and rested a hand against the wheel arch. The bandage around his head was frayed and dirty, and his eyes were bloodshot. He returned to where Wyler stood and held out the flask. The former agent took it without a word and drank deeply.

The Silkworm backed up. Tagawa guided her towards the girders at a crawl before putting her into reverse, tyres shedding clumps of dirt and slush as they revolved. He rolled her forward slowly once again, this time not stopping until the rubber kissed the concrete. Again he backed off, guiding the truck part way up the incline. The other Runners watched and waited.

Tagawa gave it everything. The Silkworm screamed, cutting up the gravel as it bore down on the chasm. The others looked on with a mixture of horror and exhilaration.

'Was zum Teufel?' shouted Brandt.

Hearst took a step forward, her fists clenched. Cassady dropped the binoculars on the track.

The Silkworm hit the girders at ramming speed and bounced along the surface of the bridge. The engine twitched and thrummed. There was a screech and the chassis shuddered as the back tyre on the right teetered between concrete and air, and Brandt and Ghazi looked away. But before it could fall, the Silkworm hit the other side of the mountain, joined the track and raced along for a few metres until red lights glowed and the engine cut out. For a moment, there was no sound other than stones clattering down the face of the gorge.

Brandt took a deep breath and cheered. On the other side, Tagawa and Victor stumbled out onto the trail and raised a couple of shaky fists. Cassady mumbled something indecipherable and picked up the binoculars off the floor. Wyler took another drink from the canteen. Ghazi said a short prayer to whichever gods were listening and wished he had even a few shreds of tobacco to smoke.

Hearst was next. Her features were blank as she climbed into the bulbous cab. The bags under her eyes were as dark as her tattoos. She'd driven further than any of them.

Cassady called Ghazi over. 'Get the Old Lady ready, will you? They'll be on us soon.'

Ghazi tried to keep the shame out of his voice. 'I can't take her over the gorge.'

'Why not?'

'I'm shot through.' He held up a shaking hand. 'If I have to do it, she'll roll.'

He held the other man's gaze. He just couldn't. It was that simple. Cassady had to understand, and he had to step up.

'Okay,' said the other Runner at last. 'I'll do it. Help Hearst line herself up. Doesn't much look as though she's about to follow the boys' example.'

As Hearst edged Orion onto the narrow bars, Ghazi stood behind the rig and watched the tyres. When he waved, Hearst nudged the wheel to correct the direction. Tagawa did the same from the other side of the gorge. Little by little, the beetle crept forward to the middle of the bridge. Ghazi swallowed. Reserves of adrenaline he didn't know he had prickled in his chest.

A frenzied shout from Cassady sent an electric shock through them all. 'They're coming.'

'Get going!' Ghazi screamed into the chasm.

Orion jogged forward, but veered right. The tyre treads began to drift off the concrete and find air. Hearst fired the engine, and the truck whined and danced from side to side as she battled to stay on the bridge. There was a heavy thump as Orion left the girders and hit the opposite bank. Victor and Tagawa stood aside as the pantech pulled in behind the Silkworm. They slapped the blood-red body and shouted their relief. Hearst didn't emerge from the cab.

The faint snarl of petrol-fired engines rolled over the mountainside. As if in sync with one another, Wyler and Brandt raced over to Telamonian. Brandt opened the rear doors and hoisted himself onto the cargo bed. Seconds later, the end of a supply crate appeared. Wyler pulled at its rope handle and heaved. Brandt appeared again, holding the handle at the other end, and launched himself out of the truck. The two men darted across to Warspite with the crate between them, threw it down by the drop hatch, and returned for the other.

As Ghazi watched them race from one rig to the other, he understood. But he didn't give the realisation time to hurt him. Instead, he ran over to the Old Lady and uncoupled the hatch, and Brandt and Wyler lifted the first crate onto Warspite's bed. Cassady appeared as they were struggling with the second one.

'What are you doing?' he asked, disbelief wrinkling his brow. 'You need to go now. We haven't got time for this.'

'Too large,' grunted Brandt. Wyler gave a final push and the crate was inside. Ghazi tied it down with bungee cords.

'What is?'

Brandt slammed the drop hatch home, wiped his hands on his trousers and nodded at Telamonian. 'She is.' He sighed. 'She won't make it across. She's too wide and the tyres are too large.'

The guttural snarls of the petrol engines forced him to raise his voice. Ghazi's eyes darted to the top of the long incline, but it was still clear. They had seconds left to get away.

'I don't understand.'

'I'm staying here.'

Cassady gaped at the old man, confusion souring to anger and then helplessness as he searched the corners of his mind for an alternative that didn't exist. The lines on Brandt's face were deep with pain, but he radiated determination. He wouldn't be persuaded. He reached out and rested a hand on the younger man's shoulder.

'It's okay, Edward. I made it this far. That's far enough for me.'

'But we need you.'

'No you don't. You need to get the others away from here.'

Ghazi turned to Wyler and asked the question he already knew the answer to. 'Are you joining us?'

The wild man's jaw was set. 'I don't think so, brothers.'

Cassady rounded on him. 'Why the hell not?'

'Remember what I told you when we were in Prestige? We're all part of the same tapestry. I ain't leaving him to face them alone.'

Brandt squared his shoulders. 'This isn't necessary.'

'I betrayed you once. I don't intend to do it again.'

'I'm not asking you to do this.'

'I know. No more discussion.'

After a moment of consideration, the German nodded.

'This is crazy,' said Cassady. 'You can come with us. Both of

227

you.'

The old man pulled himself up to his full height and fixed Cassady with a gaze that told him to stop.

'What's your plan?' asked Ghazi quickly.

'The dynamite,' said Brandt. 'Try to buy you some time. Here, take these.' He held out his gimlet knives. Ghazi shook his head.

'They belong with you.'

'We've got to go,' said Wyler. He grabbed Ghazi's arm and pumped it. Then he pulled the crestfallen Cassady close and embraced him. 'Keep going, brother. You have to make it. Don't give up.'

'We won't,' said Ghazi.

'I'll see you in the next life.'

'Auf Wiedersehen,' said Brandt.

A shout came from across the void. Victor stood in the road, hands waving for the group's attention. The noise of the engines drowned out his words. Brandt raised a heavy hand and curled it into a fist. Victor stopped shouting. Tagawa appeared by his side, and his long, thin frame bent into a bow. Hearst left her cab and joined the pair of them on the track.

A mechanical snort sounded at the top of the incline. 'They're here,' said Wyler.

The first machines rolled into view. Four-wheeled quad bikes on oversized tyres with a pod-like cage protecting the two-person crew. Helmets concealed the faces of the riders.

The machines kicked into gear. 'Go,' shouted Brandt.

The four men ran to the rigs. Ghazi and Cassady strapped themselves in. Warspite rolled towards the girders. Behind them, Telamonian shuddered into life and pulled out into the middle of the trail. The quads scudded over the hard ground, pillion riders aiming brutal carbines over the shoulders of the drivers. Bullets fizzed and popped, but Telamonian's huge body shielded Warspite from the worst of the storm.

Warspite lurched onto the bars and the ground disappeared.

Wind beat against the tarp and whistled through the grille, and it made the Old Lady sound as though she was screaming. Stray slugs clanged off the chassis. Cassady twitched the steering wheel to the left and gave her some juice. The truck teetered.

'Calm. Calm,' said Ghazi, struggling to speak over the raw fear that clogged his throat.

Cassady did as he was told, steadying his breathing and then bringing the truck level again. The gunfire continued. Ghazi checked the mirror. Telamonian charged up the incline to meet the machines. Metal squealed against metal as it hammered into the quads, sending them spinning over the edge of the cliff. A group of sleek exoskeletons took their place at the top of the hill and began to rain fire down on the monster, which groaned as it weaved from side to side. Telamonian's windshield became spiderwebbed. Under the hood the engine howled, and the great truck swerved into the exoskeletons.

A terrible explosion sent shockwaves through the fibres of Warspite. Ghazi's mind went blank as a fireball grew in the side mirrors. Cassady held the wheel steady and put his foot down, and the Old Lady leapt towards the opposite bank. The tyres bit into the rock face and she clambered onto the mountainside. He cut the power.

Ghazi's trembling hand found the door and he forced it open. He slid out and spent a long moment bent over at the waist suppressing the urge to vomit. He staggered over to where Tagawa, Victor and Hearst stood, their faces set as they viewed the destruction on the other side of the gorge. Flames licked at the overgrowth. Near the top of the incline, the remains of Telamonian belched black smoke. A quad lay on its side, its unmoving crew a few metres away. A rumble sounded further up the mountain, and several car-sized rocks tumbled onto the trail. The path was blocked.

Orion left first. Hearst didn't speak to any of them. Victor wiped his eyes and swore into the void until Tagawa led him back to their truck and set off along the narrow path. For the first time in many days, Ghazi and Cassady were alone. Silently, they checked the crates in the back. A few bullets had made holes in the tarp, but none had pierced the wood. Both men threw back a pill. Cassady slipped into the driver's seat once more and stoked the engine. A dead weight sat on their shoulders. The Koalition had won the first battle, and the Runners had paid the price.

Part III – On the Run

1

'I'm worried about Hearst.'

Cassady pushed up the peak of his cap and squeezed his eyes shut and open a few times to chase away the ripples that appeared in front of him. He'd drifted off. The trail was dark. The roof lights lay dormant, and they were running on a single headlight to avoid being detected by any drones ghosting between the peaks. A few branches snatched at them from the sides of the trail, but the landscape was still dominated by rock. The harsh edges of the cliff-side and the skull-sized stones strewn across their path suggested the route had been cut out in a hurry and then never maintained. It was difficult to tell whether it was pre- or post-Change. In some places it became so narrow that the Old Lady had to scrape her body along the cliff, and both men in the cab would wince as the smell of rock dust and metal drifted through the windows.

Hearst. She'd been driving solo for nearly four days now with barely a break. He knew why Ghazi was worried, but he didn't have a solution. They were all strung out. 'What about her?'

'She's swerving all over the road.' His co-driver spoke in a monotone. 'She can't keep going on like this.'

'What do you want me to do about it? We don't have enough drivers to rotate.' Pain buzzed in the back of his head. He removed his hat and rubbed his temples. Light from the single lamp splashed against the cliffs. 'I guess I could ask Tagawa.'

'They'll be feeling the strain too. Better to keep them together.'

'So what's the answer?'

'I don't know. I'm just telling you.'

'She's tougher than you think.'

'But not indestructible. She's been driving since the highway. We can't push her until she breaks.'

'We won't,' he said, cutting the conversation short. He

opened his canteen and sipped the cool water they'd taken from the mountain. It had no equal. He'd forgotten what it was like to take a drink without the chlorine aftertaste. He searched for something else to say.

'You need another pill?'

'If I have one more, my heart will probably give out.'

'How's your head?'

'It feels like there's a fly trapped inside it.'

The pantech crawled along. Contact with an outcrop of rock sent more shockwaves through the chassis. Cassady's teeth chattered.

'Brandt wouldn't have made it through here,' he muttered.

'I was thinking the same thing.'

Ahead, Orion's taillights flashed on and off as the trail became more twisted and kinked.

'He and Katarina were links to the old world,' Ghazi continued. 'Soon there won't be anyone left who was born before the Change.'

'You can't stop time.'

'But once we break with the things that came before us, they cease to be real. They become part of history.'

'That's how it's always been. And always will be.'

'Right, but in our minds we're always yearning for the world to return to an ideal from the past. We want to be in Eden again. The truth we choose to ignore is that the world will never be like it once was ever again. It's gone. We're trapped in an endless cycle of trying to recreate what people before us had. We only look backwards.'

'Not when we're young. I was always looking to the future.'

'Yes. But younger minds have no say in things until they become old. And then it's too late.'

Cassady looked at the outline of his partner's dark face. It was bearded now, like his own. He didn't know what to say to him. He ran a finger across his forehead. The skin was cracked, dry and covered in grit. A sharp aroma rose from his body. Lice moved in the seams of his clothing. He was decomposing.

The cliff faces retreated and the trail became wider. They had more room to breathe.

'I was thinking about Wyler, too,' said Ghazi. 'Why he chose to stay with Brandt. Our moral compass can steer us in directions others would consider horrific, can't it? It steered him wrong even though he wasn't a bad person. It led him down a one-way street. If you can't see the other options around you because you have your nose to the wall, you start to think you're right. You fail to see the world around you, and then you're shocked when somebody pulls you away from the wall. That was what happened to him. I don't think he even thought of Renfield as a human being. Not until it was too late.'

Cassady watched Orion's headlights. 'A person should obey that moral compass of yours though. Otherwise they could end up doing anything at all, totally without context or consideration. That compass comes with boundaries.'

'Still, the moment you lay down your own rules is the moment you ignore the wider rules of the universe. Those are the ones we should be listening to. Forget right and wrong as we understand it, because it goes well beyond that.'

'I wouldn't even know where to start with that.'

'Exactly. Because life is much more chaotic than we want it to be and its vastness scares us. That's why we devise systems of what we think is right and wrong, good and bad. It's short-sighted. Life isn't there to be simplified or boiled down. Wyler thought that dying with Brandt would right a wrong. But it's not as clear-cut as that.'

Cassady was silent for a moment as he reflected. Ghazi never stopped searching for answers, not even now. 'I just hope they're having a drink up there with Kaja and Renfield.'

'So do I.'

Orion's taillights jogged from side to side and the vehicle

yelped in the dark. Cassady imagined Hearst hunched over the wheel, battling to stay alert. The track angled upwards again. Ghazi shifted the stick and Warspite groaned with the effort.

The timepiece flashed. It wouldn't be light for hours. Cassady cracked the cap on the pill bottle and shook one into his palm. His body begged for him not to take it, but he tossed it into his mouth and swallowed. It was nearly his turn to take over at the wheel again.

Orion stopped on a small plateau just before dawn. The sky was the colour of iron, and gelid clouds circled the peaks and blocked out the sun. The trail had become much steeper, and the pantechs had to dig in for every metre of progress. On their right, a sheer drop into a valley promised death if they made a wrong move.

Cassady stretched out his legs where he sat as he waited for Orion to move off again. His knees and his tailbone throbbed in unison.

'Come on,' he muttered. He glanced at Ghazi, whose eyes were closed. They'd started switching places on the hour. Every minute lasted ten. As he peered through the glass, Orion's taillights died. He pressed down on the pedal and the Old Lady groaned as she fought her way up the hill. Eventually she hit the plateau, and he pulled her in behind the beetle. Ghazi awoke with a start. He coughed and groaned.

'Trouble?'

'Hearst has stopped. I'm going to check it out.'

'I'll come with you. Let me find a fleece.'

Cassady put his cap on, zipped up his creaking flight jacket and jumped out. The air was a pane of glass that was ready to shatter into a thousand pieces. He shambled over to Orion and threw open the door. Hearst was slumped over the wheel, eyelids fluttering, chin resting on top of the moulded plastic. Her arms and neckline were bare. He held her hand between his and rubbed it.

'You okay?' Misted breath drifted in front of his face.

Without raising her head, she pointed. The Silkworm had stopped twenty paces further on.

'Why aren't you wearing more layers? It's freezing.'

'Cold keeps me awake.'

'You want me to ride with you for a while?'

She struggled to sit upright. 'No.'

'Then at least take ten. Lie down, cover yourself up. I'll go and check on the boys.'

Without another word, she slid down until she straddled the two seats. He pulled out a dirty blanket from underneath her chair and threw it over her shoulders. Then he closed the door.

'What's going on?' asked Ghazi, walking towards him with his hands tucked under his armpits.

'The Silkworm.' He jerked a thumb over his shoulder.

A weather vane was set up on the roof of the vehicle, blades spinning in the mountain breeze. Victor and Tagawa squatted at the side of the track, wrapped in heavy coats and hemp blankets that gave the illusion of bulk from the neck down. Behind them was an alcove cut into the cliff. A squat, cylindrical device was embedded in the razor-sharp rock, its end capped with a plastic plug. Next to it were two metal crates whose lids had been prised off.

Victor threw something over to Ghazi, and he caught it in an outstretched hand. It was a magazine, grey, single-stack, in good condition. He pulled out his pistol, cold hands fumbling as he released the nearly-empty clip. The new one slotted home.

'Lucky break.'

'Found a few of these, too.' He held out a bag stamped with a label: READY-TO-EAT.

'Anything else?' asked Cassady.

'Empty water flasks. Another radio.'

'Any idea what that is?' He pointed at the tube in the rock.

Tagawa lifted his head. 'It's a charger of some kind. For their batteries, not ours. We can't use it. Took the cap off, but the plug is all wrong.'

'Fine.' He crouched down next to them and pulled his collar up to his ears. The cold pooled around his ankles, trying to find a way in. 'How are you holding up?'

Tagawa smiled faintly. His lips were the colour of tungsten. 'It's a test. That's all. Just a test.'

'We're hanging in,' said Victor. 'Nobody following?'

'No. Brandt took care of it.'

'Wish I could've spoken to the old man before he went. I got him wrong.'

Ghazi scratched at his beard. 'It happens.'

The boy fell silent, but the nervous energy returned seconds later. 'What about the city? Did you see it?'

The Warspite crew looked up sharply. 'What city?' asked Ghazi.

'Between the peaks.'

He shook his head, Cassady too.

'Christ, I wish we could go back. I only laid eyes on it for a few seconds. If Hearst hadn't been on our tail, I would've stopped and taken a longer look. It was white. Blinding white. Must've been one of those five Wyler told us about. Towers and bridges and buildings all connected to one another like the whole thing was alive. Some kind of raised track running around the outside. Long, thin machines chasing each other. Didn't look like pantechs to me.'

'I don't know how I could have missed that,' murmured Ghazi.

'Guess you had your eyes on the road. Flying machines, too. Not just drones. Inflatable ships bobbing up and down and huge wings that glided between the towers. I ain't lying. Hideki saw them.'

Tagawa nodded. 'It was the future.'

'Not ours,' growled Cassady. The description unsettled him. If the Koalition had resources like those the boy had described, they had even less of a chance of making it out of Novus alive than he'd thought. While the other three continued to talk about the city, he drifted away to the far edge of the plateau. He rubbed his arms and stamped his feet, and then cocked his head and strained to hear any machines moving in the heavy dawn air. The world was dead. His hand rested on his belt. He wanted some root, a drink, sleep, anything that would take care of the pain in his head.

He coughed. It started inside his bones and rattled through his body like a banshee. He thumped his ribcage and doubled over, his chest on fire. Finally it subsided. He looked down at himself, palm resting on his chest, his brow wet. On unsteady legs, he walked back to the group.

They were still speculating. Cassady picked up one of the ration packs. 'Take one to Hearst and make her eat,' he muttered to Ghazi. 'Then lie down and rest.'

Ghazi eyed him, but said nothing. He grabbed the pack and trudged away.

'We'll head out in twenty minutes,' he said to Victor. 'I'll wake Hearst when I hear your engine. You need anything?'

'No,' said Victor. 'You okay? You look like hell.'

'I'm fine.'

'Good. We gotta make it now, Cassady. I don't want these mountains to be the last thing I see.'

'They won't be.'

'They'll be waiting for us,' said Tagawa. 'Brandt only chopped off the tail of the snake. The head is still waiting to bite.'

'I know.'

'Do you have a plan?'

'All we can do is to keep going.' Cassady's fingertips trembled. He had to get back to the cab. 'We'll find a way through. Count on it.'

'I am.'

He coughed again, this time without the burning in his chest. 'Get back inside before you freeze to death. Order yourselves a three-course meal. Forward me the bill.'

Tagawa gave a wry smile. 'Generous of you.'

As he headed back to the Old Lady, Cassady rubbed his palms against one another. It was no good. His body was shaking from fear, not the cold.

2

First the sky turned a brilliant white. Then great gouts of snow settled on hoods and roofs and windscreens, forcing the Runners to switch on wipers that fed off the juice they needed to keep moving. A driving wind buffeted them and lowered the temperature further in the cabs, and after a while the snow became so thick they slowed to a crawl. They could barely tell where the trail ended and the void began.

Ghazi sweated and shivered at the same time. His muscles were on fire from the effort of keeping Warspite on an even keel. He kept glancing further ahead to Orion. Hearst had pumped herself full of blitz pills, but they wouldn't work forever. A red flare bled fire in the middle of the track, and Warspite rumbled over it. Victor had volunteered to walk ahead and drop the sticks at points where the trail banked sharply. It was a hellish job. And it reminded them all of Katarina's final act.

In the passenger seat, Cassady leaned forward until the tip of his nose left a greasy mark on the glass. He barked instructions. Each one made the muscles in Ghazi's chest tight.

'Left! Keep left!'

'I know.'

'You want me to take her?'

'No.'

Wind rattled through the grille. They had no heating system. They couldn't have afforded the juice anyway.

'Maybe we should take a break,' he said. His eyes were dry and irritated.

'We can't. If we stop here, we won't get going again for hours. In this weather we might be able to surprise whoever's waiting for us further on.' Beyond the windshield, a pair of red eyes flashed against the white. 'Besides, we need to get Hearst off this rock. She must be keeping it together by a thread.'

The tyres slid in the snow and struggled to find traction. Ghazi slipped between first and second, imagining the shift forks being pulled back, the gears on the layshaft being engaged, the engine's power being converted and transferred to the wheel axles. It calmed him a little. Slowly, the Old Lady dragged herself up the mountain. He had Cassady pour some of the cool water into his mouth and drape a blanket over his shoulders while he kept his hands on the wheel.

An hour later he stopped the truck. Once again, Orion sat dead on the incline. He pumped the lights a couple of times, but there was no response. The wind cut a path through the blizzard and for a second the curtain parted. A human form leaned against the body of the red pantech.

'Somebody's out there,' said Cassady.

Ghazi unbuttoned his holster and rested his hand on the grip. A spectre materialised before them, long and thin and bent over. It was dressed in black. A hand wrapped in cloth banged on the door and Cassady opened it.

Snow clung to the moustache above Tagawa's lip. 'Well. Hell has frozen over.'

They made space for him in the cab. He slammed the door, unwrapped the cloth that covered his face and blew on his hands. Usually so composed, he shook uncontrollably.

Then came the news none of them wanted to hear. 'Our engine cut out,' said the Japanese.

A low gurgle sounded in Cassady's throat. 'Is it dead?'

'No. It's happened before. But it will take some time to repair it.'

'I can take a look,' said Ghazi.

Tagawa shook his head. 'No. You keep going. There's enough space on the road for you to pass us. We know our pantech like you know yours. We'll find the problem. Could be moisture. Here, let me take a look at the map.'

Cassady reached into his jacket and brought out the folded

square of cotton.

'Are you okay?' asked Ghazi.

'This is what we signed up for. I'm not complaining.'

Tagawa took the map and studied it, fingers brushing over the topographical lines. 'I think we're about here.'

'How do you figure?'

'I've been keeping track of the distance. It's a rough guess. But I'm usually right.'

Cassady gave a dry chuckle. 'Okay.'

His finger jumped to another fold. 'Is this the track Lupo told us to follow?'

'Yes.'

'And you'll take it to the end?'

'Don't have much of a choice. It should keep us out of their way. This is one of the towns Lupo said was deserted. If it still is, this is where we'll charge the batteries before we head for the south wall.'

'Then we will go there, too.'

'We can't wait for you.'

Ghazi glanced at his partner. 'Yes we could.'

'No.' Tagawa handed the map back. 'Your priority is to get out of here. If we can catch you up, we will. If not, we will see you at La Talpa.' He glanced at them both. 'Or we'll overtake you on the way.'

Despite the severity of the situation, he was still confident. Ghazi took strength from it.

'Does Victor agree?' asked Cassady.

'Yes.'

'Do you need any supplies? Tools? Spares?'

'No. We have everything we need. Except food and heat and a safe place to bed down and sleep for a week, of course.'

'Are you sure about this?' said Ghazi.

'We're not going to get the whole convoy stranded up here. You have to go.'

Cassady hesitated and then held out his hand. 'We'll see you again.' The three men shook.

'Count on it. I'll tell Hearst.' Tagawa jumped out into the tundra once more and struggled over to Orion.

Ghazi shook his head as he watched him through the windshield. 'A breakdown here. No luck.'

Beside him, Cassady exploded. 'God damn this mountain. We should never have come this way.'

He looked across at his partner in surprise. 'What other options did we have?'

'They're going to die up here.'

'You don't know that. They're not even close to giving up.'

'What hope do we have? Even if we manage to make it down in one piece, the Koalition will be waiting for us.'

'Now is not the time for this, Cass. Calm down.'

'We should throw the medicine over the edge.'

'What would that solve?'

'At least we won't be bringing it straight to them.' He hit the board again. 'Remember what Hearst said to Lupo? This really is a suicide mission. We're down to two rigs. How long do you think it'll be before she cracks? Half a day? Less? Look.' He stabbed at the battery meter. 'We don't even have enough juice to make it out of here. When they come for us, we'll be sitting dead in the road with our hands in our trousers.'

For a moment Ghazi didn't speak. Then he hit the dashboard with so much force it made Cassady jump. 'We're getting off this mountain,' he shouted. 'And Tagawa's going to get that engine running again. This isn't over yet. You want to throw it away after we've lost so much already? Kaja, Brandt, Wyler, Renfield. The least we can do is try. That's better than sitting around feeling sorry for ourselves because things aren't going perfectly.' He regained his composure. 'Get a grip. You don't have the luxury of doubt up here.'

Cassady held his gaze, the cold flames dying in his eyes. His cheeks burned. 'I'm sorry, Ghazi.' He bowed his head. The layer of grey stubble made him look much older.

'I understand, okay? I don't want to leave them up here any more than you do. But we haven't got a choice.'

'I know.'

'Once we get off this mountain, we'll stop to charge the batteries. Then we'll punch a hole through whatever they throw at us.'

'I wish I could be that confident.'

'It is not a matter of wishing. It is a matter of belief.'

'In what?'

Ghazi didn't answer. Outside, Orion edged forward. He slipped the Old Lady into gear and followed her tracks. Clumps of snow spattered the windshield and the wipers worked overtime to clear them. A few metres further on, the stricken Silkworm lay pressed against the mountain. When Warspite rolled by, Victor gave them a short salute and grinned, but kept the window tight shut. As they crested the incline and rumbled along the next perilous stretch of ground, Ghazi couldn't shake the feeling he would never see the two men again.

3

With around thirty minutes of juice left in their batteries, Orion slammed on the brakes, reversed a hundred metres and shuddered to a halt. Cassady unbuckled his harness and leapt out before Warspite's engine had stopped whirring.

Hearst half jumped, half fell from the cab with her crossbow in hand. She crouched next to the hood of her vehicle, glanced over her shoulder and waved at Cassady to keep down. He ducked as he ran. The snow wasn't as intense as it had been a couple of hours previously, but the ground underfoot wasn't stable.

'What is it?'

'Camp.' She was wired. Flecks of spit gathered in the corners of her mouth. She poked her head above the hood and scanned the road.

Ghazi joined them. Muscles twitched along his jaw. 'What's going on?'

'Hearst saw a camp ahead.'

'Then they must have seen us, too.'

She cupped her hand to her ear. 'Listen.'

'To what?' asked Cassady.

'Exactly. Haven't seen us.'

'That's a big assumption.'

Ghazi peered over the hood. 'I can see it.' He crouched again. 'There's no movement.'

'What do we do?'

'Get closer,' said Hearst. 'Check.'

Cassady shook his head. The pills were twisting her thoughts in a direction he didn't want to go. 'We should push on through in the pantechs. It's much safer.'

'No,' said Ghazi. 'Hearst is right. We don't know what kind of hardware they have in there. All we'd have to do is roll over a spike strip and we're dead in the water. We should take this chance while we have it. Like you said, they won't be expecting us to be driving in this weather.'

Ghazi and Hearst looked at Cassady, waiting for his answer. A thought occurred to him. 'I left my machete in the cab.'

'Then follow behind us.'

Hearst unsheathed a hunting knife from her belt and put it in his hand. Ghazi took out his pistol and racked the slide. They rounded the hood and jogged towards the camp. Dusk would be on them within the hour. Cassady struggled to get his legs moving properly. He expected to hear a challenge or shots at any moment. Through the white screen of snow, he could make out a few squat structures to the left of the trail and a long, rectangular building on the right. Beyond it, a tall antenna swayed in the cold wind.

'Go left,' he whispered to Hearst, and she broke away from them. He and Ghazi stayed close to the lip of the road, where the chasm waited patiently to claim them. Ghazi took the lead, his pistol flashing in his hand. The path was strewn with fist-sized rocks and he stumbled, his head ducking forward as he lost control of his body. Cassady reached out and managed to grab a fistful of his partner's shirt before he fell over the side.

'Got you.'

They stood, letting the adrenaline crest and recede as they peered into the valley below.

Ghazi slapped him on the back. 'Thanks.'

No guards were visible even after they made it to the wall of the long, rectangular building. The only sound came from the creaking antenna and the wind. On the other side of the track, Hearst stood against another building with her crossbow cradled in her arms. Cassady gestured with his hand and she disappeared around the back. He and Ghazi edged to the corner closest to the track and he stuck his head out, trusting his luck to hold. No movement. He signalled for Ghazi to follow. They padded along the track into the camp. Wary eyes rested on every contour and crevice, but still there was nothing. Ghazi drifted away to try one of the doors into the rectangular building. Cassady continued on to the antenna, which was studded with bulbs that didn't burn.

He turned at the sound of metal rattling against metal. The door Ghazi had found was on a guide rail. He pushed it to one side before pressing himself flat against the wall with his pistol held ready. Cassady crouched. Whoever was in there would have heard the noise. Hearst's knife felt lightweight and useless in his hand. He counted sixty seconds. Silence. He signalled to Ghazi, and the mechanic slipped through the doorway.

A call came from within. 'Clear.'

He covered the short distance at a jog and joined Ghazi inside. It was a dorm. Two ranks of stripped beds sat like the teeth of a zipper. Next to each bed was a storage box, all of which he could already see were empty. The rest of the room was bare.

Hearst appeared in the doorway.

'Nobody here. Found this.'

She slung a wad of bound paper over to them. The pages showed fire damage, but the flames had died before they could finish the job. He picked them up and leafed through them, but the text was in a language he didn't recognise.

'Get anything from this?' he asked, tossing it to Ghazi.

Quick fingers flicked the pages over. He shook his head. 'I bet Wyler could have.' He was about to drop it when he paused. 'Wait.' He tore one of the pages free. 'Need more light.'

Outside, he shielded the page from the snow and they crowded around. It was a map. Next to black lines that snaked over the landscape were a series of arrows and numbers etched in pencil.

'Oh, thank you,' said Cassady, closing his eyes in silent prayer. Ghazi smiled. Even Hearst looked less sour.

'I think this is our road,' said Ghazi. Cassady took out Lupo's crude map and held it next to the piece of paper. 'Yes. So this block here must be the camp.'

'Seems like they were excited about this part,' Cassady said, pointing at a brown area further along the track that had been circled and annotated with numbers.

'Ambush,' grunted Hearst.

He squinted at the page. 'That's what I'd assume, too. They're waiting for us there.'

'Why not here?' asked Ghazi.

He bit his bottom lip as he sought a likely answer. 'They can't know how many we are. The only information they have is that we smashed the Zuisudra camp and we took out their vanguard. They're taking no chances. They need the medicine so they can use it as a bargaining chip. They don't want to blow up the rigs. And they don't want us wheeling ourselves into the void if they can help it.' The meaning of his own words hit him in the chest. Knowing the enemy was waiting for them was worse than driving blind. He hid his shaking fingers behind his back.

'Go off-road,' said Hearst.

'How?' asked Ghazi. 'That's almost a sheer drop.'

She gritted a set of discoloured teeth. 'I'd make it.'

'Maybe. But we wouldn't.'

Cassady glanced at the fire-damaged map Ghazi was holding once more. 'Hang on.' With a supreme effort, he managed to keep his hand still and pointed at one of the squares on the map. 'Look. What about this?'

A thin line the width of a hair rested against the page. It emerged from their trail and curved away towards the south, bypassing the ambush point further along the route.

'Could be a pipeline,' said Ghazi. 'Electrical wiring. Anything.'

Cassady studied the page. He willed it not to be a pipeline. 'We'll check it out anyway. We've got nothing to lose. Hearst and I will finish looking over the camp. You go and leave a marker on the road for Victor and Tagawa.'

'What about the batteries? We could charge them here.'

'No.' He pointed at the line on the map. 'First this. Then the batteries.'

The remainder of the search turned up nothing useful. They embarked once more and the two trucks resumed their crawl. Cassady kept his eyes glued to the cliff edge while Ghazi drove.

'You can see it's much too steep,' said Ghazi. He frowned and nudged the wheel. 'It's a pipeline.'

Cassady shot him a look. 'Didn't you tell me earlier about things being a matter of belief?'

A long pause. 'Right.'

The snow stopped, but the chill wind continued to buffet the vehicle. As they drove, the sheer drop flattened out and a thick forest swarmed over the slope. Excitement, fear and belief bloomed in Cassady's chest. The juice bar entered the red. They had minutes left before the Old Lady stopped dead.

'There,' he shouted, slapping the top of the dash. 'Stop.' Ghazi dug in and flashed the lights.

'Back up.' The engine wheezed. 'There. See it?'

Both men stared at a lush wall of forest. Snow dripped from the trees.

'Where?'

He pointed, then rubbed his eyes to make sure he wasn't hallucinating. 'Don't you see it?'

Ghazi followed the line of his finger until his gaze rested on a crease in the ground.

'That's the trail?'

'Yes.' He was sure of it. It cut away from the edge of the road at a 45-degree angle.

'But it doesn't lead anywhere. Look. It's all forest.'

'Wait here.' He unbuckled his harness and left the cab for what felt like the hundredth time that day. The light was failing now. He crunched over the snow to the edge of the road and lowered himself over the side. On hands and feet, he half-crawled, half-slipped to the tree line. He paused, caught his breath and peered at the foliage. There. His fatigue receded and he laughed from deep within himself. They weren't done yet. Taking care not to scratch his hands, he pushed the brambles and leaves aside to reveal a wooden screen. First the wall and now this. Smoke and mirrors, just like Wyler had said. Beyond the screen was the start of a dirt path, evidently intended for quad bikes.

As he kicked the foliage aside, he spotted something threading its way through the planks further down. He crouched down and gently took a piece of wire between his thumb and forefinger. He followed it beyond the screen to the hollow of a nearby tree. Inside was a black box similar to the one Wyler had uncovered at the wall.

He scrambled back up the incline and brushed the snow from his clothes. Ghazi had already set up the turbine for the battery.

'Find anything?'

'They don't have many tricks.' He didn't try to disguise his excitement. 'There's a path between the trees. It's blocked by some kind of wooden gate that we can shift. It's tripwired, but I can deactivate it. We're going over, Ghazi.'

'It's a steep rise. She might roll.'

'Better that than the alternative. We'll charge the batteries, move the gate and clear whatever else is in the way.' He slapped his partner on the arm. 'We still have a chance.'

Ghazi didn't break his composure. 'We'd better work quickly.'

'Okay. Me and you. I'll tell Hearst to rest.'

They hooked up the batteries before piling rocks into two cairns in the middle of the path and tying a piece of tarp to a tree next to the concealed path. If Victor and Tagawa managed to get the Silkworm running again, they would know which way to go. Cassady spent a nervous minute deactivating the box by the tree, and then they set to work on the screen. They used small axes to hack away at the brambles.

'How long before they realise?' grunted Ghazi as he brought his axe down.

'We'll be off this damned mountain before they decide to come and take a look.' Cassady chopped a thorny, arching shoot in half and knocked it clear. 'There. That should do it.' Straining, they lifted the wood and dumped it by the trees. Both men were a little shaken by how much energy it cost them, but it didn't matter. The path into the forest was clear.

Back on the road, they sipped at the mountain water and shared their last two pemmican cakes with Hearst. Turbines spun silently on the roofs of the two pantechs and the battery meters shone yellow.

'This cold might be able to kill you, but at least there aren't any flies up here,' said Cassady through a mouthful of lean meat. 'I don't miss them.'

'I just wish we were here under different circumstances,' said Ghazi. He leaned against Warspite, a blanket over his shoulders, and regarded the forest. 'Look at this place. Green life spilling out in every direction, unchecked and unspoiled and beautiful. I almost can't believe this is how it once was.'

Hearst shook her head. 'Alone, tired, cold, surrounded. Still you see beauty.' She handed him the canteen of water. 'You are crazy.'

Cassady laughed.

'If we make it,' Ghazi said, and hesitated. Since they'd left the Gaean camp, none of the Runners had said a word about getting home. He cleared his throat and continued. 'If we make it and we come back this way, I'm claiming a piece of this land. I don't know how, but I'm going to do it.'

Cassady closed his eyes and his elation at finding the hidden trail faded. A spasm passed through the muscles in the backs of his legs. In a few short hours he would have to force himself back into that cramped cockpit and it would all begin again.

'Or maybe we'll be buried here,' he said, eyes still shut. 'And you'll be part of it.'

4

The trees stood in loose ranks with branches bowed as the two vehicles passed by. The path was well hidden under a layer of dead leaves and wood. During the night, the snow had mostly melted and now only a few streaks of white survived. The depleted convoy advanced slowly, Warspite in the lead with the roof-mounted lamps dialled up to full beam. The canopy overhead protected them from eyes in the sky. The whine of the engines and the murmuring transmissions sounded deafening in the heart of the forest, and the Runners drove with their fingers crossed that there were no Koalition soldiers waiting in the shadows.

Ghazi gritted his teeth and held the wheel at ten-and-two. The suspension was taking a battering despite his best efforts. The trail clearly wasn't intended for anything more than quads and exos, and more than a few times the Old Lady had groaned with discomfort. If they broke down now, he didn't know what they would do. Maybe this had been the Koalition's plan all along. Plant the map, sit back, wait for the last two trucks to shake themselves to a standstill, and then swoop in, finish off the crews and seize the medicine. He gripped the wheel tighter and did his best to clear his mind. They were still alive and they were still moving forward, and that was enough. Nothing else they could do.

'Watch out,' shouted Cassady.

He slammed on the brakes. Blocking their path was a rotting trunk with an ugly fissure running down its centre.

'Lightning strike,' said Ghazi.

'Let's get the saws.'

They had been working for a few minutes when a thick voice called to them.

'Need help?' Hearst's silhouette was a broken mannequin in

the glare of the headlights.

Cassady took his cap off and wiped his forehead. 'Get your head down for a few minutes.' She trudged back up the hill without another word.

Ghazi eyed her back. 'How much longer can she keep it up?'

Cassady didn't answer. As they worked, the flimsy handles of the saws became hot against their palms and blistered their skin. Beads of sweat left dirty streaks and settled in their matted beards. When Ghazi next paused to draw breath, Cassady was moving the saw back and forth at a slower pace.

'What is it?'

'What do you mean?'

'Why are you cutting like that?'

He stopped, the blade deep in the wood, and spat on the ground. 'To give her more time to recover, goddamn it. That's why.'

'An extra ten minutes isn't going to help her.'

'It might.'

'You're kidding yourself, Cass.'

'You're being heartless.'

'I'm being pragmatic. She's made it this far because of her. Not me, not you. She doesn't need any favours from us. The sooner we get this thing out of the way, the sooner we can get out of this place.'

With reluctance, Cassady grabbed the saw and resumed his work. He didn't slow down again until the log had been cut all the way through.

The forest was everywhere, crowding the two men, ready to swallow them without trace as soon as they let their guard down. Dawn was on the way, but the dark tree tops hid all but a few patches of cloud-heavy sky. Ghazi tapped on Orion's window to wake Hearst and her dull black eyes flickered open immediately. He pointed down the hill. She yawned once and nodded.

Back behind the wheel, he guided Warspite with care towards the trunk and the bumper nudged the pieces aside without any difficulties. They bounced over a clump of branches and then they were through.

'Easier than the last one at least,' he murmured, recalling the winches in the rain. Somewhere behind them, Victor and Tagawa followed the markers they had left. Or they had been captured or were dead.

Cassady opened a drawstring pouch, took a pinch of the contents, and offered it to him.

'Hungry?'

'Like a dog.'

While they had been waiting for the batteries to charge at the top of the slope, they had gone foraging for edible plants in the forest and found a few. He stuffed a handful of leaves into his mouth. Chickweed, fleawort, goosefoot and dandelion. It was a bitter mixture, but it was better than nothing. Cassady pressed the canteen into his hand. The water soothed the cramps in his stomach and calmed his mind. He didn't think he would ever tire of its clean taste. He had no desire to go back to dust and chlorine once this was over. Maybe he could come back, like he'd said to Cassady. Find a spot to hole away in, here in this valley of Eden. If he was smart, he could avoid the Koalition. And if he was smarter still, he could do something to subvert their control. Both Sergei and Wyler had talked about civil unrest in this land, though they hadn't seen any signs of it. It was a wild idea, but if he and Cassady could somehow contact the leaders and their intentions were good, they might be able to help. He shook his head. So many ifs. They had to get out first before thinking about getting back in.

As he went to drop the canteen in the space between the seats, Cassady bent over and coughed violently. His eyes bulged. Ghazi slapped him on the back, thinking a leaf had become stuck in his throat, but he twisted away and continued to choke. He retched. The cough lost its intensity, and he wiped his lips with the back of his hand and became quiet again.

'What was that?'

'I don't know,' he gasped. 'Third time it's happened.' He swigged some water.

'You should rest up. You're pushing yourself too hard. I can handle her for now. I'll wake you as soon as anything changes.'

'That isn't fair.'

'Just do it. You won't be much use if you get sick.'

The exhausted Runner leaned his head against the window. Moments later, his snores filled the cab. Ghazi was alone with his thoughts. That cough hadn't sounded good. They'd been pushing themselves to the limit for so many months. Lousy food, little sleep, stress, days and days hunched over in poses that made their tendons tight and their muscles atrophy. Now, with this run, their bodies were finally rebelling. He glanced in the side mirror. None of that seemed to apply to Hearst. She was keeping up just fine.

As the trees became sparser and the incline started to level out, Ghazi killed the row of lights along the top of the truck. Behind him, Hearst did the same. The world was anaemic. There was no snow now. He yawned and scratched the unfamiliar hairs on top of his head and tried to stay focused. Cassady snored into his chest. Ghazi rolled his neck and shook out his arms. Pain lanced through his stomach. The leaves had staved off his hunger for thirty minutes, but no more than that. Next time they stopped, he would crack open one of their last 24-hour packs. No need to save them. Not when they were surrounded by death.

Ashen sky filled the windshield. They had reached the end of the forest. There were no quads, exos, tanks or soldiers in sight. The trail shot out into open country, clearly marked now, cutting through undulating fields of thriving grass and metamorphic rock and thorny plants. Great white clouds piled overhead. It was a beautiful land and Ghazi took it all in. Then he saw it. In the distance. His foot slapped against the brake. His body jerked forward and the harness bit into his shoulders.

'What is it?' cried Cassady, the jolt forcing him awake.

His mouth opened and closed and it took him a second to find his voice. When he did, the words emerged in a whisper. 'A white city.'

5

Hearst, Cassady and Ghazi stood together on the trail and looked on in silence. An urban mirage glittered between the converging sides of two mountains. Massive white towers stood side by side, curved sculptures moulded by giant hands. Around the periphery, smaller buildings huddled together like children seeking the protection of their parents. Masses of greenery sat on roofs, climbed the facades, emerged from openings up and down the towers. Mutant trees grew as high as the smaller buildings, leaves like vital splashes of paint against the gleaming ivory facades. A network of walkways connected the structures, each one large enough for two pantechs to drive on side by side. Flying machines sat on sleek landing pads. And lassoing it all was an orbital six-lane road on stilts whose branches disappeared to the north, south, east and west. On the slopes surrounding the city, huge wind turbines stood in rows as precise as a military graveyard, and their vanes warped the air as they spun.

But there was something else. The city was on fire. One of the tallest towers belched velvet plumes of smoke that rippled over the city. Vehicles large and small buzzed across the walkways and chased each other along the orbital road. Two four-wheeled automobiles spun out of control and crashed into a barrier, and a puff of orange rose above the road. The unmistakable clack-clack of automatic gunfire ricocheted between the buildings. A massive explosion sent a thunderclap through the walls of the valley, and its vibrations carried all the way to the edge of the forest. Other sounds drifted across to Warspite and Orion, too. Cheering, perhaps. Or screaming. As the Runners watched, minute human shapes spilled out onto roofs and platforms. From one balcony, a brilliant red flag was unfurled, and it gushed down the side of the smooth tower and stopped just short of the tops of the mutant trees. A symbol reprinted all the way down the flag was visible for kilometres around: four black lines with a defiant fifth slashing through the others.

Cassady stood with his hands on his hips, not believing his eyes. It was too fantastic. Beside him, Ghazi uttered a warning.

'Look. Drones.'

Cassady brought the binoculars up. Cylindrical black shapes with massive wings cast v-shaped shadows on the mountainsides. When they passed over the city, jets of white gas spurted out from under the wings and drifted down onto the rooftops. The people ran back inside. The drones made a U-turn and headed east. A man dressed in red appeared on one of the landing platforms and aimed a weapon at the retreating machines. A projectile slammed into one of the cylindrical shapes and sent it spinning into the valley.

'What the hell is going on?' Cassady muttered, dropping the binoculars again.

Ghazi turned to him, his liquid eyes shining with urgency. 'Revolution, Cassady. Like Wyler said. It's happening right now.'

'Do we go?' asked Hearst.

'Just wait,' said Ghazi. 'I want to see this.'

More gunfire rattled between the buildings. A convoy of heavy vehicles raced towards the city on the orbital branch from the south. The air shuddered under the weight of the cries coming from the buildings. Thousands of voices screamed murder, defiance, surrender.

'We could help them,' muttered Ghazi.

Cassady glanced at him. 'Are you mad?' He received no response.

'No time for this,' said Hearst. 'Need to go.'

'Let's do it.' He shook Ghazi, who was transfixed by what was happening in the valley. The mechanic reluctantly tore his eyes away. 'Come on.'

They raced back to their trucks, Hearst stumbling as she

went. Cassady threw on his harness and hit the accelerator as Ghazi jumped aboard, his attention still firmly on the city. Warspite burst forward and bounced along the trail. He didn't slow down for rocks or dips. Now out of the trees, they had no cover at all. One of the branches of the orbital road loomed in the steep valley to their left, great stilts holding it aloft. His sweating palms slipped against the wheel. In the distance, the trail disappeared over a ridge. He hoped they would find cover beyond that.

Ghazi tracked the battle through the binoculars.

'What's going on? Have they seen us?'

'No. Men and women on the rooftops dressed in red. Same colour as the banner. They're firing everything they have onto that convoy arriving from the south.' He thumped the dashboard. 'A revolution. They're fighting to live.'

Cassady's attention didn't leave the trail. 'Calm the hell down. Any reinforcements beyond the convoy?'

'On the circular road, yes. Quad bikes, same as the ones that cornered us by the bridge. And a few six-wheeled vehicles, similar to Orion. They look like battering rams. There's a real fight going on. I wish we could get closer.'

'What in the hell is wrong with you?'

His question was met with silence once again.

'Just keep an eye on what's happening overhead. If those drones come back, we've got no place to hide.'

Something exploded behind them. He glanced at the side mirror in time to see Orion lurch to the left. One of the tyres threw out shredded rubber. The rig threatened to tip over. Cassady caught a glimpse of Hearst wrestling with the wheel before the pantech turned side-on and drove head-first off the trail. It picked up speed as it hurtled down the slope into the valley.

Warspite bit into the earth and the two Runners dived out and raced to the edge of the incline. The gunfire sounded like rainfall. More vehicles appeared on the orbital road.

'Get control,' shouted Cassady.

The red pantech crunched over loose rocks and patches of grass. The bare wheel squealed. The taillights flared for a moment and then died. It rocked from side to side, four of its eight tyres leaving the floor.

'Brakes are gone,' whispered Ghazi.

'She's going over.' Cassady held his breath.

Somehow Hearst brought Orion back under control. The wheels hit the ground and locked in unison. One of the rear doors popped free and swung outward. The vehicle slithered along the shale and shuddered as it approached the stilts that held up the orbital road. The underside of the cab thudded into a boulder and it stopped dead with a sickening crunch. A hissing noise rolled up the slope. White smoke rose from under the hood.

They waited. The cab doors remained shut. Ghazi still held the binoculars in his hand. Cassady grabbed them and held them up.

'Do you see her?'

He didn't respond. He trained his sights on the driver's door. Open it, he thought. Wake up and put your hand on the handle and push it open. Show us you're okay and we'll come for you. But the only movement came from the wisps of smoke spiralling out from underneath the hood.

'Cass.'

'We have to get down there.' He threw the binoculars back to Ghazi. His fingers dug into his thighs. He paced at the edge of the trail, looking for a way to descend the slope. He would have to slide through the gravel and mud and hold on to the exposed plant roots.

Another explosion sounded and his gaze was involuntarily drawn to the city. The fire in the tall building had reached the lower floors. The wind snatched more screams from the streets and dumped them on the trail.

'Help me find a way down,' he said.

'We can't,' said Ghazi.

'Why the hell not?'

'She's gone.'

The two words hung between them.

Cassady launched himself at Ghazi. They fell back, landing heavily on the track. He swung blindly with his right and clenched his teeth against a sudden hot pain in his knee. A fist struck him in the temple and streaks of white flared before his eyes. Another blow took the breath out of his lungs. Ghazi rolled on top of him and he felt his arms being pinned. A white-haired silhouette blocked out the rest of the world.

'Don't be stupid,' Ghazi panted. 'We have to get out of here.'

'No chance,' he managed to hiss through the pain.

'Either you come with me now or I leave you here.'

'That's my rig.'

'I'm going on. We're not throwing this away now. Every minute counts.'

'I don't give a damn about those scientists.'

'Neither do I. This is about our own survival. We need to get out of here. Climb down into that gulley and you lose your life. Look how close those stilts are. She's practically underneath the road.'

'They can't see her from up there.'

'You can hear what's happening. You saw the drones. The Koalition isn't going to stop sending reinforcements. They'll be all over this hill before we make it down. I'm sorry about Hearst, but she knew the risk. She wouldn't sacrifice herself for you and you know it. Let her go. Or I'm gone.'

'Ghazi,' he pleaded.

There was no response. He looked into the man's eyes. He wasn't lying. The person he'd come to rely on the most would leave him if he had to. Survival trumped compassion. So why not let him go? It was over anyway. Show him you can face death alone, without the fear that seized you so long ago and never relinquished its grip.

'Okay,' he gasped.

'Okay what?'

'Let me up. We'll go.'

'Co-seat.'

'Yes.'

Ghazi stood and hauled him to his feet. Cassady took a last look at the stricken pantech at the bottom of the valley. The smoke had stopped. Everything was still. He shielded his eyes with his hand and peered at the cab doors, willing them to open. Warspite's engine murmured and the wheels rolled.

He ran to his rig, jumped onto the running board and yanked the door open. Ghazi didn't look at him as he clambered into the co-seat. He pulled his jacket around him, feeling more powerless than ever. A reflection of the city smouldered in his mismatched pupils.

'That's no way for somebody to die. She deserved better than that.' He looked at the man he no longer recognised. 'We're next. You know that.'

'We may yet save ourselves.'

The truck threaded across the open ground and over the ridge. A copse of trees stood out in the distance. The ivory buildings glittered. The red flag with the symbols fell without ceremony and landed in the trees. More drones appeared in the sky and released their gas over the landing platforms. Bodies fell from the roofs. Another convoy of heavy vehicles swung around on the orbital and raced towards the towers. Neither Cassady nor Ghazi passed comment. The track they were on arched right and then down into a crease in the earth. The city disappeared and the dense wood welcomed them. They were invisible again. And they were alone.

6

Ghazi sat in the cab with his whittling knife and the chunk of basswood. The elephant was nearly finished. He ran the blade in the direction of the grain. Shavings fell into his lap. He blew on the newly cut area and rubbed a thumb over the wood. He held it up to his eye. Yes. It was ready. He set it down on the dashboard and the inanimate animal stared back at him, no more alive than anything else in the vicinity.

They were close to the border. After the white city, they'd headed for the town Lupo had said was abandoned. It had taken all their remaining juice. The mud trail had joined a steep single-lane asphalt road that looked as though it hadn't been used in years, and they'd followed it without encountering anybody as it had wound its way down the elevated terrain. The town, a patchwork of dilapidated brick and mortar buildings, had appeared on a hillside at dusk. Other than the green puddles of grass and weeds that stretched across the streets, it was devoid of life. After making a reconnaissance with the binoculars, Ghazi had guided Warspite into a building that offered a good view of the road in both directions, and they had set up tripwires around the perimeter. A short while later Cassady had disappeared without a word.

It was quiet. He should've been pacified, but something bothered him. One of the batteries, the unit Sergei had given them at the stockade, was playing up. He'd had to spend ten minutes tinkering with it before the yellow LED light switched on. He didn't know what was wrong with it, and there wasn't much he could do about it now. At least it was charging. Tomorrow, when they hit the border, they would probably need all the juice they could get. There was no Wyler to show them a back door this time. He prayed the unrest would keep the Koalition occupied until they were out. They just needed another few hours.

He slipped one of the last blitz pills into his mouth and swallowed it dry, then grabbed the wooden elephant and left the cab. His boots left prints as he wandered through the rooms. Faint, painted lines on the floors suggested the building might have once been a workshop or a garage. Now it was the realm of dust balls and sand. There was no furniture, no provisions, nothing they could use or scavenge. The smell of mould and slow decay caught in the back of his throat. In one room he found an adjustable spanner in a pile of rubble, but its jaws and screw were rusted solid. He stood it upright in the pile. On a whim, he took the elephant from his pocket and placed it next to the spanner. He said a prayer for Hearst and asked for her forgiveness. Then he went outside.

It was already dark. The wind turbine spun silently on the roof. He spotted Cassady sitting with his back against a wide, one-storey building whose doors had been removed. His legs were stretched out in front of him and his shoulders were slumped. He looked thin. Worse, he looked defeated. Ghazi felt underneath his own shirt. If he'd wanted to, he could've counted the ribs.

Cassady didn't lift his head when he approached. 'Find anything?'

'Place is dead.'

He found a spot on the ground beside Cassady and stifled a yawn.

'I failed them,' his partner muttered. 'They're dead because of me.'

'That's not true.'

'Hearst, Kaja, Brandt, Renfield, Wyler, Victor and Tagawa. The list is much too long. They trusted me. I was supposed to get them through.'

'Victor and Tagawa could still be alive.'

Cassady shook his head. 'Why pretend?'

'It isn't over yet.'

'You're right,' he snarled suddenly. 'All we have to do now is find a way over the border and through land we've never laid eyes on to get to a place that might not exist.'

'You knew that from the start.'

'I didn't think we'd be the only ones left.'

'Lupo did. Faustine did. That's why they sent four trucks.'

'Goddamn it.'

Ghazi rubbed his eyes with the heels of his hands. The artificial kick of the pill couldn't shift his bone-deep tiredness. 'I'm sorry about Hearst. Truly.'

'You were quick enough to leave her.'

He hesitated. 'If we don't obey our will to survive, what chance do we have? I listened to my instinct. It told me to go. That's why I'm sitting here talking to you now instead of lying dead on the mountainside.'

'You're so sure of death.'

'No, there are no certainties. But the likelihood was there all the same.'

'How can you be so detached?'

'I'm not. But I can't afford to give in to my emotions now. Not while we're still in danger.'

Cassady grunted and turned to him. 'Would you have used that gun on me?'

Ghazi didn't avoid his gaze. 'You know the answer.'

They looked at each other, not saying anything. Finally, Cassady nodded.

'Okay.' The word was equal parts resignation and resolve. He shivered and scratched at the greasy hair on the sides of his head. 'Do we have any food left?'

'The rations Tagawa found on the mountain and a 24-hour box. Everything else is gone.'

'Let's break open the box. We'll eat it all.'

Ghazi checked on the battery before they ate. The LED was

still on, but it wasn't charging. He disconnected the lead, cleaned the end and checked the port. He plugged it back in again and watched, but it remained unresponsive.

'One of the batteries took some damage,' he said when he joined Cassady out on the deserted road. 'Charge won't reach halfway.'

The Runner pushed half the contents of the ration box across to him without changing his expression. 'It doesn't matter now. Eat something.'

After they'd finished devouring the virtually tasteless packets, Ghazi lay back with his head against the concrete. His stomach complained at the sudden influx of food, and the blitz pill made it difficult for him to clear his mind. But at least things were straight between him and Cassady again. That was enough.

Cassady cleared his throat. 'What was with you back there, by the city? You looked hypnotised.'

Ghazi propped himself up on an elbow. 'I don't know. I saw something. A spirit I haven't seen in the north for a long time. Something more than a desire to just survive.'

'What do you mean?'

'They were working together. Pulling in the same direction, fighting for something worthwhile. Not like us with our uneasy truces that crumble as soon as they meet the first bump in the road. We collaborate for survival's sake and nothing more. What we saw was a movement. It made sense to me, and I wanted to be part of it.'

'You don't even know what they were fighting for.'

'No, but Wyler said enough to make me think they were on the right side. Imagine if they win against the Koalition. Novus could be our Eden, Cass. With the technologies they have, the water reserves, the manpower, we could start again. Export it into the surroundings and rebuild. Slowly, but surely. It'll take decades, maybe even centuries, but at least we'd be moving forward. All we're doing now is prolonging the inevitable.'

'You're too quick to trust. Let's say they do win, whoever they are. What if they take this place for themselves, man the borders and destroy anybody who comes too close? New management, same procedures.'

Ghazi didn't respond straight away. When he did, his voice was quiet. 'All the same, it'd be worth finding out, don't you think?'

Cassady didn't answer. Ghazi didn't push it. The white city burned in his eyes, and he relived the moment when the crimson banner with its five slashing lines raced down the outside of the tower and hung there, defiant, vital, able to be seen for kilometres around. A surge of excitement momentarily displaced his exhaustion. That was where he needed to be. He was sure of it.

Half an hour passed in silence. The cramps in Ghazi's stomach subsided and his thoughts settled enough for his eyes to close and his head to drop to his chest. Then a noise at the top of the hill shook him awake.

'Hear that?' whispered Cassady, the tension clear in his voice.

'Yes.' He swallowed. A vehicle was approaching the town. Together, they jumped up and ran to the building where Warspite slept and hid by the door. Cassady blinked rapidly, one hand curling around the handle of his machete, the other flat against the doorframe. Ghazi pressed up close behind, the pistol grip slippery between worn-out fingers. The fact that he had a full clip to loose on whoever was out there offered scant comfort. An engine whined and the crunch of tyres against gravel filled his ears until it became white noise. The dusty leather of Cassady's flight jacket was undercut by the sharp tang of sweat. Twin beams turned the road a sickly yellow and light seeped through the open doorway. They had come this far, but they couldn't run any further. They could only die. He readied himself for the end and hoped it would be quick.

'Wait,' said Cassady.

'What?'

'That engine.'

Without another word, he stepped out into the middle of the road and held up his hands.

'What are you doing?' hissed Ghazi. But he wasn't listening. He walked towards the light.

Ghazi held his pistol out in front of him and left the cover of the building. The hood of a large rectangular vehicle hid behind a pair of powerful headlights. It stopped a few metres away and the transmission whined and died. The doors swung open and an elegant form leapt out from the driver's side, a rifle slung over its shoulder. On the other, a body limped down the steps to the road. Together, they approached the two men standing with their mouths open in disbelief.

Tagawa's face was grimy and his dark uniform was spattered with mud. A cut graced his forehead. Victor's arm lay in a sling and he grimaced as he walked. There was no trace of the boys who had left the stockade.

'Told you we'd see each other again,' said Tagawa by way of greeting.

Cassady smiled and stuck out his hand. 'I didn't believe you for a minute. I'm glad I was wrong.'

Ghazi grinned too, but quickly became sober again when he saw the expression on Victor's face. 'What is it?'

'We got Hearst in the back. She's in a bad way.'

His stomach turned over and a dread he'd never known wound its way around his skull. Cassady let out a strangled cry.

'She's alive?'

'For now.'

The Runner pushed past the two younger men, stalked to the back of the pillbox and threw the doors open. Ghazi stood, rooted to the spot, staring at nothing. The blood ran hot in his veins. He'd made a terrible mistake.

Victor winced as he bent his injured arm. 'What happened

out there?'

Ghazi looked into the eyes of the men standing before him. 'I don't know.' He struggled to draw breath. 'I thought she was dead.'

'She ain't got long. We tried to make her comfortable. She's flat out on a stretcher.'

'Wh–where did you find her?' he stammered.

'On the trail. When it came out of the forest and hit the open country. Picked her up before we were attacked.'

He wavered on his feet. 'She climbed back up the valley.'

Tagawa had been watching him through narrowed eyes, and now he reached out and placed a hand on Ghazi's shoulder. 'Take it easy. There'll be time enough to talk about this later. We should get her inside. Is there somewhere we can hide the wheels?'

Ghazi glanced at the Silkworm, dents and damage all over its body, and was overwhelmed by an image of Orion hurtling down the slope before coming to a sudden sickening halt. His own words rang in his ears. She knew the risk. She's gone. Only she wasn't. Not yet. 'Three buildings down on the left,' he said in a monotone. 'A garage. That's where we are. There's room enough for you.' Cassady hadn't reappeared since he'd climbed into the pillbox. 'I'd better go and help him.' He imagined the form lying in the back and felt the terror that came with the moment of reckoning. He wanted to pray, but no words came to him. He was alone in this.

'Calm and easy, Ghazi,' said Victor.

Tagawa held out his arm for his partner, who leaned against him for support. Together they limped back to the Silkworm. Ghazi followed on leaden legs.

7

Cassady stood frozen in the metal sarcophagus. Something had burned through the roof and created a ragged hole and the night sky was visible above the woman's head. He wanted to help her, but his body refused to respond to his commands. He tried to speak, but his trachea was pinched in a vice. Nothing could go up or down. He struggled to draw in air. Panic ballooned in his chest and exploded and sloshed around his stomach. Then he could breathe again, and he sucked in great ragged gulps that made him dizzy. Her face was a mask of blood. As he stared, heavy eyelids opened. A hand quivered and rose and thick fingers curled towards him. She needed his help, but he had none to give.

Footsteps sounded on the road and the cab doors slammed home. A voice came through from the front.

'Hold on, Cassady,' said Victor. 'We're taking her inside.'

The engine awoke with a sigh and with it his control over his body was restored. He dropped to his knees and grasped the hand that had reached out for him. Hearst's breath emerged in hot, painful spurts. The pantech swayed from side to side and rolled forward at walking pace. With care, he wiped at the red film covering her eyes, nose and cheeks and searched for the source. She had a deep wound at the top of her forehead. Her clothes were torn and her left leg was a mess of black and red.

Heavy boots clanged against the rear step as somebody jumped onto the moving vehicle. He didn't have to turn around to know who it was.

'She's alive, Ghazi,' he growled.

'I know.'

'You left her.'

'This isn't the time. Once Tagawa pulls up, we need to get her out of this box.'

Cassady's vision blurred and he gripped the hand tighter. Hearst's head rolled from side to side. He hated the man. But it could wait.

The Silkworm struggled up the ramp into the garage where Warspite slumbered. The engine clicked off and Victor and Tagawa climbed out.

Cassady moved to one side and gestured to Ghazi. 'Help me lift her.'

They grunted with the effort of hoisting the stretcher, but managed to manoeuvre Hearst to the doors. She whispered something about Orion that neither man understood. Victor stood by the rear door, his injured arm pressed to his chest, and watched as they lifted her out and placed her on a litter Tagawa was still throwing together. When he was done, the Japanese crouched next to Cassady and spoke in a quiet tone.

'Do you still have your med kit?

'Yeah.' His mind was working in slow motion.

'We need it.'

Cassady placed Hearst's hand in Tagawa's and went to Warspite. He turned on the headlights. Twisted shadows merged and broke apart on the wall opposite. In the cab, he popped the lock on the storage bin and threw aside canteens, boxes and tools until he found the kit. When he returned to the litter, he found that Ghazi had cut Hearst's trousers off. For the first time, the Runners saw the intricate tattoos on her legs. A tree with roots that curled and blossomed, a sliver of moon, a supernova star, an ornate bow with an arrow. The geometric patterns on her skull were designed to repel; these tattoos were a glimpse into something much deeper. The dichotomy caught in their throats. In the end they hadn't known her at all.

Tagawa pressed a rag to Hearst's forehead and whispered to her in Japanese as she drifted in and out of consciousness. Cassady cracked open the med kit. Despair boiled inside him. All that remained was a bottle of painkillers, a pair of soiled gloves and a tube of superglue. They'd used the gauze and the bandages and the drugs to try to make Kaja comfortable. There was nothing left for Hearst. He held it open to Tagawa.

'Does the Silkworm have one?'

'No. It was destroyed when we were attacked.'

Ghazi took one of the rags from the floor and ripped it into shorter lengths before wrapping it around Hearst's green-grey thigh. Gently, he moved Tagawa to one side and bound her head. With the livid wound hidden from view, she looked more like herself. Next, he sliced through her sodden shirt and peeled it away from her skin to reveal a wound in her stomach. His body went limp.

The heat from Warspite's headlights splashed against the backs of their necks. Hearst groaned and her eyes fluttered for a moment and then closed. Her breathing became steady. Cassady looked at the three men in turn and asked the question that didn't have an answer. 'What can we do for her?'

Ghazi shook his head. 'Nothing. Stomach acid's been seeping out of there for hours. We can't do anything about the infection.'

'That's it?'

He bowed his head. There was no response from the other two.

Cassady picked up a blanket and laid it over her. She moved her head from side to side, but her eyes remained shut. Her lips were dry and brittle. He ground his teeth and swallowed to get rid of the thick taste of blood. He pressed the back of his hand to her cheek. It wouldn't be long. But the fact was she was still alive. He hadn't gone down into the valley after her. He'd allowed himself to be led away like a dog, and his punishment was to stand and watch the life ebb out of the one person he thought could never be killed.

The silence stretched, broken only by her unconscious sobs of discomfort. 'What happened?' said Victor finally.

Cassady ignored the question, so Ghazi took up the slack.

'When the trail left the forest, we saw the city on fire, so we stopped. It was after we picked up again and made a break for it that her tyre exploded. The one she replaced after the Zuisudra. She tried to control it, but it was too much. Took off downhill and her truck hit a rock.'

'And then we left her,' said Cassady tonelessly. The others looked at him. 'We left her when she needed help.'

'Come on,' said Victor. 'You couldn't have known.'

'We could've climbed down the hill to check. We could've waited longer than we did. We could've done something.' He threw a venomous glance at Ghazi. 'But instead we saved ourselves.'

Tagawa rubbed at the downy hairs under his chin. 'Nobody can make the right decision every time.'

Hearst groaned and her eyelids trembled and snapped open. She looked around, trying to understand where she was. Cassady moved into her line of sight and reached under the blanket for her hand.

'You're safe,' he said, making an effort to sound as calm as possible. 'You made it.'

'Where am I?' she asked in a skeleton whisper.

'With us.'

'Don't remember getting here.' She grimaced. 'Water.'

Cassady lifted a canteen to her mouth. The water spilled around the corners of her lips and pooled in the crevices of her neck. She shifted her head when she'd had enough. Her voice regained a little of its edge.

'Puncture.'

'We saw it,' said Ghazi.

'Hit my head.' Her eyes opened wide and she tried to sit up. Cassady placed his hand on her shoulder and pushed her back against the litter.

'Orion.'

'Don't worry about that now.'

'Water,' she croaked. Cassady held the canteen up to her lips again.

'Alone. Fire and screaming. Dead ground all around.'

Cassady held her hand between his. 'You're not alone now. There's no fire. Just us.'

Her breathing became faster. She looked from Cassady to Ghazi and back. 'Death is coming.'

Cassady bit his lip. He didn't know what to do.

'Where is Katarina?'

Ghazi took her other hand. 'She'll be along soon. Be calm.'

Her breathing continued to increase. She looked beyond the pair of them and recoiled at an invisible presence. Her hand was cold and the tips of her fingers were grey.

'Be calm,' Ghazi said again. Hearst's chest heaved once. Her lips parted and surprise registered in her eyes as they turned to glass. Her eyelids slid down and stopped halfway.

Cassady placed her hand by her side, stepped back and wiped his cheek with his sleeve. He hated himself. He hated Ghazi. And part of him hated her for returning from the dead. She'd come back to haunt them, as if to prove she was stronger all along, and now he had to deal with whatever came next.

'Goddamn it.' His voice cracked. He had to stop himself from falling to his knees.

Victor's head dropped. Tagawa's gaze fell to the body on the litter.

'We can't afford to lose it now,' he said to all of them.

'This son of a bitch run.' Victor raised his head again and looked at Cassady. 'I'm sorry.'

'For what?'

The younger man flinched. 'For the way it turned out.'

Ghazi brushed Hearst's eyes closed. It was enough of a provocation. Cassady walked around the litter, pulled back and slammed an iron fist into the mechanic's chest. He went sprawling across the floor. Cassady approached on shaking legs, only half-aware of what he was doing.

'Don't touch her.'

Ghazi rolled to one side, but made no move to defend himself. 'I made a mistake. I'm not going to fight you over this.'

Cassady spat on the floor at his feet. 'You and your damn single-minded beliefs.'

Before he could make up his mind to do anything else, Tagawa pinned his arms and dragged him backwards.

'Control yourself.'

Victor stepped in front of Ghazi. 'It wasn't his fault, Cassady. It was a judgement call. Anybody could've made it.'

'I'm done.' He shook himself free of Tagawa's grip and went to the litter again, where he rearranged the blanket around Hearst. His body still shook. He stood with his back to them all, his cheeks burning with anger, shame and impotence.

Victor hauled Ghazi to his feet and the three of them retreated to the corner of the room. They spoke in low voices, but Cassady could hear them all the same.

'What happened on the mountain?' asked Ghazi.

'We worked on her for a few hours straight,' said Victor. 'Damn near froze to death. Never thought I'd say it, but it made me realise: give me hot days and warm nights. Least I know how to cope with them. Anyway, we got her started and we reached that camp. Was it empty when you got there?'

'Deserted. But Hearst found a map.'

'Which told you about the trail through the forest.'

'Exactly.'

'Figured one of you had eagle eyes or something.' Victor grimaced as he recalled the ride through the forest. 'It was choppy. I was sure the engine would give out again, but it held. The city jumped out at us after we broke away from the trees. Every building was on fire, it looked like. The ring-road, too. Some sight.'

Tagawa cut in. 'It was the drones that made me stop and

think. They were like a swarm of flies, and they dropped bombs and gas and foam on anything that moved. I don't know how anybody could have survived in there. Wyler talked about how the Koalition controls the state, but being prepared to destroy a city and everybody in it is a special kind of fanaticism. Nobody should have that power.'

'Is that when you were attacked?' asked Ghazi.

Victor nodded. 'Yeah. While we were dead on the hillside taking it all in, two drones peeled off from the swarm and headed straight at us. It was too late to turn her around and get her back into cover, so we made a run for it over open ground. Hideki went into the back with the rifle and I held her as steady as I could.'

'I hit one,' said Tagawa. 'But they kept coming.'

'The first dropped its guts right in front of us,' said Victor. 'Bombs hitting the ground, flames covering the windows. I was sure we were dead. The vibrations damn near shook my arms off. But I kept my foot down and prayed the engine wouldn't break down. The second one dumped foam on us. Corrosive as hell. Most of it missed, but some ate into the back.'

Ghazi rubbed the new bruise on his chest. 'I saw the hole.'

'Victor hit the brakes and the drones turned back towards the city,' said Tagawa. 'I suppose they had nothing else to attack us with. And that's when I saw her struggling up the incline. She didn't even respond when I got out and called to her. She just kept climbing.'

Cassady flinched as he listened to Tagawa's account, but he forced himself to remain silent.

Victor lifted his bound arm slightly. 'That's how I did this. I slid down the hill to get her and landed on it like an idiot. Might be broken. Hurts like hell in any case.'

'You were lucky.'

'I guess. Anyway, we managed to get her up onto the track as quick as we could and bundled her into the back. Hideki took the wheel after that and we gunned it away before anything else decided to try to call time on us.'

Tagawa's tone became more sombre. 'I don't know if you noticed, but the foam that ate through us landed on the medicine crate. I used the water to try to flush it out. It didn't work. The supplies are destroyed.'

None of the men spoke for a few moments.

'Two cargos in a day,' said Ghazi.

Tagawa rubbed his hands together as he tried to remove the dried blood that stained his palms. 'That's how it is. At least you still have Brandt's.'

'We could transfer it to the Silkworm.'

'No, keep hold of it,' said Victor. 'We're open to the elements now. We'll run bodyguard for you.'

'How are your batteries?'

'Working as well as they can.'

'One of ours has bitten it.'

'Then you've gotta swap with us.'

Cassady's impassive gaze left Hearst's body and he turned. He couldn't keep quiet any longer. He called across to the three men. 'I won't take it.'

Victor wasn't deterred. 'Our engine might not hold and we have no cargo. If you've got a dud, you've gotta let us help you.'

'I'm not condemning you to death as well.'

'You have not condemned any of us,' said Tagawa in a measured tone. 'We make our own decisions and we know the goal. Survival is a bonus.'

Cassady had heard enough. He walked away, out through the open doorway of the garage, along the road, between gutted homes and empty stores and other monuments to a long-dead culture. No footsteps echoed behind him. He stumbled blindly through the streets, not caring where he ended up, and turned onto an avenue of buildings that were silver and yellow-grey in the darkness. A tall one with a concrete staircase draped around its exterior called to him. A vicious kick sent a gate that hung from its hinges crashing to the floor, and he shuffled up the stairs to the roof. Animal faeces and plastic flotsam coated the floor. Cylindrical metal drums congregated in the centre. Panting, he dragged one to the edge of the roof, wiped the rust from his hands and sat down. He balled a grime-streaked fist and pressed it against his forehead. A coughing fit shook him up and down until he was exhausted. He spat between his legs. It was frothy and streaked with something darker.

He looked out at the uneven mass of concrete, but saw only the massed faces of the dead. A few stars winked blue and white, millions of kilometres distant. The trees on the mountains hissed. A deep bass rumble forced its way over the rocky hills, landed on the deserted town and dispersed. When the air had become calm again, a bird whistled from one of the rooftops. Alone and unwatched, Cassady allowed the grief to bleed out. His body trembled and his cheeks became wet. After a time, he growled at himself to stop. He rose from the metal drum and made for the stairs. He wasn't yet ready to join the ones he had failed. But the hour was close. Of that he was certain.

8

As night disintegrated and the sky turned a morose grey, the four remaining Runners placed Hearst's body on top of a meagre pyre and lit it. Cassady was the one to push the flaming torch into the pile of kindling, and the flames snarled and spat as they explored the rags. Smoke twisted into dark braids. When the air became ripe with the smell of burning flesh, it was time to go.

They had moved the rigs out of the garage and onto a steep road that would take them clear of the town. The Silkworm sat behind Warspite, its rear doors held together with a length of chain wrapped around the handles. The men walked from the pyre to their vehicles in silence, each one lost in thought.

As Tagawa brought his foot down on the cab step, he turned to look up the hill. His eyes narrowed until only two flashes of white were visible. Slowly, he dropped his foot back to the floor, filled his lungs and barked a warning.

'They're here.'

Ghazi jerked his head around. Two humanoid machines, each with a single pilot, stood side by side on the road near the top of the hill. Exoskeletons. But they were nothing like the patchjob exos in the north. These ones were large, yet streamlined, with aquiline armour plating on the arms and legs. The pilots were barely visible behind the roll cage and harness and heavy chest plate, and their faces were encased in black helmets.

The two machines leapt forward at a frightening speed. Pistons rose and fell. A sinister mechanical wheezing filled the air.

'Go,' shouted Ghazi.

The doors to both vehicles flew open and then slammed shut. Cassady pumped the starter and flung Warspite into gear. Both rigs picked up speed as they rolled down the hill. The machines hammered the dirt and made a booming noise with each mechanised step. Ghazi kept his attention on the reflection in the side mirror. The Silkworm chased their tail as the machines bore down on the pantechs. Realisation gripped him. They didn't have the head-start they needed to outrun the exos.

'They'll catch us.'

The response came through gritted teeth. 'I know.'

As Ghazi watched, the Silkworm's headlights flashed and the vehicle stopped dead. Without thinking about it, he pulled the ugly pistol free of the holster, flung open the door and jumped clear of the truck.

'What the hell are you doing?' shouted Cassady after him.

But Ghazi was already charging up the hill, away from Warspite. The pistol was a dead weight in his hand. The full clip Tagawa had thrown to him on the mountain sat in the grip, ready to be unleashed. Screeches and thumps landed like bombs. Helmeted heads bobbed behind the roll cage. The exos powered forward. Breath exploded from his lungs. He raised the pistol, but the front sight jerked up and down as he ran. Victor leaned out of the window and shouted something at him that was drowned out by the sound of metal striking the earth. Now the exos were close enough for him to spot a coloured insignia on the chest plate. The one in front raised an arm and bullets spewed out that rattled the Silkworm's rear doors. He stopped in the shadow of the pantech, his finger dropping from the trigger guard, and he aimed at the exo and squeezed until the clip was empty. The slugs left impact marks on the chest armour. The last round split the pilot's helmet and the exo fell to one side, a knee joint digging into the tarmac while the arm swung outward and emptied its bullets into the wall of a nearby building. Ghazi dropped to the floor and rolled underneath the truck.

The Silkworm's top hatch flew open and a thin, pale figure dressed in black emerged. Tagawa plugged the old bolt-action rifle against his shoulder and aimed it at the machine that was still standing. Before it could bring its arm up to fire, the rifle roared and the pilot jerked in his harness. The legs of the beast became twisted. Tagawa cycled the cartridge and fired again. A mechanical arm reached out wildly and grabbed the top of the truck. The Silkworm groaned and sank on its suspension. A third shot at point blank range hit the pilot in the neck. The exo toppled over, tearing a piece of the Silkworm's roof off as it fell. It whined pitifully in the dust. Ghazi rolled out from underneath the pantech, scrambled to his feet and, with his practised gaze, searched the machine for a control panel. Finally, he flicked a heavy switch on the arm and the exo fell still. From the first machine came the guttural moan of a man dying.

'Are you hurt, Ghazi?'

He glanced up at Tagawa, who stood on the roof with the old rifle's muzzle pointing at the sky.

'No. Good shooting.'

'Yes. It was.'

Victor climbed out of his truck and limped over to the machine Ghazi had taken down. He grimaced as he spied the gaping wound in the side of the pilot's head. The man groaned.

'Hideki, hand me your knife.'

Tagawa tossed it to the floor. 'Too much death. I hope it's worth it.'

Ghazi turned away. He didn't want to watch. Warspite idled near the bottom of the hill. Cassady hadn't gone far without him. He poked his head out the window and made a circle with his index finger. Ghazi returned the gesture.

When the moaning had been cut short, he removed the helmet from the pilot that Tagawa had killed. A well-fed face stared back at him through frozen eyes. Small tattoos ran down his left temple and cheek. He turned out the pockets of the pilot's uniform and found a plastic card with a chip. He carried nothing else.

'Look,' said Victor. He pulled a rifle free from the arm of the exo. Sleek and compact, it was light enough to hold in one hand.

'Yours has one too.'

Ghazi unclipped it and ran his hands over the weapon's contours. Compared to his crude pistol, it was a surgeon's scalpel intended for precision work.

'Automatic?' asked Tagawa from the roof.

'Yes.'

'One for each pantech.'

Ghazi made a quick search of the rest of the machine, and found two extra magazines and a container of water in a storage cavity at the rear.

'Can she still move?' he asked, nodding at the stricken Silkworm.

'She'll be fine,' said Victor.

'Then let's get going.'

Ghazi tucked the rifle against his arm, pocketed the magazines and set off down the hill. His adrenaline was spent. Exhaustion reached out with a thousand invisible hands, indiscriminately twisting and pulling on every fibre. To dispel it, he tried to summon an image of the scientists hiding deep underground. Silhouettes in a white mist were as far as he got.

The engine was already singing. He placed the rifle between the seats and stowed the extra magazines. The seat pressed against his back, legs, arms and head; this was his own exoskeleton. Warspite left the deserted town behind.

'That was stupid.' Cassady kept his eyes on the road as he spoke. 'Now you're suddenly ready to sacrifice yourself for the others?'

Ghazi placed his hands on his knees. They were stained and calloused and the veins stood out like mountain ridges. 'It isn't the right time for this.'

'You just risked your life to save them.'

'Or to save us.'

'Why them and not Hearst?' insisted Cassady. 'Are they worth more than she was? Where do you draw the line?'

The trail bent away from the rocky landscape. It flattened out and joined a gravel track that cut a meandering path through lush greenery. Cassady opened Warspite up.

'Do you even have an answer?'

Ghazi let out a low breath that collected on the window pane. 'I could say my mistake will haunt me until I die. But you know that already. Talking isn't going to bring her back. And neither is your loss of faith.'

'Faith,' Cassady spat. On either side of the road anorexic trees leaned in to listen. 'You're always talking about faith, but you're a hypocrite. You speak of people like they're there for you to study, like you can see something I can't. Let me tell you something. Spirituality means nothing if you throw it away in an instant of self-preservation.'

'You could've gone down into that valley without me.'

'And you would've taken the rig. My rig.'

'We've gone over this already.'

'You twist situations to meet your world view. That's all you do. And she's dead because of it. The blood is on your hands. You understand that?'

'Do you want to hit me again? Do it if it helps. Stop the truck and kick me to pieces.'

Cassady looked over at him. 'Goddamn it. Why do you have to talk like that?'

'Because I'm on your side. We're still in this together.'

The other man's voice cracked. 'Just leave me the hell alone, Ghazi. I don't want anything to do with you.'

The town on the border had been left to wither in the shadow of the metal-and-concrete wall that separated Novus from the southern lands. Nothing stirred. No soldiers, no civilians, no wildlife. The two vehicles approached without caution, gunning it down a sharp hill until they reached a vantage point overlooking the town.

On the roof of Warspite's cab, Cassady held the binoculars to his eyes and bit his bottom lip. Ghazi waited beside him. Sweat collected in the tough strands of his beard. They had finally emerged from under the bank of cloud and now the cold of the mountains was already fading into memory. This area of the state evidently didn't fall within the Koalition's pre-Change protection net. A familiar sun warmed the metal and the tarp and drew out its musty scent. Beyond the wall, a great sea of sand and scrubland lapped against the defences. Vehicle carcasses and a few rock formations sat under an infinite blue dome that made everything else feel insignificant. Other than the sand, it wasn't much different to the north. Somewhere out there was a road that would take them to La Talpa. He cupped his hand to his ear and listened. The only sounds were Cassady's breathing, the wind and the heartbeat of the Old Lady.

He broke the silence that had been in place since the exo attack. 'See anything?'

Cassady didn't answer immediately. The binoculars swished left and right. 'I don't see a way out.' He swept the area. 'Wait. That's it. Over there.'

He pointed. On the western edge of the town, two rusted gates interrupted the wall. A tarmac road ended a few meters before the gates, flanked by two forlorn watchtowers and a sagging guardhouse.

'We'll try for it,' said Cassady. His features were set.

'The streets could be tripped.'

'We're going down there.'

He jumped to the ground and went to the Silkworm. Ghazi looked again. Some of the buildings closest to the wall were damaged. The ramparts near the gates showed signs that people had once tried to gain access to Novus from the south. But now the Koalition didn't even station soldiers here anymore. Either they didn't have the resources, or there weren't enough people left alive in the desert lands for it to matter.

Cassady called up to Ghazi. 'Let's go.'

The Silkworm shook, waiting for Warspite to lead off. Ghazi strapped himself in.

'What if the roads are mined?' he asked again as they rejoined the track.

'I don't give a damn.'

They rolled past sandblasted buildings whose roofs had caved in. Sand and plastic piled against doorways and on windowless frames. Rebars poked through fleshy stone like snapped ribs. Faded black marks against the masonry spoke of fighting that had ended long ago.

The hood trembled. Ghazi peered beyond the front of the truck and winced. 'Do you see that?'

Cassady nodded. 'Let's just get to the gate.'

The road was littered with hundreds of bones that had been bleached yellow-white in the sun. Warspite ground them up under its wheels. The sickening noise reverberated around the cab. Ghazi glanced in the mirror to see the pillbox close behind, its front mangled, the roof dented and deformed. The silver symbol no longer glittered. He retrieved the automatic rifle from between the seats and stashed the two magazines in his pockets. He wanted to be ready.

Warspite turned a final corner. The belt of tarmac terminated at a pair of sturdy gates spotted with rust and moss. Cassady kept his foot steady on the pedal until they drew level with the subsiding guardhouse.

'Cover me with that thing.'

They slipped out of the cab and into dry and chalky surroundings. Ghazi held the rifle in both hands, fingers tight against the grip and body. He aimed at the watchtowers and the ramparts, but they were as dead as the rest of the town. Chunks of rubble had been cleared from the road and pushed into piles. At the wall, Ghazi backed up against one of the gates and felt the cool metal through his damp shirt. The Silkworm idled some way behind Warspite with its top hatch flung open. Tagawa held the captured rifle to his shoulder and scanned the nearby buildings for movement.

Cassady studied the gates. 'They're rusted shut. Too heavy to open by hand. If we can get that bar off and hook the winch up, we should be able to pull them open.'

Ghazi put the rifle on the floor and gripped one end of the bar that bound the two gates together. Cassady took the other.

'Ready. Go.'

They lifted. Ghazi grunted and screwed his eyes shut. They were weaker than when they'd set out, and both men dug deep for reserves of strength they weren't sure they had. The bar scraped against the metal. Flakes of rust dropped onto their hands and arms. Their chests heaved. Veins pulsed in their necks. With a final screech the bar came free.

'Drop it,' Cassady managed to gasp.

The bar fell to the floor with an undignified thud. They leaned against the gate and sucked in air. When Ghazi had recovered enough, he scooped up the rifle and staggered away to get the tow cable. Just before he reached the Old Lady, he froze.

Three black shapes stained the sky. They were sleek and tubular, and they cut through the air with purpose.

He shouted a warning. Tagawa jerked around 180 degrees and called down into the cab. Victor punched the accelerator until the Silkworm was alongside Warspite. He stuck his head out the window.

'Get the gate open. We'll keep them busy.' Ghazi opened his mouth to reply, but the younger man cut him off. 'We ain't got time to discuss it.'

'Then take this.' With some effort, he hefted the rifle and threw it up to Tagawa. The extra magazines followed. The Japanese slammed his fist down on the roof and the Silkworm rolled backwards. Victor threw Ghazi a short salute from behind the glass and grinned. The pillbox reversed to the end of the street and screeched around the corner. Ghazi watched the drones become larger in the sky and peel left when they spotted the moving truck.

Allowing his mind to go blank, he unhooked the frayed cable from the spool above the bumper and dragged it back to the gates. Cassady peered past him to the corner where the Silkworm had disappeared.

'Where do they think they're going?'

'They're buying us some time.' Ghazi looped the cable through an eye. His partner didn't move. 'Help me.'

Together, they fed the cable through the brackets that had held the metal bar. Controlled bursts of automatic gunfire electrified their movements. Ghazi pulled on the cable, releasing more from the winch, and passed it to Cassady, who tied it off.

'Okay. Done.'

They ran back to the truck. One of the drones rose, arced and swooped down towards the town. A hatch opened and a plume of smoke drifted down onto the buildings. Tagawa's automatic rifle crackled in response.

Cassady punched the ignition and guided Warspite backwards. The cable rose from the ground, became taut. The truck creaked. The gate shivered and shed a coat of rust as it opened a crack. Cassady put his foot down further and the wheels dug in. The whine of the transmission became more urgent. Wisps of white smoke caressed the windows.

'You're going to blow the engine,' said Ghazi. Cassady ignored him. They continued to inch backwards. The band of daylight became wider and the gate shrieked as it was finally torn from its mate and dragged all the way open. Cassady released the pedal and shifted into first. Warspite rolled forwards and the cable became slack.

'Now the other side.'

An explosion made the earth vibrate. Both men held their breaths, assuming the worst. But the sharp crack of the rifle resumed. Ghazi leaned out of the window and looked behind him. A column of dirty grey smoke spiralled among the roofs. Two drones remained in the sky.

The minutes slipped away while they unhooked the cable from the open half of the gate. The noise of the battle intensified. Somewhere back there, Tagawa was firing round after round at the drones and they were returning fire with bullets of a heavier calibre, each one making a dull thumping noise as it left the barrel. As Ghazi listened, his hand slipped and the cable scraped the skin from his palm. Blood welled from the gash. Concentrate. Do your job. His eyes burned and his shirt stuck to his arms and back. The cable came free from the gate with a snapping sound and Cassady set to work looping it around the closed half. Freedom lay just beyond. Tapering mountains, an expanse of dying scrub, tyre tracks leading somewhere. Decomposing vehicle frames showed where so many people had sought to gain access to Novus in the past. Now it was the other way around.

'Go and start her up,' shouted Cassady. 'I'm almost done.' Ghazi retraced his steps for the fifth time. Before he made it to Warspite, a drone came in low over the buildings at the end of the road and swept towards him. He broke into a run. His eyes were on the fat gun mounted to the underside of the thing's body and he watched as it began to spin.

The Silkworm fishtailed around the corner. Tagawa aimed the rifle and fired. Bullets spattered against the drone's wing. Victor slammed on the brakes. The flying machine wobbled and tried to rise, but Tagawa's intervention had been fatal. One of its engines fired and the burst of energy sent it hurtling towards the wall.

Ghazi turned in time to spot his partner dive through the open gate. The drone clipped the ramparts and smashed in the scrubland. Lumps of concrete fell to the floor where Cassady had been standing a moment before. Without gesturing to Tagawa, he ran flat out to the wall and skidded through the gate.

The drone was a crumpled mess of parts and circuitry sounding its death rattle. Cassady lay unmoving near the wall, his eyes closed. A line of red ran from the side of his head into his matted beard, and brick dust coated his skin and clothes. Ghazi checked for a pulse and found one. The gash on his head was deep. His right ear was split at the top. But his chest rose and fell and no other wounds were evident. On the other side of the wall, the dance of gunfire resumed.

Ghazi pinched the dusty skin of Cassady's forearm, but he didn't stir. He leaned over and spoke into one ear and then the other.

'Wake up, Cass.' There was still no response. Ghazi ignored his mounting despair and dug his fingers into his partner's collarbone. Heavy eyelids fluttered open and a bleary pair of mismatched pupils focused on him.

'What's going on?'

Ghazi looked up at the sky and thanked Cassady's guardian. 'The drone went down. You got knocked out.'

'My head.' A pale hand went to test the wound, but Ghazi snatched it away.

'Don't touch it.'

'Is it bad?'

'It could be worse. Can you walk?'

'I think so.'

'Then let's go. We're not out of this yet.'

He lifted Cassady to his feet and together they staggered back through the gate. The Old Lady waited patiently next to the guardhouse. Victor and Tagawa were nowhere to be seen. Ghazi glanced at the cable as they passed it. Cassady had tied it off in three places. He hoped it would hold.

When they passed the guardhouse, Cassady fell to his knees and muttered something unintelligible. Ghazi hauled him upright once more and half-dragged, half-carried him to Warspite. He pushed him up the steps into the cab and then took his seat behind the wheel.

'Take it slow,' Cassady managed to whisper. His fingers grasped a scrap of cloth under the seat and he pressed it to his head. 'Slow and steady.'

'Sit back and be quiet. Put the harness on.'

The bursts of assault rifle fire had stopped, replaced by the dull roar of Tagawa's old bolt-action rifle. Ghazi dragged the stick back. The cable rose and levelled out. The steering wheel resisted him as best it could. He kept his eyes on the gate, willing it to give way. He pushed the pedal down further. Warspite rumbled and snorted and the cable quivered. There was a squeal as the gate swung wide open on its rusted hinges.

The road to the south was clear.

For a moment he sat with his arms locked against the wheel, not believing it. He switched off the engine. The Old Lady became quiet.

'Stay here. I'm going to get that cable off. Then we're leaving.' Cassady slumped in his seat with his eyes closed.

Outside, the last of the three drones strafed the streets with its heavy-calibre weapon. Tyres squealed on the blacktop. Ghazi jogged to the wall. Victor and Tagawa only had to hang on for another minute and then they could make a run for it. The drone couldn't have much ammunition left. His throat was parched, but he didn't have enough saliva to spit out the sour taste of brick dust and sweat. At the wall, clumsy fingers worked to remove the cable. The braided wire refused to come free easily. His fingernails bent back and broke against the last of the knots and he cried out in pain and frustration. From somewhere in the town came the sound of metal crunching against metal. Then a horn, unbroken, like the call of an animal in pain. Angrily, Ghazi pawed at the sweat that dripped into his eyes and nostrils and mouth and stared at the final knot that was preventing him from getting out.

'Use this.' He whirled around. A groggy Cassady, face a

mask of pain, held out his machete. Ghazi took it and plunged it into the knot. He levered the blade back and forth and the cable jerked upward and he pulled on it until it twisted free from the gate's clutches. He clapped Cassady on the back.

The Silkworm's horn continued to blare. Back at the truck, Ghazi reeled in the cable and ignored the darkness that swirled at the edges of his mind. Bound metal strands snaked through the dirt and wound themselves around the spool. Cassady shuffled to the rear of the vehicle, a hand held against his head, and looked to the corner at the end of the road. No more gunfire echoed between the buildings. The sky was blue and clear.

Ghazi wound the winch handle a final time and joined Cassady by the tailgate. 'She's ready,' he said quietly.

The horn stopped. The two men stood side by side, the nascent silence pulling their nerves taut. They waited for a glimpse of blonde hair, a dark uniform, a pair of hollow faces wearing conquering grins.

Ghazi's eyes burned. He had to be the one to say it. 'We've got to go.'

'Just a minute,' muttered Cassady.

'They're not coming.'

'Give them a chance. The one you never gave her.'

The seconds ticked by. A breeze bent the column of grey smoke. Ghazi walked a few paces further along the road, straining to hear footsteps or voices. Something dark shimmered in the distance, emerging between the tips of the mountains with purpose. More drones. He turned away.

'Come on.'

'We could go back,' said Cassady weakly. 'At least see what happened to them.'

He shook his head. 'More drones are coming. We have to leave.'

The wounded man allowed himself to be led to the cab. At the gate, Ghazi stopped and blasted the horn three times. He opened his door and leaned out, his gaze sweeping the road. But there was no movement.

The truck passed the smoking wreck of the flying machine, weaved through ancient hulks and joined the tyre tracks engraved in the dirt. The wall and the smoke and the smudges in the sky receded in Warspite's mirrors until they became part of the horizon and were no more.

9

Flames scorched his back. The remains of his truck were strewn across the road. He staggered along the asphalt, gripping the wound in his side that belched hot, sticky blood over his hands. Overhead, drones circled like vultures, waiting for his legs to buckle. His foot had been crushed, but he felt no pain. He followed the faded white line that dissected the road. A rig, blue and silver, idled a few metres away with its front facing him. Without warning, the headlights flashed and it jolted into life. He waved to the driver. It would save him. The rig picked up speed. He waved again. It was coming in too fast. He tried to drag himself out of the way, but stumbled and fell to the floor. He had no breath to cry out. The grille was a metal fist preparing to strike. Hysterical eyes sought the face of the driver, but the windshield was crowded with the faces of the dead. He flung his arms out to protect himself.

Cassady groaned. Burning red light filtered through his half-open eyelids. He was soaked. The stinking rag he'd used to bind his head stuck to him like wet mud. Aching fingers probed the tender area around the wound. It was swollen, but at least the bleeding had stopped. When the light stopped hurting, he peered out of the window. The Old Lady followed a set of tyre tracks that ran to the end of the world. The desert lay all around them with no vegetation in sight. The sun blazed on the horizon, probing, taunting, irritating and always out of reach.

It was only when he checked the mirror for a glimpse of the Silkworm that he remembered. Three wrecks had charted their progress through Novus and now the convoy was no more. Yet somehow he and Ghazi still lived. They didn't deserve to. Losing Tagawa and Victor hurt him even more than Hearst. At least the others had been on the road long enough to live a life; the boys hadn't. They were just starting out. Not only that, but they'd sacrificed themselves to give Warspite the chance to get away. And he and Ghazi had left them on the road for the worms.

Most of the mechanic's face was hidden behind a makeshift keffiyeh and a pair of sun goggles. Had he been tormented by the same thoughts? Did he care at all? He'd been the one to turn his back on the Silkworm first, just as he'd left Hearst to bleed out. He didn't know the man anymore. Perhaps he'd never known him at all. It didn't matter now. He coughed.

'Awake?'

'Yeah.'

'How are you doing?'

'Been better. Where are we?'

'En route.' Ghazi's voice was dull and rasping.

'Can you be more specific?'

'No. Lupo's instructions say to follow the trail until it hits a crossroad and then take the eastern fork. Still haven't reached the crossroad.'

'Anything in pursuit?'

'No. We passed a settlement a couple of hours ago. I saw it from a distance.'

'A city?'

'Tents. Thrown together. Looked like it could be broken down in a hurry. If they spotted us, they didn't do anything about it. I haven't seen a soul out here since.'

Cassady pulled on a pair of goggles. His dull gaze rested on the golden sea. He wasn't surprised by the lack of activity. He reached for a canteen lodged between the seats and washed out the dust and clammy heat from his mouth. It hurt to breathe.

'Better take it easy with that. It's all we have left.'

'What happened to the rest?'

'We drank it, Cass.'

He frowned. He shook the canteen. The water sloshed freely around the insides. Another groan escaped his parched lips. He was being boiled alive. 'You got a plan?'

'We should continue through the night. If you can drive.'

'What about the juice?'

'I took a break for an hour. I figured it was safe enough and I was getting dizzy. It didn't take long to charge the battery with the PVs in this sunlight.'

Cassady stared at the tyre tracks again. He was still in a stupor, but Ghazi sounded as though he was on the verge of collapse. He had to take over. All he had to do was keep the rig in a straight line until they hit the crossroads.

'You don't want to pull up here and start out in the morning?' he asked. 'We can both rest some more.'

'Tomorrow will be hell in here. If we still haven't reached La Talpa by midday, we'll have to stop anyway and wait for a few hours until it's cool enough to get going again. Better to drive through the night while we still have the strength.'

That was true, realised Cassady. The air would be thicker than axle grease tomorrow. His hand sought the canteen, but he forced himself to put it back between the seats. There wasn't even enough for him to wash out the head wound again. He tried not to think about how quickly it could become infected.

'Okay. I'll take her now. You can rest.'

'Only if you're up to it.'

'I am.'

They switched places. The headrest was saturated and the steering wheel dripped. Cassady adjusted the goggles that pressed into the top of his cheeks. Sitting upright in the driver's seat was painful, but he wasn't about to complain. Slowly, Warspite got underway again. He kept his foot steady on the pedal.

'The tracks disappear under the sand sometimes. Watch out for that.'

He grunted. He didn't need the advice.

Ghazi placed his elbows on the dash and rested his chin on his knuckles. 'Strange to think this land was green, once upon a time,' he muttered. 'I read about lakes and cities and rich soil. A land where people could grow all the crops they needed to survive and thrive. Now everything's been buried.'

'Same as almost everywhere else.'

'Not Novus.'

'Desperate to go back?'

'No. Not yet, anyway. But it's an option, like I said before. It could be the start of something.'

Cassady sighed. The words meant nothing to him. It was something he could never be part of, not even if he'd wanted to. The light in some of the corridors of his mind was failing. His body was begging to be laid to rest, yet Ghazi was talking about the future, a joint future, as though one could exist.

Almost on cue, the coughing started and his body fell against the wheel. Fire scorched the inside of his chest. The Old Lady swerved, kicking up sand against the windows. Ghazi made to grab the wheel, but Cassady pushed him away. He regained control and wiped his mouth with the back of his hand. The phlegm was streaked with brown.

'Again?' asked Ghazi.

He didn't answer.

'How bad is it?'

'I don't know. More blood than last time.' He spoke in a monotone. He wasn't scared. Fear no longer controlled him. It was all inevitable, like the death of the Earth itself.

'Let me take over again.'

He shook his head. 'No. I can do it. I'm not that weak yet.'

'When we get to La Talpa, their doctors will take a look at you. They'll find out what's wrong. And you can rest for as long as you need to.'

'It isn't as simple as that. I'm sick, Ghazi. I can feel it. It's not something any amount of rest will cure.' He rubbed his chest. It still burned.

'Their doctors will help you,' the other man insisted, not

looking at him.

He hit the wheel with the heel of his hand. 'If La Talpa even exists. You really think there's going to be a community of scientists living underground, waiting for us to arrive? Goddamn it, wake up.' He spat the words out.

Ghazi's voice was quiet. 'If you didn't believe in the place, you'd never have left in the first place.'

'I went because something told me this would be my last run. And that something was right. It had nothing to do with the cargo. And it had nothing to do with belief.'

'Your nihilism has no place here. Not after all of this. They trusted you. Hearst, Brandt and the others.'

'Don't.'

'They followed us and now they're dead. That can't be for nothing.'

'They all had their own reasons to go. We don't owe them anything.'

'Yes we do. We owe it to them to believe we're going to make it.'

'How do you do it? We're in the middle of the desert, we have no water left and we don't know where the hell we're going. How can you tell me to believe?'

'Because I have to. These are trials of the body, that's all. As long as I keep pushing towards the light, I'm confident I'll find what I seek. It's been the same all my life. La Talpa will be there. And its people will help you.'

The challenge hung in the air. Cassady bit his lip. He had no response. Whatever it was Ghazi believed in was too strong for it to ever be shaken.

The silence stretched. Eventually, the mechanic fell asleep and his head nodded in time with the vibrations of the vehicle. Cassady flexed his arms and twisted his neck and ignored the pain in his head and chest. His body was on tenterhooks, waiting for another coughing fit to shake him. After the sun melted away below the horizon, he stripped off the goggles and rubbed his eyes. The light faded from indigo to grey to black. He switched all of the headlights on, and yellow beams built a wall of light that separated Warspite from the darkness and gave him peace of mind. The tyre tracks slithered through the hard sand. As the timepiece ticked over, he imagined the others watching him. He did owe them, of course he did. But whether he had the strength to make it over the line was another matter.

A chill settled on his skin. With one hand on the wheel, he scrabbled around under the seat until his fingers brushed coarse fabric. He pulled it out. It was a blanket. Dark stains covered the surface. He'd wrapped it around Hearst before she'd died. A different coldness spread through him. He wanted to throw it out of the window, but he draped it over his shoulders. A sour smell rose from the fibres.

The crossroad appeared some time later, a wooden cross marking the point where two sets of tracks intersected. He slowed down, peering out of the window to see whether there was a cache next to or under the stake, but the ground was unmarked and undisturbed. He eased Warspite onto the eastern fork. Lodged next to the speedometer was a slip of paper with instructions scrawled on it. He held them up to his eyes and muttered to himself. They had to follow the eastern trail for several hours. When it broke to the right by a ruined cluster of buildings, they had to leave the trail and keep going, straight as an arrow, until they hit a bank of rock. Once there, they had to pray somebody was still breathing at La Talpa.

He stretched his arms again and slapped himself around the cheek to banish the fog seeping into his brain. The creaks and murmurs of the Old Lady reassured him. She'd emerged from Novus with little more than a few scratches. He drew new strength from the five tons of metal under his command. She would outlast him, just as she had outlasted his father. Perhaps she would outlast Ghazi, too.

Near dawn, his resolve faltered together with the engine. The heart of the Old Lady skipped a beat and she wheezed. The headlights winked out. There was a clank, and then she freewheeled along the sand for fifty metres before drifting to a gentle halt. Hot metal ticked under his feet. The only other sound came from Ghazi breathing into his keffiyeh.

Cassady sat stock still, hands still on the wheel. He blinked rapidly, battling the exhaustion that was determined to overwhelm him. What did he need to do? Try the engine again. He held the locking key up to his face. The long piece of twine which he usually slipped over his neck tickled his skin. Slot it home, turn it, hit the starter and drive on.

The key found the access point and he twisted it. He pushed the starter button. Nothing happened.

He tried three more times and gave up. He leaned over the wheel and rested his cheek against the sweat-streaked plastic. An invisible hand was holding a match to the wound on the side of his head. The world no longer existed outside the cab. There was only blackness. He could see his own reflection against the glass, distorted, ugly, fading. He closed his eyes. He would give Ghazi another five minutes and then wake him with the news.

Something shook him and barked in his ear. The steering wheel cut into his forehead. He coughed and lifted himself off it. His shoulder was dead, his shirt soaked through. The side of his head throbbed in unison with his heartbeat. His watery eyes focused on a dark, bearded face.

Ghazi spoke thickly, his dried-out tongue slapping against the insides of his mouth 'What happened?'

'What do you mean?'

'Why are we sitting here?'

He struggled to piece together his thoughts.

'What time is it?' The muscles in his throat were swollen and dry and lacerated, and he choked.

'Late morning.'

He wrinkled his nose. 'It can't be.'

'Take a look outside. You can see where the sun is.'

He rolled down the window and leaned out. The air came at him in boiling waves.

'Christ. I only put my head down for five minutes.'

'Why did you stop?'

His useless struggle with the starter in the dawn came back to him. He forgot the heat. 'The engine. It died while I was driving.'

For the first time since he could remember, fear was plain to see in every line of Ghazi's face, and he sat back in the co-seat, body curling inward like plastic in a fire. Cassady's eyes watered at the pain in his throat. The engine could wait.

'Where's the water?'

'There are a few mouthfuls left in the can. That's it.'

'You're sure there's nothing else?'

'There's nothing back there except the medicine.'

'I have to drink. I can't swallow.'

'Do what you have to do.'

He shook the canteen. He'd be able to finish it in a second if he wanted to. He unscrewed the cap and held the rim to his lips. When a few drops wet his tongue, he took it away. It did little to relieve the pain.

'Did we reach the crossroad at least?' asked Ghazi.

'Yes. Eastern fork. I went until dawn. The engine died before the sun came up. I wanted to wake you. But I must have passed out.' He stared at the dials and the needles that sat at zero. 'Christ. I'm sorry.'

'Forget it. It isn't going to help us now. Look at the juice meter. The battery's fine.'

'Could be the controller then. Or the potentiometers. Dust and sand clogging up everything.'

'I'm going to check.'

'It's over 45 degrees out there.'

'Not much different to in here.'

'We need to get under the rig. Wait it out.'

'No. We need to do this while we still have the strength. Understand?'

The wound on his head itched. His vision was clouded. He wanted to lie down and let the darkness wash over him once more. But Ghazi spoke the truth. 'Okay.'

The mechanic adjusted his keffiyeh and goggles. Cassady slid between the seats to the cargo bed. Every movement was an effort. The crates of medicine were still strapped down, utterly useless to them. The storage compartments were mostly bare. He stripped off the sodden rag covering the gash and found another semi-clean piece of fabric that he wound around his head. He used another length to cover his face. The cab door slammed shut and the hood creaked open. He strapped on his goggles and climbed over the tailgate. Despite the protection, the sun hit him so hard he thought he might fall to the floor. There was nothing to see in any direction. Just sand and sky and the heat haze. He tried not to retch. On weak legs, he dragged himself to the front of the rig, taking care not to come into contact with the boiling metal.

Ghazi leaned into the engine. 'Connections are corroded,' he said in a muffled voice. 'We'll start there. Pass me a screwdriver.'

He'd forgotten the tool kit. He returned to the cargo bed and untied the bungees that held the kit in place. Back outside, he cracked the box and handed the screwdriver over. The air was a battering ram that pummelled them with every breath and sucked the moisture from their bodies. Ghazi forced the tip of the screwdriver under the caps on the controller and pulled out the three yellow wires on top. He spent minutes inspecting, cleaning and reattaching them to the housing. Cassady handed him tools as he asked for them. When he was finished, Ghazi closed the hood and retreated to the cab. Cassady stood back from the engine and watched while he readied himself in the driver's seat. He pushed the button. Nothing happened.

The sun rose higher while they worked. Ghazi remained bent under the hood, his face obscured from view, stopping occasionally to rub his temples and rest on the bumper. The pressure grew under Cassady's skin and the wound itched until it became torturous. Each time he looked at the body under the hood, it took his eyes a few seconds to focus. The sound of his own breathing rattled through the crevices of his skull until he thought he might start to scream. The cloth around his head rustled with every movement. At some point, he lost all sensation in his hands and dropped the tool box. He wiped his fingers across the back of his arm, entranced by the movement. His body had stopped sweating. He balled his fist and pressed it into his stomach. Nausea wouldn't leave him alone. Part of him registered that he had heatstroke. His mind and his limbs were trapped in quicksand, but he wasn't sure he wanted to free himself. He glanced at the horizon again and breathed in another mouthful of burning air. The ground was inviting. He could lay himself out on the floor, take off the keffiyeh and wait for the sun to fry the few circuits that were still working. It would be easy. Instead, he reached into the box and handed Ghazi another tool.

In the early evening, Ghazi straightened up.

'You called it,' he whispered. 'The potentiometers.'

Cassady leaned against the body of the pantech, no longer able to hold himself upright without support. Ghazi ran a rag across the metal cylinder, bent the terminals back into place and made sure the shafts lined up. He reattached them to the cable that emerged from the accelerator pedal and closed the hood gently. If it didn't work he wouldn't open it again.

He climbed into the cab. The door hung open. Cassady pushed himself away from the truck and fell onto the hot sand. Behind the glass, Ghazi looked up at the roof of the cab and said something. He ran his hands over the wheel and pushed the starter.

Warspite shook itself into life. A faint whirr drifted out from under the hood and was swallowed by the desert.

Ghazi switched off the engine and sat without moving for several minutes. When he was ready, he slowly climbed out of the vehicle and walked around to where Cassady sat. Tears cut through the grime on his cheeks.

'I'll make sure everything's in place. Then we can go. Hang on, Cass.' He turned, lifted the cover and dipped his head into the engine again.

A dot shimmered on the horizon in the east. A mirage. Cassady closed his eyes and found the energy to open them again. It was still there. The dot became larger, black, moving at speed, surrounded by deformed air and puffs of sand. Cassady tried to work up enough saliva in his throat to call out, but it was impossible. He dragged himself across the sand and his shaking hand wrapped itself around Ghazi's leg. His partner croaked something, but didn't emerge from the engine. He looked to the east once more. The dot had turned and was moving towards them. He was sure of it. With his remaining strength he raised his fist and hammered it against the radiator grille. The Old Lady shook. Ghazi lifted his head out of the engine and was about to speak when he, too, spotted the blur of movement on the desert plains.

'Look,' he whispered.

Cassady nodded. He rested his head against the bumper. It was hot.

'It's coming towards us, Cass.'

There was the sand, the sky, and a vehicle that rode the line between the two. The wheels were as large as Warspite. A rounded body hovered above them.

'We need to get back inside the truck.' He could hear Ghazi's voice coming from somewhere. The bumper continued to burn through the cloth covering his head. He made an effort to move his legs, but they were too heavy.

'Get up, Cass.'

He saw the others. Hearst, alone, abandoned and mortally wounded at the bottom of a valley. Brandt and Wyler charging at death, the sound of a lit fuse in their ears. Tagawa and Victor clearing the skies. Now it was his turn. Not with a bang but a whimper, surrounded by nothing, with not even enough energy to get to his feet. His blurry gaze settled on the endless sand. What had the world looked like before this?

Rough hands grabbed him underneath the armpits. His head rolled from one shoulder to the other. He was being dragged backwards. The heels of his boots left twin trails in the sand. The hands let go of him and he fell onto his back. He closed his eyes. A banging sound filled the air and an inner voice told him it was the tailgate being dropped. He forced his eyelids open. Ghazi stood over him.

'Stay awake.'

He made to nod, but Ghazi was already bending down to grab his arm. He felt a shoulder being wedged into his chest and Ghazi heaved as he tried to lift him up. He pushed with his legs and he left the ground. All he could see was the floor and the backs of Ghazi's trousers. Then he felt himself being lowered again. The back of his head hit the cargo bed with a soft thud. Walls of heat collapsed all around him. There was no air left to breathe. A final shove brought him level with a wooden box. He couldn't remember what was inside. The tailgate slammed shut. He was alone. This was his coffin. He'd run as far as he ever would. And it was okay, he told himself. It was okay.

10

The foreign vehicle sailed over the sand as a ship on a yellow ocean. There was no whirr, no whine, no creaking. The wheels were easily three times the size of Warspite's. Perched atop them was a cockroach-like metal shell lined with PV cells. The windows were tinted.

Ghazi stood with his back to Warspite and unravelled his keffiyeh. Sand billowed around his feet. The day hadn't been real. Time had stopped. He'd been tested to breaking point. His body shook with fatigue, his thoughts were scattered, but he still stood, and now he waited for what would come next.

The vehicle stopped. Rope ladders dropped down from either side of the cockroach shell and slapped against the sand. Two figures in dark jumpsuits and headscarves emerged and climbed down. Long-barrelled firearms were visible against their backs. They approached the immobile truck with caution.

Ghazi held his arms above his head, palms out, and made a full revolution to show he was unarmed. Then he lifted his goggles from his eyes. His vision swam. He couldn't see their faces.

A female voice called out to him in a language he didn't understand. He shook his head.

'Identify,' said a male voice. His accent was strong.

'Supply run.' His vocal cords shuddered with the effort of speaking. 'Sent by Giacomo Lupo to La Talpa base.'

The pair glanced at one another. They took a few steps closer.

'You are here,' said the female voice disbelievingly.

His arms fell to his sides and he closed his eyes. It wasn't a dream any longer. It was real. His thin legs wavered and blood rushed to his head. Before he went down, he felt a strong grip against his arm. His eyelids fluttered open. The two strangers in the dark jumpsuits were beside him, and they held him upright.

'Easy. Take it easy.'

They guided him to their vehicle and sat him down in the hollow of one of the great wheels.

'Drink this.' The woman unclipped a long, thin bottle from her belt and handed it to him. He put it to his lips. 'Slow.' She took off her headscarf to reveal a pale young face with a patchwork of scars on her left cheek and temple. Her gaze never left him as he drank. The liquid inside was sweet.

'What is it?'

'Electrolyte solution.'

'My partner's in the back. He's in a bad way.'

'I'll see to him,' said the man, heading over to Warspite. The woman spoke again.

'How long did you drive?'

'I don't know.'

'Medicine?'

'It's there.' He took another drink and set the bottle down beside him. The dizziness receded, but his body was still ready to shut down. 'Is there anybody left?'

Even with his blurred vision, he could see a muscle twitch by her jaw when he asked the question.

'There have been deaths.'

'How many?'

'Enough.' She crouched down so they were eye to eye. 'But please. We did not expect you to come. You have done a great thing. We take you now to La Talpa. Use the medicine. Then we rebuild.'

Time slowed once more as he processed what she had said. His heartbeat rose. Though she tried to disguise it, he heard the resignation in her voice, as though all the energy that had once driven her had been wrung out until there was not a drop left. He wanted to get back on the road and drive away. He didn't care where. His head dropped.

She placed a hand on his shoulder. 'What is your name?'

He looked up. 'Ghazi.'

'We owe you.' She struggled to find the correct term. 'We owe you a debt.'

He shook his head. 'No, there are no debts in this world,' he whispered.

'How many with you?'

'There were nine of us. We are the last two.'

Warspite's tailgate clanged shut and the man returned and exchanged a look with the woman. 'We have to get you to the base. Your friend needs a doctor. I've done what I can for him.'

Ghazi nodded. He collected his energy and forced himself to stand. His legs quivered. 'I'll follow you.' He felt nauseous with every movement, but the pressure in his head had eased off.

'Are you sure?' said the man. 'I can take your vehicle.'

'I brought her this far. I'm not handing her over now.'

'Okay. The drive is thirty minutes. We'll follow the tracks. Your vehicle will sink if we return the same way.'

'Take this,' said the woman, handing him another bottle. 'Use the horn if you must stop.'

Dusk had fallen while they had been talking. Ghazi focused on keeping his legs steady as he walked back to the truck. Thirty minutes. He could make it. He had to. With a supreme effort, he pulled himself into the driver's seat and took a few seconds to get his breath back. There had been casualties. That's what she'd said. But he couldn't dwell on that now. There would be enough time later. He looked between the seats. Cassady lay on the bed, skin shiny and unreal, eyes rolling in his head. He was muttering to himself. The huge desert truck spun in the sand and joined the barely visible trail. Ghazi twisted the key and pushed the button. She started first time. He put the Old Lady into gear, eased the accelerator down, felt the vibrations in his body and pulled away from the spot where he'd been so sure they would die.

He kept as close to the other vehicle as he could. Before long the track entered a cluster of dead single-storey structures and broke right. They left the tracks behind. There were no markings to follow, no vegetation, no islands of rock to disturb the landscape. He wound down the window and listened to the sand being kicked up by the tyres. He took another drink of solution from the bottle. Cassady whimpered in the back.

'Hang on, dostem,' he said. 'We're almost there.'

When a set of lamps on top of the desert truck flicked on, he reached for the switch next to the steering column. The left-hand lamp sputtered and died. He patted the dashboard and asked the Old Lady to hold on. She was keeping it together just for them.

Dusk turned to night and still they drove. The thirty-minute mark passed without the other vehicle showing any signs of stopping. Ghazi kept his eyes on the two red lamps floating ahead of him. He rolled the window up. It was becoming cool. He finished the last of the solution. He hadn't eaten for nearly two days, but he wasn't hungry.

A shout came from the cargo bed. 'All of them!'

'Just hold on,' he said. There was a murmur and a scraping noise. He turned to see what was happening.

The ghost of Cassady's face hovered between the seats. He stared at Ghazi with an expression of complete lucidity.

'The surface of the earth is soft and impressible by the feet of men, and so with the paths which the mind travels. How worn and dusty must be the highways of the world, how deep the ruts of tradition and conformity.'

A grin slashed Cassady's face in half and a high-pitched laugh filled the cab. His eyes rolled into the back of his head. Fear caught Ghazi by the throat and threatened to throttle him.

'Stop,' he said. 'Lie down. Please, Edward. Lie down.'

The pitch rose and the sick howling rang in his ears.

'Please,' he shouted. He balled his fist, ready to bring it down on Cassady's skull.

The laughter ceased. The face disappeared. Another groan rattled around the cargo bed and then the only sound was the hum of the transmission. Ghazi breathed deeply and released his grip on the wheel. Ahead, the desert truck slowed down. He shifted into second.

A wall of sheer rock appeared without warning. The sea of sand crashed against it. The vehicle stopped, and Ghazi pulled up behind it. A rope ladder fell to the ground once more and the driver climbed down, rounded the tyres and disappeared for a few moments. When he returned, he waved to Ghazi and pointed over his shoulder before shimmying back up the ladder. As Ghazi watched, the vehicle moved off and was swallowed by darkness.

Part of the rock had given way. Beyond it was the mouth of a tunnel that sloped sharply down into the earth. Ghazi didn't waste time admiring it. As Warspite passed beyond the rock face into the tunnel, his attention was drawn to a complex series of cogwheels spinning on both sides of the opening. Once the truck was safely inside, the wall swung closed again with a thud.

A smooth concrete track led the two vehicles down into the earth. Spotlights overhead illuminated rough stone walls and a metal lattice that held the ceiling in place. The deeper they went, the wider and higher the tunnel became. Ghazi kept the Old Lady going at a steady pace, following the desert truck further and further into the subterranean gloom. They passed a checkpoint of some kind, manned by figures wearing the same dark jumpsuits as the vehicle crew. Pillboxes on either side of the track bristled with automatic weapons, all aiming at Warspite's tyres. The number of lights beaming down increased and the concrete gave way to metal slats that groaned under the weight of the ancient pantech. After a few minutes, the incline evened out and the tunnel opened into a large chamber with smaller passageways leading away from it in multiple directions. The desert truck rolled to a halt without making a noise. Warspite rattled and sighed as Ghazi shut her down. His hand was a dead weight on top of the gear stick. He stared dully at the vacant, floodlit chamber. He'd made it. And now he would find out if it had been worth it.

11

The crew climbed down from the shell of the gigantic vehicle and beckoned for Ghazi to join them. After looping the key around his neck, he squeezed through the seats into the back and rested a hand on the unconscious Cassady's brow. It was sticky with sweat and blood.

'We're here, dostem,' he muttered. 'I'll get you some help now.'

He eased himself over the tailgate. The air was warm underground, but the temperature was far from the hell that had brought him to the brink in the desert. His boots rang against the metal planks as he rounded the front of the Old Lady. Each of the smaller passageways was blocked by a heavy metal door, and each one was too narrow for anything larger than a quad. He joined the crew standing in the shadow of one of the tyres.

'La Talpa,' said the woman.

'What now?' he croaked.

Before she could answer, the door nearest to the desert truck opened and a pallid man with an elaborate moustache emerged. Dressed in a smart white uniform with a grey cape, the crew visibly stiffened at the sight of him. He was followed by four men in grey overalls bearing a stretcher between them. The man in white spoke quickly to the crew and then turned to Ghazi. His movements were precise and authoritative.

'I understand you have a wounded man,' he said in a lilting accent.

'In the back of the truck.'

The uniformed man clicked his fingers and the four-man team went to Warspite's tailgate and dropped the hatch. Two jumped inside with the stretcher, and seconds later a prone form was hauled from the truck. As the stretcher passed between the great wheels, Cassady's hand shot out and grabbed Ghazi's wrist. The uniformed man clicked his fingers once more and the stretcher bearers stopped. With a superhuman effort, Cassady lifted his head and stared at Ghazi with frantic eyes.

'Did we make it?'

'We made it, Cass.' He gripped the other man's arm and used a sleeve to wipe the sweat from his brow. 'Lie down now.'

Cassady looked desperate. His lips twitched and his breathing became rapid. The men in the grey overalls stood impassively, waiting to take him away.

'We failed them,' he whispered.

'Don't think about that now. Be calm.'

'No.' He tried to grab Ghazi by the collar, but it was too much effort. He began to slip below the surface once more. His eyes closed and his breathing slowed.

The uniformed man nodded, and the stretcher bearers disappeared through one of the doors, which slammed shut after them.

Ghazi composed himself and addressed the authority figure. 'Where are you taking him?'

'To our medical wing. He will receive the best treatment possible.'

'I want to go with him.'

'As you wish,' said the man in his lilting accent. 'May we take the cargo from your vehicle?'

'Do what you want with it.'

'Then please follow me.' He issued a flurry of instructions to the crew. The young woman with the scarred face turned a pair of pained eyes onto Ghazi.

'Thank you for what you have done.'

He could only nod his head, too empty to do anything more. The uniformed man entered a code on a panel beside one of the metal doors and it slid open to reveal a narrow, twisting corridor hewn into the rock, its walls and ceiling supported by a network of metal beams and steel wire. The floor looked to be made of a dull plastic mesh. As they walked, it sloped gradually downwards. The sound of their footsteps ricocheted off the rough walls. The stretcher bearers were a few paces ahead. One of Cassady's arms slipped out from the side of the stretcher and bounced up and down with the forward momentum until a bearer gently lifted it back onto the board.

'This is a miracle, you know,' said the uniformed man. 'We had given up hope.'

Ghazi said nothing. He wasn't in the mood for miracles. The passage branched off into other corridors, some of which ended abruptly in sealed metal doors, others which curled away into the rock. For all he knew, La Talpa could stretch for tens of kilometres under the baked earth. It certainly seemed that way. Their small party continued straight on, following lamps wired together along the ceiling.

'My name is Omero,' said the man. 'I am the coordinator of the facility. You were sent by the four riders?'

'Yes.'

'Are they still alive?'

'Only Lupo. At least he was when we left him.'

'Such a waste,' muttered the coordinator, and ran two fingers across his moustache. 'Please, what is your name?'

'Ghazi.'

He gestured. 'And the man on the stretcher?'

'Cassady. We lost another seven good men and women getting here.'

Omero took his arm and they stopped in the middle of the corridor. His cape flowed like water behind his shoulders. 'I am sorry. Truly I am. And I speak on behalf of the entire community here. For a long time we did not want to ask for help for fear that something like this would happen. Yet these are the decisions we make. I do not expect you to take comfort from it, but their deaths were not in vain. I promise you.'

They started walking again. The coordinator's words rang in

Ghazi's ears. There was something the man wasn't telling him, but his mind was slow and he couldn't work out what it was. He was a memory of his former self. His bones cracked and his eyes slapped together in sticky exhaustion and his skin was oily with dirt and sweat. He stank of the road. Only when he'd dug his way out of that hole would he be able to look around and see the situation for what it truly was.

Colour-coded people passed them at intervals. Some kept their eyes to the floor, while others threw quizzical glances at the unconscious form in the stretcher and then at the grizzled man walking next to one of La Talpa's most important figures. Finally, the stretcher team halted outside a thick metal door with a red painted stripe across its midsection. One of the men typed a code on a panel set into the wall.

'The medical wing,' said Omero mildly.

The door opened. The medical wing was a large, cave-like space with air that was much cooler than outside, processed by a large, sleek conditioning unit that whirred rhythmically. Three women and a man in bold blue tunics buzzed around the wing, not yet acknowledging the presence of the new arrivals. Cots stood like a dull row of teeth protruding from the rock. Four were occupied. Two men and two women, all with their eyes open, all lying still. Equipment had been pulled close to these cots, giving each patient their own artificial audience.

Omero cleared his throat. Now the staff in the blue tunics noticed the small party clustered by the entrance. One of the men directed the stretcher bearers to a corner of the room distant from the other patients, and they deposited Cassady on a cot. All four medical staff clustered around the stricken Runner, removing his clothes and hooking him up to IV drips and attending to his head wound. Ghazi stood back while they worked, leaning against the rock and closing his eyes against the dizziness that washed over him.

'Please,' came the lilting voice. Ghazi stirred. Omero stood in front of him, gesturing towards the four patients on their cots. 'I wish to show you why you came here.'

He approached with some hesitation. The patient closest was female. She wore a light shift across her midriff, but was otherwise naked. Her head was propped up on an uncomfortable pillow. Dark blue bruises covered her neck, arms and chest. Speckled green eyes watched as he came closer, and he stared back, feeling an echo of the pain she was surely in. Her lips pressed together, but she did not speak. Omero hovered at his shoulder.

'Don't worry. You won't be affected once we synthesise the serum. And the chances of contagion are low anyway.' He paused. 'Albeit not low enough.'

'She's awake.'

'Yes. Insomnia is the earliest symptom of the disease.'

A vague memory stirred at the back of Ghazi's mind. 'Lupo mentioned something about that.'

'This patient is at stage two. Localised bruising around the sternum and on the upper arms. This is followed by internal bleeding. Then expiry.'

Ghazi looked down at the suffering woman and suppressed his fear and sadness. 'How many people have you lost?' he whispered.

'More than I care to think about at this moment.'

A wrinkle broke the placid surface of the woman's forehead and her eyes closed for a moment.

'She's hurting.'

'Yes. But thanks to you, she will survive. All of these patients will.'

'Will the supplies be enough for everyone here?'

'Your vehicle was full?'

'More or less.'

'Then I believe so. It takes only a small amount to counteract the symptoms and inoculate an individual from contracting the disease in the first place. We simply did not have the supplies we needed, and we paid the price for it. Until now, it has been a lottery. We wake up in fear, wondering if today is finally the day when the sleeplessness sets in and the small bruises appear on the arms and legs. Each night spent without waking is another victory, yet each morning looking out onto an empty desert makes us more and more certain we have been left to our fate. You cannot imagine how it has been, being held hostage by an invisible enemy. But now you are here. We are hostages no longer. And though we have suffered terrible losses, we shall rebuild.'

There it was again. Rebuild, recover. Ghazi pushed it to the back of his mind, instead heading over to where Cassady was being treated for a nasty injury on his arm that Ghazi hadn't even been aware of. The Runner was virtually unrecognisable under the beard and the dirt. Thin and frail, with sunken eyes and skin burned red by the sun.

Omero consulted one of the medical staff who was busy sealing Cassady's clothes in a bag. While he waited for the verdict, Ghazi took Cassady's hand and squeezed it. The mismatched eyes didn't flicker.

'He has been sedated,' said the coordinator. 'He is lucky. The injury to his head is infected but is not yet bad, they tell me. It will take some time to heal. His arm will be fine once it has been cleaned. He also has a problem with his respiratory system. It has taken quite a beating and now his trachea is bruised and bleeding. Antibiotics should clear it up. With a steady course of fluids and nutrients, he should be out of bed in two or three weeks.'

Ghazi didn't take his eyes from his friend. 'He'll be okay?' he asked, hearing the disbelief in his own voice.

'Yes.'

The last of his strength left him, and he grabbed the cot as his legs buckled. Omero reached out and held him under the arm with a muscular grip. The medical staff turned, alarmed, but Ghazi shook his head.

'I'm okay. I just need to rest.'

'You're sure?' asked Omero, still holding him. 'Please allow our personnel to look you over.'

'Later.' He pushed himself upright once more and let go of the cot. Omero released him. 'If you take me back to my vehicle, I can rest there.'

Omero issued a command to one of the staff. The man approached with a device in his hand.

'What's that?' asked Ghazi.

'It'll take a blood sample. If we do this now, we'll be able to see what your body needs and have it ready for later.'

Ghazi rolled up his sleeve and the man pressed the device to his arm. The circular end was cold against his skin. He felt a pinprick of pain, and then the man pulled the device away.

'That's it?'

'That's it.' Omero directed Ghazi to the exit. 'Please follow me. We have a room for you. I believe it may be more comfortable than your vehicle.'

Ghazi took a last look at Cassady before following the coordinator back into the corridor. After a few hundred metres they left the main atrium and took a narrow, curving tunnel that had a series of identical metal doors on both sides. Each door had a number near its centre.

'Sleeping quarters for this section,' explained Omero. 'For the medical staff and our food growers, mainly.' His cape swirled around his legs. 'Several are empty now,' he added.

One of the doors stood open, revealing an empty room within. Omero marched inside without ceremony.

'These are your quarters,' he said. 'Somewhat basic, but perhaps more luxurious than what you have been used to.'

Ghazi hesitated at the door, unwilling to touch anything for fear he would contaminate it. Everything was pristine. A wide sleeping cot was set up against the far wall and looked more comfortable than anything he'd ever slept in. Warm light poured from a thin strip in the ceiling, adding to his drowsiness. A separate cylindrical cubicle sat against another wall, perhaps a shower of some kind, and there was a basic toilet next to it.

Omero strode over to a metal locker by the head of the sleeping cot and flung its doors open. A handful of coloured tunics and robes hung from hooks inside.

'You will find clothing in here. Wear whatever you wish. We will wash your clothes in the meantime.'

Ghazi stumbled into the room. A terrible pressure was growing in the back of his head. His legs were in danger of giving way again. Omero frowned, noticing his discomfort, and went to a small rectangular cabinet built into the rock on the opposite side of the room. He opened it to reveal two shelves loaded with drinks and concentrated bars of food. He handed Ghazi a long, thin bottle similar to the one the scarred woman in the desert truck had given him, and the Runner drank from it. Almost immediately, the pressure in his head receded. His legs found new strength.

'Drink one of these every hour. And eat as much as you need to. You will still need to be examined by the medical personnel. When you're ready, of course.'

Ghazi managed a small smile. 'I hope this food is better than the pills Lupo gave us.'

Omero frowned again. 'What do you mean?'

'They worked fine for a few days, but after that they did nothing for our hunger.'

'I must apologise. The pills only have an effective life of a few weeks. By the time Lupo made it to you, they would have been close to expiry. After that they are quite useless unless they are re-synthesised. And it is only possible to do so here.'

'In other words, the old man played us.'

'He was desperate.'

Ghazi waved the excuse away. 'I don't hold any grudges.'

The coordinator bowed slightly. 'I must let you rest.' He pointed to the control panel next to the door. 'Press this button if you need anything. I will attend you in person.'

'Just let me know if anything happens to Cassady.'

Omero paused on the threshold, clasping his hands together. 'Please feel at ease here. You are among friends.'

The door hissed shut. Ghazi eased off his boots and his fetid clothes and left them in a heap by the door. He staggered into the small cubicle in the corner. Concealed nozzles blasted cold green water at him from eight directions at once, and when the cycle stopped he felt cleaner than he ever had before. Naked, he went to the cot and collapsed onto it. He was asleep before the first drips had fallen onto the foam.

A low chime roused him. He didn't know how long he'd been out, but already he felt a good deal better. The light set in the ceiling became brighter and a screen next to the door switched on to reveal a cluster of faces in black and white. Controlling the fear that bloomed in his chest, he took a plain robe from the locker and shrugged it on before opening the door.

Omero, stood at the head of the group.

'Is it Cassady?' Ghazi asked immediately.

'No. Your friend is stable. We wish to speak to you about something else. May we enter?'

Ghazi stepped aside. Two men and two women wearing identical blue tunics with gold braid on the shoulders followed Omero into the room. The last member of the group was an older woman dressed in flowing white robes. Silver hair cascaded down her back. Sharp lines were etched into her forehead and around her eyes. She could have been a sister of Katarina.

'I hope these quarters are sufficient. Are you rested?' asked Omero.

Ghazi nodded, unwilling to engage in small talk.

The coordinator took the hint. 'I will get to the point.' He gestured at the men and women accompanying him. 'These are our most senior scientists. They are the driving force behind this facility.' He nodded at the woman in white. 'This is Isa, our lead scientist. She is responsible for continuing the work on the machine that was started by others.'

The woman bowed. 'You have our gratitude for what you have done, Ghazi.' Her accent was strong, but there was steel in her voice. 'The people here were ready to give up. We have suffered many losses since the four riders departed from La Talpa. Your arrival with the medicine has given them hope again. Already the mood here has changed.'

Ghazi nodded. He thought he knew what was coming.

'Some of the council do not agree with me, but I do not wish to keep any secrets from you, which is why you should know our previous lead scientist died three days ago. He was unable to fight the disease any longer. We learned what we could while we had the time, but his genius sadly died with him.'

'What does that mean?'

'The situation is complex. The machine is at an advanced stage, but it is not yet ready. Our work now will involve finding the answers to the final questions standing between us and its operation. Now that our survival here is assured, we are confident we will be able to do so over the coming months and years.'

Ghazi swallowed. So they had been too late. She watched his reaction. 'The sacrifice of your companions will not be in vain. I promise that. La Talpa has been saved because of you. And one day we will use our technology to save humanity.'

She took a step towards him and placed a hand on his shoulder. 'Rest now,' she said. 'There will be time enough to discuss this.'

The coordinator ran a finger over his moustache. 'I will come by again later.' He opened the door, waited as the blue-uniformed scientists filed out, and then followed.

On her way out, Isa took something from a pocket in her robe and placed it on the table. 'When we analysed your blood, we found traces of something we did not expect,' she said. 'I thought you might want this.' She strode out of the room and the door slid closed with a cough.

Sitting on the table was a small metal box with no markings on it. Ghazi hesitated for a moment before picking it up. He turned it over between cracked hands, and the light collected on its surface. The scientist's words filled him with a dull uneasiness. Open it. It can't be worse than what you endured in the desert. And if it is, then you'll deal with it.

He moved to the cot and flipped the box open. Inside was a match tipped with blue and a single fragile paper stick. Copper shreds poked out of the end and they trembled when he breathed on them. He brought the stick to his nostrils and inhaled. A sweet scent he thought he'd forgotten made him gasp. His disbelieving eyes devoured the filter and the discoloured paper and the plug of cured leaves until he could taste the memory that had lain dormant for so many years. He reached over for the mug of water beside the cot and drank slowly until his lips and mouth were moist. Then, with trembling fingers, he pushed the stick between his lips. For a long moment he didn't move. He simply savoured the presence of the tobacco, dry, unlit, waiting for him to choose when to fire it and inhale the beautiful silky smoke. Sitting on the cot, he looked around the room, noting how the rock's sharp edges had been rubbed down to form a mottled wall, how the wires for the lighting and the door mechanism were on display, how the smooth air conditioning unit left the room feeling filtered and unnatural. And already he wanted to be away from this subterranean base in the desert. It was not his world. He had done his part to preserve it, for all the good that had done, but he did not belong. Static, surrounded by rock, subject to the rules of a community of men and women working to unlock the secrets of the world and then use technology to control them. No, he belonged with Warspite. Out there, in the dirt and mud, where the real struggles were happening.

The vision of the white city in flames appeared once more and obscured the features of the room. He'd seen it more than once in the desert, as he'd looked out at the horizon, and he'd believed himself to be hallucinating. Now he wasn't so sure. He saw the people fighting on rooftops, unfurling their flags, shooting drones out of the sky. Their cries of rebellion rang in his ears. Despite the processed air, he could smell only acrid smoke and urgency. Even now, having rested for only a few hours, he wanted to be with them, caught in the slipstream of revolution, helping people like Wyler break rank and wrest control of the beautiful state from the Koalition. Novus was the real key to humanity's survival, not a machine.

The matter was clear. When Cassady had recovered his strength, he would ask his friend to take him there in Warspite. It would not be an easy sell, but they had no future at the base, not that he could see. Both of them were done as Runners now, too. And he, at least, had a bigger part to play. If the struggle was still happening when they reached Novus, he would fight. And if it was over, he would help to shape its future.

Fingers burned a deep brown by the sun reached into the metal box and withdrew the blue-tipped match. The head scraped along the rough edge of his sleeping cot and a perfect flame burned brightly for an instant before slowly eating the matchstick. Ghazi brought the flame up to the cigarette and lit the end, and then pulled until his throat was scratchy and his head swam and his blood danced and there was nothing left of the cigarette but the yellowed filter and another memory.

12

He was sick of looking at the walls. Rough, grey-brown, covered in some kind of chicken wire to stop them from collapsing and killing everybody. He'd looked at them for so long they'd started taking on different shapes. A pantech crushed on one side, a three-legged dog, a skull. It was enough to make a man go crazy. There wasn't even anybody else in there with him. The last patient had shaken his hand and walked out two days ago, fully cured.

His head itched like hell. He wasn't allowed to touch it, but he'd found that pressing on it with the base of his palm helped. A tube snaked out of his arm, down by the wrist. He'd pulled it out a couple of times in confusion, but they always put it back in. Whatever was in the bag hanging from the hook above his cot made him drowsy, gave him nightmares he couldn't wake himself up from no matter how much he screamed. He saw them all: Renfield, Kaja, Wyler, Brandt, Hearst, Tagawa and Victor. They stared back at him through eyeless sockets, heads blackened, blistering or bleeding, mouths contorted into silent screams. They blamed him for failing them. He did not want to sleep anymore.

A woman in a blue tunic appeared by the side of his cot. She was the only one who spoke the same language as he did. He felt the warmth of her smile on his skin.

'How are you feeling today?'

'Like a piece of meat being left out on a hood to dry.' Her brow wrinkled. She didn't understand. 'I feel fine.'

She nodded. 'Good. Soon you will be okay again.'

'I'm okay now,' he protested.

'No, no.' She waved a finger at him. 'Soon.'

'It's always soon.'

'You should be happy. You are healthy again.'

He pointed at his body. The ribs stood out clearly under his darkened skin.

'Does this look healthy to you?'

The woman simply pursed her lips. She busied herself with his tubes before handing him a small control attached to a wire.

'Click if you need anything.'

'I need to get out of here.'

She flashed him a smile and left the room. That woman. She was something. If he ever managed to get out of the medical wing, they might have a nice time together.

He settled down, trying to get comfortable. His head prickled again, but he ignored it, focusing instead on the walls and their hidden visions. There was a low chime and the door slid open. A man entered. Clean-shaven and dark-skinned with a grey strip of hair that ran the length of his otherwise stubbly scalp. He approached the cot and stood at the foot of it.

'Hello, Cass,' he said.

Cassady's mismatched eyes saw every line on the man's head. The itching sensation in his own head ceased.

'Ghazi?'

'How are you doing, dostem?'

'Is that really you?'

A thin smile appeared on the serious face. 'Yes, it's me.'

Cassady raised himself into a sitting position. Since he'd woken from his coma, neither the medical staff nor Omero, La Talpa's coordinator, had told him any news about Ghazi, and he'd been too afraid to ask, so he'd buried it deep within himself. Even so, the question of where Ghazi was had hung over him and followed him into his dreams each night. And now his friend stood before him in the medical wing, not a scratch on him, looking rested and well-fed and as immaculately presented as Omero.

Ghazi chuckled. 'Surprised to see me?'

'More than a little. Have you been here the whole time?'

'Yes. Kicking my heels underground for the past two weeks. I heard you were up and about.'

'For four days now.' He left his next question unspoken, opting instead for a pointed silence.

The mechanic understood. 'I'm sorry I haven't been by before. I don't know. I wasn't sure if I could.'

'Why not?'

Ghazi hesitated. And suddenly Cassady knew the reason. 'It's because of them, isn't it?' he said quietly.

Mournful eyes looked him over. 'Yes. I didn't want to be reminded.' Ghazi rounded the side of the cot and sat on a stool usually reserved for the medical staff. He rubbed the strip of grey hair. 'And how we left things at the end, when it all fell apart, I wasn't sure you'd want to see me again.'

That surprised him. He shook his head. 'You saved me, Ghazi. You got us over the finish line. Not me. I was out of it.'

'But the others.'

'Whatever happened out there happened and there's nothing we can do about it anymore.' There was an edge in his voice. 'Everybody did as they were asked, but we were luckier than the others. They didn't do anything wrong, didn't drive any better or worse than we did, didn't make any decisions that were stupid. Luck. That's all it is. Theirs ran out, ours didn't. So did La Talpa's when they lost their genius.' He lowered his voice. 'I've had time to think about this. It's all I've been doing, lying here, waiting for my body to recover. I don't believe in anything else, not like you do. As far as I understand it, life's just a random series of events that we adapt to as best we can. And we go on like that until the circumstances overwhelm us. You can be the best Runner in the world, but you can't anticipate a blowout when there's nothing on the cards.'

He hadn't meant to summon the memory of Hearst, but there it was. 'I don't blame you for anything that happened. And I don't hold any decisions against you.'

The two men held each others' gaze for long enough to relive the convoy's painful disintegration. The silence in the room was broken only by the hum of the machines next to Cassady's cot. Ghazi bowed his head and extended his hand. Cassady took it.

'Glad we're back on the same side,' said the mechanic.

He smiled. 'Better that way. You're all I've got.'

'Have you seen anybody else besides the doctors?'

'Omero has been by a couple of times.'

'He comes to my quarters every day. Updates on your recovery, information about this place, that kind of thing. He likes to talk.'

'He's filled me in. Pretty impressive specs. And he's desperate to learn about the north.'

'I know. But I haven't been in the mood to answer all his questions.'

'I don't mind them. Makes me feel pretty useful while I'm lying here like this.' Cassady paused. 'What do you mean by not in the mood?'

'I've had something else on my mind.'

'Do I have to ask?'

'It's complicated. I was going to wait until you were back on your feet.'

He narrowed his eyes. 'My mind is working just fine.'

'Okay. But then hear me out.' Ghazi leaned forward in his seat, a fire already being kindled in his eyes. 'I want to go back to Novus. I can't get the image of that city out of my head. I've tried, but it won't shift. The fire, the struggle, the banners, the drones, all of it. It's so alive inside me it's like I'm there every time I think of it. More than that, I remember the mountains and the green and the ice-cold water all around. It was alive. I mean truly alive. No clay, dust or desert anywhere. This is something I never thought I'd see, and it was hiding behind a wall the whole time. I just want you to think for a minute about what Novus means. About what we could do in a place like that. It's a second chance. For us and for whoever wants it. We can join the people fighting against the Koalition and help them take control. Then we turn Novus into a sanctuary for anybody prepared to help keep it that way, and roll out the technology and the infrastructure to the surrounding areas. It'll be a new beginning. We can turn the world into a place worth living in again.'

He sat back. Cassady looked on, incredulous, trying hard to stifle a grin as he digested the words. He ran through a handful of arguments, but settled on a few words to sum up how he felt about the matter. 'You're crazy as hell.'

'Am I? What's crazier: returning north to run cargo as though nothing ever happened, or seeing if we can shape some kind of future from all this? '

'I thought that's what we did by coming here,' Cassady said quietly.

'Yes. But our work isn't done yet. In fact, it was just the start.'

'How do you know the Koalition hasn't crushed the resisters since we've been down here?'

'Omero. They listen to the shortwave and keep tabs on what's happening. The fighting is still going on, but the people are on top. They'll win.'

Cassady decided to be blunt. 'Emotion's clouding your judgement. I said this to you before – you don't even know what they stand for.'

Ghazi waved the statement away. 'We'll find out. What else do they want but to live free and not have to struggle every single day?'

'Maybe they want to control Novus. Maybe they'll build higher walls. Maybe they'll kill you before you get the chance to open your mouth.'

A trace of irritation was evident on Ghazi's face. 'Yes, maybe. But if we thought like that, we never would have come here in the first place. We were right to make this run. Now I'm making that leap again. I've made up my mind. Either I go with you, or I go alone. I've already agreed things with Omero. They'll give me a vehicle to get me to the border. I have to do this.'

Cassady sighed. The determination was unmistakable. He'd seen it in the man more times than he cared to count. He didn't have to agree with Ghazi's plan, but he would accept it. And now it was time to have the conversation he'd been rehearsing since he'd emerged from his drug-induced mist. 'You don't need to take one of their rides.'

Ghazi brightened. 'You'll come?'

'No,' he said slowly. 'You can take Warspite. She's yours.'

The liquid eyes became wider. 'I don't understand.'

'I'm giving her to you. I'm all done. The road nearly killed me. That was my last run. I told you I wanted to prove I wouldn't flinch when my time came. That I'd have both eyes open. I did it. But I'm not going back out there. I'm staying here. When you feel the fire of hell on your back, you don't turn around. You run in the other direction.'

'You're serious?'

'Straight down the middle.'

Ghazi groped for the right words. 'What are you going to do?'

'You're not the only one who's spoken to Omero. He's offered me a job. He wants me to take over as head of their scout and barter units. Says I know more about the road than all of their crews put together. I'll get back in the driver's seat, but it'll be short haul. And I'll have a place to come back to each night.'

'You've never needed that before.'

Cassady offered a thin smile. 'But I need it now. I don't want to die. Not yet, anyway. And not in the same way the others did. You might not believe it, but I found peace out there, at the end, when I thought it was over. I wasn't scared anymore. You know how many years it's been since I could last say that? And the feeling was still there when I woke up in this damn bed.' He paused. 'That's got to be something to hold on to.'

Ghazi made a steeple with his fingers and nodded his head slowly. 'It is.'

'I knew you'd understand.'

'You're really not going to come with me.' He said it with finality.

'You don't need me for this.'

'But Warspite's yours. She's always been with you.'

'We all have to move on some time or other.'

Ghazi stood up and held out his hand, which Cassady took. 'I accept.'

It was done. And it had gone as he'd hoped. There was just one more favour to ask. 'Can you wait a day or two before you leave? I want to say goodbye to her.'

Ghazi's features softened. 'Of course, Cass. I'll wait for as long as you need.'

Warspite sat at the bottom of the tunnel, her nose directed towards the incline that would take her back up into the world. Spotlights splashed yellow-white lustre onto the hood and roof until she glowed. Every faulty or broken part had been replaced with the newest variants in La Talpa's inventory. Her cargo bed was laden with water, food, clothing, weapons and other amenities that the people of the underground base had urged Ghazi to take with him on his journey. Her silhouette had changed slightly to incorporate the upgrades Lupo had promised the convoy an eternity ago in the Gaean stockade. She was ready.

Ghazi was standing by the cab, speaking to one of the vehicle scouts, when Cassady, wearing a robe that stopped above the ankle, hobbled out of one of the side corridors with Omero and a cluster of bodies in tow. His head was still bandaged and he was sweating with the effort, but he was out of the medical wing and that was all that mattered.

Ghazi broke into a grin. 'How are you feeling?'

'Like I should still be lying in that clean bed being waited on like a prince.' He smiled weakly. 'But I didn't want you to have to sit around forever. How does she look?'

'They've done a job on her. New armour, new batteries, new tyres, new everything. They even switched out the wind turbine for a hybrid solar-wind unit. Like the ship of Theseus.'

'Can't change her spirit,' said Cassady.

'Right.'

'Got everything you need?'

'Yes. I'm as ready as I'll ever be.'

'Good. I'll ride with you to the top.'

Omero stepped forward and gave a short bow. 'You'll always have a place here if you ever decide to come back. Thank you again for all that you've done.'

Ghazi accepted the invitation with good grace. 'How about getting him back down from the surface?'

'We will send a transport up for him when he's ready,' replied the coordinator. 'Our cameras will see him.'

Cassady laughed. 'You don't need to worry about me anymore. Now let's get this over with.'

While Ghazi made his goodbyes to the group of people in the chamber, Cassady went to the front of Warspite and pulled himself slowly up the metal steps. He fumbled with the handle, but finally managed to prop open the door and slide into the co-seat. The cab was just as it had always been: worn, cramped, home. He reached over to touch the bruised housing of the steering wheel, and his hand drifted over the levers and dials before coming to rest on the gear stick that served as proof of the Old Lady's great age. His foot brushed something under his seat and he leaned down and pulled it out. His cap. Spotted, faded, bent out of shape. He thought he'd lost it. He stuffed it into a pocket in his robe as Ghazi jumped aboard.

The Runner ran through his checks in silence before slotting the key home, punching the ignition and easing the vehicle onto creaking metal ribs that kept the ground from cracking under the weight of the tunnel's traffic. Cassady stared in wonder. The oesophageal structure contracted as they climbed, its walls and ceiling drawing closer as though collapsing in slow motion. They passed checkpoint after checkpoint, each station manned by grim faces that nodded when Warspite rolled by, and then the metal ribs gave way to dull concrete and the creaking ceased.

At the top of the tunnel, Ghazi touched the brake and the Old Lady trembled. Great cogs built into the wall squealed as they rotated, and a gate concealed in the rock face opened to reveal a sky of vivid blue glass. A brutal late-afternoon sun hammered an unbroken desert landscape that extended to the horizon. Hot, heavy air overpowered the artificial climate inside the tunnel and forced its way into the cab, and for a moment both men were back out there, leaning into the guts of their broken vehicle as they tried to coax her back to life in time before they, too, expired. A quiet strength ran through the pair of them. They were still alive.

On stiff, sensitive legs, Cassady eased himself out of the cab. He allowed his hand to drift over her body, tracing her dents and scratches and lesions until he'd made a full circuit of his rig. He stood back and took in the sight of her. He was ready. Ghazi waited by the hood, chin high and shoulders back but unable to disguise the pain in his eyes.

'Okay,' Cassady said. His voice was calm. 'You'd better saddle up. No need to stand on ceremony.'

Ghazi said nothing. Cassady limped over to where he stood.

'This is not my calling. My place is here now.' He pointed at the shifting grey sands. 'You're not done with it yet. When you are, we'll meet again.'

They gripped forearms. 'I'll look after her,' said Ghazi.

'I know.'

'Take care of yourself, Cass.'

'Khoda hafez.'

Ghazi pulled himself into the cab and slammed the door

shut. The keening under the hood started and Cassady stepped aside as the great vehicle rolled out of the tunnel and onto the boiling sand that held firm under the tyre tracks. It moved off at a rumble, gradually picking up speed as it headed towards a horizon shimmering with uncertainty and guarded hope. A dark arm emerged from the window, fingers curling into a fist, and Cassady raised his own in response.

A terse wind plucked at his robe and sent grains of dust into the air, and they sounded like faint rain when they peppered the rocks next to him. The scent of the day, burned and withered, filled his lungs and made him giddy, and he shuffled out onto the sand and then faltered, as though unsure whether or not to continue. The sun touched his exposed head, and sweat collected at the nape of his neck, but he did not return to the shade. He carried every long year spent alive in his bones, and he could feel them, heavier than ever, doing their best to weigh him down. But now he carried something else as well. Something that went beyond his beaten flesh and made him look upon the future, his future, with quiet expectation instead of fear.

When she was no more than a dark smudge in the distance, the Old Lady loosed a defiant cry that rolled across the plain. Then she was gone. The former Runner stood at the mouth of the tunnel, his gaze fixed on the point where yellow met blue, and he did not move for some time.

About the Author

Grant Price is a writer and translator. He was born in Plymouth, England, in 1987 and currently lives in Berlin, Germany. *By the Feet of Men* is his second novel.

Other works

Static Age
ISBN-10: 3741898600

In a hostile city, barfly Clark divides his time between drinking, brawling and ignoring his inner demons. That is, until public humiliation twice in one weekend opens his eyes to how much of a punchline his life has become. Over the next seven days Clark pushes back as he overcomes his apathy, chases an elusive girl all over town, gets even with those who have wronged him and forces himself to change his nihilistic ways until he reaches breaking point.

Available in paperback and ebook format.

COSMIC
EGG
BOOKS

FANTASY, SCI-FI, HORROR & PARANORMAL

If you prefer to spend your nights with Vampires and Werewolves
rather than the mundane then we publish the books for you. If
your preference is for Dragons and Faeries or Angels and Demons
– we should be your first stop. Perhaps your perfect partner has
artificial skin or comes from another planet – step right this way.
If your passion is Fantasy (including magical realism and spiritual
fantasy), Metaphysical Cosmology, Horror or Science Fiction
(including Steampunk), Cosmic Egg books will feed your hunger.
Our curiosity shop contains treasures you will enjoy unearthing.
If you have enjoyed this book, why not tell other readers by
posting a review on your preferred book site.

Recent bestsellers from Cosmic Egg Books are:

The Zombie Rule Book
A Zombie Apocalypse Survival Guide
Tony Newton
The book the living-dead don't want you to have!
Paperback: 978-1-78279-334-2 ebook: 978-1-78279-333-5

Cryptogram
Because the Past is Never Past
Michael Tobert
Welcome to the dystopian world of 2050, where three lovers are
haunted by echoes from eight-hundred years ago.
Paperback: 978-1-78279-681-7 ebook: 978-1-78279-680-0

Purefinder
Ben Gwalchmai
London, 1858. A child is dead; a man is blamed and dragged
through hell in this Dantean tale of loss, mystery and fraternity.
Paperback: 978-1-78279-098-3 ebook: 978-1-78279-097-6

600ppm
A Novel of Climate Change
Clarke W. Owens
Nature is collapsing. The government doesn't want you to know
why. Welcome to 2051 and 600ppm.
Paperback: 978-1-78279-992-4 ebook: 978-1-78279-993-1

Creations
William Mitchell
Earth 2040 is on the brink of disaster. Can Max Lowrie stop the
self-replicating machines before it's too late?
Paperback: 978-1-78279-186-7 ebook: 978-1-78279-161-4

The Gawain Legacy
Jon Mackley
If you try to control every secret, secrets may end up controlling
you.
Paperback: 978-1-78279-485-1 ebook: 978-1-78279-484-4

Readers of ebooks can buy or view any of these bestsellers by
clicking on the live link in the title. Most titles are published
in paperback and as an ebook. Paperbacks are available in
traditional bookshops. Both print and ebook formats are
available online.
Find more titles and sign up to our readers' newsletter at
http://www.johnhuntpublishing.com/fiction
Follow us on Facebook at https://www.facebook.com/JHPfiction
and Twitter at https://twitter.com/JHPFiction